Nightmare's Revenge

Moonlit Memories: Book Two

By H. J. Harding

This is a work of fiction. Any resemblance to real people or events is a coincidence. Some places are borrowed, but all were returned more or less intact. No Werefoxes, Faes, or Vampires were harmed in the making of this story. Some humans were annoyed however. If you actually read this, please email the author at hjhardingbooks@gmail.com and let me know.

"What a coincidence. I wish to speak with your chief." Liska gave a small bow. "Please, lead on."

Both vampire guards straightened and one started walking. Liska followed, hyper-aware of the other one marching behind her. They were escorting her like they would a prisoner. Which she might well be. That hadn't been an invitation, which would grant her the safety of a guest. That had been 'Will you come willingly, or do we drag your broken, bleeding body? Please, choose the second.'

Liska deliberately did not name the chief. If Rex Magnus had been killed in the attack, mentioning him would just make the situation worse. At minimum, it would betray her lack of knowledge and upset the guards, both of whom had probably been turned by him. At worst, it would infuriate them.

As they reached the street, a dark, probably black, limo pulled up. Guard One opened the door and glared at her. Liska nodded to him and slid in as if he were a valet and it was perfectly normal for him to open her car door. Guard Two followed her in.

Rex Magnus sat across from her.

"Great Chief, may the nights be long and prosperous. I am pleased to see you." While that was not a lie, even Liska was a little surprised at just how relieved she was to see him. Rex Magnus disliked her for unknown reasons, and he was too arrogant for her liking, but she had never wished him dead. He was at least a known quality and generally considered a decent leader.

"Are you indeed?" His words were bitter vinegar. The car started to drive. Liska ignored the way she was currently trapped, even while mentally kicking herself for not informing Ryoko-Sensei of her suspicions and whereabouts.

Author's Note

There were a few things I wanted to make known to anyone wishing to read this story. This is the sequel to *Secrets of the Moon Fox*. Whenever I see the sequel, I wonder if it is possible to read it without having read the original. In this case, no. *Nightmare's Revenge* not only reveals most, if not all of the plot points of *Secrets of the Moon Fox*, but will make little to no sense without that foundation. I'm sorry, but the story had to be written that way.

Also, a slight warning. There is a part in this story where an assassination is performed, using fireworks as cover for gunshots. This part was written years before the Los Vegas mass shooting, and I really can't change it. The scene is not graphic, but it is important.

Acknowledgements

Anyone who claims to have written a book without help is lying or remembering incorrectly. Thank you to my editor, Petticoat Betty. Thank you to my brother who loves the characters almost as much as I do. Thank you to my mother who agreed to quickly read the book so I could second-guess everything. Thank you to everyone who asks me, 'How's the book coming?' even when I can't remember which book I told you about.

Thank you everyone who reads this book, buys this book, or persuades another to buy this book. If you've done all three, thank you thrice.

Last but certainly not least, thank you to my Lord and Savior. No accomplishment can be made without You, and if it could, it would be meaningless. May this book honor You.

Chapter One

Who are you when no one is watching? – The Kikitsutai Book
of Wisdom

Kira stood, a silent sentinel, watching her cousin finish her last-minute packing. If she didn't say anything, maybe Sakaki wouldn't know how worried she was. Maybe she wouldn't guess about the iron that had set up permanent residence in Kira's stomach, or the gall that Kira tasted when she let herself think about Sakaki's recent behavior. It was a vain hope, she knew, but it was all she had. Sakaki had given her a lot of reasons to worry.

Sakaki reached left-handed for a book, even though the right hand was closer. She was still favoring her right wrist. The one she had broken a few weeks ago, fighting a psychotic vampire. The bone would have healed by now, but Sakaki was Sakaki. She pushed too hard, too fast, and re-injured it a week ago while trying to get it back to full strength. Thankfully the bone hadn't broken again, but she would need the brace for a while longer.

Kira rubbed at her nose, trying again not to let it twitch at the smell of fox permeating the room.

The room wasn't saturated in it, but it was strong. A long-time scent. Sakaki must have been using her fox form a lot, probably to sleep. She wouldn't be the first or the last of the skulk to use that trick to avoid or lessen the intensity of nightmares. If the compact of pale powder on her dresser was any indication, it wasn't working completely.

But the most worrying thing, the thought that had Kira actually frightened *of* her cousin, not just *for* her, was that Sakaki hadn't said anything, not a single word, about learning the entire skulk had lied to her. Everyone, well, everyone over twelve or so, knew Sakaki had been Tisiphone, the dreaded assassin. Then, after her breakdown, she blocked the memories out, and everyone hid the truth from her.

Sakaki was smart. When she was forced to re-remember Tisiphone, surely she had put together the pieces. Realized the whole skulk had actively conspired to keep her in the dark. Or had she? It wouldn't be the first time she chose to use denial rather than deal with something painful. That was what caused this whole mess in the first place, though Kira would rather bite out her own tongue than say that to Sakaki.

Kira had never been afraid of Sakaki before. Not when she was Tisiphone, not when she was Liska, not any of the other names Sakaki used. She never thought she would be afraid of her. Never thought she wouldn't be able to read her. But right now, Kira felt like she might as well be trying to translate the Voynich manuscript. Was Sakaki mad at her? Mad at herself? Mad at everyone? Was she in denial again? Which was worse? Was it really a good idea for Sakaki to go back to America, away from almost everyone in the family right now? Or was distance exactly what she needed?

"Is there something in my hair, or are you practicing your x-ray vision?" Sakaki asked without turning around.

Kira smiled; a small, tired curl of the lip. "Just thinking. Are you finished packing?" Normally Sakaki finished her packing well in advance. Had she put it off because she was unsure too? Or did she want to get away from everyone?

"Almost. Yes, I'm done." Sakaki reached around to grab the powder from the dresser next to Kira, close enough that Kira could just barely see the circles under her eyes that the powder was meant to hide. Kira said nothing about it. Let it be Sakaki's secret, like the teddy bear whose nose had barely peeked out from beneath a shirt until Sakaki zipped the suitcase up.

"Good. Are your parents going to see you off?"

"No. Father had to go to the mainland for a couple days. Mother was going to come, but you heard Aunt Tomo arrive ten minutes ago. I don't think she'll be able to get away. You'll walk with me, right?"

Aunt Tomo knew Sakaki was leaving. It seemed at least borderline rude to show up now, forcing her mother to have to choose between slighting a powerful woman of the skulk or not seeing her daughter off. Possibly a power play. At least Sakaki didn't seem upset by it.

"Of course." Kira eyed her cousin. Sakaki was Liska now. Liska was fine as a working persona, but it always struck Kira as sad that Sakaki sometimes found the need to be Liska around family.

Kira took Sakaki's suitcase, leaving her with the backpack, and the two Werefoxes left after saying a quick goodbye to Sakaki's mother and Aunt Tomo. 'Aunt' Tomo was not a close relative to either girl, but in a group as small and inter-related as the Kikitsutai, relations were assumed and everyone was referred to as family.

"Is Tora flying you back?" Kira asked as they made their way to the island's airstrip, greeting various skulk members along the way.

"Partway. He's taking me to California, but he has things to do there. Tomorrow I take a flight to Florida."

"You hate flying commercial." They all did.

Liska shrugged. "That's the way it goes sometimes. He's piloting the long flight, I can handle a short trip. I'll be fine."

She was right and Kira knew it. But it was also her prerogative to worry. "Call me after your flight. Both of them."

"I will. Or email if it's really late here."

Kira rolled her eyes, not really worried about 'late'. They boarded the small suborbital plane, where Tora took one look at them and said he needed a few more minutes for flight checks before closing the door. Whether he truly needed the time or her betrothed was giving them privacy, Kira neither knew nor cared. "So, another semester in college. Will you need me to take your place again?"

Liska laughed as she took the suitcase from Kira and stowed it out of the way. "I doubt it.

Though you did well on my exams. If you want to take them again...?"

"Not a chance." Both girls knew she would if necessary. "Though if you expect me to take your place, you should probably keep a journal so I know what's going on. I managed last time, but that was only because everyone was distracted by finals and I could spend a lot of time studying."

"Not a bad idea. Hopefully we won't need it though." Kira fought back a smile at the pondering look on Liska's face. That was her cousin. She'd be keeping a journal from now on.

"Luck favors most those who depend on it least," they said in unison.

The plane engine kicked into gear making both girls stifle a jump. Liska looked like she wanted to say something, but Kira spoke first. "I'm going to miss you. Be careful."

"Same to you. Both of those. Don't worry. I'll be fine. You better go."

Kira gave her a hug and disembarked from the plane. Moving to a safe distance, Kira made sure she could be seen by both Tora and Liska. When Liska shut the door and sat down, Kira waved. The small sub-orbital took off, taking them from Japan to California. Kira watched until it was out of sight, unable to shake the bone-deep conviction that her best friend and closest cousin was anything but 'fine'.

***

At her request, Tora informed her when they were half an hour out. Liska used the time to pull up her

Anna Andrews persona, the one she was using for school. It was harder than she remembered, but that was why she was getting started now. Tora had seen most of her personas before and didn't care who she pretended to be, and the chances of running into anyone she knew from Florida in California was slim. Even if she did, no one was at their best traveling.

It was Anna Andrews who spent a night in California before navigating airports to land in Miami. Anna Andrews who took the two-hour Tri-Rail trip to West Palm Beach then a taxi to the school. It was Anna who went through check-in; a tedious process that she almost suspected to be the result of some faculty having a private bet about how many lines they could get students to wait in.

After check-in, she had to get her key from her Resident Advisor. Karen, the RA, took one look at the brace on her wrist and offered to help carry the luggage upstairs to her dorm room. Her wrist was throbbing, but Anna said no. After offering one more time, Karen gave in and handed her the key. Anna took it with a smile and concentrated on not showing pain while in public.

Public. So much of her life lately was what did she look like in public. Three more steps. Two more steps. One more step. Then she was at her door. Anna unlocked the door, and Liska closed it behind her. The sense of relief was strong enough to almost take her breath away. No one was watching her. No one could hear her. No one could judge her right now.

Even if the room had been bare and empty, she would have been glad to have it right now. But seeing her belongings sitting in boxes waiting for her was a relief she hadn't expected. She hadn't been supposed to return here. *Sensei* had brought her things back from Japan when he returned to the States a few days ago, but she had thought that she would have to pick them up from him tomorrow. Apparently, he had taken advantage of the school being mostly closed to bring them back. She would still have to unpack, but unpacking was easier than moving boxes.

Not that she needed or even could do that tonight. No, she didn't have enough energy to even *think* about unpacking everything right now. Priorities. First priority was contact. It was too late to call Japan, and she didn't really feel like talking to anyone anyway. But email was a marvelous invention. A quick note to her parents and Ryoko-*Sensei* informing them she had arrived safely and was back at her dorm, one to Kira saying she'd call later, and a note to Tora, thanking him for the flight, offering a favor at a later time.

Messages sent, Liska looked at her luggage. Everything she needed for tonight or tomorrow was in her backpack, so her suitcase could wait. Even after a painkiller, her wrist was achy and she had promised not to push too hard again. Why was her wrist so bad today? She had been traveling, not weightlifting. Instead of pondering that, Liska unpacked her backpack. Clothes for the night and the next day or two, toiletries, a book, and her teddy bear.

Ryoko-*Sensei* had considerately left a set of sheets out in a bag marked 'linens' so she didn't have to go rooting through boxes to make the bed.

Unless she was mistaken, they were one of his spare sets, not hers. She'd return them once she had hers unpacked. Making the bed didn't take more than a couple minutes, finishing with setting her teddy bear, Inari, next to the pillow.

Liska flopped onto the now made bed and stared at the ceiling. Now what? There was nothing. Nothing that needed to be done now. No family she had to reassure. No job to focus on. No strangers she had to be normal for. Nothing but her and her thoughts.

The thoughts and memories she had been avoiding for the last month rushed in like a flood, painful in their diamond sharp clarity. Liska barely managed to scramble off the bed and into the bathroom before the nausea and tears overwhelmed her.

She had been an assassin. She had seriously injured, possibly killed a child. She had broken down to the point of attempting suicide. When that failed, she repressed the memories. And everyone in her skulk, everyone she trusted, had *known*. Known and conspired to keep her from finding out, hiding everything so she wouldn't remember.

Sakaki was no stranger to lies. She gave them easily and expected them in return. She took almost nothing as given, nothing by faith. But there were foundations she had based her life upon. When everything else crumbled around her, she trusted her skulk and herself. But both had failed her.

Her skulk had, not betrayed her, not truly; but how could she trust them the way she had before? Now that she knew they could and would conspire against her? Even knowing it was on her behalf, it left a sour taste in her mouth and a painful throb in her ribcage.

That, however, paled in comparison to how badly she had failed herself. She couldn't afford failures on that scale. It was too dangerous. *She* was too dangerous. This couldn't be allowed to happen again.

Rising from the cold linoleum, she flushed the toilet before splashing water on her face and washing away the last remnants of evidence of her breakdown. Once she wiped her face dry, she looked her mirror self in the eye. "There aren't going to be any more hidden personalities or dangerous secrets. One way or another, I will make sure of that." Liska glared at the mirror, ignoring Sakaki's deep shudder.

***

A thirteen-hour time difference between Japan and Florida meant that Kira woke up before Liska was ready to sleep. Before Liska could call Kira, Kira called her. Talking to her helped, like it usually did. Kira was surprised but pleased to hear that her belongings were back in her room. After once more reassuring her cousin that she was fine, Liska hung up the phone, ready to collapse.

It was Saturday and classes started on Monday. Which meant she needed to be mostly past the jet lag and time difference by then. Well, eight-thirty wasn't *too* outrageously early for bed. Unusual for her, but she had been having a little trouble sleeping lately. Or maybe more than a little.

Liska hadn't told anyone about the dreams. Oh, everyone had some vague ideas that she had been having some nightmares lately, but everyone dealt with nightmares sometimes. Especially in her skulk. It wasn't a big deal, so why mention it?

When she had been forced to remember being Tisiphone, everyone seemed to be under the impression that she remembered everything about it at once. She had done nothing to discourage that idea. But in truth, she had remembered only a small fraction of Tisiphone's memories and had slowly been gathering more fragments ever since. Many came in dreams, confused kaleidoscopes of blood, tears, and broken glass. Then she would have to sort through them and try to remember which parts were real and to what extent, and which were just fun bits of horror for her psyche to play with.

Right now, Liska thought she had about half of Tisiphone's memories sorted out, though some might have been dreams and some real memories she might have discarded as fake. Worse were the blank spots, the foggy bits, that were probably important but she couldn't remember a thing about them. Maybe she could get a list of the jobs Tisiphone pulled and where they were. She knew such lists existed, but asking for one would cause questions and put her under *more* scrutiny.

Exhaustion finally quieted her racing mind and she fell asleep. Liska didn't remember her dreams, but she woke with tears in her eyes and the sound of fireworks ringing in her ears.

Chapter Two
The wise fox knows when not to be alone. – The Kikitsutai
Book of Wisdom

It was morning. Very, very early morning. On Sundays the cafeteria didn't even open until ten, and it was currently almost six. Liska stretched out and wiped her eyes. If she wasn't going to sleep, she might as well do something productive. If she buckled down, she might even finish unpacking today. Oh, and she needed to buy her textbooks.

Anna Andrews had been registered for classes before the whole mess of almost being withdrawn from school. But when it didn't look like she would be coming back, she hadn't bothered ordering textbooks. By the time it was decided she *would* go back, there wasn't enough time to order them online. So, she would help support the campus bookstore. That sounded much nicer than saying she was going to willingly get ripped off by the textbook manufacturers.

Liska had two boxes and her suitcase unpacked by eight and was in her third box when she found her inline skates tucked into the bottom. She stroked the side of one skate, considering. Four more boxes to go, though two were small boxes, probably books. It would take maybe an hour or so to get her textbooks, depending on lines. Her wrist was just starting to wake up and ask her what she thought she was doing. She didn't know where her helmet and safety gear were.

With a sigh, she set the skates aside. Then she found her safety gear in the next box. Liska put her brace on as a precaution before packing her shoes, some food, and a water bottle in a small backpack and heading out.

As soon as she stepped outside, she was slapped in the face with a wave of heat. Ah, yes, how could she have forgotten West Palm Beach's lovely 'temperate' climate? Weres don't have as many sweat glands as humans so she had to be more careful about not overheating. Still, it was early in the morning. That would help.

For safety's sake, she didn't put on her skates until she was at the bottom of the staircase. Then she took another check of her equipment. Knee guards were snug, same with elbow guards. Helmet was secure, and mouth guard was in place. Liska stood up, pushed off, and tried to outrace the wind.

Off campus, she headed for the bridge that separated West Palm Beach from Palm Beach. She wouldn't go all the way to the ocean, there was nowhere to skate on sand and this area didn't have a board walk. Or maybe she would. She could switch to her shoes and have a picnic on the sand.

As she crossed onto the pedestrian walkway of the bridge, she saw the ship about to cross under the bridge. Large enough they would have to raise the bridge for it to pass, and she would probably be kept waiting about ten minutes or so. Oh well.

The view from the bridge was nice enough. Even over the car scents, she could smell the salt. Closing her eyes for a moment, she just inhaled. Salt, water, gas fumes, fish, pollution, and people scents. Other than two cars, she currently had the bridge to herself.

Liska continued until she reached the limit of how far she could go. The bridge in front of her was almost to its' zenith, and the ship was just starting to disappear underneath. Waiting, Liska turned to stare at the water. Far below, she could see the broken reflection of her face. The ship moved, casting the reflection into shadow. A memory snagged.

She was on a bridge, looking down at the river. It was dark, night. Something hit the water, shattering her reflection. She felt nervous, jittery. Just reach the hotel room, and everything would be fine. Just get there. *A voice called her, breaking her concentration.*

"There you are! I've been looking for you."

The convergence of memory and present day startled Liska badly enough that she spun to see who was there, forgetting momentarily that she was wearing skates. Her feet went out from under her, and it was only a desperate grab at the rail that kept her from hitting the ground. Of course she hit her bad wrist making that grab, and several muscles were protesting such an awkward stretch without sufficient warm up. She might have been better off falling.

With a wince, she carefully pulled herself to a standing position before facing a rapidly approaching, apologetic Shahara. "Sorry, sorry. I didn't mean to scare you. Are you okay?"

Anna. Shahara would be expecting Anna. "I'm fine. I do worse than this all the time." To her relief the words came out with the British accent that Shahara would be expecting from Anna.

"Is that how you got the brace?" Shahara eyed it with a mix of concern and chastisement.

"No, that was from falling on ice, back home. It's mostly healed now. I only use the brace when I'm doing something that might strain it." She had used that as an excuse at the airport in California and decided it worked for the official story.

Shahara shook her head. "I'm glad you're okay, but if your wrist is bad, then you shouldn't be skating. What if you fell and hurt it again?"

She was right, and Liska knew it. Besides, she wanted some time to interrogate that memory fragment. It was definitely one of hers, not her pathetically weak retro-cog abilities. "You're right. I shouldn't have even tried. But I haven't been able to skate for weeks and I missed it." She could switch out her skates for shoes and continue taking a walk.

Apparently, that wasn't a good enough compromise for the Jamaican girl. "*Are* you okay? You seemed really out of it. And you're pale and not sweating much. Those aren't good signs in this heat."

No, they weren't. Weres were more susceptible to hyperthermia, but Liska doubted she was anywhere near the danger zone yet. "I had a bad case of food poisoning a couple days ago. Just getting over it. I guess I haven't gotten my color back yet."

"I still think you're overheated." Before Liska could stop her, Shahara's hand was on her forehead. "You're burning up, girl! I'm calling Jamal."

Internally, Liska flinched. Externally, she remained calm. "I'm fine. I run hot normally." Normal healthy temperature for her was about 100.8 Fahrenheit, but anywhere from 99.5 to 101.9 was considered 'safe'. The chances of her really having a fever without knowing about it were low. Though she hadn't reacted quickly enough to stop Shahara from checking her temperature, when she really should have been faster. "Maybe I did have a little too much sun, but I have water." She fished her water bottle out of her backpack and drank some to prove it. "I'll just go home and rest. I might have overdone it a little, but it's not serious."

Shahara frowned. "Okay, but I'm going with you. Make sure you get home alright. I swear, you wind up in more trouble than anyone else I know!"

Liska carefully didn't look at Shahara, knowing she wouldn't be able to resist laughing hysterically if she did. Shahara had *no* idea. "Deal. So, why were you looking for me? When I left, I wasn't supposed to come back. You knew that." Liska started skating slowly so Shahara didn't have to jog to keep up. It was actually more difficult than normal skating.

"I know, but I kept hoping you would anyway. Then Marsha said she saw you at registration."

Liska mentally rewound her school database, trying to remember a 'Marsha'. Oh, yes. "Tall fashionista, usually wears feather earrings?" They had shared English 101, but Liska certainly wasn't going to claim to 'know' her, nor would she expect

Marsha to bother to pay much attention to her. Thinking back, she did vaguely recall seeing the girl during check-in. They weren't close enough to talk, but she might have nodded a greeting. Or she might not have. Her brain was a little fuzzy still.

"That's her."

"I didn't know you knew Marsha."

"She's my roommate."

That would do it. It also explained the faint cross-over scent. "My father did want me to stay home, but we talked it over, and he agreed I should finish my education here." Not entirely true, but accurate enough, and better yet, plausible.

"So you're staying here? Great! Does Todd know?"

"Yes, actually. I emailed him a couple times." Five times. Besides, he was with her in Japan when the matter was decided.

"And he didn't tell me? That lousy bum." Shahara shook her head. "I'm going to have a talk with that boy."

"In his defense, things could have gone either way almost up to the moment I left." Until Father left for the mainland the day before her own departure, Liska kept half expecting him to change his mind. "He may not have wanted to get your hopes up in case things turned around. Did you stay in touch over break?"

"Yeah, we live near each other. He's been really quiet this break. Maybe that's why. We even threw him a party when he got back from Russia, but it didn't cheer him up much. Did you hear about that?"

"Russia? I heard a little bit. Something about an art competition," Liska lied. They had manufactured the contest to give Todd an excuse for being in Russia. Poor Todd really wouldn't be able to talk about the art competition he had supposedly been to and certainly couldn't say much about what he had really been doing. Which begged the question... "What did he tell you?"

"He went to the Hermitage and will talk your ears off about it if you give him half a chance. He mentioned a few cathedrals, not much else. All he says about the art contest is that he didn't win. Won't even talk about the ones that did. And he didn't take *any* pictures. Can you believe it?"

Liska made a mental note to talk to him and help him get his story straight. She'd tried to help him with that before he left. Obviously not enough, though. "Well, this is my dorm."

Her words stopped Shahara's rant on how could *anyone* go to a foreign country and not bring back any pictures or souvenirs other than some food wrappers written in Russian? Had he kept his trash from the train ride? Liska tried not to sigh. She had made a point of telling him the best places to get Russian souvenirs and even made sure he had some money for it, but she hadn't been able to go with him. It would have helped his cover story. "Are you sure you're okay?"

"I'll take my temperature, and rest for a while. Promise." Liska sat down on the stairs to take off the skates. She could go up or down steps wearing skates but it was dangerous, difficult, and generally unnecessary.

"You had better. Hey, want to meet up for lunch later? About one?"

Late lunch. But it was Sunday, and Shahara was a Christian. She probably intended to go to church. If Liska hadn't done a spot-on impression of heat stroke, she might have been invited. "Sure, that would be nice. Oh, Happy Belated Birthday. I got you something in England. I can give it to you then."

"Aw, you didn't have to do that." The rare dimples came out. "Thanks. What is it?"

Liska laughed and hoped it didn't sound as fake as it felt. As every laugh had felt in almost a month. "You'll just have to wait to find out. See you then."

She felt eyes on her until she shut the room door behind her. Even though she was certain she wasn't sick, she checked anyway. She had promised, and she hadn't been at the peak of health to begin with. Liska definitely did not need to get sick or heat stroke now. 101 degrees. Probably a tad elevated from the sun.

Liska drank some cold water, then took a cold, wet washcloth and laid it over her eyes and forehead as she relaxed on the bed. Couldn't hurt, and it might help her headache. Trawling through old memories was painful enough.

Now that Shahara knew she was back, she'd tell her brother, Jamal. Todd already knew. To the best of her knowledge, they were the only ones at school who knew she might not be coming back. Good, now she just had to focus on becoming Anna once more. Shouldn't be too hard. After all, she was used to living a lie.

***

"You, mister, are in serious trouble."

Todd turned to see Shahara glaring him down, hands on her hips. "What did I do?" He was pretty sure she wasn't as angry as she was acting, but she was definitely annoyed and he didn't know why.

"Wrong question. It's what you *didn't* do."

"Well, that certainly narrows it down." Todd frowned, trying to figure out what this was all about.

Shahara rolled her eyes when Todd didn't magically divine her meaning. "Guess who I just ran into?"

Sakaki! She was back. Maybe. "S... Anna?" *Keep it straight, Kensworth.* Sakaki had been gracious enough, and at times had no choice but to let him into several of her secrets. Unfortunately, he was well aware that made him a weak link. Maybe she was used to keeping massive secrets from everyone, but he wasn't. He couldn't slip like that, for her sake.

Fortunately, Shahara didn't seem to notice his slip. "Yes, Anna. And do you know what she told me? She said you already *knew* she was coming back." Shahara scowled at him. "And you said nothing."

"I wasn't sure. Not until you said you saw her." Sakaki had hinted that her father wasn't quite pleased with her decision. Reading between the lines, she didn't seem completely sure about it either. "I didn't want to say anything..."

She scowled at him a moment longer before relenting. "Fine. But don't go keeping secrets like that from me again."

Oh, Shahara had no idea about secrets. He needed to talk to Sakaki, as soon as he could get some privacy. The end of last year had dropped several bombshells on both of them, and he wasn't sure how she wanted to handle all that information. At very least, he needed to talk to her about his blog and what the official story was. He couldn't believe his silly little blog had almost gotten them both killed. But whatever stories Sakaki was spinning, he needed to make sure he didn't ruin them by saying something different. "When did you see her?"

Their usual meeting time was after the Kendo classes he taught, but he wouldn't be starting those up again for at least another week. At least he was recovered enough that he could actually teach again, not just supervise. If he never punctured a lung again, he would be very pleased.

Todd knew where her dorm room was, but he'd rather not bother her there if it could be helped. Things had been so awkward before he went home. Maybe she didn't want to be friends with him anymore. Maybe she blamed him for helping her enemies find her. But she had emailed him. More than once. He just needed to talk to her, so he could *know*, rather than deal with circuitous thoughts. If Shahara knew where she was...

"A little before nine." Right, that didn't do him any good. "I'm meeting her for lunch. Want to come? Jamal will probably be along soon."

Not ideal for a private conversation, but it would have to do. "Sure."

Sakaki arrived at the cafeteria about thirty seconds after they did. Todd let out a small, silent sigh. Somehow it wasn't real until he saw her. Then she turned, saw them, and smiled. He smiled back. Judging from Shahara's quiet snickers, his smile might have been a bit goofy. He ignored her.

Todd was the first one to get his food, so he grabbed a table. The girls joined him a moment later, and Jamal a few minutes after that. Shahara started the conversation and kept it moving while Todd found himself surprisingly tongue-tied.

It was difficult, remembering that the Anna in front of him was so different from the Sakaki he had spent a week with over Christmas break. He could only imagine what it was like for her.

Sakaki had remembered that Shahara had a birthday during break and gave her a small wrapped box that she said she'd picked up in England. Since they hadn't actually stopped in England, Todd wasn't sure where it came from, but Shahara loved the delicate butterfly necklace. She also had two boxes of Christmas Crackers that she claimed were a traditional part of the English holiday season. She gave the larger box to Jamal and Shahara and a smaller one to Todd. "I wouldn't recommend setting them off here, they can be quite loud."

"I've seen these in movies. They looked like fun," Shahara enthused.

Sakaki chuckled. "Don't get too excited. The prizes are usually pretty chintzy. I tried to get a nice set, but still..."

Shahara tried to plan a mini Christmas party where they could, among other things, pull the crackers. Sakaki demurred and changed the subject to what everyone did over break. After the third time Todd had to stop himself from bringing up something Shahara and Jamal didn't know about, and probably shouldn't; he tried to just keep his mouth shut unless asked a question. But that just led to Shahara and Jamal wondering what was wrong. "Nothing. I'm just tired." It was a lame excuse, but it was all he could think of.

Shahara shook her head. "Must be going around. You're feeling better, right? No fever?" She turned to Sakaki to ask.

"I'm fine. I checked. My temperature was slightly elevated from the heat, but once I cooled down, I felt much better. No relapses."

"Were you sick?" Jamal asked. Of course the pre-med student would wonder. Though Todd was concerned too. Sakaki said she didn't get sick often, but when she did, it hit hard. Was this a rare illness, or was she covering for something?

"I had a very nasty but short-lived flu a couple days before leaving." Sakaki took a sip of water. "I'm past the illness, but still a little run down. Apparently travel took more out of me than expected. The sun drained me too. I'll be fine in a day or two."

"Then you shouldn't be skating until you're better. And *where* is your brace?" Shahara asked.

Todd gave Sakaki a quick scan. What brace?

"I don't need it all the time. Just when it's achy or I might strain it. I had it on for protection. Good thing, I banged it when I lost my balance." Sakaki glared at her right wrist. To Todd's inexperienced eye, the wrist might be a little swollen. "I put some ice on it. Ironic, considering."

She gave a small smile to Todd and Jamal. "I sprained it falling on some ice. It's almost healed. Shouldn't be much more than a week, I hope."

This time, Todd knew she was lying. After all, he had been there when her ex-fiancé broke it. Though it shouldn't be so bad still. Liska said that Werefoxes healed from broken bones much faster than humans did. She had outright said that it should be back to normal before she came back to school. Well, now he knew the official story. Not that he planned on telling anyone that a rogue Werefox working for a megalomaniac vampire had kidnapped him and tried to kill her.

Todd started when Shahara stood up suddenly and addressed Jamal, "Hey, we'd better go if we aren't going to be late."

Jamal looked at her. "Late?"

"Yeah, you know, to the thing?"

Jamal stared at his sister for another moment while Sakaki buried her head in one hand and Todd felt his ears going red. "Oh, yeah. That. Gotta go, guys. Anna, nice to see you again. Thanks for the crackers. Happy New Year."

"You as well," The ninja responded with an amused smile. Once they were gone, she turned to Todd. "Well, that was subtle."

"Oh, yeah. Big time. Though we *do* need to talk."

Sakaki frowned, eyes darting about the cafeteria. The lunch rush had faded, but the room was still about half-full. "Not here. Take a walk with me?"

"You okay for that?" Todd asked, even as he stood up, gathering dishes and trash.

"I'm fine."

Did that mean the illness was a cover, or that she was refusing to admit weakness? With her, it could be either. Maybe that would be one of the things to talk about. Maybe not.

Since he didn't have any plans on where to walk to, he let her lead. Sakaki paused as they left the cafeteria before heading towards the intracoastal. They didn't go quite that far, but they did end up on the edge of campus, across the street from the waterway, next to one of the campus fountains.

"The water from the fountain will make it difficult for anyone to eavesdrop, and we'll see anyone coming." She took a seat, facing the campus.

Todd angled himself so he could see her and the area behind her. "So, were you sick?"

"No. But my recovery has not been... as smooth as I would like. Shahara caught me in a moment of weakness, and that was the best explanation I could think of."

"I'm sorry. What happened?" She gave him a cool measured look. "Uh, I mean, I hope you feel better soon."

"I'm fine."

Todd didn't believe her, but it wasn't worth arguing over. It would only make her angry. "How about your wrist? I thought it was supposed to have healed by now?"

The Werefox glared at said appendage. "Relapse. It should be back to normal in a week. Or two. I don't think I set it back today."

"Good." Todd took a deep breath. "Um, I don't remember if I apologized, but about my blog..." What did he even say? 'I'm sorry my blog almost got us killed?'

Sakaki shrugged. "I found out about it months ago. Admittedly, I didn't expect Atolatar, or anyone else, to find me that way, but I did know about it."

"You never said anything."

"At first, I didn't want to do anything to encourage your 'Cats-eye' investigations. Nice name, by the way. Then it just didn't seem important compared to everything else that was happening." She twirled her neck as if to stretch it, then turned to look at him. "It wasn't your fault, you know."

Yes, it was. "I can take it down, if you want."

Sakaki frowned and shook her head. "No, that will just draw attention. You have a decent sized audience and your friends and family know it's important to you. If it makes you feel better, we can find ways to make your blog, shall we say, less hazardous?"

"How?" Todd dipped his hand in the fountain before running the wet hand over his forehead. The water wasn't drinkable, but it was cool.

"You could ask me before putting information on your blog. Or I could give you information for it. Not all information would be accurate, but some would be."

"Would I know the difference?"

She shrugged. "Somewhat up to you. I really can't tell you everything, even now. But I could probably at least tell you if something is accurate or not."

"Can I think about it?" He didn't like the idea of deliberately passing on lies. Oh, he could see the necessity, but it churned his stomach.

"Take your time. After all, the horse already escaped."

That threw him for a second, before he caught the reference to locking the barn door and winced.

"Not your fault." Sakaki dipped a leaf in the fountain and splattered him lightly with water droplets. "Things happen. Besides, if he hadn't targeted me, I wouldn't have started investigating him. Atolatar somehow managed to slip under our radar, it's possible no one would have figured out what he was up to in time."

"I guess. It's hard keeping the different stories straight. How do you manage?"

She rolled her eyes. "It wasn't easy. I've trained myself to have near perfect recall. I do *not* recommend you try my method. Acquiring it was a painful, brutal process. And there are many things I would prefer to forget."

Remembering her breakdown less than a month ago, Todd nodded, hoping he wasn't turning as pale as he felt. "So, you don't forget things?"

"Not that simple. I can mentally rewind and pull up my subconscious memory, which notices things I don't consciously realize. It doesn't always work, and it can take up to a few seconds to rewind, but it's accurate enough. The things I think are important I make a mental note of, basically the equivalent of sticking a bright, flashing light onto it, so I can find and retrieve it easily."

"Okay." Sounded a little like the 'memory palace' technique one of his psych books had talked about. He hadn't had much luck trying that, but he could practice.

"My method isn't the only one out there. Everyone has their own technique. I believe *Sensei* uses mental databases. He compared them to Rolodex. Kira tries to link important memories to smells or musical trills. You just have to find the method that works for you."

"I'll look into that." Todd eyed the leaves floating in the fountain while he tried to decide if he was really brave enough to ask what he most wanted to know. If he didn't ask, he'd never know. Taking a deep breath, he hoped he wouldn't mess up, or offend her, or... "You said that Yoshiro was your betrothed."

"Yes, that's right." Sakaki seem slightly surprised he was bringing it up, then she stilled.

"I'm sorry about his death."

She nodded, not saying anything. Sakaki had confided to him that she didn't get along with Yoshiro, but that didn't mean she wasn't upset at his death.

"Your parents arranged the betrothal?"

"Father, mostly."

That wasn't a surprise. "Are you betrothed to someone else now?" It wasn't quite what he wanted to ask, but he needed to know.

"Not at this point. Since Werefoxes mate for life, it is considered wisest to have it arranged so everyone knows who they are *supposed* to fall in love with. It doesn't always work, but it's probably better than the alternative. Unfortunately, if something does interfere, it can be difficult to re-arrange things. In addition, I passed on my right to be leader of the skulk, and Father is trying to get Kira more involved with running things. She may have something else planned. Perhaps a treaty, either with another skulk or some other group." Sakaki shrugged as if the idea of being forced into marriage with a stranger was of no consequence.

"That doesn't bother you? That someone else could choose something that important?"

"I've *always* known that. Do you have any idea how rare it is to choose your own spouse in my skulk? I can only think of a handful of occasions off the top of my head. And that includes my parents. Besides, Kira would never force me into a marriage where she thought I would be unhappy." She eyed him, measuring, searching. "You want to know if there's a chance now. A chance we could have a relationship."

"Yes." No point in hiding it.

"So ask me."

Of course she wouldn't make it easy. Todd smiled. If she would, she wouldn't be her. "Is there a chance for us?"

She didn't say anything for a moment, just looking at him, before looking at their reflections in the water. "A chance. Nothing more, nothing less. Kira would allow it. My father... would not be pleased. He might, eventually, be persuaded, but it would be difficult. More importantly, are you sure?"

Todd opened his mouth, closed it, and let out an exasperated breath. When he was in Russia, he was certain he was in love with her. Now, he was back to doubting. "I do care about you. A lot. I think it's love. But I'm not sure. I'm not sure if I know what love is. I'm not sure anyone truly does. But the question isn't 'am I sure', it's 'are you willing to take the risk', isn't it?"

Sakaki nodded once as she stared into the water. "That's a good question." Her eyes went back to his. "Did you know that three different members of my skulk told me you were good for me and I shouldn't let you go?"

Todd tried to force his heart rate back to normal. "So..."

Sakaki smiled impishly. "So, convince me." She jumped to her feet and started to walk off.

He stared for a moment before calling after her, "May I escort you to dinner tonight?"

She looked back at him. "I think I'd like that. Six?"

"Six o'clock." It might take him that long to quit grinning like a loon.

Chapter Three

The enemy you know nothing about is more dangerous than one hundred enemies you know well. – The Kikitsutai Book of Wisdom

As Liska had suspected, Ryoko-*Sensei* admitted to moving her things back to campus when he returned to the States two weeks earlier.

"No point in having you borrow my car and move everything back when you were tired from your travels," he said, shrugging off her thanks. "Besides, I was certain you would need some things right away, and I doubted you would appreciate my rummaging through your belongings to figure out what would be a priority. No matter how well-meaning that rummaging might be."

He was right on both counts, especially the second one, so Liska dropped the subject. One of her objectives for the visit was to see if she could talk her great-uncle into a spar. The older Werefox turned her down, with a glance to her wrist. Perhaps he could smell the lingering pain.

"It isn't *that* bad," Liska protested.

"And the last thing you need is *another* relapse."

She carefully didn't sigh. "Yes, *Sensei*."

Still, it was nice to visit. Over the last semester she had averaged two visits a week. But he had gone back to the United States more than two weeks before she had, so this was the longest she had gone without seeing him in months.

"Do you think this semester will be quieter than the last one?" Ryoko-*Sensei* asked her, watching carefully over his tea cup.

"Too early to tell." Liska snagged a tea biscuit. "I thought last semester would be quiet, but some people had other plans." Which was a polite way of saying she had been arrested, nearly killed more than once, and forced into a nervous breakdown. There were less polite ways to say it, but she didn't hold to that kind of language.

"True. But he is dead now, correct?"

"*He* is dead," Liska sighed, remembering the encounter. She still hadn't told anyone how badly facing Atolatar had shaken her. "But we know he had at least one follower or ally somewhere near here. Someone had to be sending the notes." Yoshiro had confirmed that for her, before dying. Probably it would be best not to mention that. As much as she had disliked Yoshiro, she had at least been able to forgive him in death. Ryoko-*Sensei* seemed to be holding a grudge, feeling Yoshiro had betrayed them too far to come back.

"You have a point." Ryoko-*Sensei* stroked his chin, dislodging biscuit crumbs from his beard. Liska didn't crack a smile. "So, with Atolatar gone, would he try to carry on with whatever plans Atolatar had...?"

"Or will he fold like a puppet? I honestly do not know. Did Atolatar even have plans for alternate contingencies? He barely seemed to have a grasp on the plan he did have. Which could mean several things, most of them bad. How desperate is this follower? Or has he, or she, changed their mind? Like it or not, this has to be investigated." Liska put down the biscuit that she just realized she had been making 'walk' across her fingers. Her mentor kindly ignored the stress reaction.

"Very true. But I had hoped it was over."

"It's never over, *Sensei*. You know that." Liska cocked her head, like she might in fox form upon hearing a strange noise. "I should check with my contact at the local Blood. If Atolatar's follower is another vampire then either he belongs to the Blood or they'll be watching him. If he isn't a vampire they would probably keep an eye on non-vampires that vampires are in regular contact with." Vampires were notoriously territorial, and Rex Magnus, the leader of the local blood, was paranoid.

"A good place to start."

Liska made a mental note to call Van when possible.

"So, you met with the Kendo boy today," Ryoko-*Sensei* said to his empty teacup.

Danger zone. Proceed with caution. "Yes. We are friends. Besides, we needed to iron out our cover stories. Some things should not be put into writing."

He nodded at that, then put down the teacup to watch her. "That was all?"

"*Sensei?*"

"He is... attracted to you."

"Yes. I am aware of that." Nor was that entirely one-sided, as Ryoko-*Sensei* had undoubtedly figured out.

"This is not a good thing. There is a very large gap between your worlds. Most humans do not adjust well to changes in what they perceive to be reality."

"Also true," Liska admitted. Mother had managed, for the most part, but Liska strongly suspected there were times that Anne Johnson regretted ever meeting Sejou of the Dragonclaw, let alone getting involved with him and moving to Japan where she was the only human among Werefoxes. Father was chief of the skulk, so Mother had to be treated with at least lip service respect, but for many it didn't go deeper than that, and Mother knew it. She always seemed to feel at least a little left out and never did understand some of the standard Werefox mindset.

"It would be wise to avoid unnecessary contact with him. No point in becoming too attached. It would only hurt you both."

Oh yes, *Sensei* would *love* to hear about this afternoon. He had an excellent point though. "I will be as cautious as possible." She poured herself some more tea, inhaling the fragrance. She'd got more out of the smell than the taste. Her sense of smell was nearly four times better than a human's, but her sense of taste was about a third.

Over the scent of properly brewed tea, *Sensei*'s displeasure wafted over to her nose. But he didn't argue with her. "I hope you are."

"I intend to. Five-thirty? I have to go. I'll keep you posted about Atolatar's follower." She stood, taking one last sip of tea. "I promised someone I'd meet them for dinner."

"Who?" Ryoko-*Sensei* asked as she hurried out the door. Liska didn't answer, hoping he'd assume she didn't hear. Unlikely, but possible. At very least, he'd probably forget to ask again.

***

Todd knocked at Sakaki's door at about five minutes to six. Hopefully he wasn't too early. Or too late. He had agonized for almost an hour on what to wear, how to treat this. Was this actually a 'date' date, or was this part of a probationary period, or what? He didn't want to act too casual and give her the impression that he wasn't treating this, or her, seriously. But on the other hand, he didn't want to act like he was expecting far more than she was ready to give. They were having dinner at the school cafeteria, for crying out loud!

Final choice was a pair of tan slacks and a blue and red button-down shirt that he had gotten compliments on before. It wasn't the fanciest outfit he owned, but it wasn't like he could go to the cafeteria in a tux either. Even a suit would seem odd. The shirt was a little nicer than he usually wore around campus, but it wasn't too noteworthy. Jamal had noticed, giving him a funny look, but Todd hadn't bothered to try explaining.

"Just a minute!" Sakaki called from inside.

Okay, maybe a little early. "No problem. Take your time."

Todd gripped his pocket flaps to stop himself from running his hands through his hair or pulling at his shirt. Why was he so nervous? He had taken Liska to a fancy dance before. But that wasn't a date, it was a way for her to break into a police evidence locker.

He had followed her to Russia where she would confront a murderous vampire. This was just dinner. It shouldn't be in that league. But it was a date. A real date. He thought.

The door opened. "Hi. Sorry, I was visiting my uncle and got back a little late." She smiled at him and his mouth went dry.

It looked like he had taken the right approach to dressing. Sakaki was wearing a forest green shirt made from some subtly shiny material that frilled at the neck. Todd had been there when Shahara picked it out for her, saying she needed some dressier tops, but this was the first time he had seen her wear it. Her hair, which she almost always kept up in some kind of a bun with a hair stick to keep it in place, was still in a bun, but held in place by a rose-gold filigree bun holder that blended nicely with her red hair. Then there was her necklace. It was just a simple jade heart on a gold chain, but the only time he had seen her wear a necklace before was when she was going to the policeman's ball.

When Sakaki looked askance at him, he realized he had been staring. Probably with his mouth open. "Uh, hi. You look great."

Another smile, smaller but realer than the first. "Thank you. So do you. Shall we?"

"We shall." Todd turned and, on impulse, offered her his arm. She took it without hesitation."

"Thank you, kind sir."

"Of course, my lady."

If Sakaki wasn't so small, they probably couldn't have walked that way down the stairs, but she was and they could. Todd was trying very hard not to giggle. Some of it was probably a release of nerves, but some of it was just the thought of the two of them walking around campus to the cafeteria, acting for all the world like they were in a manor house on the way to the ballroom. Sakaki looked serene, ignoring the looks they got, like she did this every day and was used to acting and being treated like a proper lady.

He made it a good halfway to the cafeteria before Sakaki looked at him with a glint in her eye. That was it. He lost it, dissolving into giggles. Sakaki didn't lose composure the way he did, but she did laugh.

They separated arms and walked to the cafeteria normally. So, conversation. That was something you were supposed to do on a date, right? It would help if he could think of a single thing to say. "So, you were visiting your uncle? The one I've met?" Who was technically her great-uncle, if he remembered correctly, but he could completely understand her dropping the 'great' part for convenience and to be less conspicuous. Come to think of it, when he visited Japan, he probably met more than one of her uncles. Still, only one lived in the area. He thought.

"Yes."

"How is he?"

"He's fine."

Right, this was boring. "How about you? Are you feeling better?"

Sakaki frowned briefly, but then it was gone. "Some. I'm currently playing tag with an old memory. It frustrates me."

"I thought you were really good at remembering things."

"I am. But this was a buried memory."

Ah, one of Tisiphone's. "So, why are you trying to dig it out? Why not let it stay buried?"

"Because it might be important. Besides, I keep getting small flashes. Very annoying." And if the way she absently rubbed her forehead before catching herself and immediately lowering her arm was any indication, it might be painful too.

Todd took the next two steps quickly so he could hold the cafeteria door open for her. "Yeah, I bet. Sorry. Um, if you need someone to talk to..." What was he doing? Sure, he was a psychology student, but he certainly wasn't qualified to give counseling yet, and Sakaki's issues ran deeper than most. It was possible that even a fully trained psychologist would be unable to help her much.

"I may. You've helped me in the past. But let's table that discussion for another time." Sakaki hummed in thought. "What classes are you taking this semester?"

School. That was something he could talk about. They compared schedules. Todd noticed that Sakaki's classes were all required classes. Which made sense since she was a second semester freshman, but he had no idea what she planned to major in. Well, there was one way to find out. "What's your major?"

Sakaki played with her straw. "I'm undecided at the moment. I haven't really figured out what major would be the most useful for... my career path." Which seemed to be defined as 'Ninja who worked to end threats from human and non-human sources'. Gee, now why didn't the college have a major in that?

"Huh, well, probably not one of the humanities." She shook her head. "Uh, I doubt law would help."

"I tend to agree."

"Pre-med?"

"No, we have our own specialists. Testing indicates that my strengths don't lie in that area. I know some emergency first aid, but..." She waved her hands in a dismissive manner.

"Okay. How about psychology?" He could help her, if she studied that.

"Unlikely. I know a lot of the same things you do, even if I don't know the names or the history. A few courses might not be wasted, but I don't think I need a degree in it."

Todd nodded. "Fair enough. Not philosophy."

"No one takes philosophy for practical purposes."

"I'll accept that." Todd leaned back. "You aren't interested in the arts."

"Not very practical. Not for me."

"So, math, computers, and maybe the sciences. Possibly politics."

"I have thought of politics, or chemistry. I've even contemplated psychology. But," she bit her lip, "I don't know. None of them seem quite right."

"Well, you have time. I don't think you're required to declare a major before junior year."

Sakaki nodded. "I'm sure I'll figure something out."

"And who knows, maybe they'll add something useful. I remember hearing rumors that the school was hoping to expand and offer some new majors in the not-so-distant future."

"Really? I hadn't heard that. Perhaps they will at that."

"Yeah, check out 'The Lighthouse'," Sakaki looked briefly confused. "You know, the school magazine." Her face cleared. "Yeah, they always have a column on what the school will be doing in the future."

"Hmm, perhaps I should take a look. I thought they just had information on how the sports teams were doing and a pep talk from the dean."

"Well, to be fair, there is a focus on that. But there is more, too. A little history, a bit about future expansion, and usually a teacher profile."

"I see. I'll check it out then."

Okay, that subject was talked out. Subject change. "So, do you have all your textbooks yet?"

"No, I have to get them tonight. The bookstore is open until eight tonight, correct?"

"I think so. I always order online. Ever since my first semester when I had to pay a hundred dollars for a brand new textbook and could only get five dollars back for it, because they were coming out with another brand new edition. It was a math book! Things didn't change in Trig in one year." Sakaki was snickering at him. "Well, they don't."

"I know. And I would have ordered them online, but by the time I was certain, there wasn't time."

That made sense. And he didn't really want to think about her staying in Japan. "I guess there wouldn't be."

"So, did you impress all your friends with your trip to Russia?" Sakaki asked with a smile.

"Well, some were upset I didn't take pictures." Sakaki gave a silent huff of a laugh. Probably Shahara had already ranted to her. "But I wasn't the only one to go out of the country over break. One of Jamal's friends went to Luxembourg, and their pastor, Pastor Erics, S— Anna, are you okay?"

Sakaki was holding her forehead like she was trying to keep her brain from forcing its way out; she was pale, breathing like she had run a marathon, and unless his eyes were deceiving him, she was trembling. "I think... I think I really need to dig out this memory."

"What do you need?"

"Quiet, privacy."

That completely ruled out the cafeteria. If he tried to get her to her room, someone might just report him to campus security for kidnapping, she looked that out of it. She might not even make it that far. Then he had it. "I know just the place." He scooped his trash onto his tray and grabbed hers while standing. "Don't get up yet. I'll be right back."

Todd threw away their trash and deposited their dishes as quickly as he dared before forcing himself not to run back to her. A fast walk wasn't a run. "Come on." He offered a hand that he didn't fully expect her to take. When she did take it, he didn't react, just calmly led her through the cafeteria and into the elevator up to the second floor of the building.

When they got out of the elevator, Sakaki blinked, looking around. "These are offices." Had she really been so out of it, she hadn't noticed where he was leading? Todd chose not to ask.

"They're empty now. But that's not where we're going." He led her to a little room tucked into a back corner. If you didn't know it was there, it could easily be overlooked entirely. And it was empty.

"What's this?"

"They call it a prayer chapel. Basically, a place for students to have private communion with God, or the deity of their choice, though it was designed for Christians." He waved at the cross on the wall. "Shahara showed me this. People rarely come here, and the door locks on the inside. I'll tell anyone who comes that the room is occupied."

Tension went out of her shoulders. "Thank you, it's perfect. Just don't let me stay too late. I still need to buy my books."

"Do you have your list?"

"Well, yes..."

"Good. I'll get them."

She looked about to argue but changed her mind. "Thank you. Here, pay for them with this." Sakaki handed him a pre-paid credit card and her list. "I'll try to settle this quickly."

"Take whatever time you need. I'll be waiting."

"Thank you." She shut the door, and he heard it lock.

Well, he might not be able to help her trawl through her memories, but he could at least pick up her textbooks and be a listening ear when she finished.

Chapter Four
Guard your heart as you would your body. – The Kikitsutai
Book of Wisdom

Liska forced past the haze of pain to survey the room. She trusted Todd, almost as much as she trusted anyone, but if this memory was as strong and deep as it seemed, she could be vulnerable for some time. That was intolerable without *knowing* for certain that this was a safe place. Lucky for her, the room was smaller than her kitchenette. There was no place to hide.

A wooden cross hung on the wall, with a table in front. The table had a light-colored cloth runner draped across it, with a darker embroidered cross on each end. A Bible and a hymnal were on the table, a kneeling pad was underneath. No other recesses of the room. She was safe.

"Hope you don't mind," Liska said to the cross, before sitting on the floor, back against the door. There was a chair, or she could use the kneeling pad, but she wanted the floor.

Now, what sparked the memory? It was all jagged edges and hooks. But maybe if she could find the right hook, she could use that to pull it out. Metaphorically, at least. What had Todd said?

"One of Jamal's friends went to Luxembourg, and their pastor, Pastor Erics," Luxembourg. Erics. What about... Ooh. Of course.

Tisiphone strode through the streets of Luxembourg City, examining the buildings with interest. She enjoyed historic places, and much of the city looked like nothing had changed in over a hundred years. But that wasn't the purpose of this visit. No, this was business.

Luxembourg was a peaceful country, now. Sure, it got invaded several times during the European wars, but it was small and defenseless enough that the invading armies generally left the country alone, leaving the buildings intact. Now, it was quiet and calm. Even their army was under a thousand people.

And, that peace had consequences. Unlike some countries, there wasn't video surveillance everywhere openly or covertly. She could work around that, but it was nice when she didn't have to. There was talk of putting up CCTV cameras in some areas, but it was still in the talking stage right now.

Tisiphone circled the main square twice. Tomorrow would be a festival, complete with fireworks. June 23 was Luxembourg's national Independence Day. The twenty-second was a night of celebrating and fireworks. There would be concerts and merrymaking going on through the night. Parties and concerts would be in almost every public square including this one. Today, the square was just a public square. Joggers and walkers lapped it for exercise. One more walker, even one with more of an interest on the buildings, didn't stand out at all.

Leaving the square, she crossed the street, following one of the narrow alley ways. Yes, this suited her needs perfectly. Yesterday she had scouted the same building from the opposite side. Now, she was convinced it was perfect for tomorrow.

For now, she had time to kill, and evening was approaching. She was hungry and had no desire to go back to her hotel yet. Perhaps a café was in order.

Tisiphone started back towards her hotel, knowing there were at least two outdoor cafés and three restaurants on her way. She hadn't made it a block when she spotted someone who gave her a familiar tingle. Another Twilight. Judging from his reaction, he noticed too.

He was tall, a little more than six feet tall, with dark hair and an easy smile. A little older than her, she'd guess, but she'd have to get closer to know for certain. Since he was heading towards her, that wouldn't be hard.

Luxembourg had three official languages: French, German, and Luxembourgish. French, she was mostly fluent in, and she knew enough conversational German to pass as long as the conversation didn't become specialized. Luxembourgish was heavily based on German, so she could usually muddle through, especially reading it. Which language should she use here? She decided to let him choose.

As he got within ten feet, she had to restrain her reaction. A vampire? Interesting. It wasn't even dark yet. But it was getting there, and vampires had been working on a version of protective sun block for centuries.

"Forgive me, Miss. I couldn't help but notice you. Pardon my impertinence, but may I ask if you love the moon?" He asked in German.

"You may ask." She gave him a brief smile. He probably didn't even need to ask. Vampires didn't have as much a sense of smell as Weres did, but it was better than human. Enough to pick up the animal scent that all Weres had to some extent. Being a female Werefox, she always had a faint scent of violets, as well. That was enough that even some humans could pick it up.

He laughed, showing teeth that any dentist would envy. Other than the abnormally sharp canines, of course. "So coy. I am Eric. And might I have the honor of knowing your name?"

"Sakaki." The instant she said it, she was mentally smacking herself silly. What was she doing? She wasn't supposed to give out her real name. Especially not when she had a perfectly good cover planned. Leticia, the French photography student, touring Luxembourg City to get pictures of the architecture. If anyone asked, her camera was back at the hotel. There actually was a top-of-the-line camera in her suitcase, that she could sometimes take a semi decent picture with. At very least, she knew what the most obvious buttons did. Weres simply didn't come by the visual arts easily.

"Well, Sakaki, I am enchanted to meet you." He offered his hand, but when she put out hers for a handshake, he kissed her hand instead.

Tisiphone tried to force back the blush. This was ridiculous! She was betrothed, not to mention, only sixteen. There was no way he would be interested if he knew that. She should tell him that. That she was too young for him, or wanted nothing to do with vampires, or... Her stomach took that moment to remind her that she hadn't eaten for hours. "I'm so sorry."

Eric smiled, eyes gleaming. "I heard nothing. But, if the lady wishes, I happen to know somewhere nearby that serves a divine blue steak."

"Really," she drawled. Like all Weres, she generally preferred her meat less cooked. Blue steak, scorched on the outside, raw inside, was something she only liked once in a while. But it looked like once in a while was now. "I could probably be persuaded. This is Luxembourg after all."

No major vampire bloods, Were clans, fairy rings, dragon enclaves, etc. were located in Luxembourg or within fifteen to twenty miles of the country. Partly by coincidence, then later, by design as the area was declared neutral ground for all Twilights and Nights. Much like Switzerland had a reputation for neutrality among the Humans. Which meant that a vampire escorting a Were to dinner could raise a few eyebrows, but they should be left alone. Good, she neither needed nor desired attention.

It was still a bad idea. She should say no. Say she had to go home. That she had someone waiting. That... They were there. Eric led her to the underground door that led into a café. One which clearly catered to the non-human community. Not that there weren't Days there, but there were far too many Twilights to be a coincidence. So were the Days in the know, or ignorant? Better assume ignorant to be on the safe side.

As she suspected, they did get a couple raised eyebrows, but no one commented. Both she and Eric ordered the blue steak. Another interesting puzzle piece. It was difficult to guess the ages of vampires, especially with them being effectively immortal, but from her understanding, after a couple decades as a vampire, they had very little interest in human food. So, for a vampire, Eric was probably young.

Not just because of the food. But between the food, the being out before dark, and approaching her even after he realized she was a Were; he not only gave the impression of being young, he might actually be a turned human. Those were rare. Especially these days. Vampire bloods kept strict control on turning. An unauthorized turning almost always resulted in the deaths of the new vampire and the one who turned him.

It was possible, though unlikely, that because there wasn't a strong local blood, someone could slip through the cracks; but from what she had heard, until recently, things had been very stable here. She could ask him, but that would be unquestionably rude. No, she should enjoy her dinner, which was delightful; enjoy her companion, who was determined to keep her smiling; and forget the rest. After all, she would probably never see Eric again.

When he asked her what she was doing in Luxembourg, having figured out she wasn't a native, she did have the presence of mind to pull up her cover.

"Photography? That surprises me. A lot. Surely you don't develop your own photos."

"Digital. They're all digital. I specialize in black and white of course." She could explain it away as artistic reasons instead of explaining that she couldn't see in color and really only had so much of an idea of what the picture looked like.

"Ah, of course."

"What about yourself?"

"Oh, nothing much. I'm... well, vacationing."

Not the complete truth. "Vacationing from what? Are you a wanderer?" A vampire without a blood.

"No, not exactly. But it might be better to be... away, briefly."

"I see." He was avoiding someone or some place. If he had provoked another vampire, he might well have to stay clear for centuries. But Eric didn't seem concerned and it was none of her business.

When they left the restaurant, Tisiphone made note of the name and location. A restaurant like that was one to remember. She was ready to make her excuses and head back to the hotel, but Eric asked if she wanted to take a walk.

"It is a beautiful night; surely you don't want to be stuck inside four walls just yet."

"Well, maybe a short one."

It was hours before she got back to her hotel.

***

Given the choice of methods, Tisiphone was primarily a close range assassin. It was the best way to ensure that she got her target and only her target. Her 'signature' weapon was a long string of razor wire, with a wooden handle on the end. Razor Thread, she called it. She also had an interesting variety of both lethal and non-lethal poisons and various ways they could be distributed. Long, extensive practice with the sword and knife left her capable with each.

Guns were not her preference. At all. She could use them and of course trained herself to recognize the most common and best quality types; but even then, it was mostly handguns. Easier to hide, and to dispose of.

Normally, the method of assassination was at least partially at her discretion. This wasn't normally. No, she had been assigned to eliminate two targets, at the same time, and specifically told to use the sniper rifle provided: a VSK-94. At least they picked a gun she could handle easily.

The Russian-made VSK-94 was designed for urban combat. The barrel was suppressed which eliminated the muzzle flash and made it quieter than a more powerful gun would be. It was small, barely more than three feet long, fully assembled; and light, under seven pounds when unloaded. Broke down to five pieces that she could easily fit in her backpack. The trade-off was that its effective firing range was only four hundred meters, which had her a little too close for comfort.

The gun itself had been smuggled into the country months earlier. She didn't know who exactly had done it, nor did she care. As long as the rifle was in good order and had ammunition, which it was and did. She had checked repeatedly. There was also a plan in place for the disposal of the gun afterwards. All she had to worry about was eliminating her targets, and no one else. The second was a much higher risk than she liked. But she knew better than to buck orders.

Tisiphone lay on the roof of her chosen vantage building, watching the festival below. The fireworks were due to begin in two minutes. Her ear plugs were in place, the gun was assembled, and ammunition in place. For the tenth time, she made certain the location of her targets. They weren't close to each other, but that might be for the best.

Everything was in place, her plan was as foolproof as it was possible to make it. All she needed was the cover. The first firework went off thirty seconds early, taking her by surprise. One last check, her targets were still in place.

With the fireworks filling the air, the sound of two quiet gunshots blended in. Luck and practice favored her. Both her targets went down with a single shot, and no innocents were harmed. As soon as that was confirmed, she rapidly disassembled the rifle, snagged her shell casings, and scaled down the fire escape.

Tense energy had been running through her all day, but now she felt like lightning was striking her skin everywhere. Her teeth were starting to chatter. Never failed. Pull off a mission, fall apart. But she couldn't do that here. Not now. The job wasn't finished yet.

First step was a quick spray of scent concealer to help cover up the scent of cordite. Her gloves were removed as soon as she was away from the fire escape and tucked in her pocket for now. Zipping up her jacket, she left the alleyway and walked at as brisk a pace as she dared. She had passed the second block before she heard the sirens.

Another block and she ducked into a walkway, and pulled out the mostly empty bottle of cola from her backpack and tucked her jacket inside. Tisiphone doused the front of her shirt with the remainder of the cola, before heading to the gas station across the street.

The teenaged clerk was sympathetic to the poor girl who had fallen and spilled her soda, and was now covered in dirt and soda, and let her clean up in the bathroom. Though he did have a hard time not staring at her hair (a wig that was blonde with purple streaks according to her mother), her piercings (magnetic), and her tattoos (sleeves, and temporary). Good. That meant he wasn't looking at her.

She had planned ahead, buying two identical pairs of dark jeans. Her new shirt was covered by the jacket that she zipped up. The clerk might be suspicious if he realized she had a whole new set of clothes to change into. But having a jacket, well that was just good sense.

Her old clothes went in a bag that was designed to cut odors. She gave them another spray with scent concealer anyway. As well as herself after she had changed clothes. Now even she couldn't smell anything suspicious on her.

Another couple blocks and Tisiphone slipped through another alleyway, shedding her wig, piercings, and the tattoo sleeves on the way. They all went into her backpack for the moment. She also reversed the jacket and unzipped it. A knit cap covered most of her hair, thanks to a mostly involuntary haircut a couple months earlier, and a cheap pair of glasses completed the look.

This new girl was the one who took the back entrance of the building made of cheap apartments. Mostly young, student housing. The stairs were quiet as most of the inhabitants were out at the various parties around the city. No one saw her go into 312, the safe house that the Kikitsutai had set up three years earlier. It was the same place she had gotten the gun.

Her tell tales hadn't been disturbed, and there was no recent scent but hers. Still, she checked the room before relaxing. The five-gallon tub of bleach hadn't been disturbed, and Tisiphone was quick to dump the parts of the rifle in it. The tub itself was hidden in the frame of an armchair, with a board on top and the cushion on top of that. Sometime in the next few weeks or months, someone would come by and dispose of the gun.

The room had other resources in it. Fake passports. Money in several currencies. Enough weapons to arm a militia. Materials for disguises. Nonperishable food and bottled water, and a first aid kit. But she didn't need any of that, so she left it alone. It was a temptation to allow herself to fall apart here and now, but Tisiphone refused to allow herself the chance. She had little doubt the room was bugged or surveilled somehow. There was no way, absolutely none, that she could allow herself to fall apart in front of an audience. They couldn't know she was weak.

In the basement was a laundry room. Her original plan was to throw her old clothes in a washer, start a load and abandon them. But when she found two washers running with no one in the room, her plan changed. One load was darks, so she dumped her work clothes in there, with an extra dollop of bleach. Hopefully not enough to ruin the other persons' clothes. Then she added an extra token to each machine so it would run longer. Whether the owner kept her clothes, threw them away, or took them to the office, really didn't matter.

Her backpack was switched out for another of a different color and designer, and her reversible jacket was exchanged for another reversible jacket with two different colors. This one had a hood, which she wore up when leaving, without the glasses.

The shell casings, carefully wiped, were tossed down a storm grate. The piercings were thrown away in a coffee shop trash can when she went in for a tea. Tattoo sleeves were rolled into a ball and thrown away by a theater. The various pairs of gloves she had worn were tossed in a hospital dumpster, that was more than a mile from the safe house, her hotel, or the scene of the crime.

All that was left was the wig. Dovetailing from the hospital, Tisiphone headed for the river. Two rivers met in Luxembourg City. She wasn't sure if this one was the Alzette or the Petrusse, but neither did she care.

The bridge, one she had found two days earlier, was lit, but not well. Nor was it frequently traveled. Shaky legs led her up the stone bridge, stopping next to the broken lamp near the middle of the bridge. This was the darkest part. Almost done. Just hold it together for a little longer. No one was around.

Looking into the water, she saw her reflection, until it was broken by her wig hitting the water. Done. Only the ear plugs were left. The ear plugs could be tossed out at hotel, they looked enough like the ear plugs that thousands of travelers used to sleep in strange surroundings. All she had to do now was go back to the hotel and get past her nerves.

"There you are. I've been looking for you."

Tisiphone turned so hard, so fast; that she was amazed she didn't leave her skin behind. "Eric?"

He came closer, frowning. "Are you alright? You seem..."

"I'm fine." The words came out half an octave too high. "I need to—" She tried to walk, but her legs gave out under her. Eric caught her before she ended up kissing stone.

"Here, sit down for a moment." He half-carried, half-led her to a bench.

"No, I need to get back." She was going to fall apart any minute now. She couldn't do that in front of him!

"You can't right now." He sat next to her, brushing hair from her face. "What's wrong?"

"I... I... Nothing. I just..." She shook her head. "I need to leave."

"Hey, just relax. Calm down." Eric touched her forehead, probably to check her temperature. Tisiphone gasped in sudden pain, then fell into black.

***

She woke up on a bed. An unfamiliar bed. An unfamiliar bed in a dark room she had never seen before. "Hey, are you okay?"

Tisiphone startled into a sitting position, scanning the room before spotting Eric in the corner. No other current scents. No sounds of other people present. This was probably a recent apartment. None of Eric's scents were older than a couple days. "Where am I? How did I get here?"

"My apartment. I brought you here." Eric stood with a shrug. "There's no couch, so I thought the bed would be more comfortable. And I don't have your information, so I wasn't sure about taking you to the local clinic. After all, it didn't seem to be an emergency."

He hadn't wanted to take her to the clinic. That was fine, she didn't want records of her visit to Luxembourg. "Right, thanks." A few test stretches didn't reveal any injuries. No signs that anything happened while she was unconscious. She didn't like the thought of being moved to an unfamiliar place while vulnerable but being left unconscious in public would probably be worse.

"I need to get back now." She still had to report in, and the jitters weren't gone yet.

The bed was large, and it was a little more awkward than she thought to slide to the edge, especially trying not to mess up his blanket with her shoes. She stopped when Eric held up his hands in a calming gesture. "Hey, easy. What happened back there? You were panicking, then you just passed out."

That wasn't a normal part of her nerves, but she had never been interrupted quite like that before, either. "I'm fine. Just a little stressed."

"Stressed, huh?" The tone was low and deep, and his scent had changed. Tisiphone cocked her head, questioning. Eric came and sat on the bed. "Well, then perhaps we need to help you relax some."

Instincts took over, making her lean back as his hand came up. Undaunted, Eric caressed the side of her face. Warmth spread through her, as he leaned in, closer, closer. His lips were practically on hers.

Startled, Sakaki pushed him back with a cry, leaping to her feet. At the door, she faced him wide-eyed, as Eric tried to regain his balance and not fall to the floor. He started to stand, as she turned and ran, pausing only long enough to grab her backpack.

The apartment was a studio, so the door led to the hallway. The hallway had a prominent staircase. Without thinking, she dashed down the stairs, not even keeping track of how many flights there were. Eric was running behind her, so she ran faster.

When the stairs ran out, there was a large door. Sure enough, it led outside. Once outside, Sakaki froze. She had absolutely no idea where she was. Behind her, Eric came to a breathless stop.

She turned to face him. Vampires might be faster but Weres are stronger. If he wanted a fight, she was ready.

"Rotten fangs, what was that about?" Eric asked, staying at least two meters back.

"You tried to... to..."

"Kiss you, yes. Most people don't freak out about that. Or consider a simple 'stop' to be sufficient," he said dryly. Eric took a couple steps closer, stopping when she glared.

She was starting to feel sheepish. Perhaps she had overreacted some. She needed to get back into Tisiphone mode. Tisiphone could handle this. "I'm going home now."

Eric held his hands up, palms out, and took another couple steps. "Okay. That's fine. But I'm worried about you. Can I at least walk you back to your hotel?"

She glared again but inwardly had to acknowledge he might have a point. "You can walk me to the Avenue de la Liberté." There were so many hotels near there that he wouldn't be able to guess which was hers.

"Deal. This way." He held out his hand for hers, but she ignored it, pretending to look around. After an awkward moment, he dropped it.

It was a ten-minute walk to the Avenue de la Liberté. Tisiphone, which she had managed to re-establish, had figured out where she was about halfway there, but continued to follow Eric. She was now feeling thoroughly foolish for her panic. She wasn't some silly little kid. Not that she should have let him kiss her, but there were many better ways to handle it.

"So, here we are. Are you sure I can't see you to your hotel?"

"I'm sure." She took a deep breath. "Sorry about... earlier."

"It's fine. So, may I kiss you now?" Eric asked with a crooked smile.

"No." She smiled to take the sting out of the refusal. "I have to go."

"Right. Will I see you tomorrow?"

"I don't know. Maybe." Tisiphone only had one more day in Luxembourg. Maybe she'd see him. Probably she wouldn't.

"Well, I'll be here." Eric looked around. "This is the part where I leave so you can go to your hotel?"

"Yes, I believe it is." He hesitated to leave, but Tisiphone said nothing to encourage him. She watched him walk out of sight before checking for tracers or bugs. Nothing. Judging from scent, Eric hadn't even tried to open her backpack. Good. She walked the last two blocks to her hotel, sent the coded email she had been told to send, took a shower, and collapsed into bed.

***

Due to the assassination of one of the Grand Duke's ministers, and the aide of an EU official, travel in or out of Luxembourg was prohibited for a few days. Tisiphone made sure to mention that when giving her full report, one day late.

Tisiphone did not meet Eric that night, choosing to stay in her hotel room, nursing a headache. *That night she dreamed of wandering streets filled with blood.*

The next day she was too restless to stay inside so she risked going out. The hotel had given her a newspaper each day at her request, so today Tisiphone read it at an outdoor café. The assassination was, of course, the biggest story in it. According to the press, the police suspected someone ex-military turned terrorist. They had identified the building she had shot from, but if any clues to her identity had been found, then it wasn't being reported.

"Sad, isn't it?" Eric said, as he pulled out the seat across from her.

Tisiphone jumped and mentally castigated herself for letting her guard down. "Oh! Hello. Early for you, isn't it?"

"A little. But the cream works well this late in the day. You're reading about our current events?"

"Impossible to miss it. It just... It seems odd. When's the last time something like this happened in Luxembourg of all places."

Eric shrugged. "I don't know. Not for a while, I'm sure. I can't even imagine why it happened this time. They weren't ill-liked, or even particularly important."

But they were the ones who knew about the non-human community and were trying to propose laws that would eventually expose them. Tisiphone shrugged. "I'm not even from here, and I don't generally follow politics."

"Is that why you weren't at any of the parties?" *Did he suspect her?*

"I don't like fireworks."

Eric smirked at that. "Fair enough. I don't either. How much longer are you in Luxembourg City?"

"Depends on how long the 'no travel' is in effect."

"That soon?"

"Student. I have to go back to school."

Eric frowned. "Look, there's someone I want you to meet. Can you take a trip to Switzerland?"

"Um, no. I really can't." She was due back in Japan as soon as possible.

"It's important."

"Sorry." Switzerland wasn't even neutral territory. It was very much vampire country. Not that she couldn't go to Switzerland, but it would be precarious.

Eric was saying something, trying to persuade her. But Tisiphone tuned him out. There were eyes on her. Not threatening. But... Tisiphone's eyes widened as she turned. "Father?"

Father regarded them both with eyes that betrayed no emotion. "I have transportation. Are you packed?"

"Yes, Father. It would only take a few minutes to finish up." She didn't bother asking him how he had gotten in the country or how he planned on them leaving with the no travel edict in place. Nor did she ask him how long he had been there, or if he had come because he was angry or disappointed with her. In fact, she didn't bother to ask anything.

He nodded. "Then I suggest you do so."

Tisiphone stood, folding her newspaper as she did so.

"Let me help you." Eric stood as well.

Father said nothing, positive or negative. Tisiphone shrugged but didn't say no. Since she was leaving, it didn't matter that he knew what hotel she was staying at. Her hotel was actually across the street from the café. It did not escape her notice that Father remained at the café, probably to let Sakaki deal with this herself.

Eric didn't say anything until she unlocked her door. "Do you have to leave?"

"Yes, of course."

"We could sneak out. Arrange transportation. I can take you to the vampire homeland. He would never be able to make you leave. Then—"

"No!" Tisiphone gave him a look of mingled horror and pity. "I am going home."

"But I need—"

"You need to let it go." Tisiphone tucked her toothbrush in her suitcase. One more glance around the room, and she was satisfied she had everything. "Goodbye, Eric. Perhaps we'll meet again one day."

Head held high, Tisiphone walked away, not listening to his sputtering. Father was waiting outside with a car, which took off once she was inside. Silence became heavier and heavier. Finally, she spoke. "Nothing happened. With Eric, I mean."

"I know."

She flushed and glared at the floor of the car, trying to pull her emotions together. Of course he had been watching her. Or had someone else doing it, which was all the same.

But Father spoke again, in the same measured tone, "I know, because I know you."
Oh. The rest of the ride was less awkward.

***

Sakaki lifted her head from her knees, feeling tears on her face. It took at least two minutes longer than it ought to have to calm her breathing and heartrate. So that was what she had been trying to recover. Why? Why was that particular memory so insistent on being remembered? Probably because of Eric. Her first crush. Even when she had buried all of Tisiphone's memories, she hadn't completely forgotten him.

But it was just a crush; a handsome, older boy, interested in her. At sixteen, she was just coming into her sexual maturity and had been overwhelmed. It meant nothing.

There were still a few blurry spots in that mission. She couldn't remember the names of her targets, or why she had been required to use that particular method. But it wasn't important. The memory didn't hurt anymore.

Anyway, it didn't matter. She knew for a fact that Luxembourg had been a necessary mission, and heaven only knew where Eric was now. She just needed to make sure not to let memories of Eric interfere with her relationship with Todd.

Liska wiped her face clean and stood up on legs that had long since fallen asleep. "Thanks," she said to the cross, then let herself out. The past was in the past, and the future was waiting for her.

Chapter Five

Trust is the crowning jewel of friendship. – The Kikitsutai
Book of Wisdom

Todd looked up from the English textbook he had been reading through when he heard Sakaki coming. "Hey, feeling any better?"

She sat down next to him. "Some. I think I need something for this headache, but I found the memory I was looking for."

"Good?" He hoped so, anyway. Considering her memories, there wasn't a guarantee.

As if she read his mind, she smiled. "Yes, good. It wasn't that bad a memory and it doesn't hurt anymore."

"Then, good. Um, I got your books. I tried to get the cheapest used books they had. Except for one where someone covered nearly a quarter of the book with purple highlighter. Then I went for the next cheapest."

"That's fine." She took her card back, then looked at the book in his hands. "Anything interesting?"

"Well, I finished reading 'The Celebrated Jumping Frog of Calaveras County'. Almost finished with 'The Pit and the Pendulum'."

"Ah, yes. I do enjoy Poe sometimes. Creepiness and all. Though I remember being very disappointed with 'The Gold Bug'. I expected something a little more interesting. A little more... 'Poe'. Then again, not all his works were macabre, that's just what he's known for."

"I think 'The Gold Bug' was his most popular piece."

Sakaki nodded. "I read that. Personally I preferred 'The Pit and the Pendulum' and 'Loss of Breath'."

"I don't think I've heard of that one," Todd admitted.

"Not one of his more popular works, but it's actually rather funny. In a slightly dark way." She frowned. "The other story. The frog one, that was... Mark Twain?"

"That's right."

She sighed. "I have trouble with Twain. They say he was a master of dialects. Maybe he was, but I have a hard time reading them."

"Yeah, I imagine you would." Especially since English wasn't her first language. There was silence for a while. Sakaki slumped into the couch, looking tired. "Did you want to talk about it? Your memory?"

"No, not right now anyway. Maybe later. Actually, I'm not even sure why this particular memory is being so insistent."

"Memories aren't very well understood." Todd took a deep breath. "Do you have a lot of hidden memories?"

"I don't know. They're hidden. Honestly, I think I've got about eighty percent or so uncovered. Hopefully all the important parts."

"I guess it was a dumb question."

Sakaki shrugged. "Not a dumb question, just one I can't answer. Sorry, this probably wasn't what you had in mind for tonight."

Todd took a moment to try to word this correctly. "Well, I certainly didn't plan this, but I did want to get to know you a little better. I'm not going to pry, I hope. But if listening will help..."

Sakaki laughed. "Good answer. It wasn't a test though." Suddenly she jumped to her feet. "How about we put these books away and take a walk or something."

"Sure, sounds good." Todd stood, making sure he was holding more than half the books. Sakaki didn't call him on it.

When they got to her dorm, she ducked inside long enough to drop off her books and take something for her headache. "So, did you have anywhere you wanted to go?" He asked when she came out.

"No, not really." She led the way down the stairs. "Okay, I have an idea. You wanted to get to know me better, and I should work on getting to know you better as well. Why don't you show me one of your favorite places on or near campus? Then next time, I'll show you one of mine."

"That's a cool idea." Todd paused and thought about it. "It would be even cooler if I could think of someplace you might like."

She smiled. "So don't think about me. Just show me someplace you like."

"Okay, but don't say I didn't warn you."

***

Liska hadn't been sure what to expect with such a dubious warning, but this wasn't it. Todd took her to one of those small hole-in-the-wall stores; the kind that were almost invisible if you didn't know about them. Liska loved those kinds of stores. You never knew what kind of treasure you might find.

This particular store sold art supplies. Walking in the door, paint tickled her nose and she could almost taste the ink. It took a good minute for other scents to penetrate, paper, erasers, floor cleaner, and people. On the back wall, about three-quarters up there was a border of paper, turned sideways into diamonds. Even color-blind, she could tell a gradual progression of color as the grays went from light to dark. Below them were canvases in various sizes.

On a table near her was an almost haphazard display of sketchbooks in various sizes and types of paper. A spinning display on the counter had brushes ranging from too small to be mouse whiskers to larger than Shahara's biggest make-up brush. Labels identified the material, including camel, sable, and horse, along with many synthetic materials.

A bookshelf held watercolor paints on one side and oil-based paints on the other. Another table held small tins of various pencils, half marked with a B or an H and a number, the other half sorted by colors. The table next to it had pens; mostly black, but other colors and inks as well. Kits were available as one headed further in. Colored pencils, drawing pencils, charcoal, watercolors, pens, clay, etc. For the less experienced artist, there were instruction books, notices of various classes, etc.

"I don't think I realized how many materials were available to create art. But I can see why you like this place." Liska fiddled with the wooden figure of a human, seeing how many poses she could make it hold.

"That's a cheap model. They have better ones." Todd handed her a box for a deluxe model. More joints, better material, guaranteed to hold a pose, and correspondingly, much more expensive.

"What would *I* do with it?" She put it back. "So, what's with the letters on the pencils?"

"Oh, that's to tell how dark and sharp it is. The higher the H, the sharper. B's are more muted and not as dark. Though sometimes they are written as HB which is just confusing. The standard number 2 pencil? That's 2 B."

She couldn't resist. Liska scooped up a 2 B pencil and a 4 H pencil. "2 B or not 2 B?"

Todd laughed. "Here, let me show you." He took both pencils from her and found a clean spot on the testing paper before scribbling a thick line with each. "See the difference?"

"I think so. Why do you need so many?"

"*I* don't, but I don't focus on pencil drawings. Those who do need precision to get the right shading. When you don't use colors, the changes in shade become more important." Then he seemed to blush, realizing who he was talking to.

"I can see that." Liska had noticed she had a better appreciation of the difference between close shades than some people who could see in color. "So what is your focus?"

"I dabble. Both pencil and pen and ink do have their good points. Charcoals and pastels can be fun if you don't mind getting your hands dirty. I like color, so if I do use pencil, it's usually colored pencil. I've done watercolor for my paintings, but generally use acrylic. I'd like to try oil painting, but that's expensive, and a totally different technique." Todd absently leafed through the sketchbooks. Liska watched him fight a mental battle over one that had a twenty dollar price tag before putting it back with a sigh.

"What's the difference between these books?"

"Oh, lots of things. Size, quality, number of pages, the texture of the paper, etc. See, the paper in this one is very smooth. That's good if you're using pen. This one has a bit of tooth to it. Important if you're doing charcoal."

Liska felt the offered pages, nodding at the difference. "You like sketchbooks, don't you?"

"Guilty. Sketchbooks and pads. I almost always have to have one nearby, and I tend to buy them even when I don't need them." He shot one last semi-regretful look at the twenty dollar sketchbook before turning back to her. "So, do you have any idea why Shahara keeps suggesting that I should teach you how to draw?"

It took her a moment to remember the conversation. Though it was almost a month ago. She had told Shahara that she'd have better luck drawing a masterpiece than having a relationship with Todd. "Inside joke."

"Ah, right. Well, do you want to learn?" He coughed slightly. "Because I don't mind teaching you."

"I'm nearsighted and colorblind," Liska said, flatly.

"Just because I like to use color doesn't mean everyone does. Pens, pencils, even charcoals. Actually, charcoals might be best, everything's a little smudged anyway, so you don't have to be precise. Besides you can't be too nearsighted, I've never seen you with glasses."

Ryoko-*Sensei* was starting to go blind and he almost never used glasses. But this wasn't the time to bring up the Kikitsutai's tendency towards degenerative vision disorders. "You really want to do this, don't you?"

"Well, not if you don't want to. But I think..." Todd bit his lip.

He wanted to invite her into his world. This place where he was in his element, even more than in the dojo. It was almost humbling. "Don't expect much." She picked up a cheap sketchpad and strode over to the charcoal kits.

Todd was at her side a moment later. "No, you should try this sketchpad. Better for charcoals and almost as cheap." He looked at the kit she had been examining. "You *could* use this one, but I think you'll like this one better." 'This one' was a kit by a different company that included two more charcoals, and an eraser brand that even she knew was considered good quality. "I agree you shouldn't buy expensive materials before you know if you'll like it, but you want good enough quality to accurately know whether or not you'll like it."

"So, is this everything I'll need?"

"No, you need a fixative spray. I'll find one."

While he was doing that, Liska put back the first sketchpad she picked up and grabbed the twenty dollar sketchbook Todd had eyed covetously.

"What's fixative spray?" Liska called as she went to the register, handing the cashier the expensive sketchbook first, with a finger to her lips.

The woman at the register, Liska estimated she was in her late fifties, possibly the owner, wearing what was probably a very colorful dress, nodded with a smile. It was a small store, and there was only one other customer, the woman had no doubt been watching them. And since this was one of Todd's favorite stores, she probably knew him.

She put the sketchbook in a paper bag, inside the plastic bag she put the other supplies in. Todd came back with the fixative spray just after that. "Hi, Juliet. Trying to win a convert."

"I see that." Juliet smiled as she added the spray to her total.

"Right, fixative spray. Well, the whole point of charcoal is to smudge. But eventually you get the picture the way you want it, and you don't want it to smudge or smear anymore. So, you spray it with the fixative, and that holds it in place."

Liska nodded. "Was there anything you wanted?"

"No, I'm good at the moment. Hey, Juliet, do you know when–"

"I'll let you know when we get your canvases."

Todd gave her a sheepish smile. "Thanks." Then he spotted the amount of money Liska was handing. "Wow, that added up to more than I thought it would."

"It's fine." Liska took her bag and started towards the door. "Hey, want to check out the bookstore while we're here?" She could hear Juliet chuckling after them.

"Um, sure."

They compared favorite sections and books. Todd, not surprisingly, enjoyed coffee table books, non-fiction about art and artists, and detective stories and thrillers. He also liked biographies and some fantasy and science fiction. Liska enjoyed histories, some biographies, fairy tales and folk tales from around the world, the occasional thriller, and non-fiction about other places.

"No paranormal?" Todd asked, half-joking.

"They get everything wrong."

Todd laughed.

Liska let herself chuckle. "That said, I do read it sometimes. I'll read a little bit of everything. You never know where you'll get a good idea from. I actually found an amazingly useful idea in the middle of an abysmally written trashy romance novel Kira gave me as a joke."

"Oh, what idea?"

She smiled as she thought of it. "The female lead once threw off a pursuit by appearing to be in the act of changing. The people following immediately shut the door to give her time to finish, which she used to escape. I actually did try something similar once. Probably wouldn't have worked if I hadn't shrieked and thrown something at him. Naturally, the success would depend on the caliber of the pursuer."

Todd shook off a slightly glazed look. "Yeah, it probably would. Um, books?"

Liska chuckled and changed the subject. It wasn't until they were heading back to the school that she pulled out the paper bag and handed it to him. "Here, happy belated Christmas."

Todd took it on instinct. "You didn't have to do that." He looked in the bag. "Oh, wow. You *really* didn't have to do that. Uh, I didn't get you anything."

There was no one around, so she could answer as Sakaki, not Anna. "I don't celebrate Christmas. It isn't a major holiday in most of Japan, and the Kikitsutai don't celebrate at all. Well, Mother tries, but it's hard when you're the only one."

"That's... kinda sad. Celebrating alone when no one else around you does."

"A little. I try to be home for her then. Father hasn't mentioned anything, but I think he does too. I watch the specials with her." Obviously that wasn't enough for Todd. "Anyway, I know you celebrate, and I hadn't really gotten you anything. Those crackers don't count."

"You did though. You came back."

Thankfully he wasn't looking at her, because her blood was betraying her. Though he might not be much better if his ears were any indication. "Well, Happy Christmas anyway."

"Thank you. But, just so you know, it's 'Merry' Christmas."

She did know that, didn't she? "Not in England. They say 'happy' there. Makes more sense."

"That does fit in with everything else, doesn't it? I don't know why Christmas gets a 'merry' when everything else is 'happy'."

Liska took a quick rummage through her mental databases and came up empty. "Neither do

I." They were back at her dorm. "Well, I've got to go. I'm running on fumes and going to crash soon."

"Yeah, got to be ready for class. Um, do you want to have breakfast together? Before class? My earliest tomorrow is nine, so..."

She had a ten o'clock. "Okay, eight-thirty, at the cafeteria?"

"Great. See you then." Todd hesitated. "Can I give you a hug?"

It was an awkward, shy, hesitant question. It was also almost heartbreakingly sweet. "Yes, you may."

His hug was gentle, careful not to take any liberties, and brief. It was quite possibly the most romantic thing anyone had ever done for her. "Goodnight," Todd said and left.

His scent still in her nose, Liska forced herself to keep both the dreamy smile and the knowing smile off her face. *He liked her. He might even love her.*

Tonight, she would not think like that. Not now. She would wash off her make-up and go to bed.

Liska unlocked her door.

Scratch that. New plan. Deal with the irritating pest who had made himself at home on her bed, wash off her make-up, and go to bed.

Chapter Six

Love is as beautiful and deadly as the finest blade. – The
Kikitsutai Book of Wisdom

"Hello, Korvou. Are you enjoying my textbooks?"
Liska had forgotten that she had dumped the books
on her bed before going out.

"Not really. Have you *read* what they called
the causes of the Franco-Prussian War?" The dark-
haired Fae didn't so much as glance in her direction.

"No, I just got those. But I'm betting they
didn't include anything about the Fae-Vampire
alliance of 1868." That had been a disaster and a
half. Fortunately, it was short lived. Especially
considering it was made up of races that barely
aged.

"You'd be right. Nothing about the Werewolf
Insurgence of '69 either." That had happened the
next year, probably as a direct result of the alliance.

"Right. So, other than to lambaste my history
books for not having information that they aren't
supposed to have, why are you here?" Liska leaned
against the doorway, arms loose at her sides. Just
because he was acting relaxed now, didn't mean he
couldn't be a threat in seconds.

With a sigh, Korvou rolled to a sitting
position. "Is it too much to ask... Are you wearing
make-up?"

"No. What do you want?"

Liska forced herself to maintain a relaxed air as he stood and took a few steps closer. "You *are* wearing make-up. And you're all dressed up. *And* that human male walked you up. I felt his aura. Your auras are entwining. I had no idea you had gotten that far."

"Korvou!" She snapped. "Focus. Why are you here?"

"Right. Well, it wasn't to wish you luck or congratulate you. Though, good luck and congratulations." She nodded. "No, there's something you need to know. You remember my warning from earlier, that things were going to happen? It's not over."

"Is it ever?" Liska sighed, before frowning. "I do remember your warning, but didn't I deal with that?" She could have sworn it was Atolatar he was warning her about.

"Yes and no. You took care of the red and black aura, the one that was blood and death. Good job on that, by the way. But with him gone, I can see another that follows the same path, green and poisonous, like a serpent."

There was something about dealing with Korvou that made Liska wish she swore. At the moment, she was almost ready to 'forget' she didn't. But she couldn't let Korvou know that. "Atolatar wasn't calling the shots. He was being controlled."

"Manipulated. He was working of his own free will, but I think you're right. Someone else was behind it. I doubt Atolatar realized it."

"That explains a lot. A whole lot." No wonder Atolatar had banked so much on a plan that could be stopped so easily. He wasn't enough of a planner to realize how precarious his plans actually were. Whoever was behind him probably didn't expect him to succeed anyway. So, what was the real plan? "Where?"

"Not far. This state, I believe. But I can't narrow it down more than that. It's fuzzy somehow. Someone else is involved too, but I can't read that one well. Someone who doesn't know his own mind or works on impulse probably. They're hard to predict."

That made a lot of sense. "What makes an aura fuzzy?"

"Magic can. Certain types of mental partitioning, indecision. Yours is fuzzy, but I have a lot of experience reading it." Korvou smirked.

Liska deliberately didn't roll her eyes. "So, why tell me?"

"You don't think I'd give you a warning out of the kindness of my heart?" Korvou put a hand over said organ. "I'm hurt. Wounded to the quick."

"I can do that, if you like." Liska drew a dagger, rubbing the hilt back and forth slowly.

Korvou dropped his joking attitude. "Seriously? I don't know what this poisonous aura wants, but it's bad. Bad for you, and probably everyone. I know that I really, *really* don't want it to succeed. And sooner or later, it's headed for you."

"I understand. Let me know if you get anymore?"

He grimaced. "That's the other thing. I'm going to be incommunicado for a while. It's a Fae thing. I leave tomorrow and probably won't be back for six months to a year."

Now that was interesting. Korvou was undergoing a chrysalis? She hadn't realized he was that close.

For the first thousand years of a Fae's life, sometimes a little longer, they would periodically have to cocoon in order to grow and get more power. Usually happened about once a century or so until they reached their top power level. Since a Fae in chrysalis was almost completely vulnerable, the entire thing was supposed to be kept secret from non-Fae. Even among themselves, it wasn't uncommon to attempt to hide when and where one was cocooning, to prevent sabotage and attacks. The only reason she knew about this little quirk of the Fae was because her skulk made a living off of information and had frequent dealings, good and bad with Korvou's ring. They made a point of knowing these things. "I see. Good luck."

"Thanks. Keep an eye on things for me."

"I'll keep an eye on things. Period. Not for you."

Korvou laughed at that. "So, you and the human?"

"Get out."

"You're going to leave me wondering? All this time I'm away?" Korvou tried to look entreatingly at her. Puppy dog eyes really didn't work on him.

"Yup. Have a good trip. Up to a year, you said?"

"That's right. Think you can manage it?"

Liska smiled blissfully. "A year. A year of peace. Not finding you in my room. Not hassling me. Oh, I think I'll manage just fine. Take your time."

"For that, I'll try to make it less." Korvou got serious. "Look, I'm calling in my favor. While I'm gone, I need you to do something for me."

As he explained, Liska felt her eyes widen. "You don't ask much, do you?"

***

Todd was heading to the cafeteria to meet Sakaki for breakfast when a strong arm started pulling him aside. "Just the person I was looking for."

His instinctive struggles faded as he recognized the voice. Recognizing the voice's owner took a little longer. That's right, the tall black-haired man was a 'friend' of Sakaki's. Sort of. "Korvou, right?"

"That's right."

"Look, I've got to go. I'm meeting someone." He wasn't sure what the Fae wanted, but he was pretty sure that it wasn't something he wanted to be involved in.

"They'll wait." Korvou dragged him to a nook where it didn't look like they were hiding but they wouldn't be overheard. "First of all, congratulations with Liska."

"Uh, thanks. She told you?"

Korvou huffed a laugh. "Liska wouldn't tell me if it was raining fire unless she owed me a favor or was trying to make me owe her one. I read it in your auras."

"You were the one who said we had a destiny," Todd brought up their first real conversation.

"I did. I also said I don't know how long or short, or if it's good or bad. I still don't. But I do wish you the best of luck. And as much as I'd love to stick around to watch how this plays out, I have to go for a while. But I wanted to warn you first. Something is up. Something big. Something that will interfere with your relationship. Depending on how the two of you react, it could end everything or it could lead to the two of you being bound tighter than ever."

Todd blinked. "You can tell that?"

Korvou gave a dismissive half-shrug. "What can I say? I'm just that good."

"Can you tell me when or what?"

"Not a clue. It's still up in the air. I just know that forces are at work that will strain things. But I don't know the catalyst yet."

"If you're quite finished with your vague proclamations of doom, Todd has a breakfast appointment with me." Liska appeared suddenly, arms crossed, fingers of the right hand drumming on her left arm.

"I'm finished. You took care of it?" Korvou asked as he released his hold on Todd's arm.

"It's done. Now, I believe you were leaving."

The Fae smirked as Todd hurried to Liska's side. "Don't rejoice too much. I'll be back in a year or less. Try not to let the world break too much while I'm gone."

Liska rolled her eyes. "I've managed without you in the past. I can manage without you now. You worry about yourself, I've got everything else. Don't let the others eat you alive."

Korvou gave her a wry smile, a half bow, and faded into the wall.

She nodded, satisfied. "So, breakfast?" She asked in her 'Anna' voice as she turned back to a confused Todd.

"What was that about?"

"Long story. He has to be away for now. Asked a favor of me and apparently decided to hassle you before he left." Sakaki shrugged, letting more of Liska drop. "I wouldn't bother asking."

It was too crowded for those kinds of explanations. And he wasn't sure she would tell him even if it wasn't. "Right. So, um, how much did you hear?"

She just gave him a smile. "Let's get some breakfast. You have class soon."

Acknowledging that she had a point, Todd dropped the question. She probably wouldn't answer anyway.

"When are you done with classes?" Todd asked as they sat down with their food.

"I have a two o'clock. But that's also my last."

"Okay, I have a two o'clock also. After class, maybe around three, do you want to have your first art lesson? We could use the, huh, not the game room. Too noisy. The room upstairs, between the offices? Where we were yesterday?"

"That would be fine."

A thought occurred to him. "Do you know basic drawing techniques? Vanishing point? Perspective? Proportion?"

"I've heard of them." She sounded skeptical.

"Right, tell you what. I'll bring some of my pencils and we'll go over the basics before we get to your charcoals. Bring your sketchpad." She nodded. "Good." Then he noticed the clock and stifled a wince. "Sorry, got to eat and run."

"You do that," She said with a small smile.

***

As Liska finished up with the chapter review questions for history (factors in the Hundred Years war), the phone rang. Her mobile phone, not her room phone. Since only family had her mobile number, and one in the afternoon in Florida was two in the morning in Japan, her first thought was that it was Ryoko-*Sensei*. But according to caller ID, it was Kira.

"Liska's House of Mayhem and Madness, this is Mayhem speaking."

"I still think you cheated to get that one."

Good, everything was fine. "So, not that I'm not glad to hear from you, but isn't it the middle of the night over there?"

"Come on, two isn't that late." Which was true, for them. "Besides, I wanted to call when you would likely be there and awake." Of course Kira would memorize her class schedule. "How is everything?"

"Fine." No way was she going to mention Korvou and his favor. The art lessons... maybe. Maybe not. Atolatar? After she had more to give her. "I've only had two classes so far. How about you?"

"Well, I've been asked to arrange a treaty in Washington D.C. Werewolves and Werecoyotes. They asked for a member of our skulk to be one of the intermediaries. Your father thought it would be a good experience for me."

Liska felt her eyebrows raise. She couldn't remember the last time Father had delegated a task like that to anyone under forty. "Well, good for you. You'll certainly do a better job than I would." She was a little too blunt and impatient for standard diplomacy.

"Thank you. Anyway, I was thinking, since I'll be so close, relatively, maybe I could come down and see you while I'm in the country."

"That would be wonderful if you can swing it. If you can't, I understand. When?"

"About two weeks. I'll email you the dates and my itinerary. So," Her voice got more playful. "How's Todd?"

"He's fine."

"Just fine?"

Sakaki smiled. "Yes, he's still interested. He's going to try to teach me how to draw." She had to pull the phone away because of her cousin's squeal.

"Well, good luck."

"Thank you." Things really had changed if there was even a chance of her marrying a human, even an Esper, and not get ostracized. Father might have managed it, but she never thought she could.

Of course, better Todd than Eric. She never could have gotten away with marrying a vampire. Liska frowned. Why was she even thinking about Eric right now? She hadn't seen him in years, and probably never would again. Must be because of the memories she uncovered the day before.

"Are you still there?"

"Yes, I'm here. Sorry, just thinking. Anyway, I hope to see you when you come. Congratulations on being asked to do this. But I've got to go to class."

"Okay. I'll talk to you later."

***

Todd fidgeted as he sat on the couch; sketchpad and the most commonly used drawing pencils in front of him. How would Sakaki take him teaching her something? Especially being treated like an absolute beginner? On the other hand, she seemed to be a beginner in this.

He really wanted her to like this. Oh, he didn't need or expect her to become a master artist, or even love art like he did; but art was such a big part of his life that it would be sad if she couldn't share it with him.

"I'm here." Anna sat down next to him, looked around, and slowly became a little more Liska. It was funny watching the transition, but at the same time, Todd was aware that if he didn't know, he probably wouldn't have noticed a thing. Just like he wouldn't have noticed that she didn't relax as far as Sakaki. "Sorry, class got out late."

"That's fine. Mine got out early. So, what do you know about drawing?"

"That I can't do it."

Todd bit his lip so he didn't laugh. "Yet. You can't do it *yet*. If you can see, you can learn to draw. Okay, let's start at the beginning. Vanishing point and perspective." She seemed to understand the concepts easily enough, but something odd happened when she drew. "You can imitate fine, but you seem to have more trouble when I don't draw something first." Todd eyed the cubes. Hers looked very close to his, but her rectangle was much messier.

"Mother used to have me practice calligraphy either as a calming method or as a minor punishment. I can mimic, even forge handwriting. But..."

Todd nodded, ignoring the part about forging which probably shouldn't surprise him but did. It made sense that Sakaki wasn't very visual, especially considering her eyes weren't her strongest sense. "Okay, so that means to draw something, you need to be able to see it. That's fine. A lot of artists need a picture or model to work from. Can you draw that couch in front of us? Don't worry about shading or anything fancy. Just the couch."

Better. His art teacher would probably have a fit, but it was recognizably a couch. Sakaki looked frustrated with it.

"No, that's a good start. Here's how we can make it look better." They moved on to a few techniques for shading, etc. When she was done, there was improvement. It still wouldn't be eligible for an art show, but it was a respectable couch for a beginner.

"Great, you're starting to get the hang of this. I want to give you a little more practice with pencils before moving on to charcoals. How about next time I bring you a few things to draw?"

"Okay. When?"

"When's good for you?"

"Tomorrow?"

Todd smiled. She liked it at least enough to come back. "Sure. I have a three o'clock, so, four?"

"That will work. When are you starting the Kendo club back up?"

"Next week. I'm finally cleared to spar again. Will your wrist be up to it then?"

"Should be." Sakaki didn't even look at her wrist. Which probably meant that she was stretching the truth.

"Well, if it isn't, don't push it. Please? I'd feel horrible if I hurt your wrist again."

She laughed. "Okay, so you don't feel horrible, I won't spar until my wrist is better."

"Thank you. I appreciate your consideration for my tender feelings." He made a silly face at her, making her laugh again.

"I do have to go, though. I need to talk to my uncle."

"Ah, okay. Will I see you at dinner?"

She glanced at her watch. "Perhaps. I should be back by six, I think."

"Well, then I'll wait until then."

Sakaki shot him one more blinding smile, and strode off, sketchpad in hand. Todd gathered his supplies in a dreamy haze.

Chapter Seven

Fear and Hatred are the greatest enemies. – The Kikitsutai
Book of Wisdom

"You're getting better at this. Do you think you're ready to move on to the charcoals?" There was a pause. "Anna? Anna? Sakaki?"

Liska glared at him. "It's Anna."

"Then actually respond, please. Where is your mind today?" Todd paused. "Is something going on that I don't know about?"

"No. Yes. Probably." She sighed. She hadn't told Todd about Korvou's warning. *Sensei*'s reaction had been bad enough. He had almost broken his teacup. And he was stressing the need for her to talk to the blood. She hadn't yet, partially because she was still getting past jetlag, but also because there was something weird going on. "I'm missing something. I keep feeling like I know the pieces, but I'm not pulling them together, or even recognizing them, and it's driving me crazy. What time is it?"

"Five."

"I know it's early, but how about dinner? I have something I need to do tonight, and I'd like to catch a nap first." She really couldn't put off talking to the blood any longer.

"Sure. Okay." Todd started packing things up. "Anything I should know about? Or can?"

"Information gathering for now." At some point, she should tell him the truth about Atolatar. He deserved to know. But not here and now.

"If you need a sounding board, or someone to help you find your pieces; I'll listen."

Liska nodded. "I may take you up on that at some point."

"Happy to help." Todd stood and offered her his hand. She didn't need it but didn't see a reason not to take it.

Jamal joined them, since he had a meeting later. Future Healthcare Providers, or something like that. Shahara wasn't there. Liska mostly let the other two talk, letting the conversation wash over her. She didn't feel like talking, didn't even really feel like thinking, particularly about the confusing memory mess. But she couldn't stop. It was like poking a bruise to see if it still hurt. Yup, still did.

When Jamal left to go to his meeting, she excused herself as well. Todd hadn't finished eating yet, so he merely wished her luck on her 'research'. Good, he was starting to learn some subtlety.

Liska did manage a nap, waking about eleven o'clock. Perfect. Van should be awake by now. Now, the main question was would Van be able to help her, and with or without permission from the chief? One way to find out.

A few months ago, she had made arrangements for Van to have a phone, that Liska personally made sure didn't get cut off. While she hadn't called her contact often, and Van had never called her, Liska appreciated having it. It was so much easier than actually going to the Blood and dealing with Rex Magnus.

The phone rang. And rang. And *rang*. After the twelfth ring, Liska hung up. This had never happened before. True, it was conceivably possible that no one was around to answer the phone. It wasn't the fake phone that was manned by wraiths to deter outsiders. But always, *always*, when she called, Van had answered. Okay, once someone else did, but he found Van and put her on the phone.

So, if no one answered.... Possibility one, the phone got cut off or cancelled. Possibility two, something was going on there, and everyone was busy or not near the phone. Possibility three, the chief had given orders to ignore all calls or hers specifically. Possibility four, no one *could* answer the phone.

Trying to force back a very bad feeling, Liska pondered her options. While not a master hacker by any stretch of the imagination, she was good enough to check utility records. But that wasn't something she wanted on her school computer's records. Her laptop was a possibility, but it would be safer to use Ryoko-*Sensei*'s computer. Or she could go in person and get her information that way. If there was a current emergency, they might need help. If they were ignoring her calls, she'd be harder to ignore in person.

***

Liska eyed the small, nondescript building dubiously. Even in the best of times, it had never looked welcoming. To keep visitors away, the building was kept deliberately drab and dingy, no signs or labels; located in a rundown part of town. But now, it looked, and felt, deserted. From a block away, it showed no signs of life, no air of being inhabited.

She approached from the side of the building before coming to the front, trepidation growing deeper. The front doors led to the lobby, the one room that was always kept well lit, manned by wraiths who turned away any who were not to be admitted. The curious, the lost, pushy salespeople, etc. The lobby was dark. An old scent of smoke started to curl in her nose.

Adrenaline flooded her as she went to pick the lock, only for the door to swing weakly open at her touch. The smoke smell slapped her in the face and made her gag. Liska wiped water from her eyes and pulled out a handkerchief to tie around her nose and mouth. While it would be harder to smell out anything important, right now she wasn't sure she would be able to smell anything important over the scent of smoke, soot, char, ash, and melted plastic.

The scents were all over a week old, she noted as she walked in. Even in the dark she could tell the walls were streaked and smudged with soot. The desk, that had once been longer than her bed, was mostly charred splinters, with a melted blob of plastic that could have been an abstract sculpture, but she suspected was what remained of the phone.

What happened here? Obviously a fire, but why? What caused it? Did the vampires get out in time? Closing her eyes, Liska tried to filter out various scents. Ah, gasoline. And alcohol. This was a deliberate fire. And she very much doubted the vampires set it.

Vampires, like Weres, had an instinctive... hesitance of fire. Not that they couldn't use fire, they did and freely. But there was more caution and concern than the average human seemed to have. While no one knew exactly why that was, there were suspicions. For Weres, it was probably the animal instincts screaming danger. It was simply a primal reaction.

Vampires, for whatever reason, had been observed to be slightly more flammable than most other races. Sure, they couldn't die until the heart had been destroyed, but fire could do that. It just took a few minutes. Liska could think of worse ways to die, but not too many.

Standing in the middle of the room contemplating possibilities wouldn't get her anywhere. It was time to search for answers. Liska started with the desk. If anything survived, it might provide answers. But nothing seemed to survive. The largest remaining portion of the desk was a charred stick barely larger than her forearm. Certainly any papers were ash now. And in keeping with the low cost dive look, there was no computer out here. Honestly, Liska wasn't sure Rex Magnus would let his blood use a computer. He was such a traditionalist.

Something across the room caught her eye, and Liska abandoned the desk to get a better look. But as she walked away, her hand brushed the former phone. In a flash she was there.

She looked up at a noise. Ten, maybe fifteen humans were at the door. Gas! They were carrying cans of gas, stakes, and even some guns. How could they have found them? She had to warn Rex Magnus.

Stephen, her partner tried to bar the doors. She grabbed the phone and stabbed the line one button. As soon as someone picked up, she was screaming. "We're under attack. Armed Purifiers! We're under attack."

"Get inside the Heart now!"

The phone fell from her fingers as the door burst open. A loud sound erupted in the air and Stephen fell bleeding to the ground.

Run. She had to run. Or fight. Or something! The man in front sneered at her. "Earth for Humans." There was another loud crack.

She fell and everything hurt. She had been shot. Was she dead? No, not yet. But she was dying. Distantly, she heard the phone.

"Isabelle! You and Stephen get to the Heart, now!"

"They're coming," She croaked out.

Her vision swarmed, coming back to focus on the man standing over her, no compassion, no mercy, no humanity in his eyes. "Gas," he said, holding out a hand. When someone handed him a canister, he opened it and started pouring it over her.

The smell pierced the growing fog in her brain, and she prayed she died before she burned.

Liska gasped and steadied herself automatically as the vision ended. She stood panting, tears streaming down her face as she tried to sort through which 'she' she was. She was Liska, not Isabelle. She was a Werefox, not a wraith. She had not just been shot, and she hadn't been set on fire. Hopefully the lack of memories of being burned meant that Isabelle had gotten her wish and died before she burned.

That was her longest and deepest vision yet. Those poor wraiths. No, Stephen and Isabelle. That was their names, and it was only right that someone remembered them. Whether they had managed to warn the blood in time or not. Had they?

Liska left the desk and found what had caught her eye in the first place. It was a spray-painted message, obviously painted after the fire. 'E F H' in a circle. Earth for Humans. The Purifiers rallying cry. But how did they find them? Liska checked the Purifier's website frequently, and there had been no sign they knew anything about the blood. In fact, yesterday, she would have classed Purifiers as a semi-knowledgeable irritant more than a threat. What changed?

Betrayal. It was, if not the only possible explanation, definitely the most likely. But who and why?

And who would think it might have been her?

She shook her head. Focus on that later. Damage control could be done after she verified how much damage had been done. How deep had the Purifiers gotten? They couldn't have wiped out the whole blood; Rex Magnus was too paranoid not to have a way out. Or was he too paranoid to have more than one way that would have to be guarded? She wouldn't find out standing in the lobby, and it would be wise to move before she was spotted.

Down a small side corridor that was almost invisible in the dark, even with her night vision, was the door to the Heart of the Blood. It lay in shattered pieces. Clearly it had been barred on the inside, but it had been hacked down. Not a good sign.

Liska had been through part of the Heart before, but she had always been led down roundabout routes. Her sensitivity to the magnetic pole had given her a rough compass, but it still took Liska a minute or two to put together her mental map and find the clearest route.

There were no candles this time, and as good as her lowlight vision was, this was dark even for her. Rude as it might have been in normal circumstances, Liska felt justified in using her flashlight this time.

The path to the Heart had always had tapestries lining the way. Liska had kept her thoughts on the mildew scent to herself. But mildewed or not, the tapestries had been clear works of art. Now every tapestry she passed had been either slashed to pieces or burned.

Mobs. Liska hated mobs. They were dangerous, not just for sheer numbers, but because normal, reasonable people would do things they would normally find unthinkable while in the midst of one. After all, how many of that group would have believed they would literally set another person on fire, or stand by and watch someone else do it?

The leader might have. He was surprisingly dispassionate for someone leading an angry, bloodthirsty group. That made him more dangerous. Pity Isabelle didn't have a strong enough sense of smell to pick up on his scent. All Liska had to go on was his face, and that was how Isabelle saw him. He would look different in Liska's eyes, black and white and near-sighted. But it might be enough.

The tunnels didn't smell as strongly of smoke as the lobby did, probably because there was less to burn. But that didn't mean they didn't burn what they could. Soot licked at the walls and ceilings.

At last she got to Rex's meeting chamber, the furthest into the Heart she had been permitted to see. There were signs of a bonfire in the center of the room. Liska recognized one of the arms of Rex's great supposedly ebony chair, charred, but still intact. On another side was one of the legs. They probably hacked up or tore apart the chair before burning it. Here and there were scraps of fabric, mostly from tapestries. Was that a hint of Rex's cloak? Had he actually died in the attack?

Every time she had been here in the past, the room was dark, lit by the occasional candle. That was enough light for them, enough for her. With her flashlight, she could see the whole room, including the doors on the far side. An area they undoubtedly hadn't wanted her to see. Probably no one but the blood went back there.

Three doors. All broken off their hinges. She approached the first, still listening for any signs of movement, of life. Nothing. This room turned out to be a kitchen. Wraiths had more humanlike eating habits, so they need someplace to prepare actual food. Even without the wraiths, they would need a way to preserve blood.

The stove had some black streaks, and had been smashed several times with something hard, but had stood up to the punishment pretty well. The refrigerator hadn't been quite so lucky. Did someone have a sledgehammer? Isabelle hadn't seen one, but it was possible that once they were sure they wouldn't be slaughtered by vampires, the mob had come back with more tools of destruction, maybe more people.

The steel table had been left alone except for 'Earth for Humans' spray painted on it in large, messy letters. Cupboards had been torn through with the contents either scattered or dragged away to be burned. There was no one here. Nothing useful. Liska moved on.

The second door led to a staircase leading down. Hearing nothing, Liska moved on to the third door. She'd come back to this one. The third door stayed on this floor and appeared to have been an information center. While most of it had been destroyed, she could see evidence of there having been computers here. And a phone. This was probably where the warning had been received. The computer components had been smashed and scattered. Some had probably been dragged away to be burned, but she could still see shards of glass and plastic, and fragments of cords and circuits. Apparently she was wrong about how deep Rex's devotion to tradition went.

Leaving that, Liska went back to the staircases. Just in case she had missed something, she stopped at the top of the stairs, head cocked and listening. Nothing. At the landing, she did the same. Still nothing. The next flight brought her to the floor. Distantly, she could hear water running, but nothing else. Not even insects or mice, both of which she had heard here before.

Another large door, thick and strong. Barred from the inside. And apparently someone had an axe. Even partially burned, she could see that the wood had been hewn. With a sigh, Liska pushed the remnants aside with her flashlight and went in.

Another corridor, with rooms on both sides. Living quarters. From the looks of it, they lived two to four in a room. All the rooms were pretty much identical. In fact, they looked a bit like her dorm room. Or what her dorm room would have looked like if someone had ransacked the place, torn the pages out of her books, slashed up her bedding, mattresses, pillows, and curtains, hacked up the furniture, and then threw in a Molotov cocktail.

Tracking the sound of water led her to the communal bathrooms. Yes, someone definitely had a sledgehammer or something similar. All the toilets were smashed to porcelain rubble, the sinks were fragments of sharp plaster, and the mirrors were slivers of glass. The shower stalls were mostly left alone, probably because there weren't too many 'fun' ways to destroy them, but all the curtains were slashed.

The gym had clearly held another bonfire, but the exercise equipment was left alone. Probably because it was too tough to destroy. After the gym was another set of living quarters, that seemed to be either family living or rooms for the higher ranked vampires. Maybe both. The rooms were bigger and sometimes had other rooms attached. They were probably nicer than the communal rooms, but it was hard to tell because the mob had gone even crazier with them.

Beyond that, there was one quarters that was different. Obviously Rex Magnus's rooms. Equally obvious, the mob had taken special care to destroy this place. Paintings, many of them old, some no doubt valuable, had been slashed beyond recognition. Books ripped apart and burned, probably without anyone even checking to see if there was any valuable information in them. The bed had been chopped up, as had his wardrobe. She saw no signs of his fabled jewels. If he had enough warning, he might have been able to take them with him. Or maybe they had been stolen. Or maybe they were as fake as the costume jewelry rings he wore. His silks and velvets (velour) lay in a corner, slashed and, Liska's nose wrinkled at the acrid smell even through the handkerchief, urinated on. Mobs!

Liska was careful not to touch anything. Yes, it was more than likely that Rex Magnus hid one or more important things, or bits of information in his room. It was even possible that he might had hidden something and not been able to retrieve it. Possibly something survived that escaped the notice of the mob. If so, she might be able to find it.

But she didn't know if there *was* anything worth retrieving, and even if there was, it wasn't currently her job to retrieve it. She certainly had no desire to be in the mind of someone who would do this. The last thing she needed was 'memories' of committing these kinds of atrocities. Her mind was a dangerous enough place as it was.

Leaving the room, Liska tried to find some place she hadn't searched. There *had* to be another exit. Rex Magnus wasn't that stupid. If not another exit, then a panic room. Surely there was something?

It was her third rotation of this floor when she found the spot. A place in the gym where her footsteps didn't sound the same. Moving the damaged mat to the side, she noticed the flooring didn't quite match the rest. Carefully, she pried the panel loose, breathing in relief as she saw the trap door. The unbroken trap door. They *did* have an exit; one the Purifiers hadn't found.

The only lock was from this side, and it wasn't locked. At least a few must have made it out. The trapdoor opened to a ten-foot drop and a tunnel. Not a problem for the average Were or vampire. Getting back up might be slightly more difficult.

Liska pulled a small bundle of paracord out of her pocket and tied a secure knot to the nearest exercise machine, one that allowed users to go up against five hundred pounds of weight. Approximately one hundred pounds of Werefox shouldn't be a challenge. Certain her line was secure, Liska jumped.

Once in the tunnel, she saw the ladder that was evidently there to allow those inside up. Even behind the handkerchief, her nose twitched. There was something off about that ladder. She wouldn't be using it to get up.

No smoke here meant she could take off the handkerchief. Even through it, the scent of terrified vampire was clear. But the numbers weren't. For the number of scents to blur together like that, there would have to be at least ten. By her estimates, the blood had contained about fifty vampires and ten, possibly twenty wraiths. No estimate on the shades. Hopefully she was smelling so many more than ten.

The scents were too old and too blended for her to pick up on the smell of any individual vampire, and there were only two she was certain she'd recognize by scent anyway. But there was no way for her to pick out either Van or Rex Magnus in this crowd.

Fifteen feet in, just after the first curve, the tunnel was blocked with rubble. Clearly it had been mined to go off. Probably to keep anyone from following.

Liska elected not to dig through the rubble. Undoubtedly there were other booby traps for the unwary or malicious. Nor was she sure where it led. But clearly, some of the blood made it out. So where were they?

Using her cord and the narrow walls of the tunnel, Liska climbed out, back into the gym before collecting her cord. There was nothing for her in this building. She'd have to look around, find where the blood was now. Hopefully most of them made it out. Vampires don't leave a body behind, it was possible even they weren't sure how many they had lost.

Liska left the building, only to stop dead at the sight of two vampires waiting for her. Male, probably vampires for two hundred or more years. Tall and strong, they had the figures and uniforms of guards. "Our chief wishes to see you."

Chapter Eight

The line between justice and vengeance is easily crossed. –
The Kikitsutai Book of Wisdom

"What a coincidence. I wish to speak with your chief." Liska gave a small bow. "Please, lead on."

Both vampire guards straightened and one started walking. Liska followed, hyper-aware of the other one marching behind her. They were escorting her like they would a prisoner. Which she might well be. That hadn't been an invitation, which would grant her the safety of a guest. That had been 'Will you come willingly, or do we drag your broken, bleeding body? Please, choose the second.'

Liska deliberately did not name the chief. If Rex Magnus had been killed in the attack, mentioning him would just make the situation worse. At minimum, it would betray her lack of knowledge and upset the guards, both of whom had probably been turned by him. At worst, it would infuriate them.

As they reached the street, a dark, probably black, limo pulled up. Guard One opened the door and glared at her. Liska nodded to him and slid in as if he were a valet and it was perfectly normal for him to open her car door. Guard Two followed her in.

Rex Magnus sat across from her.

"Great Chief, may the nights be long and prosperous. I am pleased to see you." While that was not a lie, even Liska was a little surprised at just how relieved she was to see him. Rex Magnus disliked her for unknown reasons, and he was too arrogant for her liking, but she had never wished him dead. He was at least a known quality and generally considered a decent leader.

"Are you indeed?" His words were bitter vinegar. The car started to drive. Liska ignored the way she was currently trapped, even while mentally kicking herself for not informing Ryoko-*Sensei* of her suspicions and whereabouts.

"I am. Until I found your secret passage, I had feared the worst. Even then, there was no way to tell how many escaped. My condolences upon your losses. I hope they were few."

"Even one is too many." Rage blazoned in his eyes. If Rex Magnus discovered who caused this, not even the Vampire Laws would protect them for long.

"I quite agree." She hesitated but asked anyway. "May I ask how many?"

For a moment, she didn't think he would answer. "Fifteen are still unaccounted for. Five known to be dead. Two more presumed so."

She closed her eyes and shook her head. What a tragic waste. All because of ignorance and fear. "How?"

"*That* is a very good question." He pierced her with his glare. "What do you know about it?"

So, she was a suspect. Liska pretended surprise anyway. "I? Nothing. I called tonight, hoping for a little information. Something minor.

When no one answered, I was curious, perhaps concerned. When I arrived..."

Rex Magnus sat, slowly turning a large ring on his bony finger. There was a burn mark on his hand, probably not the only one. "I find it very curious that the 'Purifiers'," he spat out the name, "could find us, and even know directions into our very Heart."

"I agree. You must have been betrayed."

He leaned forward, a tight, ironic smile on his lips. "And why, Luna Liska of the Kikitsutai, did you betray us?"

Very aware of the guard next to her polishing a silver dagger, Liska kept her eyes on Rex. "I did not. I knew nothing about it before tonight." She forced herself not to move as the dagger suddenly hovered over her neck. It didn't touch, and there was even room to move away.

Liska made no attempt to evade the dagger or break the arm of the guard holding it. She made a point not to even look his way. "I swear upon my honor that I neither betrayed you nor know who did." There was a pause while Rex considered her words. When he seemed almost convinced, she spoke again. "I would appreciate if you asked your guard to move his knife. I'd rather not get my throat slashed because your driver hit a pot hole."

Rex made a negligent gesture and the knife was back in front of the guard. It was still out, and could be used at any time, but she wasn't likely to die in the next few seconds at least.

"You wanted information?"

"I do. I wanted to know about vampires in the area who are not part of your blood." After a moment, she added, "I am looking for a follower of Atolatar."

The vampire sneered. "Always coming when you want something. Always putting your nose in where it isn't wanted. I'm not inclined to give you anything right now. Let alone betray our kin when we are currently reliant upon them. Granted, Atolatar was too dangerous to remain, but I've seen nothing like that here."

Liska remained silent. She didn't think Rex was finished yet. She was right.

"An exchange then. You want information and to prove you were not involved in planning our destruction? Find out who betrayed us. I have questioned my people, it wasn't one of them."

On one hand, that wasn't quite fair. Rex knew, or ought to know, that she was telling the truth. She would never lie when she swore on her honor. That was unbreakable. On the other hand, any who would do such a thing was a danger to all of them, and had to be stopped at once. She was in a better position to ferret out the truth, and Rex knew that. Not that she planned to let him use her that easily.

"For the sake of those who died, for the sake of those that live, that they might not die; I will find your traitor. Not because of your accusations."

Rex nodded at that. "Agreed."

"Who else knew the layout of your den?"

"Besides you?"

"I knew no more than you showed me before tonight." No point in mentioning that she had been out of the country when this happened. Not in a time of instantaneous communication. "Yes, besides me."

"No other living outsider had seen the Heart."

Well, that would make things tricky. No wonder he had latched on to her as the culprit so vehemently. "What about the dead?"

"What? How would that help?"

Liska shrugged one shoulder. "Perhaps they left behind notes. Or told someone before they died. And how do you define 'outsider'?

The ring made three complete revolutions before he spoke again. "I will speak to my people and gather a list of all who ever had access. Only those of my people I have specifically questioned will be left off the list. It should be to you in two night's time. Van shall deliver it."

Good. Van made it out too. And that list should be a good starting point. "Acceptable."

The car came to a stop. The guard put away the silver dagger before opening the door and letting her out. Immediately, she recognized her location. She was across the street from her dorm. It was a message. *We know where you dwell. We can come for you anytime we choose.*

Vampires had difficulty crossing a threshold uninvited, but it could be done. Especially if ordered by the one who turned them. Loyalty to their 'parent' overrode almost everything else. Besides, as Korvou's frequent appearances had hammered home, a temporary college dorm room that she had no attachment to, simply wasn't enough of a home to build up a significant threshold.

So now she had another huge, urgent item on her to do list. And it was only the second day of class. So much for a quiet semester.

***

"What do you mean, gone?" Ryoko-*Sensei* asked, ignoring the puddle of tea that formed when he dropped his cup.

"Gone. The building is a mostly burned-out wreck, except for some Purifier's graffiti, which we may want to deal with at some point, and the vampires left. The majority made it out, thankfully. Rex Magnus has essentially ordered me to find out who betrayed them."

The older Werefox bristled, a growl reverberating in his throat. "Does he presume to command us?"

"He claims to believe me responsible. To 'prove my innocence' I must find the true guilty party." That, unfortunately, he did have grounds for. Long Twilight tradition allowed for the most likely, but not proven, suspect of a serious crime to have a chance to prove their innocence by finding the guilty party. A time frame was set, and if they were unsuccessful in 'proving' another responsible, they were punished as if truly guilty. A month was the typical time frame.

Rex hadn't mentioned a time frame. He might do so when she was given the list. More likely, he hadn't mentioned a time frame because he knew that he had no chance of getting away with having her formally executed. An 'accident' in his private limo that no one knew about? Possibly. But a formal charge and execution could well lead to the destruction of the rest of his blood, and possibly a war between Vampires and Weres. Peace was tenuous at the best of times, after all.

The best Rex could hope for would be the ability to prove, beyond any shadow of doubt, that she was guilty, and then demand the Kikitsutai enact justice on her. Whatever he might believe, they would, if she was truly guilty. Even Father would order her execution in that case.

"You weren't even in the country!"

"Phone. Email. Messenger. I wouldn't have to be. But, in case you were in the slightest bit curious, no, I knew nothing about it." She carefully didn't look at him.

"No, of course you didn't. Neither did I."

Liska said nothing about the fact that she hadn't been *sure* until he spoke. And certainly didn't mention that he hadn't been *sure* until she spoke.

***

"Have you found anything?" Ryoko asked his grand-niece after she had been on his computer for an hour. His eyes got drained too fast to do in-depth searches.

"Maybe. Not much, but it's something. There's nothing on the Purifier's site about who was actually involved in the attack, proving that they aren't all suicidally stupid." Not surprising. Liska was far from the only Twilight to be a member in order to keep on them. Current estimates ranged from one in twenty to one in ten 'Purifiers' was actually an infiltrator. Which was why, despite being one of the more knowledgeable hate groups, they weren't very effective. Until now.

"What did you find, then?" Ryoko squinted, trying to force the too bright pixels to reveal information.

"The one who reported the den. Remember Richard Calloway?"

"Calloway?" The name took him a moment. "The one who stood on a roof and tried to snipe at you and the Kendo boy with silver bullets?"

"Led here by an anonymous tip, you said."

"Indeed." He had interrogated the man thoroughly before hypnotizing him into forgetting everything about that day, and the address. Not much of a challenge. Ryoko was a master hypnotist, and Calloway was both an idiot and easily manipulated. Apparently someone else was taking advantage of that as well. "I ensured that he forgot everything. Nor did he have the skills or intelligence to find the den on his own. I am certain of that."

Liska steepled her fingers. "Another tip, perhaps."

"Sounds likely. Do you wish assistance questioning Calloway?" He might be old, but he wasn't that old. Besides, Liska was considerably less skilled in hypnotism; even she wouldn't argue that. Liska scowled at the computer.

"I would, but it would take more assistance than you can give me. Maybe a Ouija board would help. Calloway died in a *car accident* about five days ago. So very sad." She deadpanned.

Ryoko felt his eyebrows raise. "How... *convenient.* Any details?"

"DUI. Apparently his blood alcohol content was nearly twice the legal limit."

He sighed. "The man was an alcoholic. That means it's possible, just possible, that this was a coincidence. But the timing..."

"The timing stinks. I agree. Only good thing is he didn't take anyone else with him on his final ride."

A small consolation, but a consolation, nonetheless. "Now what?"

"Did Calloway have a family?"

"Yes."

Liska started walking a pencil across her fingers. "Did his family know about Purifiers?"

"That was not the impression I got."

"Then he probably didn't keep anything useful at the house. Though, he *was* an idiot. But chances are, whoever was manipulating him wasn't. No, he's a dead end. At least for now." The pencil went all around her hand and began again. "I have a germ of an idea. I don't like it and would very much appreciate if you could tell me I'm wrong."

"I can't tell you anything if you don't tell me your idea."

"Calloway was manipulated into attacking us, based on an anonymous tip, correct?"

"Correct." Where was she going with this?

"Not long before that, I was arrested for attacking Todd, also based on an anonymous tip. We know that the first tip came from either Atolatar or his follower, and odds are good that the second one did as well."

"A fair enough conclusion. Not a certainty, but likely." Ryoko stifled a shudder.

"If the first two anonymous tips, not to mention my anonymous notes, came from the same source..."

"Then why not the third?" It was a terrifying idea. Vampire betraying vampire was so rare as to be nearly unthinkable. Different types of Weres bickered and fought. The fae rings were in a constant struggle for supremacy, both internal and external. Ghouls had few loyalties beyond themselves. Even dragon clans had a tenuous peace.

But vampires were different. Along with the undying loyalty to the one that turned them, there was a deep bond between vampirekind. For a vampire to turn against another individual vampire, there had to be severe provocation, or being ordered to do so by the one who turned them. Even then, it was only on an individual level. There was no precedent for a vampire turning against a blood. "Your logic is sound. But not certain. I truly fear if you are correct."

The flip side of a vampire's loyalty to his kind was a brutal retribution if that loyalty was betrayed. If another vampire had betrayed the Magnus blood, there would be a slaughter. One Ryoko had no intention of standing in the way of.

"You and me both." Liska leaned back. "Then again, we don't know for certain that Atolatar's 'follower' is indeed a vampire. He had other Twilights in his following. But if it is the same person, what's the end goal? What could they possibly be trying to accomplish?" Liska glared at the computer monitor as if demanding answers from it.

"A very good question. Is it possible, though, that you want it to be the same person so that you have only one major undertaking to accomplish, not two?"

"Right now, almost anything is possible." Liska stood abruptly. "Except for finding the answers without work. I'm going to try to find the wanderers. See what they know."

Ryoko schooled his features so he didn't wince, and bit back his objections. "Be careful."

He caught a whiff of her irritation, but she was respectful. "I will."

"Have you tried using your retro-cognition?" Ryoko asked, only to be concerned by her micro flinch.

"Sort of. It wasn't deliberate, but something triggered it while I was in the den." She didn't continue until he prompted her, and when she did it was expressionless. "I was in the head of one of the wraiths manning the lobby when she saw her partner gunned down and die. She bled out before being burned. Her name was Isabelle."

Ryoko said nothing for a moment. He hadn't been aware that her ability had grown to the point that Liska could go that deep in another's head. How badly had it hurt her to be 'Isabelle' as she died? One thing he did know, Liska wouldn't admit it to him. When Kira visited the country, he was going to strongly encourage her to make the time to come here.

"I am sorry." It seemed callous to ask, but he had to. "Did you learn anything?"

"I saw a few faces. The leader, for certain. Not everyone. I'll talk to Kira tonight, she can draw him, scan it over."

Their gift. Anything Liska could describe, even in vague terms, Kira could draw as if she had seen it herself. It was not reciprocal, and neither could do that with anyone else.

"Good. At very least, he should be stopped." Pity the Purifiers didn't have a picture directory. But, as Liska said, they weren't suicidally stupid.

"Yes." Liska rubbed her hands together, as if to warm them. "Even leading a rampaging mob, he was cold, dispassionate."

That... was a very bad sign. "Liska? If you find that man? If you can? End him. A man like that has no conscience and is a threat to everyone, everywhere. Don't even feel guilty about it. Consider it an order if you like."

For a moment, she just stood there motionless, then she turned and looked at him, a wry smile on her face and a strange light in her eyes. "I'll keep that in mind, *Sensei*." She left.

Ryoko stayed, shivering, wondering if he had just made a giant mistake.

Chapter Nine

Choose your fights with care, and your allies like weapons. –
The Kikitsutai Book of Wisdom

"Anna! Hey, Anna, wait up!" Todd called, breaking into a light jog. He had seen her at lunch, but Shahara was there, and he had a feeling that the questions he wanted to ask, she wouldn't answer in public. Something was wrong. She had been distracted and on edge in a way he hadn't seen since Russia. Now, however, she appeared to be heading off campus. Maybe she'd be willing to talk.

Sakaki turned to face him, and Todd stopped as if hitting a wall. Her clothes were the same. Khaki pants, the kind he knew hid pockets from the ankle to the knee that were just big enough to stash a *wakazashi*, and a medium blue shirt with a v-neck and three-quarter length sleeves. She had added a jean jacket in light blue. Her hair was the same, the bun held in place with a hair stick, same as it was most days. No jewelry, nothing unusual. But there was an unholy fire in her eyes and a look on her face that suggested someone might die tonight. No, not 'might', would, if she had anything to say about it.

"Anna?" It wasn't quite a squeak. Or if it was, he wasn't admitting it.

Her eyes closed, and when she reopened them, they were softer, more familiar. Tension that Todd hadn't even been able to see relaxed. "Yes, Todd?"

Todd inched closer. "Hi?" He swallowed. "I wanted to talk. Are you busy?"

Her head tilted as she considered the question. "I am busy. But I think you might be able to help. If you're willing."

"Sure!" Todd took a couple steps closer, before whispering, "Um, is it dangerous?"

Sakaki smirked. "Life is dangerous. But if I was expecting trouble, I wouldn't have invited you unprepared. We're going to take a walk, on Clematis."

"Uh, okay. Do you want to walk there or drive?" The street was only about a ten-minute walk away, and was a semi popular hotspot, but he had no idea what she wanted there. The closest public library was there, as was an ice cream shop that was popular, some very expensive shops, and at least a handful of nightclubs. It was after ten in the middle of the week. The library and the ice cream shop were definitely closed, and probably most of the stores were too. He had no idea about the nightclubs. Did they even bother in the middle of the week? Even if they did, he couldn't imagine Sakaki enjoying them. They were too loud for *him*, and he didn't have her sensitive hearing. She was also allergic to alcohol and didn't seem to like crowds.

"Hm, drive. I can fill you in on the way."

"Sure, great. I'm in Lot B." It was the opposite direction from Clematis, but Liska, she was definitely Liska now, followed him without a murmur of complaint.

In fact, she didn't say anything as they got to his car, and he didn't say anything as she stopped him and checked the car over, including underneath. She was still on the ground when someone started walking up, asking if anything was wrong. Without thinking, Todd called out, "Lost a contact lens."

"Found it," Liska said, standing up. "We're good." She smiled and waved to their Good Samaritan.

The questioning student nodded, waved, and left. "Good one." Liska gave him a small smile. "You're getting better at this."

"Isn't that a frightening thought?" Todd unlocked the car, buckled up and waited for her to do the same before starting the car. "Okay, what are we doing?"

"Looking for vampires."

Todd forced himself to concentrate on backing out without hitting anything. "Well, that wasn't quite what I planned on doing tonight." His voice was only slightly higher than normal. He thought. "Why are we looking for vampires, and how dangerous is that?"

Out of the corner of his eye, he could see her one-sided shrug. "We aren't looking for a fight. Just to talk. But they're going to be on edge. I wouldn't rule out a small spat or two, but I doubt any will try to kill us. Do you have your UV flashlight?"

"Yeah. But–"

"If things get bad, stay behind me. Far enough that you aren't impeding my movement and just shine it on them. As long as you don't get me in the eye with it, it won't hurt me. And I can fight blind if I have to."

Why was he even surprised? Best to follow her advice. He wasn't completely helpless, but she was better trained, and they had never tried fighting together. Trying now would probably cause them both to impede each other. "Why are we looking for them?"

Liska let out a heavy breath. "Someone attacked the local blood recently. They lost more than a quarter of their numbers, and it looks like they were betrayed."

"Oh, ouch." Todd hadn't had any good experiences with vampires yet, but Liska said they had a truce with them. An uneasy truce, but still a truce. Besides, something like this was painful, even if you didn't know those involved. "So, you're looking to see who betrayed them?" This might be a little more dangerous than she implied. Possibly a lot more dangerous.

"Yes and no. Yes, I'm looking for who betrayed them. I've been... asked to find the one responsible. No, I'm not expecting to find them tonight, or to accuse any vampires we run into tonight of that betrayal. This is information gathering only. Also, we know Atolatar had a follower in the area. I'm hoping for some information about him. Or her."

Next time, he was going to ask how he would be helping *before* he agreed. Oh, who was he kidding? He'd still be here. "Right, what's my part?"

"One, cover. If anyone looks, we're just another couple exploring the admittedly somewhat lack of nightlife. Two, it doesn't hurt to have another reason to convince any aggressive vampires we run into not to attack us. They have no way of knowing how trained you are, but if I brought you in for backup..."

"Then presumably, you think I'm good, not hopeless."

"I *know* you aren't hopeless. True, you aren't trained as extensively as I am, but if things do get entirely out of hand, you could be helpful in a fight. I've an extra sword."

Todd pulled into a parking space. "I'm used to a longer blade, but I'll try not to let you down."

"You won't. Besides, I don't think we'll need it." She unbuckled her seatbelt.

"One more question. If so many vampires died, who are we looking for?"

"The blood was attacked and devastated. We're looking for Wanderers. Vampires that don't belong to any blood. It's a difficult life. The bloods don't trust them, watch them, but offer little in the way of protection. But there's also less to keep them in check. Their loyalties aren't assured. They are more desperate, more dangerous. On the other hand, most don't want to make waves or get noticed."

"So, to get this straight, we're going looking for the more dangerous, unpredictable vampires, who are going to be twitchy because of this terrible event where their own kind was betrayed, and go ask them a bunch of questions?"

"Exactly!" Liska beamed, sounding amused. "And to think, you could have stayed home and studied."

"Wish I had." Judging by Liska's smirk, he wasn't fooling her. "How do we do this? I'm guessing we don't ask random pedestrians if they know where the vampires are."

She huffed something that might have been a laugh. "No. Actually, depending on circumstances, we might not *talk* to more than one person tonight. I just want to find out who hangs out here."

Todd was feeling a little dumb for not picking up on the implication that vampires hung out at Clematis. He might never come here again. Liska rolled her eyes, evidently knowing his thoughts. "Why here?"

"Why not here? There's people, commerce, etc. Isn't this one of the hot spots of West Palm Beach?"

Todd shrugged. "Maybe."

"Just keep your eyes and ears open, and when in doubt, your mouth shut."

"Better to keep silent and be thought a fool, than open your mouth and remove all doubt?"

"Something like that. Actually, it would probably be best if you stayed silent and acted unimpressed. You do this every day. You're my muscle."

"You're your own muscle."

"They don't need to know that. I'm a semi-known quantity. You aren't. They may guess you're an Esper, but not what kind. All they know is that *I* thought it was worth bringing you."

Warmth filled him even as he told himself it was silly. She considered him capable of backing her up in a tight spot. Or at least bluffing others into believing he could back her up. It was a bluff, wasn't it?

On the other hand, this was the first time she had voluntarily involved him in her work. She may have needed him in order to get into the police station evidence room, but she had left him out of it as much as possible. He still didn't know exactly what she had done. She hadn't wanted to take him to Russia at all and made him promise to wait in the hotel. Neither of them had counted on him being kidnapped from there.

This time, she admitted she was working and asked if he wanted in. Did that mean she trusted him more, was trying to let him understand her better, or she was certain that there was no way he could mess it up or endanger them? Hopefully not the last.

They had parked in the library parking lot, which was one end of the street, and Liska resolutely led him the other direction. Perhaps it was knowing what they were doing, but as they passed block after block, it seemed to Todd that the lights got further apart, the buildings looked more disreputable, and the people were more alert. A couple of the pedestrians also triggered Todd's sense of recognition, meaning they were Twilights. Were they vampires?

Liska didn't seem phased. She strolled like this was a romantic walk and she was completely relaxed. Her eyes belied that though; alert and darting everywhere. As they passed a bar, a red light from the sign shone on her, particularly her hand that was pointing out a shrub. Todd got the sudden impression of blood and the unholy fire he had seen in her eyes earlier. She would spill blood tonight. He inhaled sharply.

"What did you see?" Liska spoke under her breath, leaning in like it was lovers' talk.

"Blood. On your hand. Tonight."

"Mine or another's?"

"I...I'm not sure. I think it's someone else's."

She nodded. "I'll be careful."

Well, he couldn't do more than that. Maybe he was wrong. Just like he really hoped he was wrong about someone starting to follow them.

He was jarred from his thoughts by Liska nudging him into an alley. As soon as they were in, she straightened up and separated from him. Work mode. Todd drew himself to his full height and tried to look strong and capable. Hopefully he didn't look too ridiculous.

Liska walked over to a door half hidden in the shadows and nodded to it. Todd took the hint and opened it for her. Liska swept in and marched to the counter of what appeared to be a small bar. A speakeasy? Five people were in the bar. No, five vampires. Probably.

Todd tried to size up the situation the way she probably would. One was behind the counter, clearly the bartender. He seemed young, which meant who knew what, and was tall and lanky. One weedy looking character in stained clothing sat at the far end of the bar. If Todd saw him somewhere else, he would have assumed a drug addict. Could vampires be drug addicts? The last three were at another table playing cards. One of them was huge. Not much taller than Todd, but built like a mountain, and from the look of it, that was muscle, not fat.

All eyes were on Liska as she came to a stop in the middle of the counter. Todd followed and took a ready stance two feet behind her and to her left. Liska was right-handed, so her left side was marginally weaker, not to mention closer to the closest 'opponent'. On the other hand, it was her right wrist that was injured, and that was the side with more vampires on it. Oh well, changing now would be worse than staying. He would just have to remember that if any fighting started.

"Evening, gents." Her voice rang out in the now silent room. No one responded. "What's on tap?"

"You will be, if you aren't careful." The Mountain vampire sauntered over to the counter on Liska's other side. "Pretty girl like you? You don't belong here."

Liska didn't so much as glance at him, eyes still on the barkeep. "You have a real pest problem here. Might want to clear them out before Inspection comes."

There was a ragged round of nervous chuckles. Mountain didn't like being ignored or laughed at. "Listen, you bit– Aargg!" His hand, which had been reaching up to grab her face, was now in the counter with a knife sticking out of it. Todd hadn't even seen her move. He had barely seen Mountain move.

Now Liska looked at him, a tiny smile on her face. "Wrong species. I'm no dog. I'm a vixen."

Liska stayed in place, so Todd did too. Mountain was still stuck to the counter. Everyone else edged away from them. Liska turned back to the barkeep who was nervously eyeing something under the counter. "A real pest problem."

"I don't want trouble," the barkeep said. He looked even younger, like Todd's age. Of course, who knew what that meant?

"I'm not interested in trouble either. I simply believe in being prepared if trouble comes knocking on my door." She was silent a moment. "Who owns this bar?"

"Look, I don't..."

There was a mirror behind the counter. Apparently vampires did have reflections, but Todd was watching Liska's face. She seemed... amused? She raised an eyebrow over eyes that were becoming slitted.

"He does." The barkeep pointed to the Mountain who was still trying to pull the knife out of his hand.

"Ah, excellent. I just need a word with your boss." She dropped a couple twenties on the counter. "Next round's on me." Liska withdrew the knife with a smooth motion, before pushing Mountain over to a door on the side.

Todd waited in the bar itself, since he didn't seem to be invited into this conversation. Of course, now he was in a room with four other vampires. Fortunately, they were mostly ignoring him in favor of staring at the now closed door. He couldn't hear anything from inside and wondered if they could.

It was the weedy vampire who broke the tension. "She did say she was paying."

Barkeep gave a wry smile. "Your usual?"

"Nah. If she's paying, make it the good stuff."

"Ah, of course."

A moment later, weedy guy had a glass of something that Todd very much suspected was blood. Yup, definitely blood. What made one kind better than another? Blood was blood. Then again, Liska said they seldom drank human blood, maybe some sources were more desirable than others.

That broke the ice. The other two decided to get their free round while the getting was good. After serving them, Barkeep looked Todd in the eye. "Drink for you, Sir? We've got sheep, cow, pig, rat, cat, and dog. Even a small quantity of AB+."

No, he did not want to drink blood! This was not part of the job. Before he had to say something, Liska swept out of the side room. "He doesn't drink on the job. AB+, huh? Documented?"

"Of course, legally gathered." He held up a paper, that Liska breezed through before nodding. "You, Ma'am?"

"I don't drink on the job either." She eyed up the patrons. "I'm looking for some information, and I'm willing to pay generously to get it. Needless to say, I take very poorly to being lied to." Almost as an aside, she turned to Barkeep. "Do you have a napkin?" Liska extended a hand that had a scary amount of blood on it.

Barkeep quickly handed over his bar towel. She slowly wiped her hands, still eyeing the group. "I'm looking for information about a man named

Richard Calloway. I want to know who's been associating with him."

No one said anything for a minute, before the barkeeper swallowed hard. "Um, Boss doesn't like—"

"He gave me permission." Liska gave a small, feral smile. It was all Todd could do not to shiver. She eyed the room again. "Well, if you find out, I'm sure we'll be in touch." With a small jerk of her head, Liska strode out. Todd followed.

He managed to make it a good block before it burst out. "What the heck was that?"

She was calm about his question and his hysteria. "Groundwork, mostly. None of them know anything, but they'll make a point of finding out now. And they'll discuss it in that bar. Which I just bought."

"You got in a fight with someone three times your size to buy a bar?" Todd knew he was gaping at her, but he couldn't help it.

Liska chuckled. "Good, it did look convincing. He's one of Rex's, the local blood leader? I made a deal with him beforehand. He's one of Rex's informants, but he depends on no one realizing he's part of the blood. Rex ordered him to co-operate with me. We faked a fight, as planned, and then while we were in the private room, I offered to buy his bar. It's struggling, I'm leaving him in charge, and no one knows I bought it from him, so he agreed. I don't need it in the long run, so I'll probably let him buy it back from me in a few years. In the meantime, he'll let me know all the rumors that float around there."

"That... that was all fake? But you stabbed his hand!"

"With this?" She pulled out the knife, held the edge of the blade in place and slid the hilt down.

"A retractable knife." Todd shook his head, feeling dizzy. "You used a stage prop?"

"Sure. He held it there, acted like he was in pain, and no one questioned a thing. If the bartender gets suspicious, his boss will hold him in line."

"So, was that fake blood too?"

"In a vampire bar? I'm not that stupid. No, it was really his. Had to be fresh too. He gave himself a cut, about hairline. Head wounds bleed a lot, no matter what your species. I hadn't actually planned that, but you mentioned seeing blood on my hands, so I decided it would be effective. He'll seclude himself a few days, until one wouldn't expect to see injuries."

"So it was all fake. *Could* you fight him?"

"Did you *see* him? He's more than three times my size. If I went in grandstanding like that, I would have been killed. And I would have deserved it completely. Take my word for it, if you see someone grandstanding in a fight, either they're a fool, or it's fake. If I really had to fight him, I would have used a very different strategy." She was quiet for a moment, probably thinking out a mental fight. "Probably gone for his knee or groin first. That would cripple him more effectively. What's wrong?"

His stomach was churning and there was bile in his mouth. Despite the eighty-degree temperature, he was starting to shiver. What was his problem? They got out okay. There wasn't a fight. Liska hadn't even hurt the guy. *What was wrong with him?*

"Ah, adrenaline crash. It's okay. Um, here. This way." She led him to a bench and made him sit. "Just breathe slowly. I have some water." Todd closed his eyes as he heard her rustle around. "Here. Small sips."

A small plastic flask was forced into his hand. The water inside was warm from her body heat, but he didn't complain. It took him two sips to realize that his hands were shaking. "Sorry," Todd gasped out between sips.

"It's fine." He could feel her take a seat next to him, but he didn't bother opening his eyes. "I should have considered that this might happen."

"I feel so stupid." His eyes were starting to tear up.

"Relax. It happens to everyone sometimes. I've had worse reactions for less reason. You've even seen one."

"If we're talking about the dog, I don't think that counts as less reason," Todd argued.

He could feel Liska shrug. "In any case, I'm not going to judge you."

"Do you ever get over it?"

"Yes. And no. Most of the time, my reactions aren't as bad as they used to be. Sometimes I don't react at all. Other times, well, I've learned how to hold it together long enough to get somewhere private to break down."

Todd wasn't sure if that made things better or worse. "Maybe I *should* have stayed home and studied."

He felt but didn't hear her laugh. "Do you need anything? There's a drug store on the next block."

"Another water and something for an upset stomach?"

"Sure. Wait here."

"You sure that's safe?" They were still less than three blocks from the vampire bar.

"You're almost directly under a streetlamp. If anyone gives you any trouble, threaten to throw up on their shoes."

"That might not be a bluff."

"I'll grab a ginger ale." He felt her stand up, then stop. "Here. Just in case." Todd opened his eyes to see her offering something. He took it on instinct only to realize he was now holding a switchblade. He opened his mouth to object, but she was already gone.

***

Liska blinked away moisture. The harsh florescent lighting was especially bad after the darkness of outside. The flipside of excellent night vision was an occasional sensitivity to bright lights.

The longest part of her visit was browsing through the headache-inducingly large amount of medicine. Could even pharmacists tell them apart? Really? After a minute or two, she grabbed the most promising, before snagging the promised water and a ginger ale.

At eleven on a Wednesday night, Clematis was hardly a hot spot. In fact, she was the only customer in the store. Not that it got her out any faster. The cashier, some kid who didn't look any older than fourteen, but smelled about eighteen to twenty, saw her in line, and still spent five minutes fussing with the battery display. Liska timed it.

To help her eyes adjust faster to the night, she closed her eyes as she left. Two steps out, she opened them as something tickled at the edge of her awareness. Something familiar, but that she hadn't felt for a long time. But what—

"Sakaki? It that really you?"

She jumped, spinning in mid-air. Her eyes landed on her target before widening in disbelief. "Eric?"

Chapter Ten

The one who marries heart and head stands unconquered. –
The Kikitsutai Book of Wisdom

How could this be happening? How could Eric even be here right now? Eric gave a small laugh and a smile that made something deep inside her flutter. "Wow, small world. What are you doing here? Still a 'photography student'?"

Okay, he figured out or guessed that she had lied about being a photographer. Not surprising. But had he figured out what she had really been doing in Luxembourg? Well, she wasn't going to tell him. "I'm currently attending classes at the local university."

It wasn't until she spoke that she realized they were both speaking German. Then again, that was the language they had used the first time they met. She had no idea if or how well he spoke English, and he had no way of knowing what languages she spoke. "What about you? I didn't expect to find you here."

He gave a shrug. "My 'Father' told me to come. Whatever. Not a bad place. It has some things going for it. Even more than I realized." He looked her over. "It's been a while, Sakaki."

"It's Anna, here." Did he know that she was Luna Liska? She hadn't been when they met before, but that didn't mean that he hadn't put it together. It was a small risk telling him that she was going by Anna, but not as much as telling him she was Liska. Anna was a common name, Liska was not. But if he had any contact with the local blood, he could easily find out she was Liska. Hopefully he wouldn't mention 'Sakaki' to anyone.

"I see. I'm sure there's a story there. I'd love to hear it. To hear all your stories. We should catch up. I know a few places, I'm sure you do too..." He sauntered closer.

Liska backed up, hands out. "I'm here with someone."

"Oh? My loss. Another time then?" His voice made her want to melt.

"No, I don't think so." Liska took a deep breath and gave herself a mental smack. "What happened in Luxembourg, well, that's it. Nothing further can happen."

"Oh, c'mon." His fangs glinted as he gave her a wide smile. "I'm just asking for the chance to talk. You know, two friends who haven't seen each other in years." She opened her mouth to object, but he continued. "Or, if you insist, two people who have things in common, getting the chance to become friends." Impossibly, his smile widened. "I'll even promise not to try to kiss you, if you like. Though you can feel free to kiss me."

It was the sound of her shoe skidding on asphalt that told her she had stepped back. Feelings that she hadn't been able to identify as a sixteen-year-old surged through her, and now she was pretty sure it was desire. "I... I have to go." She turned and ran.

***

Todd looked up at the sound of running. It was Sakaki. She slowed as she got to him, so chances were nothing was seriously wrong. "Everything alright?"

"Fine. How are you feeling?"

Wow, she was usually a lot better at lying than that. This was probably not the time to call her on that, though. "A little better, I think."

"Good. I got water, a ginger ale, sorry, that probably got shaken up; some pink bismuth, and some ginger pills."

"What's pink bismuth?"

Rather than answer, Liska sat next to him and handed him a small box. He tried to read it by lamp light. "Pepto-Bismol pills?"

"Generic Pepto-Bismol pills."

Todd made a face. His only memories of Pepto-Bismol were of it making him throw up. Which generally helped, but it was still nasty. "I'll try the ginger pills."

"Sure." She read the label, then passed over the bottle. "Dosage is one pill."

Todd took the bottle and the water bottle she offered, quickly swallowing the pill; before washing it down with water. "So, why were you running?"

"This is the person you're with?" Todd looked up as a shadow came over them. Another Twilight. Male, classically handsome, would make a wonderful model for an angel or a Greek hero. Dark curly hair, blue eyes, perfect teeth. Who the heck was this?

"Eric..." Sakaki let out a long-suffering sigh. "Eric, this is Todd. Todd, this is Eric. Eric, I told you... Look, I can't talk now. Goodbye."

"I'm ready to go." Todd stood, ignoring the way his nausea intensified. If Sakaki wanted to get away from the movie star handsome man who wanted to hit on her, Todd was more than happy to help.

She stood too, only for this Eric fellow to grab her arm. Irritation and jealousy sparked in Todd, becoming a roaring fire when not only did she not pull away, but she turned to listen.

"Look, Sakaki. I really do need to talk to you. Privately." Sakaki? He knew her real name? How did he know her name?

"*Anna*. Is it urgent?"

"Well, not exactly."

"Can it be discussed in under two minutes?"

"Not a chance, but—"

"Then it will have to wait. Goodnight, Eric." She shook off his hand and started walking away.

Todd followed immediately. He waited until he was pretty sure Eric was out of earshot before speaking, trying very hard to keep his irritation hidden. "How does he know your name?"

"I was young and stupid, and told him."

"Just came out and told him?"

"Todd, are you really going to dredge up the dumb mistakes I made at sixteen? *Really*? Because I've investigated you. I'm friends with your best friend and his younger sister. Trust me, I know some of the things you did at sixteen."

Almost, he said something like 'At least I was never an assassin.' He had to bite his tongue, but it didn't come out. He was *not* going to fling that in her face, no matter what. "I can understand making some mistakes because you're young and dumb. Like you said, I've done dumb things too."

"I particularly liked the story about you riding your dirt bike into a lake."

Todd winced. *Shahara.* He was going to have to talk to her. "That was an accident. And it was dangerous. But I find it... odd, that someone as paranoid and cautious as yourself would go revealing something that personal to a random person."

"Fine, he was my first crush. Happy?"

No, no he wasn't. "I thought you could only fall in love once."

"I can. But there's a world of difference between love and a crush."

True enough. "How long were you involved?"

Sakaki scoffed. "*Involved?* You make it seem deeper than it was. I knew him for four days; three years ago, while I was in Luxembourg on a job."

Three years ago. "Tisiphone."

Her stiffness answered him before her quiet affirmative. Right, so very not going there. "And you told him your real name?"

"Yes! I told him my name! We ate dinner together, met up the next day by accident, and two days later he sought me out. I think we talked for ten minutes before Father came and took me back home. Are you satisfied now?"

"You had dinner together?"

"Argh!" Sakaki stopped and took a couple breaths. "We are not going to fight in the middle of Clematis. If you want to argue, we can do it in your car."

"Fine." She had a point. They were already getting a couple stares.

The rest of the walk was silent. Todd held her door open, which she accepted with a quiet nod. As soon as he was in and shut his door, Liska spoke up. "Before you say anything, yes, I was attracted to Eric. But as I told him, then and now, nothing could happen between us."

"You told me the same thing." Todd started up the car.

"I told you the truth as I knew it. Things have changed, a little. You and I have a chance, albeit a small one. Eric and I do not even have that."

"Does he know who you truly are?"

"Heaven alone knows. I didn't tell him. He seems to know I was lying about before, but I don't know what he does know."

"But you told him your name."

"I also told him I was a photography student. You knew me better as Anna then he did as Sakaki."

Todd took a deep breath. "Alright. I trust you. Before I forget, who's Calloway?"

Sakaki huffed a laugh. "Oh, you'll love this. Calloway was the sniper who shot at us a couple months ago."

Todd blinked at that. "What? Really? He's still alive?"

She gave him a strange look. "What do you mean?"

"Well, you were so closemouthed about what happened to him, I figured he was dead. I mean, I wasn't happy about it, but he was trying to kill us, so that's self-defense, and I couldn't report it, because I had no proof, and I wasn't going to anyway–"

"Todd, breathe!" She waited until his breathing was close to normal. "That was really bothering you, wasn't it?"

"Honestly? Yes, it was." He hadn't even known how much, because he'd been avoiding thinking about it.

"*Sensei* hypnotized him to forget about us and sent him home."

For something he hadn't been thinking about, it was amazing how much of a relief it was to hear that. "So, he's still alive."

"Well, no. He's dead now. Apparently a car crash while he was DUI less than a week ago. Coincidentally enough, it was only a little after the raid on the Magnus blood, which he supposedly identified."

Todd tried to make sense of that. "So, you killed him for betraying the vampires?"

"What? Wait, first of all, *I* didn't kill him. I wasn't even in country at the time. It may have even truly been an accident; the man was an alcoholic. But I doubt it. Two, he didn't *betray* the vampires as he didn't have any loyalty to them in the first place. Someone used him to pass on information, probably betraying the vampires. I suspect they also arranged his car accident."

"Oh, okay."

"Now, why did you think *I* killed him?" The tone was casual but her posture was tense, and she was all but vibrating with suppressed energy.

"Well..." Because she had killed before. Because Todd had honestly believed she was roughing someone up for information back in the bar. Because some part of him was afraid of what she would do if she felt the need.

"'*Well*?' What does '*well*' mean?"

"Why didn't you tell me what the plan was in the bar?"

"What? That doesn't answer anything."

"Still, why didn't you?"

"Because plans change in a heartbeat. Because I needed you to believe it. You were far more effective that way."

"I almost gave the whole thing away."

"Not really."

"Would you really do something like that?"

"What? Stab someone in the hand? Sure. If I needed to. Beat someone up for information? If I had to. Normally I don't. I'm good at mind games. If I make them believe that I'll happily rip out their spine and make a necklace of their fingers and toes, they'll tell me everything I need without my actually touching them." She glared at him. "Contrary to popular belief, I'm not a *complete* sadist."

"I never said you were."

"No. Just implied it."

"Look, I'm sorry but I find it a little hard to know what to believe when I tell you that I saw blood on your hands, and you decide it's a good idea."

"Would you prefer someone really got hurt?"

"Don't put words in my mouth. You know I wouldn't." He took a deep breath and tried to calm the anger churning in his stomach. But every time he thought he had it almost settled, it sparked up again. "Did you use me?"

"I asked if you wanted to come. I didn't force you and even told you the truth afterwards. Now I'm getting accused of sadism and murder. What more do you want?"

What more *did* he want? He pulled into the parking lot by her dorm. Sakaki unbuckled her seatbelt and had the door open before she spoke. "I don't want to make this fight worse. We can talk tomorrow when we're calmer. But I want you to think about one thing, Todd Kensworth. You said you wanted to know more about me. Well, this is who I am. This is my life. If you can't deal with that, let me know now." The door slammed behind her.

Almost, he went after her. But he didn't. They were too wound up. Someone would say something, the other would say something worse, and before they knew it, their friendship would lie shredded on the floor. Tomorrow. Tonight, he had to think about if he could deal with this side of her. Maybe he *should* have stayed home and studied.

***

Liska waited until she heard Todd drive off. It was past midnight and she had classes tomorrow. She should sleep. But she didn't even bother to try. It wouldn't work anyway.

Instead, she headed back outside. It was too late to walk to the ocean, even if it was only a mile away. But the intracoastal was much closer. Looking at the water would help calm her. Hopefully.

The sea wall was only about two feet off the sidewalk on one side, but over the water it was a good five, six feet to ground. Perfect to sit on and think.

The moon was nearly full as it reflected on the water, broken by gentle waves. Salt, fish, pollution, and car smells filled her nose. Liska took in a deep breath and Sakaki let it out again.

She had to stop traveling with Todd; all their fights seemed to take place in cars. Of course, some of those were her fault. But this wasn't. She even let it drop why he thought she had been the one to kill Calloway. And answered his questions instead of telling him it was none of his business.

Really, what did he expect? She had all but spelled out what her job entailed. Tonight wasn't even that dangerous. Sure, she made it look bad, but...

Sakaki sighed. Maybe they were just too different. It was to be expected. She had said so, *Sensei* said so, and the only reason more of her family hadn't said anything was because they hadn't known he was interested. But somehow, she had let herself hope.

"There's a reason we don't mix with them, you know."

Liska didn't turn to look. "There's a reason vampires and Weres don't mix too."

"I'll grant you that one." Eric took a seat next to her. "You must like rivers. I keep finding you near them."

"I do like water. It's... soothing. Peaceful." It made her feel small, and her problems even smaller. "I should be furious with you, you know?"

"With me?" Confusion mixed with amusement. It irritated her.

"I *told* you it was Anna here. You could have made things very awkward back there." Actually, it had gotten very awkward. But it would have been worse if Todd didn't know who she was.

"Ah, then I beg your pardon, fair lady. Please allow me to make it up to you."

Liska sighed. "What are you doing here, Eric? Why did you come to West Palm Beach?"

"I was told to. Father is helping out the remnants of the Magnus blood after..."

"I heard about that. So you're helping? How long have you been here?"

"About a week. You?"

"Not quite as long. Since Saturday. When did it happen?"

"Ten days ago. I still can't believe it. Such a tragedy."

"I know. I'm not clear on details. What do you know about it?"

She felt more than saw his shrug. "Not much. There was no warning. Just a sudden attack." He gave her a grim smile. "Why do I only run into you when there's death afoot?"

"I guess either I'm bad luck or you are."

"Who are you really, Sakaki?"

Several different answers came to mind, but in the end she only said, "I don't know, and you'll never find out. Goodbye, Eric."

Liska spun to get up, but a wave of sudden dizziness had her almost lose her balance and fall into the water. Eric caught her, helping her to her feet. "See, here you are falling head over heels." He didn't let go.

"What do you want, Eric?"

"We had something in Luxembourg. Don't tell me you felt nothing."

She could deny it. It would be a lie, but she was used to that. "Immaterial. This isn't Luxembourg. I'm not who I was there. You have your responsibilities, your loyalties, and I have mine. Our paths don't join."

"But here we are. Twice in just three years, thousands of miles away."

"It's a small world."

"Do you believe in fate?"

"No."

Eric laughed. "Just determined to shoot me down, huh? Fine, fine. How about friends. Can we do that? You could always use more friends."

She could. Another contact, another connection. But this was playing with fire in a way that others weren't. "Fine, but just friends. I have classes tomorrow. I have to go." Liska jogged back to campus, not caring whether or not Eric was watching.

Chapter Eleven

Problems are inevitable. Attitude is everything. – The Kikitsutai Book of Wisdom

When Liska woke up the next morning, she felt lousy and it took her a few minutes to remember why. Why was it that emotional confrontations always took more out of her than physical confrontations? She wouldn't have felt like this if she had just gotten into a bar brawl at, what was the name of that bar again? Oh, yes. 'Devil's Fang'. Whose brilliant idea was that? She could change it, being technically the owner now; but she didn't want anyone to know that. Besides, that was the least of her issues.

Eric was in town. She would have thought it very interesting that he should show up just as she uncovered that memory of him, but she had figured it out last night. He must have been hanging around before their encounter last night. Subconsciously, she had been picking up on small signals that drove her to uncover that memory. There was no proof of her theory, but it fit. He may have even engineered their little run in. Not that she would likely ask him.

So what did he want, and what was she supposed to do about him?

Well, Eric could be dealt with later, after she found out what he knew about the Magnus blood. Todd she had to deal with today. What did she do about him? Should she apologize? Had she done anything wrong? Not that the one necessarily had anything to do with the other, but both needed an answer.

Perhaps it wasn't quite cricket to expect Todd to be her backup without enough of an idea about what she was doing that he would know if something went wrong. Perhaps she would have told him more if she wasn't so used to improvising under pressure. But he had to understand, this was the kind of thing she did and that wasn't going to stop as long as she was physically capable of doing her job. Last night was an easy job where no one got hurt. It was often much less pleasant. Liska would be the first to admit that she had done many things she wasn't proud of for the sake of her work. Just because last night's adventure didn't require force, that didn't mean tonight's, whatever tonight might bring, wouldn't.

Deep breaths. No point getting worked up again. Talk to Todd, see where things go from there. Liska got dressed and opened her door... only to stop at the sight of a small pot of violets sitting on her doormat.

She squatted to pick them up, sniffing carefully before touching the wrapper. Violets, dirt, plastic, a hint of old blood... *Eric.* So he had been watching. Not really a surprise.

Liska brought in the plant. There was no note, but she didn't need one. Violets, huh? Werefoxes, particularly vixens, usually smelled a bit like violets, as a carryover from foxes. Even some humans could smell it. Todd could, he had mentioned it. Then again, since all her soaps and toiletries were unscented, perhaps it wasn't surprising that the violets were the most noticeable smell.

Some time ago, she had studied the language of flowers. Mostly for fun, but she had used it a few times. Violets, depending on color, stood for modesty, daydreaming or faithfulness. Did Eric know that? It didn't seem like much of a message. Perhaps he only picked it because she was a Werefox. Or perhaps because he liked it, or it was on sale. She had to be careful about reading too much into things.

It didn't matter. She shouldn't be taking flowers from him at all. Still, Liska put the potted plant next to her aloe. Her rosemary plant had died a month ago. Maybe she'd remember to water this one. At least the aloe was thriving.

Start of day, take two. This time, Todd was standing at the base of the stairs. Having no desire to shout back and forth, she went to him. He spoke before she could.

"Hey, I wanted to say I'm sorry. I don't know why I reacted so badly last night. Part of it, well, I don't think it all felt real to me. Which is really dumb, considering what I've already seen. I mean...I don't know what I mean." Todd took a breath and ran a hand through his hair. "I'm sorry. I trust you. Really."

"Thank you. I'm sorry too. I probably should have told you a little more. Forgiven?"

"Forgiven. Um, here." He held out a hibiscus flower, probably picked from a bush on his way over. "I didn't have time to visit a florist."

Liska laughed. She couldn't help it. It seemed absurd. "I love it. Thanks." She took the flower and tucked it behind her ear. It didn't stay, so she took a bobby pin from her pocket and pinned it in place. "There. How does it look?" Probably a little silly. Hibiscus flowers are large blossoms. She didn't know what color this one was, but it wasn't white, so it probably clashed with her hair. She hadn't looked in a mirror, so it was probably crooked.

"Perfect. Absolutely perfect. May I escort you to breakfast, fair lady?"

"You may, kind sir."

Hibiscus stood for 'Rare and delicate beauty'. Todd probably didn't know that, either, but he seemed to believe it true.

***

"I'm sorry, but did you really say what I think you just said?" Kira held the phone between her shoulder and ear as she rolled up clothes to pack for her trip.

"That depends on what you think I said." She could *hear* Liska's smirk.

"Oooh, you! Okay, did you really say that you have a date tonight? A Saturday night date?"

"Hm, maybe. That sounds a little like something I might have said."

"Sakaki!"

Her cousin's laugh was slightly distorted over the phones. "Yes, I have a date with Todd tonight. A *date* date. On a Saturday. And what does the day have to do with anything?"

"Saturday dates mean more."

"That's silly. Why is that?"

"No idea, but it's common knowledge."

"Can't be that common. I didn't know about it."

"What do you know about dating? I will eat my boots, the pair you keep trying to steal from me, if Yoshiro ever asked you out on a date."

"Eh, whatever." That was a 'no'. "So, he's taking me to some fancy restaurant. He won't tell me where, though. Said he wanted it to be a surprise."

"And you're okay with that?" Kira flopped onto her bed, staring up at the ceiling. Like most homes on Kikitsutai Island, it was literally built into the mountain, so her ceiling was stone. Sometimes she could swear a stalactite was forming in one corner, even though she knew that was impossible without water.

"Let him have his fun. True, I don't like surprises, but I understand why he wants to surprise me, and I won't ruin it."

"That's... amazingly laid back for you. You already know, don't you?"

Sakaki laughed again. "I've narrowed it down to two possibilities. I'll leave it alone from there."

That was still a surprising amount of trust for her. Kira could barely get away with surprising her with birthday presents. It wasn't that Sakaki was a control freak, she was just too paranoid to be happy following another person's plans. And she was a bit of a control freak.

"Sorry to kill the mood, but any luck with the blood?"

"No." Sakaki bit out. "I haven't been able to match your sketch yet. No one knows anything useful about Calloway. I've heard a few rumors that his death wasn't an accident, and a couple suggested it might be about retaliation instead of to shut him up, but nothing definite or even promising. Can't track motivation either. Rex Magnus is about to start spitting nails, and I can't blame him in the slightest."

"Me neither. Your father was infuriated when he found out about it. Of course, part of the reason he was so angry was that it took over a week to find out. He feels we should have known in time to warn them."

"Ideally, we would have. But we didn't."

"True," Kira sighed. "Anything else going on?"

"Hm? No. Not really."

Kira frowned. Okay, that was a lie. "Sakaki?"

"I've got to go. It will take me a while to get ready. You'll be in the States Tuesday, right? Call me then?"

"Yes, of course. But–"

"Got to go." Kira was left listening to a dial tone. What was that about? What was Sakaki hiding now?

***

Todd knocked on Sakaki's door, wondering how many 'first dates' they were going to have. The dance wasn't a 'date', since she only went because she needed to get in the evidence room. Nor was he sure if escorting her to meals in the cafeteria counted. But this was totally and unarguably a date.

He had finally broken down and told Jamal and Shahara what was going on. Sort of. He told them that Anna was giving him a chance to convince her that they could have a relationship.

Jamal had clapped him on the back and wished him luck. Then the coward disappeared, leaving him in Shahara's clutches. Shahara interrogated him on everything from what clothes he was wearing, to how was he doing his hair, to was he giving her flowers and what kind?

"Does it really matter?"

"Yes. Anna knows the language of flowers. I'm sure she knows you don't, but you don't want to accidentally send her a message that you hate her, right?"

No, he didn't want that. It had sparked an idea, though. After swearing Shahara to secrecy about everything, he had scoured sources looking for the meaning of common flowers to find the perfect message.

Todd was torn from his thoughts by the door opening. "Hi. Is this sufficient for your restaurant? I forgot to ask about a dress code." Sakaki was wearing a sapphire-colored blouse, shiny, with a slight v-neck, and a black swishy skirt that went down to her calves. She had on a pearl necklace and matching earrings. They must have been clip, because he knew for a fact she didn't have pierced ears.

"It's fine. You look beautiful." In truth, it might be just a hair too dressy for where he had in mind, but she looked so good, he wasn't going to tell her no.

"Thank you. You're not so bad yourself." He was wearing a dress shirt and tie with slacks, but not a suit jacket.

"Thanks. Here, for you." Todd handed her the white carnation he had picked out earlier and tied with a metallic gold ribbon. A symbol for innocence, pure love, faithfulness, and meaning sweet and lovely.

"Thank you. Is this white?"

"Yes. Does it matter?"

Sakaki gave him a slightly odd look as she shrugged. "Just curious." It was long stemmed, so she tucked it into her bun instead of behind her ear. "How does it look?"

Todd minutely straightened it. "There, lovely. Ready to go?"

"I am."

He had prepared by checking ahead of time about food allergies (strongly allergic to chocolate and alcohol, sensitive to grapes, raisins, and nutmeg), and her food tastes (spicy was fine, she was not vegetarian, but not opposed to the occasional vegetarian meal, international was fine, and she liked chicken, beef, and seafood, as well as some more exotic choices). So he was fairly confident that she would be okay with Pearl of the Sea, a fancy Mediterranean style restaurant. It was a place he associated with good memories. Hopefully tonight would bring a few more.

When they arrived at the large building, designed to look like an Italian Villa, Sakaki said, "Hmm, I've never been here before."

"Do you like Mediterranean?"

"Certainly," She smiled.

Todd returned it. "Good. C'mon, we have reservations."

He didn't know anything about having a 'good' table, and wouldn't claim he did, but he was satisfied with the one they were given, not far from the middle of the room, under one of the fancy chandeliers that looked like one crystal would pay his tuition. Todd bet they were plastic or glass though. To his slight amusement, Sakaki immediately moved to the chair facing the door. He took the hint and held out the chair for her.

Through his uncle, Todd had experience interacting with various police officers. Once thing he had heard repeatedly was that most of them hated sitting with their backs to the door. It only made sense that Sakaki was the same, but he had never noticed it before.

Taking his own seat, he eyed the row of silverware with only a slight bit of trepidation. Work from the outside in. Hopefully that would be enough to keep him from making a fool of himself. He had only been here with family before, and no one cared if he used the wrong fork. Maybe Sakaki didn't know either. Yeah, right. That was probably one of the things she had training in, like astronomy and horse riding (he had been a little surprised to learn that was still considered important enough to teach in her clan). She knew how to pass as a fancy lady. Certainly better than Todd could as a proper gentleman.

"Todd?"

He snapped up realizing she had been talking. "Sorry. I, um, got distracted."

She was polite enough to hide her smile behind her hand, but he still knew it was there. "I asked how you learned about this place."

"I've been here a few times. When Mom got the promotion she really wanted, for my eighteenth birthday, getting my black belt in Kendo, graduating high school, when I won an art competition, celebratory times.

"How nice. To have a place with such memories."

The waiter came by then. "Would the gentleman and lady like to see our wine list?"

"No, thank you." They were both underage, and she was allergic. "I'll have a water to start, please."

"The same, please," Sakaki chimed in, before looking at her menu. As the waiter left, she turned to Todd. "As I said, I've never been here. What do you recommend?"

"The pumpkin soup is awesome. They serve it in a little hollowed out pumpkin shell. I've never had anything bad here, but I haven't been here that many times, and I usually get the lime cilantro shrimp."

"That has potential." She breezed through the menu. "But I think I'll go with the herbed mussels with pasta."

"Mom got that at least twice. She loved it."

The waiter returned with their waters. "Are the gentleman and lady ready to order?"

Todd looked at Sakaki, who nodded. "Yes, I think so." Then he shut up to let Sakaki order.

"Yes, I would like the herbed mussels with pasta. Can I get that with angel hair?"

"The lady may."

"Perfect. Oh, is there wine in the sauce?"

"There is." He named something that Todd guessed was supposed to be the vintage.

"May I have it without?"

"Of course. Would the lady like soup or salad with her order?"

"The pumpkin soup, please."

"Very good. And for you, Sir?"

Todd handed over the menu. "I'll have the lime cilantro shrimp on rice, also with the pumpkin soup, please."

"Very good." The waiter took their menus and left.

Todd was suddenly left feeling very awkward and unsure what to say. Then Sakaki smiled at him. "So, how come you rate a 'Sir', and I'm 'the lady'?"

"No idea. Maybe because he's not sure if you're a miss, or a ma'am, or didn't want to pick a foreign language equivalent. Sir is just simpler. Or not. Who knows?"

She shrugged. "Doesn't matter. I was just curious. So, how are your classes going?"

From there, they had a conversation. Nothing particularly exciting, but a conversation. Until Sakaki frowned at her watch. "Does it normally take this long?"

"Food in these kinds of restaurants always take a long time."

"Yes, but forty minutes? I would expect the food by then. And we should have had our soup ages ago.

"Huh, you do have a point." Todd made eye contact with their waiter.

The waiter came straight to the table. "Would the gentleman and lady like their check?"

"We'd like our food first," Todd protested.

The waiter looked at their table, probably seeing their clean dishes. "Ah, yes. What did you order again?"

"Two orders of pumpkin soup, the herbed mussels with angel hair, no wine, and the lime cilantro shrimp?" Sakaki said, inflection making it seem a question.

"Of course. Have you had your soup yet?"

"No, nothing." Todd looked at their table. "Not even a basket of rolls."

"And I would like some more water, please."

"Let me fetch you some rolls. The food will be ready in a trice." The waiter disappeared towards the kitchen.

"He's lying. I don't think they've started our food yet." Sakaki shrugged.

"Oh, I'm sure they have."

She shook her head. "Nope. He didn't have a clue. Somehow, we slipped through the cracks."

The waiter returned with a basket of rolls. "Fresh from the oven. Your food will be ready shortly."

"Thank you," Sakaki said to his retreating back. She reached out and took one. "I hope he comes back soon with my water."

Todd took a roll too. Sakaki had taken a bite and was frowning. One bite and he knew why. The center was dough. "Yours' undercooked too?"

She nodded. "I think they all are. Do we say anything? They're still edible."

"I don't know." He took another. It was raw almost all the way through. "Yeah, I think we should. I mean, I hate to complain, but this..." This was supposed to be a nice date at a fancy restaurant, not a comedy of errors.

"Fair enough. If nothing else, they should probably check their oven settings."

It was almost fifteen minutes before their waiter made another appearance. He refilled Todd's water, which was still half-full, but ignored Sakaki's empty glass even as she pushed it over and didn't seem to hear their attempts to talk to him. Then he disappeared again.

"I swear, I've never had a problem like this before." Todd held up his hands.

"I'm not blaming you. I am, however, thinking that our waiter will probably *not* be getting a good tip."

"Well, it might not be fair to blame him for a kitchen mix-up or half-baked rolls; but he's ignoring you, and being rude, which is definitely a problem. I guess we aren't fancy enough for him."

"Yes, I knew the type." She smirked. "Would you be terribly opposed to my putting on an act?"

"No knives involved this time, right?"

"Only to cut the meal." Humor and anticipation were rolling off her.

"Go for it." Todd leaned back. This should be good.

Sakaki gave him a nod, then went silent and closed her eyes. She made some minute shifts to her posture, then opened her eyes. Turning, she sought out the waiter, making eye contact with him. He was at her side in seconds. "Ma'am?"

"Yes, I would like another water. And I'm afraid these rolls are not done to our satisfaction." She ripped her roll open, revealing it to be more raw than cooked. "You may wish to check your oven's settings." The man was white-faced now. Sakaki tilted her head slightly. "Or perhaps what I have heard of this restaurant has been overblown?"

"I shall inform the chef immediately. More water? Of course." The basket of rolls left with the waiter.

Sakaki turned back to Todd. "They'll probably give us a discount on the check. Frankly, I think they should."

"Because of the rolls?"

"Because of the rolls, the rude waiter, and the fact we've been sitting here for over an hour and haven't even gotten our soup yet."

"Okay, can't argue with that."

Sakaki's water and a new basket of rolls appeared as if by magic. "Your soup shall be along presently."

This time the waiter was right. The soup arrived only a minute later. Unfortunately, it was the wrong soup. "We ordered the pumpkin soup, not," Sakaki sniffed the air, "rabbit stew."

"Of course. I merely read the wrong entry. My apologies." He took the soups away.

Sakaki shook her head as she took a roll, ripping it open to check. "Fully cooked this time."

"Oh, good. We're going to get our food tonight, right?"

"Maybe, maybe not. Something's gone wrong in the kitchen, but I can't tell what." She sniffed. "Fire."

"A kitchen fire?" Todd whispered despite wanting to shout. "Shouldn't we evacuate?" Kitchen fires were some of the most dangerous.

"No, they seem to have it under control. It's almost out."

There was nothing telling them to evacuate, no smoke alarm blaring. He couldn't even smell smoke. If they left, they would have to explain why. He'd have to trust her for now.

Their soups arrived. "Two pumpkin soups. Our head chef would like to offer you both a gelato after the meal. Our compliments. Simply let me know when you are ready."

"We will, thank you." Sakaki nodded graciously. After the waiter left, she turned to Todd. "Okay, maybe he will get a tip. We'll see."

"Yeah, the meal is still young." Todd took a bite of his soup. His tongue and nose tickled. Pepper? He didn't remember tasting pepper in this before. He tried another bite. Definitely pepper, and lots of it. With his third bite, he sneezed. Sakaki was frowning at her soup. "Is yours peppery too?"

"No, not pepper. Nutmeg. There's a ton of nutmeg in mine. Here, try it." She took a clean spoon and offered him a bite of her soup.

While Todd might not have been able to positively identify the spice as nutmeg, he could tell there was a lot of it. "Didn't you say you were sensitive to nutmeg?"

"Yes. I can't eat this. It would make me sick. Trade soups?"

"Not sure you want this one." He mimicked her by offering a bite with a clean spoon.

She made a face. "I see what you mean. How disappointing." Once again she did her magic 'summon waiter' look. He was there instantly. "There appears to be a problem with our soups. Someone appears to have dropped the contents of a pepper shaker in my companion's soup, and mine has a far too heavy dose of nutmeg."

Todd stirred up his soup to show the preponderance of black flakes. The waiter didn't quite scowl. "I see. I'll have these replaced."

"We appreciate it."

Todd was pretty sure it was supposed to be his job to deal with the waiter about these kinds of issues. Both to be gentleman, and because he had invited her. On the other hand, Sakaki was so much better at it, and it was amazing to watch. Idly, Todd wondered if she could teach him how to do that.

Their replacement soups arrived at the same time as their entrées. While nothing was obviously wrong with them this time, Todd was certain he remembered the soup being better than this. It was okay, but nothing better than that. "I know this tasted better last time."

Sakaki gave a graceful shrug. "I wouldn't know. How about your shrimp?"

Todd popped one in his mouth and bit down. Instantly, his eyes started to water as his mouth and sinuses burned. He took a few sips of water and hastily ate a roll. "I don't remember cayenne pepper in this. And if I didn't know better, I'd swear someone doused it with ghost pepper sauce."

"Oh, dear. What do you want to bet there's wine in my sauce, too?"

"No bet."

She twirled a small amount of pasta in her fork and sniffed it delicately. "Yes, yes there most definitely is." Sakaki raised her hand slightly and their waiter hastened to their table. "I believe I ordered my dish without the wine. Someone appears to have misunderstood that as 'extra wine'."

The waiter, undoubtedly with visions of no tip floating through his head, tried to cover. "Surely the lady knows that the wine adds flavor."

"The lady knows she has severe food allergies and no desire to visit the emergency room." The plate was practically yanked away from her. "And my companion was wondering if the recipe to his dish has changed, as he does not recall either cayenne pepper or ghost pepper being a predominate part."

The waiter's brow furrowed. "In lime cilantro shrimp? There's no cayenne or ghost pepper in that."

"There is in this one," Todd said.

"I can smell it from here," Sakaki added.

"I see. I will get to the bottom of this." The waiter took Todd's entrée as well.

"At least the soup is edible." Sakaki dipped part of a roll in said soup.

"I wanted better than 'edible', I was hoping for special." He stirred his soup around, trying to hide his disappointment.

"Todd, look at me." He did, on instinct. "This *is* special. Yes, problems are happening, but that's not your fault. Things just happen sometimes." She gave him a small smirk. "I'm not going to refuse to see you again just because Murphy is determined to vent his spite on us tonight."

"I know that! I just..." Just part of him kind of thought she would. Or should. He knew it was silly. Like she said, none of this was his fault. But Sakaki had been so hard to convince in the first place that part of him was still expecting her to back out at the first hint of anything going wrong.

She was gracious enough to not call him a liar to his face and let the subject drop. They discussed classes and art lessons until their promised entrées returned.

***

Liska thought she was doing a good job at not showing her irritation. It got harder as the night wore on and things got worse, but she was determined not to take it out on Todd. It wasn't his fault and he was upset enough.

The second attempt entrées weren't nearly as bad as the first, thankfully. Not exceptional, but that could be due to her lack of taste buds. However, Todd seemed disappointed too. She was going to be having words with someone.

If she didn't know for a fact that Tora and Ryo were on a separate continent right now, she would have half suspected them to have snuck in and be pranking them. It would be their style. Almost. They wouldn't have slipped her anything potentially dangerous. No, this wasn't them.

The promised gelato was fine, though colder than she expected. About halfway through desert, Todd reached for his pocket. Then his other one. Then the two behind him. All while smelling of dawning horror. His wallet.

"Could it have fallen out in the car?" Liska asked.

"How did you...? Never mind. Maybe. I'll go check. I know I had it, I made sure before picking you up. Wait here? Um, you can finish the gelato."

Liska took another couple bites. Then a few more because it was melting. As she was pondering whether or not she really should finish it, the maître d' came by. She had been expecting this.

"We would like to apologize for the issues you and your companion had today. Tonight's meal is on the house. I would call it complementary, but I doubt you feel complemented."

"No, not truly. I was quite disappointed. I had heard good things about this place."

"Yes, well, we would also like to offer you half off your next visit. We promise you, these issues will not happen again." The man was sweating.

It wasn't his fault, so she let him off the hook. "No, I don't imagine we will. Thank you, we *will* try again at some point."

"Certainly, Ma'am. Please just present this upon your next visit." She was handed a piece of paper, made of cardstock that was about the size of a playing card. It offered the bearer half off their next check. No exclusions, no expiration date. She must have really scared them.

"I will." The maître d' left. Liska took the last few bites of gelato and left a five on the table. The waiter didn't deserve a large tip, but he should get something. Then she left to find Todd.

He was frantically rooting through his car, looking up in surprise when she came over. "I can't find it. I *know* I had it."

"They gave us the meal on the house and a half off voucher for our next visit. I left tip."

He relaxed a little. "Why?"

"So we didn't get a reputation as troublesome customers. Don't get me wrong, the waiter was a bit of a problem on his own, but better to leave him something."

"Well, thanks." Todd leaned against the car. "I am so sorry. I just don't know what happened tonight."

"I have an idea. May I borrow your shoe?"

Todd looked at her like he wasn't sure he had heard her correctly. "My shoe?"

"Exactly."

With a shrug, he moved to standing on one foot and slipped off his left shoe. "I *am* getting this back, right?"

"Pretty sure."

She could see him debate for a second before warily handing it to her. Liska took it with a nod, turned, and threw the shoe as hard as she could at the branches of a nearby swamp cypress.

Todd's cry of protest turned to shock as Eric crashed out of the tree and hit the ground. Liska stalked over to the slightly dazed vampire. "You, Sir, have caused enough trouble tonight."

Eric shook her head before focusing on her. "Oh, come on. It was just a little fun."

"You ruined our meal, and two of your 'additions' were dangerous to me."

"I knew you'd realize as soon as you took a bite. If it got *that* far. No harm done." He grinned, teeth glinting.

Liska didn't crack a smile. "Give Todd back his wallet."

Eric rolled his eyes and tossed the small leather object carelessly. Behind her, she could hear Todd making an awkward catch. "Happy?"

"Now give back what you took out of it."

The vampire gave a heavy sigh and handed her some cash, at least one card, and some pictures. Liska didn't look at them. "Now you are going to get lost. We are on a date, as you well know."

"I do know. But seriously, a human?"

"Goodnight, Eric."

He stood, cracking his back and knocking branches away. "If I leave, can I talk to you in private later?"

"You get one hour at a time and place of my choosing."

"Fine." Eric bent and picked up the shoe. "Nice throw. You're a pitcher, aren't you?" He gave it an underhand toss, letting her catch the shoe easily. Liska didn't say anything. "Tough crowd. Well, you two lovebirds have a good night." Eric gave them a mock bow and left.

Liska watched until she was sure he was gone before shaking her head and walking back to Todd.

"I'm sorry about that. I'm pretty sure he was behind ninety percent of tonight's mishaps." She offered Todd back his shoe.

He looked confused. "Um, Sakaki? I don't speak Russian."

She blinked and thought back. "German actually. Sorry, I didn't realize I had changed languages." Eric had answered her first sentence in German and she had automatically switched.

"How could you not know?" Todd took his shoe and tried to get it back on. She moved closer so he could use her for balance, but he stuck to the car.

"Father wanted me to be multi-lingual and knew little children learn languages the easiest. So he tried to teach me one a year from... birth, basically."

"How'd that work?"

"Not well. I was slow to talk, and ended up with lots of vocabulary, some rules of grammar, and no earthly idea of what belonged to which language. By eight, I could barely talk without mixing at least three languages and no one could understand me. Well, Kira almost always knew what I meant, and Mother was pretty good at guessing. By nine I stopped talking altogether."

Todd winced. "What happened?"

"Mother put a moratorium on my learning any new languages until I had this straightened out and *wanted* to learn more. Then she and Father arranged for several members of the skulk to agree to always, only, speak to me in a certain language, then when I finally started talking again, encourage me to use that language with them. I didn't speak for almost a year and a half and I was twelve before I didn't need that anymore. While I've picked up some more languages since, I still sometimes forget what belongs to what language, especially if it isn't one of my better ones. But I'm not always aware that I'm switching languages."

"I'm sorry."

Liska shrugged. What was, was. Without Father's pushing, she certainly wouldn't know as many languages as she knew now. She probably wouldn't be anyone close to who she was. Whether or not that was a good thing was yet to be determined.

"So, he was responsible for everything?"

This was so close to her thoughts that it took Sakaki a second to realize Todd was asking about Eric and tonight. "Pretty much. I mean, unless Eric is a telepath or empath, I doubt he had anything to do with the waiter being rude in the beginning, but certainly most of the rest. Though vampires are charismatic, it is possible... Never mind. Oh, here." She handed him the contents of his wallet that Eric had taken out. As she was holding it out, one of the pictures caught her eye. Using her free hand, she fished it from the rest of the pile. It was them, dressed up before the Police Ball. "I didn't know you had a picture of me in your wallet."

Todd blushed. "Yeah, hope you don't mind."

Liska thought about the significance of such a thing. "No, I don't mind at all."

Chapter Twelve

The words of a loved one can hurt worse than the swords of a thousand strangers. – The Kikitsutai Book of Wisdom

"Anna? You okay?"

Liska pulled herself from her thoughts and looked up from the book she was supposed to be studying. Shahara was standing across from the library table, radiating concern. "Hey, Shahara. Yeah, I'm fine. Why do you ask?"

Shahara sat down across from her. "Well, you seem distracted. You've been staring at that page for about five minutes, and Todd said that there was some complication with your relationship, but he wouldn't give any details."

Clearly, she was expected to be more obliging. Why Shahara thought she'd be more likely to talk about it than Todd, she wasn't sure. On the other hand, she wanted to talk to *someone*. Ryoko-*Sensei* was out. She still hadn't told him that she was giving Todd a chance at all. Kira had just landed in Washington D. C. a couple hours ago and would probably be half-dead from the travel. Besides, if she was so distracted that she didn't notice Shahara watching her for several minutes, then something clearly was wrong.

"It's... complicated. You know that Todd and I are trying to date. I'm still not convinced it will work, but we're trying."

"Right." Shahara learned forward, vibrating slightly.

"Well, I ran into someone I didn't expect. My first crush, actually. He... wants to pursue things."

Shahara's eyes bugged wide. "What did you say?"

"That I'm with someone."

"And he..."

"Keeps sending me flowers." Mostly violets. It was a rare morning she *didn't* find something on her doorstep. The other girls in her dorm were starting to notice. She had heard more than a few comments about a secret admirer.

"Oh, wow. You know I'm on Todd's side. But that there, that's really romantic."

"Many say the same of *Romeo and Juliet*, but I'd rather not live it."

Shahara sobered instantly. "You don't think... He's not a threat, is he?"

Eric? A threat? "No. I don't see him as dangerous." That said, she didn't see him as completely safe either.

"Whew." Shahara let out a breath. "So, what do you feel? Honestly. Promise I won't tell a soul."

What did she feel? "Conflicted. I like Todd, I really do. But we keep arguing lately, and I just don't know." There had been two more fights since the 'date that shall not be named', and both of them made their argument at Clematis seem friendly. "And as loathe as I am to admit it..."

"You're still attracted to this guy." Shahara said knowingly.

That was an understatement. When she wasn't near Eric, she could be reasonable and logical about how impossible the idea was, and his faults. When she was near Eric, she could barely think straight, and he almost had her convinced it was possible. "He was my first crush."

"You never forget that."

"No, you don't. But, if it would be difficult building a relationship with Todd, it would be all but impossible with this guy." It might be best not to give his name.

Shahara caught the omission but let it slide. "So, what are you going to do?"

"I'm not sure what more I can do. I told him nothing was going to happen, I continue trying with Todd, and I work on my assignments. One of those is also driving me crazy." It might not be a school assignment, but finding out who betrayed the blood was still an assignment, and she was making no progress.

"Can I pray for you? I mean, I already do, but more?"

Liska shook her head briefly in disbelief. "Sure, go ahead. I need all the help I can get."

"Alright. Oh, and, Anna, you know I'm hoping things work out between you and Todd. But even if they don't, I'll still be your friend."

She had to blink at that. The library was dusty; it was making her eyes water. "Thank you. I appreciate that."

"I mean it. But could you do me a favor? If things don't work out with Todd, would you please try to be gentle with him? I don't think I've ever seen him act like this with anyone else."

Fair enough. Todd was Shahara's friend first. "I swear upon my honor, I will do my best not to hurt him."

Shahara might not have known the depth of her vow, but she seemed satisfied with the sincerity. "That's all I ask."

"Okay, changing the subject now. No more talk about relationships." Now what? Was she really this inexperienced at having friends? Or at least, friends who weren't also ninja? "Out of curiosity, what's your major?"

"Cosmetology and textile design. What's yours?"

"Still deciding. I've got a few ideas that are near fits, but nothing that's quite right."

"Hey, can I ask you something?" Shahara seemed serious but not overly so.

"You can ask." Nothing said she had to answer truthfully. Or at all.

"Why did you choose *this* school? I mean, Jamal, Todd, and I all chose it because it was close, and we have friends here. But you're from England, you didn't know a soul. You haven't picked a major, so wasn't for a specific program. You aren't on a sports team, so you weren't scouted. Was it the beach?"

Well, she couldn't tell Shahara it was because there was a Twilight/Night medical clinic nearby or that Father wanted a better read on the Rex Magnus blood. Since she had made contact with them before, she was a good choice. But Father had left the decision completely up to her, only stipulating that she had to choose a college or university in the same city as a Twilight/Night clinic, and had to be fluent in the official language. Though to be fair, that was more of a strong recommendation than an order. "I may have never been here before, but my parents did have a connection or two in the area. Besides, I had heard a few good things about the school. I wanted some distance. It had to be far enough that I wasn't in my family's shadow. Honestly, I'm not sure why exactly this school. I had other options." Which was true. "It just appealed to me on some level. Maybe the beach was a small part of it." That part wasn't true. "I don't regret coming here." Which was mostly true.

"Well, that's something at least. Should I be letting you study?"

"I'm not sure I was studying before you got here," Liska admitted. "So I don't think your being here is much of a drawback."

Shahara chuckled. Then she spotted Liska's copy of the school's magazine. Liska had seen it by the cafeteria and decided to check it out. "Did you see that they're adding a new school?"

"No, I hadn't. Haven't actually read the magazine yet. Do you mean a new campus location, or a new area of study that they are calling a school?"

"The second. Within a couple years, they are hoping to open the Wilkinson School of Forensics. Forensic Chemistry, Forensic Biology, Forensic Physics, Forensic Anthropology, etc. Anna?"

"Where was that article?"

"Page twelve."

Sure enough, there was talk of the new school of forensics. Inspired by the growing need and interest in the forensic career track. "Interesting."

"Seriously? You want to study dead bodies and stuff?" Shahara sounded like she was trying very hard not to sound grossed out. It wasn't working, but Liska appreciated the effort.

"Your brother's pre-med. He studies 'dead bodies and stuff', doesn't he? And while profilers don't actually do the forensics themselves, they do depend on it being done. Forensic Chemistry could be very practical." They didn't have any specialists in forensics in the skulk. Several knowledgeable amateurs but no experts. A practical niche, in one of her interests? And a very good reason to stay longer than the original four years? This could well be perfect.

"Well, if you want to." Shahara didn't sound like she could understand why anyone would want to.

"I'm not running out and changing my major today. But now I have some ideas. A potential goal to work to. Maybe things will change, and I'll do something else. Or maybe not."

"Who knows, maybe you and Todd will find ways to work together."

Liska gave a tamer version of her 'evil' grin. "I assure you, I never thought anything of the sort."

"Oh, no. Of course not."

***

"You're in a good mood."

"I'm making progress. Almost broke through her defenses. She should be very *receptive* tonight."

"I don't care about your little games. I need her here."

"I'll get her."

"You had better. I don't care how you do it, just do it. Soon."

"I will."

***

"You're in a good mood."

"I should be. The peace treaty was straightened out in record time. I have plenty of time to come down to visit you once I finish here." Liska smiled at the thought. It would be good to see Kira. "You sound like you're in a good mood, too."

"I am. Todd and I are trying again. We're basically pretending last Saturday never happened." Not to mention a couple fights. "I'm sure we'll be able to laugh about it in the future, but for now..."

"Might be for the best. So, forensic chemistry, huh? Are you sure?"

"Certain? No. But it would be useful."

"True. I think it could be a good match for you. But will it be available by the time you leave school?"

"It's a graduate degree. I would probably get a Bachelor's in Chemistry first. That's at least three years. And even if it isn't ready here, now that I have a potential goal, I can find another school that does have it when I'm ready."

"True. Well, I'll probably be down in a day or two unless you need me earlier."

Liska laughed. "I think I can manage that long. Oh, there's the door. I have to go."

"Have a good time. Don't do anything I wouldn't do. Unless it's really cool and you take pictures."

"Goodbye, Kira." There was another knock as she hung up the phone. "Coming!" She hurried to the door. "You're early, To– Eric?"

"Hello, Sakaki. Can we talk? You did promise me an hour."

***

"You're in a good mood." Todd looked up from the mirror at his roommate's voice.

"I am. We're trying another 'first' date."

"Ah. Say 'hi' to Anna for me." Jamal went back to studying.

"Sure, I'm going to mention my roommate while I'm on a date." Todd closed the door as Jamal chuckled.

Humming slightly, he bypassed the elevator in favor of the steps. Taking them two at a time might have been a bit much, but no one was watching. It was a little early, but hopefully Sakaki wouldn't mind.

He had gotten her primroses this time. Soon, perhaps tonight even, he'd admit that he had been studying the language of flowers to find the right meanings for her. Maybe she'd even accept his message.

It was all he could do not to skip on his way to her dorm. Most of his good mood vanished when he saw Eric talking to her at her door. Probably best to let her deal with this. Todd stood back, hoping not to be noticed.

***

"Eric, I don't have time now," Sakaki argued.

"You promised me an hour. I know you don't want to go back on your word," Eric pushed. She was close, he could feel it.

"An hour when it was convenient to me. At a time and place of my choosing. This is neither. Which I'm quite sure you know."

Of course he knew. But he had to stall her a little longer. Not yet. Not yet. "Are you going back on your word?"

"Eric! You're twisting the situation." She was irritated. That wasn't what he wanted. He wafted a little more lust at her. Something he had been steadily doing whenever he was close enough to affect her. But he had to be careful. She was too smart and aware of the possibility of empaths. Eric had to make sure she thought it was all her feelings.

"C'mon, I've been waiting forever. You've been avoiding me." Almost time.

"It's been a week. And I'm not avoiding you. I'm very busy." Huh, she really hadn't been avoiding him. There was no guilt, nothing that would indicate a lie.

Didn't matter. The human had finally arrived. Watching. Just barely on the edges of Eric's awareness. The irritation and jealousy in the human came naturally, but Eric fanned the flames. He was easier to manipulate. For some reason, even when manipulating her emotions, Sakaki's actions were a mystery. Either she had deeper shields than he thought, or she was trained not to follow through on her emotional impulses. Possibly both.

The human, Todd, was much easier prey. He didn't have the same defenses, and when he was argumentative, Sakaki responded in kind.

Sakaki hadn't noticed the new addition yet. Pitching his voice to carry, Eric spoke. "What about Todd?"

He could feel her confusion, and a little more irritation. "What *about* Todd?" Her voice was normal speaking level for her, which was soft and quiet. The human wouldn't have heard her.

"What do you tell him?" The human's curiosity was almost higher than his jealousy.

"What are you talking about?"

Hitting Sakaki with another wave of lust, Eric leaned forward and stroked her face. Torn between confusion and lust, Sakaki didn't pull away as Eric gently kissed her.

***

Todd was trying to stay back and let Sakaki deal with this. Until Eric said, "What about Todd?" Yes, what about him?

He couldn't hear what Sakaki responded. Whatever she said, Eric followed with, "What do you tell him?"

What did she tell him about what? Did Eric know something he didn't? No, he was getting paranoid. He'd talk to Sakaki when the vampire left. Which might be faster if they knew Todd was there.

Todd started towards the stairs. Only to stop frozen. They were kissing. When he had asked Sakaki if he could kiss her, she smiled and said she didn't kiss on the first date. Maybe he was just the wrong species.

He didn't realize he was squeezing the bouquet of primroses until his nails met his palm. Opening his hand, he let the crumpled flowers fall and walked away. It looked like she had made her choice.

***

With as much lust as he had shoved in her direction, Sakaki accepted the kiss for a good ten seconds. Then she pushed him away. "Todd," She breathed.

Anger flared within him. "I know you don't know much about kissing, but it's very rude to call out another man's name after a kiss."

"Ruder than forcing a kiss on a lady? I doubt that. Go away, Eric. I will not talk to you. Not tonight, or any other."

How was he failing this badly? He should have her eating out of his hand. Rotten fangs, she should have been happy to strip for him by now. Eric had been certain it would last long enough to get into her bed. Still, it was enough.

The human was gone. If Eric could swing by and bolster up the human's hurt and wounded pride, he wouldn't be willing to talk to or even listen to Sakaki. Who knew, maybe he'd get another chance while Sakaki was hurting from the inevitable fight?

"I'll leave, for now. But you promised me an hour. And I intend to collect." Sakaki slammed the door in his face, rather than talk to him.

He didn't spot the bouquet of ruined flowers until he was almost down the stairs. They felt of betrayal, hurt, sorrow, jealousy, and anger. Eric smirked as he deliberately stepped on them. Oh, yes. It might not have been what he had in mind, but there was still a chance of a little fun tonight.

***

Liska kept touching her mouth, scolding herself for it, trying to stop, and doing it again. What on earth had Eric been thinking? Surely she hadn't done anything that would suggest she welcomed such an action. It was rude and wrong. And her first kiss. And it came from the wrong person.

She shook her head to clear it. Where was Todd? He should be around soon. At least he hadn't seen that bit of drama. She had to get control of herself. After a few minutes, Liska was satisfied that she could get through the evening without betraying emotional turmoil. But where was Todd?

After another few minutes, Liska decided to go looking for him. It didn't take long to find him. Todd was in the middle of the green. Talking to a bush? Perhaps trying to rehearse a speech.

The wind wasn't in her favor so he spotted her before she could hear what he was trying to say. Todd was silent as she approached. So she had to initiate conversation. Grand.

"Todd? I thought you were coming to pick me up?" She tried to sound neutral. What was wrong?

"Right." Todd took a deep breath and let it out loudly. "I've been thinking. A lot."

Liska arranged her features in a neutral mask. She could already tell she was not going to like this. She was right.

"You warned me that there were a lot of differences between us. Between our lives. I... I think you may have been right. I don't think I can handle your life."

"I see." It must have been her voice that said that, but she didn't feel it. Didn't remember telling her mouth to open or her tongue to speak.

"I hope we'll remain friends. But I think that..."

"I understand." Distantly she felt herself smile. Just a little, as if her face would crack if she moved it. "Friends. I can do that."

He gave her a smile in return, mixed sorrow and pain. "It might be best if we gave each other a little space."

"Yes. You're right. We can talk tomorrow. Goodnight." Liska nodded at him and walked away, head high. Never let them see your pain.

As she got to her dorm, she spotted some crumpled, trampled flowers. Primroses. Symbols of eternal love. Not sure why, she scooped them up. Then Liska walked upstairs and let herself into her room.

The primroses were dropped on her desk, as she blindly dialed a familiar number.

"C'mon, you can't have gotten in trouble already." The words were light. She couldn't bring herself to respond. She had no air. "Sakaki? What's wrong?"

"I need you." She gasped out.

"When?"

"Now." Yesterday. As soon as she could get her.

"I can be there in the morning." There was the sound of hurried movement on the other end.

"Drive safe." Slow and safe was better than fast and dead.

"Can *Sensei* help?"

"No." Definitely not.

"Are you hurt?"

"Not physically."

"Fine. Stay where you are. I'll be there as soon as I can."

Maybe she said goodbye, maybe she didn't. She couldn't remember for sure. She did know she hung up the phone. Then Sakaki walked over to the bathroom mirror.

"You fool. You complete and utter fool. You *knew* this would happen. You *knew* he would change his mind. But you *had* to go and fall in love! Now he'll leave, and you will never love another. And you deserve it completely, you little idiot!" Only then did she break down crying.

Chapter Thirteen

Never underestimate the revenge of a loved one. – The Kikitsutai Book of Wisdom

Kira veered into the parking lot and was out of the car almost before the engine finished turning off. Bypassing the valet and the baggage assistant, Kira half-ran to the ticket counter, aware that she was attracting a lot of attention.

Even at nine o'clock at night, the airport could be busy, so she was fortunate that only one person was in line in front of her. Kira vibrated with impatience and pretended not to see the security officer who was 'casually' arranging to be in earshot. As soon as there was the option, Kira darted to the lady at the counter.

Knowing he would be listening anyway, Kira made sure her voice was pitched to be heard by the security officer. "I need to get to West Palm Beach immediately. It's an emergency. My sister needs me."

It was only slightly an exaggeration. Since their fathers were identical twins, genetically, they might as well be half-sisters. More importantly, Sakaki had only once called her sounding like that.

It was a time Kira tried not to think about it, and Sakaki had actively repressed.

"Do you have a ticket?" The lady asked, seeming slightly in shock.

"No, I need one. I'll pay all your emergency fees, rent a plane, whatever it takes. Just, please. I need to get there."

"Um, well, we don't have any flights going to Florida until tomorrow. The closest we could get is Atlanta. You'd have to rush, it leaves in about an hour."

"I'll do anything. Can I get a flight from there?"

The lady typed some more. "Yes, but not until about five-thirty in the morning. You'd be in West Palm a little after nine."

"Deal!" She had grabbed her one suitcase on her way in, just in case there wasn't time earlier. Uncle Eiji lived in Washington D.C., he'd probably be willing to deal with the rental car for her. Or know someone else who would.

There were a load of fees that had to be paid for the last-minute tickets, and Kira knew they were doing extra security checks on her and her luggage too, but she was able to board the plane with minutes to spare. That was all the really mattered.

***

Kira stretched the kinks out of her back as she left the airport. While she wasn't as bothered by it as some in her clan, she didn't like flying commercial. Too noisy, too slow, too many people, and no control. A six-hour layover in Atlanta hadn't helped her nerves either. The only thing that kept her there was the knowledge that it would take even longer to drive. Still, she had gotten to West Palm Beach. She would have taken dog sled if that's what it took.

Nine-thirty, Sakaki might not be awake yet, especially if she was upset last night. Or she might not have slept. There was no way to know.

A taxi took her to the campus and she tipped enough to be a generous tipper without being memorable. Early for a weekend, the campus was quiet. On the ride up, Kira had tied back her hair, put on a baseball cap, and sunglasses. As long as no one who knew 'Anna' caught a good look at her, everything should be fine.

No one paid her the slightest heed as she walked up to Sakaki's door and knocked. Quietly in case she was asleep. The door was opened in seconds. Sakaki stared blankly at nothing briefly before focusing on Kira. Her eyes were bloodshot and her clothes rumpled.

Kira gently shepherded her inside, following and closing the door. Reaching into one of the dresser drawers, she found Sakaki's anti-eavesdropping device and turned it on. "What happened?"

Sakaki opened her mouth, closed it and thought. Then she tried again. "Todd said that he believed our lives were too different. That we were better off as friends. He said... that he can't handle my life." Kira hugged her, wondering if it was a bit of an exaggeration to call her down for this. "And I was the *utter idiot* who went and fell in love with him."

No. "Are you sure?"

Sakaki's head was buried into her shoulder, but Kira felt the nod. No, this couldn't be. Weres only fell in love once in their lifetimes. Todd knew this. How could he have thrown her away like that? When she got a hold of that boy, she'd...

"Does he know?"

Sakaki shook her head. Okay, maybe she wouldn't kill him. Maiming was still a possibility though. Possibly castration. But first things first. "I'm so sorry. What can I do?"

"I don't even know. I just... I wanted you here."

"Here I am. As long as you need me." What could she do? How could she fix this? Was there a way?

Sakaki was drooping. Kira got an idea. "Hey, I didn't sleep last night, and I don't think you did either. Let's get some sleep. Things will look better when we wake up. Don't they always?"

Sakaki shrugged but let herself be led to the bed. One bed. Kira took a few minutes, checking to make sure the blinds were shut, the lights off, and the door locked. Then she stripped and changed into a fox. Sakaki followed her lead. Within minutes, the two foxes were dozing on her bed.

***

Kira woke up a little cold and completely alone. Judging by scent and the absence of residual warmth, Sakaki left about an hour ago. She stretched, yawned, and jumped off the bed, changing back to her 'human' form. As she collected her clothes, she spotted the note on Sakaki's dresser.

It was written in a code they hadn't used in years, but Kira remembered it easily enough. *I went out to buy groceries. Don't keep dinner.* Sakaki was investigating something and wouldn't be back until evening.

It was a little worrying that Sakaki was going out on her own right now, but it was a good thing she was concentrating on work. Though heavens only knew what she was doing. There were some papers on the desk relating to the Wanderers in the area. Nothing stood out to Kira, but she put the papers inside a drawer anyway, so they were out of sight.

More importantly, Sakaki wasn't on campus right now. Meaning Kira could be 'Anna' without worrying about running into anyone who knew Anna was elsewhere. Good, because Kira had something very important to do.

Sakaki's wig, made from her own hair, was in her closet along with the most important information Kira would need to impersonate her cousin. Paranoia could be a blessing sometimes.

She read through the information twice, trying to commit it to memory. Kira might not have Sakaki's memory techniques, but hers weren't bad. Throwing on one of Sakaki's shirts and getting the wig on properly didn't take long. The fake eyebrows took a moment longer. The whole time, Kira tried to set 'Anna Andrews' in place. Satisfied she could pass, she unlocked the door and went looking for Todd.

***

"Seriously, T-man, you've been bummed since last night. What's up?"

Todd didn't look at Jamal, being a little busy sketching the water. "I don't want to talk about it."

"You were in a good mood when you left. Did something go wrong on your date?"

You could say that. "Long story."

"I could get Shahara to talk to you." It wasn't an idle threat. "Or I could ask Anna."

"She won't tell you." Todd shaded in some waves. Maybe he should throw in a ship.

"One way to find out. Hey, Anna."

Todd rolled his eyes at the attempt to bluff him. Only to drop his pastel when Jamal was answered. "Hi. Look, sorry to be rude, but I *really* need to talk to Todd. Privately."

Todd managed to rescue his pastel from falling into the water then turned to see 'Anna' talking to Jamal. But something was off. On second glance, he realized it wasn't Sakaki. Kira? Sakaki had mentioned that Kira hoped to visit, but he thought that was a few days away.

Jamal held up his hands in mock surrender. "Go ahead. He's too moody for me anyway. Maybe you two can make up and he'll be much happier."

Kira smiled. "Good. Thank you." She waited until Jamal had crossed the road before turning to Todd. "You, with me."

"Look, Kira—"

She glared at him so heatedly that he was slightly surprised he didn't ignite. "Did I say you could talk? No? Then walk."

This would probably be a good time to follow her lead. He had packed up his pastels while Kira was talking to Jamal anyway, so he only had to put the sketchbook in his art box. Then he followed her past the bridge towards a building that wasn't labeled. Apparently, Kira wanted them away from the water. Probably a good idea. They didn't go inside the shack, though Kira did lead him past a 'no admittance past this point' sign.

By then she seemed to have decided they were far enough past anyone who might hear. Which might be a bad thing, because she looked ready to murder him. "First off, how did you know I was Kira?"

"Because you clearly aren't Sakaki."

"How did you know that?"

The same way he knew which greens went with which blues. He looked and knew. "I looked. There was something off. You aren't her."

"So you think you know her so well?" Clearly Kira was leading up to something, but Todd wasn't sure what.

"I know a lot."

"Oh, good for you. You know her a lot." The words dripped with sarcasm so heavily that he almost looked for droplets at her feet. "Do you know that Weres mate for life?"

"She mentioned that, yes." Which was one of the many reasons that he was so bitter about seeing her kissing a vampire.

"So you knew that, encouraged her to trust you, let herself love you; and now, now you decide you don't want her?" Kira poked him in the chest, looming over him. The fact that she was actually several inches shorter than him did not deter her.

Todd backed up a couple steps. "Look, she made her choice, and it wasn't me." He was not the bad guy here, dang it.

"Oh, yeah? That's not what she told me."

Okay, he had been trying to keep it quiet, but he wasn't going to take all the blame for the break-up. "Then why did I see her kissing a vampire last night?"

Kira stopped in her tracks. "Alright, she didn't mention that."

It didn't feel as good as he thought it would to hear that. "So what did she say?" Todd asked, kicking at a stray can.

"That she loved you."

Todd froze, feeling like he had been punched in the gut. "What?" He croaked out.

"She believes she fell in love with you." Kira repeated, her words were daggers slicing his flesh. Judging from her grim smile, she knew exactly what she was doing. "I don't think you understand just how badly I hate you right now. No one hurts my cousin and gets away with it. *No one.* I could cheerfully kill you right now, and believe me, I'd get away with it. But if anything happened to you, that would hurt Sakaki. So, for her sake, I hope you live a long, healthy, *miserable* life."

Kira started to walk away. "Wait! She loves me? Are you sure?" Todd grabbed her shoulder, only to suddenly find himself lying on the ground, stars in his eyes. Kira was standing on his arm.

"I may not be an active ninja like Sakaki, but I've had much the same training. Touch me again; and you'll lose that hand." That was probably not a bluff, either.

"Right, sorry." Todd held his hands out and didn't move. "What do I do?"

Kira scoffed, even as she backed up so she wasn't standing on his arm. "Stay away from her. Maybe she's wrong and it's just a crush; one that will fade if she's not near you. Don't even think about trying to stay with her out of pity. She'll reject it completely no matter how she feels about you."

"But—"

"No more chances. *If* and only *if*, you're ready to commit to her, forever; should you do anything more than say hi, and *maybe* an apology. I'll try to talk her into transferring schools." Kira looked down at him as if he were a disgusting bug that was just too big to squish. "Don't follow me. I'm not sure I'll hold back again."

Todd didn't get up until she was long gone.

**

Todd actually spent a very long time lying in the mud, just trying to think. His eyes told him Sakaki had kissed a vampire. Her cousin said she loved him. Which did he believe?

Would Kira lie to him? Certainly. About that? Probably not. If Sakaki *didn't* love him, then Kira had no reason to want him around. Sakaki had no reason to lie to her cousin and say she was in love if she wasn't. Besides, if Sakaki could sniff out a lie, it stood to reason Kira could too.

Assuming Kira was telling the truth, at least as far as she knew, what about what he saw? He hadn't actually gotten up the nerve to ask Sakaki about it. Could there have been an explanation that he wasn't aware of?

Todd found himself rubbing his breastbone. It hurt, a lot. Sure, part of it was Kira knocking him down, but not all. It hurt to even think about Sakaki kissing that handsome vampire. Not that he could think of much else.

Last night, if he had tried to talk to Sakaki about Eric, they would have fought. Probably enough that they would still be considering themselves broken up now. But maybe, just maybe, they could stay calm and discuss it today.

If there was a good excuse for last night, then he owed her an apology and an explanation. If not, well, she probably owed him one. Not that she'd likely give him one, but one way or another, he'd know.

Todd dragged himself upright and tried to clean the dirt and mud off himself. He was only partially successful. The prudent thing to do would probably be to take a shower and clean up first, but he decided he'd better go talk to her before he lost his nerve. Besides, if she was laughing at him, maybe she wouldn't get so mad they would fight.

Hoping he didn't look *too* ridiculous, he limped his way to Sakaki's room, cursing himself for *still* not having her number. It would make things much easier.

Todd knocked on her door. After a few minutes, he knocked again. Still no answer. Okay, if Kira was roaming around campus pretending to be Anna, then she must have been pretty sure that Sakaki wouldn't come by and ruin it. Which probably meant that either Sakaki stayed in her room, or she wasn't on campus at all. If they weren't ignoring him and they were off campus, the most likely place to find them would be at her great-uncle's place. If they weren't there, he might know where they were or at least give him Sakaki's number.

He hadn't been there too many times, and he had only driven there on half of those trips, but he still found the place easily enough. When he knocked, Kira, no longer in her 'Anna' costume, was the one to answer. "What are you doing here?" She demanded. "And give me one good reason why I shouldn't use you as target practice."

"I need to talk to Sakaki. One of us is wrong about something important. If it's me, I owe her an abject apology."

Kira eyed him, looking like she was mentally planning three different ways to murder him and how to hide the body. Eventually she must have decided it would be too much work. "She's not here. We're waiting for her to get back."

"Back?"

Kira said nothing. Right, he wasn't going to be privileged with information. Todd tried again. "May I wait here?"

Their great-uncle came up behind Kira. "You may wait. If Liska doesn't want to talk to you, you will leave."

"Fair enough and thank you."

Kira looked like she wanted to object, but she moved silently to the side. Todd walked in and forced down his instinct to run. He was now in a house with one ninja who actively wished terrible suffering on him, and another who didn't seem to know what was going on but was clearly on Sakaki and Kira's side. Not that he expected anything else.

"There is a shower upstairs. Kira, look through my clothes. See if you can find something that might fit him. No point spreading dried mud everywhere."

Ah, yes. He had forgotten about that. His car was going to be filthy. "Thank you, Sir."

Kira was silent as she led him upstairs, pointed out the bathroom, and dropped off what were clearly work clothes. They were covered in paint, worn, and had a few holes in them. Ah well, he was a college student, he wasn't picky.

His shower was quick, especially since the hot water never came on. Something he suspected was deliberate on the part of at least one of the Werefoxes. Not that he planned to confront them.

The older Werefox, Ryoko, let out a long-suffering sigh when he saw Todd's clothes. Todd thought he saw a small smirk on Kira's face, but it was gone before he could tell for sure.

Then they sat there. No one spoke. Kira glared at him while carving what appeared to be the start of a small wooden javelin. Worryingly enough, she barely looked at what she was doing. Ryoko also sat opposite him, hands pressed together; staring at Todd as if trying to read his soul.

Todd, for his part, just tried to pretend they couldn't kill him and bury him in the basement, and that this wasn't the most awkward situation he had ever been in. This even topped introducing his uncle to 'Anna' after she was arrested for supposedly trying to kill him.

What was he even doing here? Sakaki would go back to school eventually. He could talk to her there. Alone. Anything he said here would be overheard by the others, unless they chose to leave.

So why was he here? Because she was that important. He had to know what was going on. Oh, he hoped she would be back soon.

His hair was dry, and he was feeling increasingly sick when there was a knock at the door. A heavy knock. Much too heavy for Sakaki.

Ryoko went to the door. Todd and Kira stayed in the sitting room, just out of sight. When the older man opened the door, he spoke in an exaggerated accent. "Yes? Can I help you?"

"Are you Ray Takano?"

"Yes, Officer. Is there a problem?"

"Did you lend your car to a Diane Russell?"

Kira was turning gray. Todd waved, catching her attention, before mouthing, "Liska?" at her. She nodded.

"I did. This afternoon."

"What is your relationship to Ms. Russell?"

"Family friend. What is this about, Officer?"

"I'm very sorry, Mr. Takano. We recovered the car on I-95. She appears to have driven the car into the embankment. Ms. Russell was probably killed on impact. We don't know the cause of the accident yet. There was a fire. She had her license on her, but we're going to need dental records or DNA to confirm."

Ryoko seemed to buckle. Kira dropped her knife. Todd swallowed bile. More words were said, but he couldn't hear them. Couldn't understand them. Dead? She couldn't be dead. It had to be a mistake. This was just a nightmare.

Somehow, Ryoko convinced the officer to leave, and shut the door. Kira leapt to her feet. "It can't be. It's not possible! Why Diane Russell anyway? She wasn't using that one. It's not even a complete identity."

"Diane Russell is the only one of her identities that had an American driver's license. She may have had it on her because she was borrowing the car."

"But the body can't be confirmed without dental records or DNA?"

"Yes, it sounds like a cover up. Has she said anything about needing to disappear?" Ryoko asked, collapsing into a chair. For the first time since Todd met the man, he truly looked old.

"No, nothing."

"You have to tell me what you find out." Todd bit his tongue a second later. They had forgotten him. Now, they remembered.

Kira turned on him, a volcano that finally had somewhere to vent. "We don't have to tell you *anything*. Get out. Get out, now!"

The door slammed shut in his face. He had no memory of moving.

Chapter Fourteen

Necessity makes for strange allies. – The Kikitsutai Book of
Wisdom

Todd sat in his car, watching and waiting. And
waiting. And *waiting*. It took more than three hours,
but his patience was rewarded. Kira, once again
dressed as Anna, left the house and headed for the
campus. Meaning she passed his car. "Need a ride?"

Kira gave him a poisonous glare. "Why would
I want to get in a car with *you*?" She asked, making
him feel like a combination of a leper, a giant insect,
and some sort of vile slime.

"I have a proposition for you."

Apparently, it was possible to scoff a laugh.
Interesting. "This ought to be good."

"One that might be best not to broadcast."

She hesitated for another minute, before
opening the door and climbing in. But only after
giving him a look of such disdain that it seemed to
fill the car. "Fine, what's your proposition?"

Todd started the engines and rolled up the
windows but didn't take the car out of park. "You're

taking Sakaki's place as Anna, right? Until you find out what happened."

For a moment, Kira said nothing. Then, "That is a *reasonable* assumption."

"You managed to pass last time, but that was for a couple days while everyone was concentrating on exams. It's going to be harder now. A lot harder."

"Sakaki left notes."

Somehow, that didn't surprise him. "I'm sure she did. But that won't cover everything. Not little things like who she knows, and what they expect. As it happens, the three people on campus that know her best are me, my best friend, and his sister. I can help you keep your cover."

Kira was silent, considering it. Then she eyed him warily. "And in exchange?"

"In exchange, I want to be kept in the loop. What you find out, what really happened, etc."

It took her a couple minutes, but Todd was pretty confident she'd agree. Which she did. "Fine. You make a decent point. Now, I'm told the two of you were dating?"

"I didn't tell anyone what happened last night. I doubt she did either."

"I'm quite sure she didn't. So, 'we' had a fight."

"Makes sense. We've had a few recently. And now..."

"And now we're 'cooling off' slightly. We're trying to be friends without dating, see if that eases things."

"Okay, good. That works." It put less pressure on Sakaki when she was back and meant he didn't have to 'date' Kira. "Careful of Shahara. She likes 'us' together."

He could see Kira trying to place the name. "Jamaican girl, tall, likes fashion?"

"That's her. She's my roommate's sister. Probably the female Anna associates with most. She considers Anna one of her best friends."

"I see." The tone was cold. Was Kira jealous? "How perceptive is she?"

"More than you'll like. Both her and Jamal, her brother. Jamal joked that Sakaki was Cat's-eye the first time I told her about my blog. But I'm sure he has no idea he was right." Only then did it occur to him that Kira might not know about his blog. But she nodded, as if she understood perfectly. So either she knew, or she wasn't willing to admit ignorance. Six one way, half a dozen the other.

"Any information I need to know? Inside jokes? Important information that might have been imparted?"

"Um, Anna claimed her mother was half-something. It wasn't Japanese, but it was one of the Oriental countries. When Shahara was doing her hair, and said it was the wrong texture for a white girl."

"Vietnamese. She put it in her dossier."

"Oh, okay. There's also the fourth of July."

Kira gave him an odd look at that. "Your Independence Day?"

Todd chuckled. "Yeah. Shahara asked if they had the fourth of July in England. Sakaki answered no, they skipped from the third to the fifth." Kira smirked at that, no doubt familiar with her cousin's sense of humor. "So Shahara changed it to do they *celebrate* the fourth of July in England. Sakaki said something like, 'You mean, "Oh, goody, we got rid of them" day? It's our biggest national holiday'." His attempt at Anna's accent was terrible even to his own ears, but it made Kira smile, just a little. "Jamal and Shahara like that answer a lot. It's come up a few times since."

"I think I can manage that."

"If I think of anything else, I'll let you know. Your turn. What do you know?"

Kira got serious and took a long time to answer. "*Someone* is dead in that car. But when we went looking for 'Diane Russell's' dental records, they had been tampered with. The computer records don't match the paper copy we have of Sakaki's. They do, however, match the dead body. Also, whoever she was, she was strictly human."

"It's not her." Relief made him giddy for a few seconds, before other considerations took over. "I mean, not that I'm glad someone else is dead, but..."

"I understand. I feel the same way."

Now came the questions he wasn't sure he wanted the answer to. "Would she do something like this?"

"You're asking multiple questions." Kira looked out the window. What she was seeing, Todd had no idea, because they were still in park.

"I am?" He thought it was only one question.

"Yes. First question, would Liska fake her own death? Yes. She has in the past, and I doubt she'd hesitate about doing it in the future. Second question, would she kill someone to fake her own death?"

Todd shuddered but kept quiet. The idea had occurred to him.

"The answer is no. She would not kill someone *solely* to fake her own death. Third question, would she take advantage of a body that was already dead, or use someone she had to kill for another reason to fake her own death? Probably. She's rather... practical, that way. But the most important question is the fourth."

"What's the fourth question?"

"Would she fake her own death, especially in a way she knew would get back to us in this manner, without informing someone ahead of time, or as soon as possible afterwards? The answer is no. She would tell us. She would tell *me*." There were almost tears in her voice.

For the first time, Todd could see how badly Kira was hurting right now. Her beloved cousin and best friend was missing, and no one had any idea why or where she was. Todd remained quiet for a few minutes to give her time to compose herself before asking, "Where does that leave us?"

"I don't believe she left voluntarily. She's in trouble. We *are* going to find her, and I'll make sure she has a role to come back to. If she wants it."

"I'll do anything I can to help."

"Then suppose you actually drive us to school?"

Todd put the car in drive. "Do you have her keys?"

"I have the set she copied for Ryoko-*Sensei*."

"You'll have to get a new student ID. She probably had hers on her, and half the things at school require it. The office will be open tomorrow, but only until three, because it's Sunday. They'll charge you ten dollars for a replacement. I can swipe you into the cafeteria tonight."

"I have cash. Thanks, though."

"What about Eric?"

"Who?"

"The vampire. The one she kissed."

Kira frowned. "That's just not like her. And she didn't say anything about it to me. For now, we say nothing. If he shows up, I'll try to read context clues, see what he expects. Until we can talk to one of them, it never happened."

He nodded, as he pulled into the street. "How long can you pass off as her?"

Out of the corner of his eye, he saw her shrug. "As long as it takes."

***

'As long as it takes' was taking longer than Kira hoped. Even ignoring the implication of Sakaki's disappearance, pretending to be Anna was harder than she thought. It had been five days, and Kira was lamenting that Sakaki's notes, while wonderful on classes, were slightly lacking in human interactions. Like the name of the pretty Hispanic girl who sometimes partnered with Anna on projects in Humanities. Or that the Math teacher expected her to be running into class just in the nick of time. Or the cafeteria lady who believed Anna was anorexic and tried to give her pamphlets about eating disorders and rehab centers. That probably had as much to do with Anna always taking small portions as her apparent weight. Werefoxes simply didn't eat much at one time. Good thing the lady didn't know Sakaki, or Kira's, real weight. Werefox bones were lighter than human bones, so a Werefox would always weigh less than a human of the same body size and type. Probably only by five or ten pounds, but still.

All these were things that Sakaki probably considered too minor to mention. All things that could have wrecked her cover if Kira wasn't so well trained on improvising. Sakaki was better, but she wasn't here; and Kira thought she was doing a pretty good job.

Other than Todd, only one person seemed to really notice the 'change' in Anna. Shahara. Maybe Sakaki had more encounters with her than her brother, or maybe she had confided in the girl more than Todd expected, but Kira kept picking up on occasional scents of confusion or suspicion. But where was she failing? If she couldn't figure out what was tipping the other girl off, how could she stop doing it?

Right now they were at dinner. Todd, Jamal, Shahara, and her. "Hey, are you still taking art lessons from Todd?" Shahara asked her.

Sakaki had mentioned art lessons. But Kira could draw just fine, thank you very much. "When we have time. We're both kind of busy right now."

"Well, don't let it go too long. You're supposed to be creating your masterpiece, remember?" There were hints of an inside joke there, so Kira gave a small smile, hoping it was a proper response. Todd looked a little confused, so he didn't know that one. Too bad.

But he did change the subject, asking Shahara about a project for one of her classes. The other girl was distracted and the moment passed. For now. She was going to have to be very cautious around Shahara.

***

Shahara turned down Jamal's offer of walking her to her dorm. She wanted to think. Something was wrong with Anna. For the past few days, she had just felt something was off about her. Something Shahara couldn't put her finger on. The first two days she ignored it, but it was getting worse.

Marsha said that Anna seemed a little spacey, like she was always thinking, and on two occasions, she didn't seem to remember something from last semester. So, Shahara tested it, slipping in inside jokes, conversations they had had, trying to get a normal reaction. But there was something off about her responses. Even when Anna responded the 'right' way, there was distance there. True, Anna wasn't the most open person in the world, and it took time to get her to let you in, but why did she suddenly throw the walls back up?

If it wasn't so ridiculous, Shahara might think that it wasn't Anna at all. But that was silly. Who else could it be? Why would anyone try to impersonate a British ex-pat college student? Besides, Todd would see through it in a heartbeat.

Then again, they had broken up right around the point where Anna started acting weird. Maybe to keep him from digging too deep?

No, she was just being silly and paranoid. Anna was probably just reacting to the break-up. She just had to give her time. But Shahara would be watching. Yes, she had to be careful with Anna.

***

Ryoko wasn't sure how his living room became their 'war council' but he wasn't upset about it either. At least this way, he knew what was going on. He still didn't know what had happened between the Kendo boy and his grand-nieces, but they had mutually decided it wasn't important right now.

For security purposes, it was decided that outside the three of them, only Sakaki's parents and Kira's would be informed of what happened. That Sakaki was missing and Kira was currently replacing her at the school while the three of them tried to track her down and find out what kind of trouble she had gotten into. As far as anyone else was told, Kira was in town to assist Sakaki and Ryoko in uncovering what happened to the Magnus blood. It wasn't a bad cover, as they did still have to do that. It wasn't like they could tell Rex Magnus that Sakaki had stopped investigating because she had disappeared. He'd likely use that to declare her guilty. While he couldn't get away with executing her without causing a bloodbath that he was undoubtedly desperate to avoid, there was a lot he could do to make life miserable and difficult for her and the skulk. Besides, vampires usually played a long game. It came with millennia long life spans. So *everyone* had to believe Kira was Anna, was Liska, was Sakaki.

"I received the accident report today." Ryoko knew that would get their attention. "It has been determined that the brakes failed, causing the crash. 'Diane' died of a broken neck. The car exploded, burning the body. We may never find out who died there."

The boy was somber at that. Kira simply nodded, focused on other things. "Any sign of Liska?"

"The fire was probably to destroy any evidence. The brakes didn't fail on their own, but the report gives the impression they did."

"How did she seem when she came to borrow your car?" The human asked.

"I was not home. She left a note. We have a long-standing agreement that she can borrow the car when she needs to, provided I am not needing it. I was just surprised she didn't take her bike."

Kira straightened. "May I see your note?"

Ryoko had kept it, putting it in a drawer in the end table. He handed it over to them, not needing to re-read the message he had already memorized long ago.

Uncle Ray,

Needed to borrow your car for a job. Should be back by dinner.

Anna

"Why'd she write in code?" the boy asked.

"In case someone else saw it," Kira answered. "So whatever information she found or thought of, while she was in her room, she decided she needed a car to get to and couldn't wait long enough to talk to either of us first. That's not like her."

"Isn't it? I mean, it seems like her. From what I've seen, she's independent and can be impulsive," the boy said.

"She can be, but she also knows better than to run around chasing her tail when it comes to work." Ryoko took back the note and put it carefully back in the drawer. "I would feel better if one of us had seen her before this happened."

"Alright, another question. Why was she identified as Diane Russell? Is that another persona she's using? Is there any significance to it?"

Kira shrugged. "Pretty sure she's had it for about two years now, but it isn't an active persona. She doesn't live as Diane Russell. She only uses it to acquire information and things. I don't think she even has a full bio for it. Diane Russell had a driver's license, memberships to several museums and libraries, and was an intermediary for certain communications or deliveries." Kira suddenly got very tense. "Diane Russell was also the name she used to join the Purifiers."

Now that was interesting.

"I'm sorry, join them? I thought she didn't like them. And vice versa."

"Exactly," Ryoko said. "But how do you think we know what they do? We infiltrate. Many of their members are actually Twilights, with a few Nights, who managed to get referred, allowing them access to their site, and sometimes more. You knew she accessed their site, did you think it was open for anyone? They are smarter than that. Liska was referred by another member of the skulk and was able to refer at least two others. But with 'Diane Russell' being dead, her account could end up closed." He turned to Kira. "Do you have an account?"

"No, I never needed one. And they have a one month probationary period before you can get any real information after you join." She sighed. "Ryo, Tora's twin; doesn't he have a membership? I can get him to refer me and pass on information in the meantime."

"Um, question." Todd raised his hand like he expected to be called on by a teacher. "Wasn't Liska looking into some Purifier who supposedly died in a car accident?"

"Richard Calloway." Ryoko flexed his stiff fingers. "Yes, she was. You find it unlikely that they both supposedly died in car accidents?"

"Just saying. It seems a bit odd."

Kira frowned. "Possibly, possibly not. Car accidents are relatively easy to fake, and done right, leave little evidence. Also great if you don't want a body identified. Not to mention, they happen frequently enough on their own that most people don't think much about it."

"I saw the report of Calloway's autopsy. There were pictures. While not as certain as I would be if I had actually gone and smelled the man, there seems little doubt that it truly was Calloway, even if the method of his death might be under dispute. However, it is worth considering that it could be someone's M.O." Ryoko nodded at him. Thought should always be encouraged. Especially when it was potentially useful.

"So, it could be related, but it might not be. How do you ever figure out anything?" Todd asked in exasperation.

He stood up and started pacing. "Okay, everyone agrees that Sakaki was upset and acting in ways that were at least slightly out of character for her. Then she is declared dead, but we know for an absolute fact it wasn't her body in the car. It's been a week and she hasn't contacted anyone. At least, anyone we know about. It is extremely out of character for her to deliberately be out of contact and leave her family worrying. If she needed a little alone time, she would have said so, and asked Kira to take her place for a while. So, either something is so wrong that she feels she *can't* talk to anyone, she's so mixed up she doesn't *want* to talk to anyone, or she's being prevented from contacting anyone." Todd stopped and tilted his head. "Or she has amnesia, or something. Which I'm guessing would be really bad with having to transform."

"If she had amnesia, she would have ended up in a local hospital. I've been watching those records." Ryoko left out that he was watching morgue records too. "Unless someone took her in and lied to her. Which would be much the same as preventing her from contacting someone. And, yes, transforming would be bad. She changes in three days. Though, if she is being contained somewhere, that might give her a chance to escape."

"Unless they knew and prepared for it. We are pretty much assuming that she is being physically prevented from contacting anyone, right? Especially with the convenient dead body in your car." Todd asked. "That about sums up our options."

"Essentially," Kira drawled. "Why? Any theories from the future profiler?"

Ryoko closed his eyes briefly. It may have been a mistake to throw down a challenge.

Todd's jaw tightened. "Well, most of the evidence was damaged by fire, but I find it hard to believe anything happened while Liska was driving. For whatever reason, she was probably out of the car when whoever took her... took her. We all know how good she is at defending herself, so she was either caught by surprise or completely overpowered quickly. Or we'll find them badly injured. I doubt this all happened on the side of the highway. Too many cars. Perhaps she had gone to meet someone, and it turned out to be a trap. Her cellphone was shattered before the explosion, because it's a lot of blobs, not just one. Perhaps to erase evidence of a call or text. As for the kidnapper?"

He was silent as he made a complete circuit of the room. Neither Kira nor Ryoko said anything to interrupt. "Sakaki's paranoid. She wouldn't let down her guard unless she thought it was safe. Either she knew her attacker, or she went willingly with him, not realizing she wouldn't be able to come back, or he was so much stronger or faster than her, that anything she could do didn't matter. Or he might have had a hostage. Possibly even the woman who he used to fake her death. Though once she was dead, Sakaki wouldn't have any reason to go along calmly."

The boy turned and walked the other way. "This was planned. He had a body ready, who was about her height and size. Sakaki is not a common height or size. He hacked the records. Sakaki was not chosen randomly. Chances are high that he knew she wasn't human. Probably been watching for a while, but carefully, or she would have noticed. He's pragmatic, not squeamish or sentimental. No qualms about either dealing with a dead body or killing someone else for his purposes. Detail oriented, and technologically aware enough to know about checking dental records, and hacking computer systems. But that's old school now. They're more likely to check fingerprints or DNA now. But Sakaki would be more careful about those, and he probably knew that. So, pragmatic, long-time planner, who can change the plan when need be, detail oriented, probably a little old school, confident. It was risky grabbing her in broad daylight in pubic. He was certain of his abilities. Could have used force, but I don't think he did at first. He uses something else until he's close or has no choice. He likes having more than one option."

Another turn, and he headed the other way. "He likes to pass himself off as urbane and cultured, but he has a brutal streak that he doesn't mind indulging or has an underling that does. 'Sadist' might be a stretch, or it might not be." Todd closed his eyes. "He uses a philosophy like Nietzsche's Uberman to justify his actions. He truly believes he is superior to other people and therefore shouldn't be held by their petty rules. He should be allowed to do whatever it is he wants, because it's *him* doing it. How's that?"

Kira looked at him skeptically. "How much of that is a guess?"

"Absolutely certain that this was planned, he's pragmatic, detail oriented, keeps at least somewhat up with technology, and he was confident. Pretty certain he didn't just use force.

Less certain about the rest, but I bet most of it's accurate."

Ryoko cut in before it could become a fight. "Impressive. But how did you reach these conclusions? I can see where most of the first part came from, but I do not see some of the others."

"It's difficult to explain. I can't even use the standard profile of a kidnapper because we don't know why she was kidnapped. Some of it is intuition, other times it's inference. The body was damaged to the point that dental records were needed. Unless he managed to get a woman who looked very like Sakaki, he couldn't take the chance that the accident would leave her face intact, so he would have to brutalize it beforehand. Which fits the report. Her skull was crushed in. On one hand, that's practical. On the other, judging by the completeness, I think he enjoyed it on some level. Perhaps he's the type to not get his hands dirty, so he assigned someone else the task, and they enjoyed it. As for the Uberman? Okay, if he's been planning this for a while and knows she isn't human, then he knows that this masquerade won't fool anyone who knows she's a Werefox. But he isn't concerned about that. Either he didn't think we would figure it out, which is just plain stupid, or he doesn't care. He is confident in his success, that no one will find her and stop his plan. It doesn't necessarily lead to a superman complex, but it certainly implies it."

His conclusions were not without logic, but it made him more frightened for Liska's sake. "What does he want with Liska?"

Todd slumped and took his seat again. "No idea. The only thing we can rule out right now is ransom. He took a lot of time and effort to fake her death, so he plans to keep her alive for a while. I think she's still alive—"

"I know she is," Kira interrupted. "I would know if she died."

Todd nodded and continued, "But that doesn't tell us what he wanted. It could be information, revenge, or well, anything. There was a specific purpose, but I don't know what it might be."

"How about where?" Ryoko asked. The boy might be a stronger Esper than he realized.

"Sorry, I'm completely at sea. I have no idea."

It was difficult to quietly sniff around and find information about someone who wasn't supposed to be missing. The last thing they wanted was to attract attention. Kira had to be even more careful around Sakaki's contacts. They were much more likely to spot the substitution than her classmates were. Ryoko had a few contacts of his own, but general inquiries revealed nothing, and he was afraid to get more specific.

Which meant that all they had for certain was that she probably didn't leave voluntarily, and now a potential profile of the attacker. Not a clue about motive, what Liska was going through right now, or where she was. That girl aged him more than any three others of her generation combined.

"I think we've done what we can tonight. We have to get back to the school before we're missed." Todd stood reluctantly.

"Oh, you think we're done? We have nothing! We know nothing! Sakaki will be gone forever at this rate!" Kira snapped at him.

Todd, grief surrounding him, just asked quietly, "Do you have any other ideas?"

The ire faded and she slumped like an empty puppet. "No."

"Then I suggest you follow his advice. We *will* find her. But we must keep everything in balance in the meantime. That means acting normally at the school." Ryoko didn't mention the way he wandered through random neighborhoods hoping to get a whiff of her scent. He'd be going again tonight. It wouldn't surprise him if Kira did too.

"You're right, *Sensei*. It's just so hard!"

Todd nodded in agreement, while shyly offering Kira his handkerchief.

"I know, Kits. I know."

Chapter Fifteen

Desperation gives strength to the weakest. – The Kikitsutai
Book of Wisdom

Kira glared at the dorm room, ready to tear her hair out. She had been through every lick of information that Sakaki kept in her room and still had no idea. Everything she could decipher anyway. There was a notebook under the bed that seemed to be written in some made-up language and encoded beyond Kira's ability to interpret. Then there was another notebook that included a list of names that Kira didn't recognize, but there wasn't enough information to tell what they were supposed to be. The last two were written with a different pen than the three before so they were probably the most recent. 'Stephen' and 'Isabelle', but it meant nothing to her.

There were no phone calls to the room phone, no emails, and no calls to her mobile phone. A text was possible, but they couldn't find out if there was one or what it might have said. Even with all three of them brainstorming, they were no closer to figuring out what caused Liska to go off right then when she could have had back-up just by waiting.

While there were notes that tracked what Sakaki was doing, the most recent was a couple days before her disappearance, and they were almost exclusively about school. Even her index card about what she was wearing was a day out of date, which was beyond out of character for Sakaki. Meaning she might not have been thinking straight that day. Or that she was wearing the same clothes for a second day in a row.

There was a random line in her notes about a favor for Korvou. Nothing about what the favor was, just that there was a sealed envelope for him. Kira had examined the envelope and was pretty sure it was a specialty key, maybe to a safe deposit box. But she left it alone and didn't open the envelope. It wasn't her business.

The notes where Liska detailed how she acquired a vampire bar made her smile. It was just like her. For all that Liska liked working in the shadows, every once in a while, she loved to cause a scene. Kira hadn't gone back there yet, but she would probably have to soon.

Sakaki's art supplies, Kira had left alone. That was private. But she could tell that Sakaki had enjoyed learning to draw.

Kira sat up suddenly. Art supplies. Drawing. Maybe just maybe... It was a long shot, but she'd take any chance she could get.

Quickly, she rummaged through her bag for *her* sketchbook. Ever since Kira had learned to draw, her best drawings were the ones that she drew based on something Sakaki described. It was almost as if seeing from her eyes. She had tried it with forty other people, once they learned what they could do, but while she could draw a decent picture, it wasn't the same as what they had seen.

But Sakaki wasn't here to describe anything right now. She couldn't say what the room looked like, or where it was, or who took her. But Kira had to try.

She flipped her sketchpad to a blank sheet and sat, pencil poised, eyes closed, trying to capture an impression of something, anything, that could be useful.

Nothing came.

Kira narrowed her focus. A face. *Please, Sakaki. Show me what he looks like*. Nothing. Okay, maybe she could prime it a little. Kira drew an oval. How wide was the face? How long? Nothing. Alright, what about eyes? She tried to draw an eye. But the whole thing just looked grotesque.

With a growl, she tore the page away and started again. "Fine, if you can't show me a face, can you show me a place? Are you inside right now? Outside?" Inside was much more likely. It was easier to contain a person inside, and harder for others to find them. Most Weres, when outside on the ground, had some impression where other nearby Weres outside, on the ground, were. Not to mention, she was supposed to change tonight. A fox could slip bonds that a human couldn't.

So, supposing she was inside, what did the room look like? Dark? Light? Was she in a basement? An attic? A spare room somewhere? Or someplace worse?

It wasn't good for Weres to be inside too long. Something in their genetic make-up made them crave freedom and the outdoors. Those who were stuck inside all the time usually suffered from nutritional deficiencies, general malaise, mood swings, sometimes aggressiveness, and once in a rare while, mental issues.

That was all kept a secret from Non-Weres. There might be a rare few who knew, but not many. Probably not the person who kidnapped her. They had to find her quickly.

Kira went back to her drawing. If this was a room, where were the walls? She tried her best, but the end result was a sheet of crooked eraser marks, one of which had started to tear a hole in the paper. For some reason, she couldn't seem to draw the room straight.

She jumped at the thunder crack. A storm had moved in. Not a surprise. That happened a lot here. Kira stood and went to the window, looking outside. Despite being mid-afternoon, the skies were dark as night, and the rain pounded down in sheets. A perfect bolt of lightning struck the ocean, the thunder joining it soon after.

"I don't know where you are, but I hope you aren't out in this." Kira bit her lip. "We *will* find you. I just don't know *how*."

***

Todd watched the storm from his dorm lounge. He hadn't seen one this bad, this close in months. The skies lit up, only to roar in protest a moment later.

"You know, lightning can travel through glass. It's bad enough watching through a window. You're sitting in front of a glass door." Jamal stayed in the hallway as he spoke.

"Storm's at least a mile away."

"Do you know far lightning can travel?"

Todd smiled. "Then maybe you should back away."

Even though Jamal was behind his back, Todd could almost *feel* him rolling his eyes. "Seriously. This is potentially very dangerous."

"Yeah, a little. But have you seen this storm?"

"I can hear it." Jamal came in a little. "It's very... wet."

Todd groaned. "That's kind of what rain does. Besides, you know as well as I do that it will dry up within a couple hours when the sun comes out."

"Great. Then we can leave it."

Todd gave Jamal a side look. "You *that* worried about lightning?"

"I'm worried about *you*. Period."

"Me?"

"Yeah, you." Jamal poked him in the shoulder. "You're depressed lately. You disappear a lot, and considering you aren't dating Anna, you're still spending all your time with her. But it isn't making you happy."

Todd sighed. "It's complicated."

"What isn't?"

"Good point."

"Anna's acting strange, too."

Oh, dear. "Huh?"

"Yeah, haven't you noticed? She's more closed up, more distracted, almost spacey at times.

But you aren't noticing. Odd, that. Shahara's concerned."

Of course she was. Jamal and Shahara were far too perceptive for Todd and Kira's good. But what could he possibly tell them? "Anna's got some family issues right now. I don't know all the details, but she's really concerned. That's probably what's going on. You know she's really private, and doesn't like to share much."

There was a lightning flash, and a crash of thunder while Jamal considered it. "Fine, I won't ask her about it. But we are here if she, or you, wants to talk. Remember, Anna is not your only friend."

With that, Jamal left Todd sitting alone in the lounge, feeling as if he really had been struck by lightning.

***

Ryoko barely looked up when the front door opened. It would be Todd this time. Kira was away for now. "In here," He called, letting the boy know where he was. Kira would be able to tell, by scent or sound. Todd lacked that ability.

"Hey," Todd greeted, then offered him a choice of muffins. Ryoko took the blueberry. "Can I ask a potentially rude question? I mean, you don't have to answer if it's offensive, or information I'm not supposed to know."

"You may ask."

"Where is Kira, and why did she go away for a couple days? You said it wasn't new information..."

But there was still a tinge of hope as if he thought they might be lying about that.

Ryoko put aside his reading glasses. "It is not exactly a rude question, though the answer is not one that most outsiders are aware of." But Todd wasn't an outsider anymore. For all that Ryoko had discouraged Liska from developing a close friendship with the boy; he now knew more about them than any human who wasn't married to a Were. Did he tell him?

Todd nodded, and opened his own muffin, orange poppy seed. While still curious, he wasn't going to push.

That was what made Ryoko decide. "I do not recommend saying anything about it to the girls unless one of them brings it up." Todd looked at him, alert attention. "This is the time of year that foxes in this area go into heat."

Confusion gave way to comprehension and embarrassment, as Todd choked on his muffin. "But you aren't animals. I mean–"

"I understand what you mean. And you are correct. We are not." Ryoko took a deep breath. "Liska never mentioned the differences in reproduction between Weres and humans, did she? I thought not. Well, then this should be very interesting." And probably embarrassing to both of them.

"There can't be that many differences. I mean, Sakaki said her mother is a human."

"Yes, and yes. If Liska were to go to a human gynecologist, she could do so without revealing that she was non-human. Provided they didn't take samples to test. The organs are the same and mostly work the same way. I trust you know how human reproduction works."

Todd nodded heavily, face dark and sweat starting to form.

"Excellent." This was actually almost fun. "Now, there are a few major differences. To begin with, a sexually mature human woman releases an egg from her ovaries approximately once a month until menopause, correct? Also, the age of sexual maturity can vary a great deal. For Werefoxes, and many other Weres, sexual maturity is almost always reached in the sixteenth year, give or take a couple months. No one knows why, so don't bother asking. Are you following so far?"

"Yes?"

Ryoko ignored that it was a question, not an answer. "Also, a female Werefox usually releases two or three eggs over an approximately six-to-eight-week period. These times are also often rougher on the female in question than the average human woman's would be. I know Liska used to get intensely ill on her first day. I believe she outgrew that but still tries to arrange her schedule so she can avoid having to leave her house more than necessary at the time."

Todd tentatively raised his hand. "Not to change the subject, but I'm going to change the subject a little. If they usually release two or three eggs, does that mean Weres are usually born as twins or triplets?"

"Twins are the most common outcome, followed by triplets, then single births. Four or five is uncommon, but not unheard of."

Todd sat back, shaking his head. "Wow. But Sakaki and Kira are both only children, aren't they?"

"As you pointed out, Sakaki's mother is human, and not prone to multiple births. While she clearly loves her daughter, she's never shown any interest in having other children." It was probably more complicated than that, but he had no proof. "As for Kira, she did have a twin brother, but he was stillborn. The pregnancy almost killed her mother, who was advised not to try again. That is one of the many reasons the girls are so close. They were the only ones their age without siblings."

"But Sakaki could easily have a lot of kids?"

"Could, and may well want to." It wasn't *quite* indoctrination that encouraged Werefoxes to have many children.

"Any other differences?"

"Yes, we did get off topic slightly. The other major difference is that around the same time foxes go into heat in the area where the Werefox is currently living, the females undergo something similar. Most prefer not to call it 'heat' but an alternate name has not been generally accepted yet. They are especially fertile, producing a lot of pheromones, and are particularly interested in sex. In order to deal with this and prevent a major mistake from being made because of hormones, the females generally isolate themselves during this time. Back home, they have a separate island where they go. From girls a year or two too young, to ones that have passed that stage. They say that the hormones are controllable when there are no suitable males around. I do not know exactly where

Kira has gone, but it will be someplace where she will not be exposed to men."

Todd nodded slowly, his face gradually resuming its' normal coloration. "So they do this every year."

"Mostly. The girls seem to look forward to it, even if they rarely discuss specifics. Sometimes a couple, especially newlyweds, will take a vacation by themselves instead." He smiled in remembrance. "My Yumi and I did that a few times."

"Yumi? Your wife?"

It was a reasonable question, but it was still hard to separate memories of Yumi from the pain. "Yes, my wife. She died many years ago."

"I'm sorry. You must miss her a great deal."

"I do. Her death was losing part of myself."

"I know you aren't a visually based people, but do you have pictures of her?"

He did, even here. But did he really want to go tearing up old scars right now? "Some other time, perhaps."

"Of course." Todd went back to examining the papers, but Ryoko could smell his curiosity. It would get the better of him sooner or later.

"Ask."

"What?" Todd looked up, startled.

"You have a question. Might as well ask."

"You don't have to answer if you don't want to. But, how did she die?"

Ryoko closed his eyes in pain. "She was effectively murdered. Hunted down by dogs. I can't talk about it."

Todd's pencil broke, but Todd didn't seem to notice. "Was Sakaki there?"

He had hoped for years that she didn't remember. "She was. Please don't tell me she remembers."

"According to her, she remembered everything but who the woman was and how they got into the situation in the first place."

Ryoko let his head fall into his hands. "I had hoped she didn't remember. She was only four at the time." If she remembered that, did she remember how he had treated her in the aftermath?

"What did happen?"

"I do not know. I wasn't even in the country at the time. Sakaki's father recalled me when Yumi died." Even knowing that there was nothing he could have done, he still blamed himself for not being there at the time. Yumi had needed him, and he had failed her. Then compounded his failure by blaming Sakaki, the child Yumi had given her life to protect. Yumi would have scolded him so soundly, his ears would still be ringing these fifteen years later.

Todd looked like he had more questions, but Ryoko had reached his end. "Please, it may have been years ago, but it is still painful. I thank you for informing me that Sakaki remembers, I will need to talk to her. But I cannot discuss this now."

"Right, sorry. I didn't mean to reopen old wounds."

"With the amount I have, that's inevitable sometimes. The same with Liska. The point isn't, 'do you push each other's buttons'. Of course you do. The point is, 'do you ever deliberately hurt each other' or 'how do you react after your buttons are pushed'. That is far more important."

"I'll keep that in mind." Todd stared at the table, his left hand petting the small fox keychain that he said Sakaki had bought him as a joke. "I'm going to apologize to her. When we find her. Whatever was happening, I should have at least asked her before reacting."

Ryoko still didn't know what had happened, but now he thought that was probably best. He had become surprisingly close to Todd during this time, and the last thing he wanted was to be drawn into a conflict between Todd and one or both of his nieces.

"We will find her."

Todd nodded. But Ryoko knew they were both thinking the same thing. *Seventeen days.* Odds of recovery went down every day she was missing. Even if they found her now, she would probably be hurt, possibly seriously. And every single lead they could find or think of was dry.

***

Twenty-six days. It was a mantra that Kira found running through her head at various times. Sometimes she couldn't believe that Sakaki had been missing for so long. Other times, it felt like it had been much, much longer.

She was now certain that Shahara was suspicious, but she didn't know why. Kira tried avoiding her as much as she could without being noticed. Of course, because the other girl was suspicious, it was hard to keep her from noticing.

Jamal might be suspicious, though not as much as his sister. But Kira wasn't sure exactly what they thought the truth was.

She was also avoiding Eric. He hadn't made a diligent effort to talk to her, but she had seen him around a few times. Maybe someone had shortened his leash. It was definitely possible.

Todd shared her mantra. It was evident in the slump of his shoulders that he fell into when not thinking about it, the sad look he had when he didn't think anyone was looking, and the way he alternated between listlessness and restlessness.

But they had nothing. No clues. No leads. No direction to look. Kira was taking any long shot she could think of, including wandering random neighborhoods or large crowds hoping for a hint of her scent. Nothing.

Kira took another bite of... salad. How pathetic was it that she had to actually check what she was eating?

"Hey, sorry I'm late." Jamal slid in the booth across from her, next to his sister. "Got held up." He set down his tray. "Some group was just outside of campus passing out flyers. Not sure what it is. Sounded like a LARP or something."

That caught her attention. While LARPs or Live Action Role Playing was a common pastime, her skulk wasn't the only group to use it as cover for something else. "Oh, what about?"

"Something about the planet being infiltrated by invaders who can masquerade as human and could cause humanity's downfall."

Now she was definitely interested. It wasn't an uncommon theme in stories, but... "Can I see that flyer?"

Todd shot her an odd look that she ignored. Jamal handed her the paper, one that was probably some bright color. The large EFH on top had her riveted.

Do you truly know the people around you? There are those among you who aren't human. They are a danger to all of us. Learn to recognize them and take back our planet. Earth For Humans. Mondays at eight o'clock.

There was an address that Kira quickly memorized. It *was* a LARP, but one the Purifiers were using to find new recruits. How very clever.

Kira handed it back, letting Todd and Shahara read it. "Are you interested?" Shahara asked after a minute.

Jamal shrugged. "Don't know. Might be interesting."

"I wouldn't. I've heard of this group. This might be a game, but the organization? They're... shall we say, xenophobic? This is how they find recruits," Kira warned him.

Jamal froze. "Are you sure?"

She nodded solemnly. "Yeah. Seriously, be careful."

Jamal picked up the flyer, ripped it in half, then in half again, and continued shredding it until he had a small pile of confetti by his plate. Kira wasn't surprised. Xenophobes were often racist as well.

"Is that even legal?" Shahara asked.

"Well, do remember, *this* is a game. To about ninety-five, ninety-eight percent of people involved, it never gets beyond a game. They'll have no idea that the group itself can be darker." Kira shrugged. "Then you have to actually prove that they are doing something illegal. Free speech and all."

Shahara snorted in disgust. "Awful. All of it."

"I agree." However, this might be exactly what she needed. If she could make it work.

Kira was quiet during most of the meal, waiting. When Todd left, she made her excuses and followed him.

Todd noticed. "I have class."

"Skip. This is important."

He looked at his watch. "Three minutes."

Good enough. Kira pulled him to the side. "I need you to join that LARP."

"What? But you said–"

"We need someone on the inside and bet you anything you want that they have a way to recognize the most common Twilights. They will know me if I go. It's much, much harder to identify an Esper. You're the only one who can."

Todd bit his lip. "You really think this will help?"

"*Someone* knows something. We just need to find out who. This is currently our best shot."

He sighed. "Okay, I'll do it."

Her conscience pricked her. "Make sure you pay attention to your instincts. Get out if it seems dangerous. Sakaki would never forgive me if I let you get yourself killed."

Todd almost laughed. "Fine. For your sake, I'll try not to die." He looked around. "Can I go to class now?"

"Go." Kira stepped back, letting him leave. She was starting to understand what her cousin saw in him.

Chapter Sixteen

Even the best mask is just a mask. – The Kikitsutai Book of
Wisdom

"Here, to join the group. Memorize this."

Todd took the plastic card Ryoko-*Sensei*
handed him on instinct before looking at it. It was a
driver's license. The picture was his, but the name
and address weren't. "A fake ID? Will I need this?"
Todd asked, even as he tried to commit the
information to memory.

"You may." Ryoko stroked his chin. "If they
are indeed looking for recruits, which is likely, then
they will want to know who you are and how they
can get in touch with you. When you do leave the
group, it would be best if they cannot find you
again."

"Okay, but what if someone I know is there?
They were advertising just off campus."

"That is one of the reasons we left the first
name the same. If someone you know is there,
hopefully they won't know your last name, or you
can convince them they were mistaken. If someone
knows you well?" Ryoko shrugged. "Use your best

judgement. If you *do* give out your real information, let us know. We can hack their database later. You remember your cover story?"

Todd took a deep breath and nodded. "Right. I'm checking out this game because I'm bored and it sounds interesting. Personally, I think it might be a metaphor for immigration which needs to be more stringently regulated. I enjoy science fiction stories about clever humans repelling a hostile alien force and this might be more of the same." He was beginning to see what they meant about the cover having to be similar and different. Todd, having immigrants as best friends, was in favor of more liberal immigration rules. He did enjoy science fiction stories, even a few of that type. However, he also enjoyed ones where humans and aliens worked together.

"Good. Good. Remember, Kira will be nearby. Signal her, and she'll cause a distraction and you can leave. After we get a feel for what they are doing and how advanced they are, we might be able to wire you. But we can't take the risk this time."

"Because you don't know if they'll be looking for that." Todd nodded. They had been over this all before. He wasn't sure if the older Werefox was trying to reassure him or himself. While agreeing with Kira's plan, Ryoko-*Sensei* had been gravely displeased at the idea of sending in a civilian. "I think I'll be okay."

Kira strode into the room. "Well, in case you aren't, wear this." She handed over a clunky looking watch. "If you get in trouble and want help, press the button on the side. The one that looks like the tuning knob. It gives off a sound that isn't in the human hearing range, but is in ours. We can track it up to half a mile. But it isn't connected to a locater, so the Purifiers shouldn't notice."

Todd put the watch on quickly. "Thanks." He let out a heavy breath. "So, it's time?"

"Are you armed?" The Werefoxes asked at the same time.

"No. Well, I do have the switchblade L... that she gave me. I forgot to give it back to her. Pretty sure it's illegal to carry though."

"Then don't pull it out unless it's an emergency." Kira shrugged, unconcerned. "What did you tell Jamal?"

"Nothing. He's studying. I just said I was going out. I don't want to lie to him if I don't have to, but I couldn't think of a good reason to explain why I'm going to a group that you said might hate his guts. Besides, he's my roommate, not my mother. He doesn't need to know where I go."

"I'm not actually sure if the group would have a problem with him or not. But it's probably best you don't tell him. Though having backup..."

"Time to get moving, Kits," Ryoko cut in. "Good luck."

Kira grabbed a battered backpack that looked very different than the one she used on campus to carry books around. Todd wasn't sure he even wanted to know what was in it. "If you don't hear from us by ten, something went wrong."

Todd held the door for Kira and tried not to think about all the different ways things *could* go wrong.

They drove to the address, Todd letting Kira out a block short at her request, before going into the nearest fast-food restaurant and changing his clothes. Kira had insisted. His old clothes went in a bag in the trunk, and he'd change back later.

The game met outside a community center. Todd found a place to park and looked around the group. About twenty or thirty people, ranging from his age to maybe forties, predominately guys, with a few girls mixed in. The way the flyer had been printed probably wasn't as successful with women. Fortunately, there was no one he recognized, so he could give the fake information.

Before getting out of the car, Todd took one more look at his information. Todd Johnson. 12 Flagler Drive, West Palm Beach. Birthday was December 7th. One month after his real birthday. He wondered if they had done that on purpose. Probably. It was easier to remember that way.

He could do this. For Sakaki. He *would* do this. Todd climbed out of the car and wandered over, trying to look a little confused.

A man, probably mid-thirties, smiled at him. "Hey, first time?"

"Yeah. I saw a flyer at school?"

"Sure. We love first timers. It's a good time to join, too. We're about to start a new campaign. You register at that table there so we can keep you in the loop, and there's a handbook. Rules, character creation, etc."

"Great, thanks." Did he know the real purpose? Or was he one of the people just in it for the game?

Todd went over to the registration table, manned by a friendly-looking woman who had a large black lab at her feet. The dog was covering his ears but still looked up when Todd approached. The woman smiled. "Hello, I'm Sandy."

"Todd. Um, I've never done anything like this before." He took a moment to let the dog sniff his hand. "Can I pet your dog?"

"Sure. He loves people. Don't worry about being new. You need to sign up here. Name, phone number and email. That's how you get the updates. Then you sign this waiver. Basically that you are aware we are not liable if you get hurt playing, and this stating that you read the rules and agree to follow them."

"Hurt?" Todd looked up from the dog.

Sandy shrugged. "It's a game. Some people get a little into it. We've never had a serious injury, but a few falls, some scrapes, stuff like that. We're just being safe.

Todd stood to the side, taking a moment to read the waiver and rules before signing anything. The waiver was pretty much what Sandy said. EFH was not liable for the actions of its members, for injuries acquired while playing. and was definitely not advocating illegal actions like trespassing or breaking and entering. The rules were similar. Nothing illegal, no real weapons, no attacking anyone, remember that it was a game. Nothing Todd would have a problem with. Good.

He remembered, barely, to sign the fake name, give the phone number to the burner phone that Kira had acquired somehow, and the email address that was set up deliberately for this purpose.

"Awesome. Here's your handbook. Details of the campaign, full list of rules, and a little of the history are in here. Also, some advice on how to create your character. If you want or need any help, you can talk to anyone wearing one of our wristbands." Sandy held up an arm, showing off her black wristband with EFH embedded in blood red letters. "You'll need to wear one of these for the game." She gave him a white wristband with EFH in black letters. "Everyone wears one during the game so you know who's involved."

"Thanks." Todd slipped on the wristband, took the booklet and retreated to read it. Skipping the history for now and only giving a cursory look to the full list of rules, he concentrated on the scenario. Scouts from an alternate dimension had come to earth, analyzing the weaknesses in preparation for an oncoming attack. These scouts were able to mostly pass for humans, but there were certain signs they weren't. Different types of scouts had different weaknesses and strengths. The Beastials had animal traits: usually very good hearing or sense of smell, but poor vision, particularly with color; often had unusual eye colors; and sensitivities to certain foods or metals. Gee, Todd wondered who *those* were supposed to be based on. On the other hand, Beastials were also supposed to be stupid, violent, and driven by instincts.

The Blooders had an obsession with blood and were supposedly much smarter than the Beastials, who they used as grunts because the Blooders couldn't tolerate sunlight. May be driven away by bright lights, strong smells, or religious iconography.

Then there were the unclassified. Not explored enough to describe. Ways to identify one of these dimensional scouts included odd eye colors, senses in the uppermost or lowermost part of human range, unwillingness to be out at certain parts of the day or certain days of the month, not knowing common or pop culture, or they just gave you a weird feeling.

Todd tried to suppress a chill, even as he heard a few others complain about how they ripped off Werewolves and vampires for a sci-fi setting. Yes, yes they had. But that didn't make it any less dangerous.

Right, remember, this was supposed to be a game. A game that he was supposed to play in such a way that they thought he might be receptive to more. How was he supposed to do that anyway? First things first. Create a character.

Kira and Ryoko-*Sensei* had tried to help him create a character that might work in a game like this. Because they didn't know what the game would entail, they came up with a few general directions that he could pick from and narrow when he got there. Praying that at least one of their ideas would work, Todd read the character creation rules.

You have recently discovered or strongly suspect you have discovered a non-human trying to pass as human. Further investigation led you to find out about the scouts. You are now trying to find like-minded people in the know, without being thought of as crazy. How did you discover this? What do you believe should be done about the menace?*

* No player may play as a scout or a double agent for the scouts without specific permission from moderator.

Todd sighed in relief. This was perfect. The Werefoxes had suspected something like this and gave him the perfect cover story. His character was an amateur bird watcher, which is how he noticed this one guy who went down to the park every day. Even though he didn't feed them, the birds always 'flocked' to this guy, who just so happened to have golden eyes. Following him would be enough to explain finding out about the scouts. His character, Jackson Brand, sometimes called Fire Brand by his friends, supported rounding up suspicious characters and interrogating them about their plans. It wouldn't be pretty, but the future of humanity was at stake, so there was no time for tiptoeing around.

"Need any help?" One of the volunteers, a man about five years older than him, asked as Todd was finishing up. He was wearing a black wristband, and a name tag that said 'Mike'.

"No... Well, maybe. I've never done something like this before. How is this for a character?" Todd handed over his sheet.

The man skimmed through the sheet, eyebrows quirking a couple times, before handing it back with a small smile. "I think it's about perfect. How did you come up with the bird whisperer?"

Todd gave the answer the Weres had coached him in. "Oh, I knew someone in high school. Well, knew of. People called him Bird. His eyes were almost yellow, and birds and squirrels tended to come to him. Of course, he did feed them. Sometimes anyway. Made gym class interesting."

"Really? Are you in touch with him?"

Todd gave a shrug. "No, I never knew him well, and he moved before I graduated. I don't even know his real name. But honestly, if I had been doing this then, well, I'd probably think something weird of it." Todd tried to look a little confused. Not convinced that it was possible, but not entirely convinced it wasn't either.

He'd been a little concerned with this cover story, that he might be giving away too much information, but the Werefoxes said he wasn't. For one, there was no such person. Two, the Purifiers already knew that many Weres had unusual colored eyes, or weird responses to animals. Three, despite stories, there was no proof anyone could turn into a bird or a squirrel. Wererabbits and Werefoxes were apparently as small as they got. Most Weres were considerably bigger. Considering how badly they were violating the law of conservation of mass to get *that*, perhaps it wasn't a surprise.

"Well, I think you've got a good set up. Look forward to seeing how this plays out. If you have any questions, feel free to ask." Mike nodded to him and went off to talk to someone else.

Todd tried not to let out a breath of relief. He had laid out the groundwork. Now he had to convince them that he was worth taking a chance on.

***

According to Sakaki's notes, she was on good terms with a motel owner, who called her Mary. Sakaki hadn't said exactly what she had done to ingratiate herself to the owner, just that she had. But the fifty-year-old man clearly loved 'Mary' and insisted on telling her about his young granddaughter and how well she was doing thanks to Mary's help. Whatever Mary wanted, she got. Be it a room, information on who was in the motel, or for the owner to be very busy somewhere else while Mary did *something*. No, nothing illegal, why would you even suspect that?

From the bits and pieces she got, Kira suspected that the girl needed some kind of medical treatment that the family couldn't afford, and Sakaki paid for it. Since the girl in question was about three, it really didn't surprise her at all. Some things, Sakaki was a very soft touch about.

When Kira had shown up and said that she needed a room that overlooked the community center for a few hours, and would need it on a weekly basis, he had been happy to show 'Mary' the room, and leave her alone to it. Didn't ask why she needed it or would need it on multiple occasions. Tried to refuse to let her pay, too. Finally, they agreed that she'd pay a deposit on the room to let her use the room indefinitely, but she'd pay more if damage occurred or if she used the room for more hours than her deposit covered. Kira doubted he'd ever charge her more than the hundred he had reluctantly taken from her.

Anyway, the room had a good view of the yard, and Kira used binoculars to identify and memorize the faces of everyone she could, and a parabolic mic to listen in. Todd seemed to be setting up good groundwork. This would be so much easier if she could actually be there to read the situation. But she couldn't.

Kira had no intention of going near the Purifiers little game if she could help it. If they were responsible for Liska's disappearance, then they would recognize her face. Even if they weren't involved with that, they had ways to tell she was a Were. Like say the dog at the registration. Most Twilights didn't smell quite human. Espers, however, smelled perfectly human because they *were* human.

Both Werefoxes had made a point of putting on scent concealer before Todd came by. Between that and changing his clothes, Todd didn't smell enough like fox to rile up the dog. Good. He also wasn't reacting to the box that was emitting a high pitched squeal just above human hearing range. That dog must be in pain. Kira was over a block away, and she could hear it even before she pulled out the parabolic microphone.

Because they were meeting outside, with dark fast approaching, there were lots of lights around. Some of them were UV lights, specifically designed to help seasonal depression. Undoubtedly that was to keep the vampires away, but it worked against a few other things too. Kira would bet money that there was a line of purified salt at every entrance. That would keep out shades and make vampires and fae more reluctant to enter. Though in the last two cases, they had spread the rumor that it was more effective than it was.

The game came to a stop around nine-thirty. Kira sent *Sensei* a text to let him know they were heading back before packing up her equipment. She still managed to get to the rendezvous before Todd did. Probably because he had stopped to change his clothes back.

"We'll talk when we get back to *Sensei*'s," Kira said before Todd could start.

"Fine."

Sensei was waiting for them. "It went well?"

"I think so." Todd rubbed at the back of his neck. "I caught someone's interest. His name was Mike, but I don't know his last name. Mid-twenties, maybe? Short and stocky. Pretty sure he's a true believer, but I'm not positive."

"We'll look him up in the database." Kira made a mental note to ask Ryo to do that. "You used our story?"

"Yes. I tried to seem open, but not like I believed it yet. He just said it was good and he looked forward to finding out how it went."

Sensei nodded. "He would not tell you anything yet, and it is better you do not press. Slow, steady, don't come on too fast. He will be watching to see if you have potential."

"Right." Todd let out a breath through clenched teeth. "Is it a good thing or a bad thing that I feel slightly sick?"

"Both," Kira said. "It's good you don't feel very sick. It's good that you don't like pretending to be one of them. It's good that you aren't a hardened liar. It's bad because you are going to have to keep doing this. It's bad because the harder you find this, the harder it will be for you to keep it up."

"You did well tonight. Concentrate on that." *Sensei* took the papers Todd offered him and spread them on the table.

Kira tried to skim them quickly upside down. She snorted when she read the descriptions of the Beastials and Blooders. It wasn't hard to see what their main targets were. Interesting what information they had and didn't have.

"Any idea why they think the Blooders are smarter than the Beastials?" Todd asked. "I don't have much experience with vampires, but vampires and Weres seem about equally smart and both at least on par with humans."

"We are. It's possible that this is a story element. Or maybe they assume because we have ties to animals, we simply aren't as smart. More instinct than intellect," Kira answered.

"Actually, there have been a few attempts to convince groups like this that Weres are truly less intelligent. It was considered a form of protection. One doesn't take as many precautions to outsmart an idiot. That has been mostly phased out, but some still use it," *Sensei* corrected.

She hadn't known that. Strange, usually they were taught what disinformation had been spread. "Any other ideas on who might have been a true believer, versus just in for the game?"

"Not sure. No one else stood out. They have a two wristband system. Everyone wears a wristband so you know they're playing. Most of us had white, and we were told to talk to those who had black bands. While all the people with black bands might not be true believers, I'll bet most of the believers would have the black bands."

"Good. We'll concentrate on them. I took a lot of pictures." While she hadn't concentrated on the black bands, with luck, between her pictures and Todd's memories, they would have most of them. If not, there was always next week.

"If they are using old information, that Weres aren't that smart, does that mean we're looking at someone with old information? Maybe a long-time Purifier?" Todd asked.

"Possible. Though, like I said, some still use it. And, as Kira suggested, it may just be a story element."

Kira thought she heard Todd muttering something about going to elves for advice, but she ignored it. Elves were notoriously unhelpful.

"Is the vampire still in the background?" *Sensei* asked.

"I've seen him in the distance from time to time, but he's made no move to talk to me. I don't know if he suspects or not. Or what reaction he would expect from Sakaki." Kira sighed. Thanks to Todd's description, she could identify him, but he never got close. Which she was honestly grateful for.

"I've seen him a few times too. But he doesn't want to talk to me either."

"We will find her," *Sensei* said.

"Yes, we will," Kira agreed.

"I know. I just hope it's soon." Todd sighed.

Twenty-nine days. And they had <u>nothing</u>.

***

Thirty-six days after Sakaki disappeared, and Kira was beginning to wonder if this was an unending nightmare. Between her and *Sensei*, they had checked every neighborhood in a five-mile radius for her scent, some more than once, but there was never even a vague hint. Rex Magnus was demanding a meeting with her by the end of the week to know what she had discovered. He called it an 'update', so he wasn't expecting everything yet, but she had nothing to tell him. A face with no name, no address, nothing. Tonight she'd go to the Devil's Fang and see if Sakaki's groundwork had borne fruit. If so, it would be the only thing to have gone right in a month.

She was absolutely certain that Jamal and Shahara *knew* something was off. But she was going to ignore it until they confronted her. Besides, what could they possibly come up with as an explanation that was stranger or worse than the truth?

Todd, at least, was always there. He shared her desperation for clues, drove her anywhere she wanted to go that might be helpful, listened when she needed to vent, and loved hearing all her stories about Sakaki. Tonight he'd go to his second LARP meeting. One more way he was becoming her rock. Kira had even forgiven him for hurting Sakaki and was hoping Sakaki could forgive him too.

But first, she had to get through the school day. It wasn't that the classes were difficult. She knew most of the material already or at least had enough of a foundation to follow along. But they all seemed so *completely pointless*. Who cared about Boyle's Law when they had a family member missing? So what if Washington Irving was a huge fan and contemporary of Charles Dickens? Did that tell her who betrayed the vampires? And if she had to hear her history teacher make one more mistake that a read through of the textbook would fix, she might scream. She could understand him not knowing the true history, but shouldn't he at least know what the textbook said? He picked the stupid book!

"Anna?"

It took Kira a couple seconds longer than it should to remember that she was Anna. She tried to cover by rubbing at her temples. "Shahara?" She looked up to see the Jamaican girl standing over her library table.

"Hey, you okay?"

"Headache. I haven't been sleeping well lately."

"I'm sorry. School stress?"

Kira shrugged. "Among other things. What's up?"

"You need to relax. Take a break. C'mon."

No, the last thing she wanted was to get dragged into something. She didn't want to be scrutinized, to have to be careful of her mask. "I'm busy now."

"You're always busy. Todd's almost as busy as you. You are both taking a break. C'mon." Shahara took her book as Kira's sleep-deprived reflexes made her just too slow to stop her.

"Not in the mood. I'm bad company right now."

Shahara crossed her arms. "It's my birthday. We're celebrating."

Kira tried to quickly run through Sakaki's notes in her head, but she couldn't remember when Shahara's birthday was. It didn't feel quite right, but Kira couldn't tell for sure. Shahara was definitely up to something, but Kira didn't know what. "Is it?" Shahara didn't say anything, no change of face or scent. Nothing to go on. "Happy Birthday." If it really was Shahara's birthday, then refusing to celebrate would be rude. "I didn't get you anything."

"Don't have to. Just come."

Now she didn't have a choice. But she still wasn't sure about this. "Alright. Where are we going?" Kira stood, gathering her belongings at the same time.

"Not far." Shahara offered to take some of her papers, but Kira waved her off. "Coming?"

"I'm coming. I'm coming."

As they were leaving the library, Shahara spoke up. "I haven't seen you skating recently."

Kira forced her expression to remain neutral. Sakaki loved skating, often comparing it to flying. To her, skating was about freedom. She didn't bother trying to learn the names of moves, or how one competed; it was just her and the skates. Sometimes she went for speed, sometimes distance, and sometimes for trying crazy stunts. However she did it, Sakaki loved skating.

Kira, on the other hand, considered it death on wheels. She couldn't keep balanced on inline skates and had no interest in regular skates. Even if she had the inclination to skate, anyone seeing her would know in an instant that she wasn't Sakaki, who could probably compete if she was willing to follow rules. And wasn't trying to stay anonymous. "Haven't felt like it."

"Are you depressed?"

Yes, yes she really was. And she had excellent reason to be. Kira shrugged. "I think I'm just stressed."

"You must be." Shahara started fiddling with her butterfly necklace. She wore that one a lot. Must like it.

Kira ignored the unspoken invitation to talk about it. Shahara led her to one of the classroom buildings. Science and Medicine. Interesting. "Why here?"

The Jamaican girl didn't answer until they were on the staircase. "The school of Medicine has a private study area for students. Jamal reserved it for an hour."

A study room? Why there? True, most of the dorms were restricted by gender. That would limit the amount of places that Shahara could plan her party or anything if she wanted Jamal, and likely Todd, maybe a few other people to join. But a study room?

They reached the study room to find Jamal and Todd waiting. It definitely didn't look like a party. Jamal looked grave, and Todd was confused and concerned. Every instinct Kira had was screaming at her to run.

Shahara closed the door and locked it before taking up sentinel position in front of it. "Who are you and what have you done with Anna?"

Chapter Seventeen

The truth is a dangerous weapon. – The Kikitsutai Book of Wisdom

The instant the lock clicked shut, Kira knew exactly what was going on. Shahara's words only confirmed it. In that breath of time, Kira could see multiple paths but didn't like any of them.

If they were confronting her, they were absolutely certain of their conclusions. The room had no windows, and only one door. Which meant that to get out, she would have to get past Shahara and the locked door. It could be done, but not without seriously harming Shahara, and probably Jamal, who would certainly come to his sister's defense. Todd would refuse to stand idly by while his friends were injured, but she wasn't quite sure what he would do. Therefore, neither flight nor fight were an option except of absolute last resort.

Confusing them, convincing them they were wrong was extremely unlikely. But by trying, maybe she could at least stall them long enough to figure out what to truly tell them. If she found out what they knew, she could tailor a story for them that they might believe.

Kira put on a face of confusion. "What? What are you talking about? This isn't funny."

"No, it isn't," Jamal agreed. "So suppose you tell us the truth."

"Guys—" Todd tried to interrupt.

"No! I'm not sure how you're so blind you don't see it, but this isn't Anna. Probably hasn't been for weeks." Shahara pursed her lips. "I said today was my birthday. Anna gave me this for my birthday back in January." She tugged at the butterfly.

"I'm sorry, I've been really stressed. I forgot all about that," Kira said.

"You haven't skated in forever," Jamal said.

"You told her not to while her wrist was bothering her," Todd said.

"Except, I haven't seen any sign of a sore wrist in ages, have you?" Shahara asked.

"It goes in stages. Sometimes I'm skating all the time, sometimes weeks go by without any interest," Kira lied, still trying to project innocence and confusion.

"You don't recognize inside jokes," Shahara accused.

"I'm stressed and tired all the time. Sometimes I'm amazed I remember my own name!" That one was much less of a lie. Come on, a story. There had to be something she could tell them. Sakaki would have a story by now.

"Anna fiddles with things when she's thinking or nervous. Pencils, pens, silverware, her bracelet. You tap your fingers quietly," Jamal said. They were leading up to something.

Sakaki was more likely to fiddle with things when trying to think, but she tapped her fingers too. "I've always tapped my fingers, and I'm trying to stop fiddling with things. It can get... problematic." Especially since sometimes Sakaki fiddled with knives.

"*And* you don't have Anna's scars." Shahara was on the brink of tears. "So tell us what you did to Anna, or I swear, we will have the police on you so fast—"

Kira held up a hand. "Fine. I'm not 'Anna'. But it's complicated."

Shahara pulled out a cell phone, only to go ashy when Kira snatched it out of her hands. "You can't—"

"I have no intention of threatening anyone here but at least listen to what I have to say before calling the police. That is why you brought me here, isn't it?"

Jamal moved, probably to distract attention from his sister. Kira shifted slightly so she could clearly see them both. Jamal held his hands up. "We'll listen, but this had better be good. And stop pretending to be Anna."

"Fair enough." She dropped the accent and removed the wig. The eyebrow prosthetics could stay, because those were a pain in the neck to get right.

"You still have her face," Shahara objected.

"You're out of luck there. It's my face too." What in the world did she tell them?

"Tell them the truth. Please. You can trust them," Todd said, ignoring the way they stared at him, and the accusations thrown his way.

Kira bit back several swear words. "Everyone have a seat. It's a *loooong* story." She sat first and waited until everyone else was seated. "I can't tell you everything. Don't expect me to. But you're right, I'm not Anna. Anna... doesn't exist. She never did. The girl you knew as Anna was my cousin, Sakaki."

"How do you look like her? What's your name?" Jamal asked.

"My name is Kira. Our fathers are identical twins. Genetically, we're almost half-sisters. I was born a month ahead of her, and we've always looked alike. And we cultivated that. We can and do pass for each other. Granted, usually not for more than a few hours."

"Why are you pretending to be her, and why is she attending school under a fake name? And where is she?" Shahara demanded.

"We have enemies. The whys and wherefores don't matter for the moment, but we do. Enemies that would gladly see us dead. Sakaki chose to come here for an education, but for safety's sake, had to use a fake name. A little over a month ago..." Kira took a deep breath. "She called me, asking me to come to her. I was in this country anyway, so it wasn't difficult. She was extremely distraught." She could smell Todd's guilt and remorse without looking at him. "I came down and tried to comfort her. I had traveled all night, and she hadn't slept, so I suggested we both rest. She was gone when I woke up, leaving a note saying she wanted to check on something and would be back late. No, I don't know what she wanted to check on. She borrowed a car from another relative of ours in the area."

"I thought she didn't have any family here," Shahara said.

"She lied." Kira shrugged. "She lies to everyone, so don't feel bad." That might not have been the best way to put things. "In her defense, there are many things that she simply cannot tell anyone. In any case, she borrowed the car. A few hours later, police came to the door, saying that 'Diane Russell', the name the license is in, had died in a car crash."

Shahara gasped, covering her mouth, and Jamal looked pale. Kira continued. "We know for a fact that the body in the car wasn't hers. But that's all we know for sure. We haven't heard from her. We can't find her. I'm sure she's still alive; I'd know if she died. I'm sure she wasn't responsible for this. She wouldn't do such a thing. But I can't find her. I know she's in trouble, but..."

"Er, sure there's a reason for this, but why haven't you contacted the police? I mean, maybe she'd be in *some* trouble for the fake ID, but..." Jamal sputtered.

"We can't. It's... *complicated*. Nothing to do with the fake ID."

"No, I'm sorry. I need more than that. Whether she was lying to me or not, she was still my friend, and I'd like to think I was hers. Even if she wasn't a friend, you believe she's in trouble. If she's been kidnapped, by someone willing to *kill* to cover it up, then I need something more than *complicated* or I'm going to the police!" Shahara practically had steam coming out of her ears.

Kira made eye contact with Todd. "If this goes wrong, I'll have to tell *Sensei*." Todd swallowed hard but nodded. "Right. Okay. We can't call the police, because this isn't something the police are equipped to handle." Nor did she want them to be yet. "The reason we know the body wasn't hers, was because the body was human." She paused to let the obvious implications sink in.

Jamal croaked out a, "What," that somehow wasn't a question.

Shahara was more verbose. "And you're what? Martian?"

Despite the circumstances, Kira snickered at that. "Wrong genre. No, I'm from Earth. My kind have been here as long as humans. We think. Are you sure you want to know this? You can leave now, accepting only that 'Anna' is missing, and I'm trying to find her while making sure she has a role to come back to. Just believe I have good reasons for not calling the police in."

Shahara pulled her chair in front of the door, sat down and folded her arms. "Not a chance. You aren't getting rid of me that easily."

Jamal looked to Todd. "You know this, whatever she has to say, don't you?"

"Yeah. I've known for months."

"You knew she wasn't the same person. Probably helped her pass." Todd nodded. "Is it bad? What I'll learn if I stay?"

Todd bit the corner of his mouth. "It changes *everything*. You won't look at life or anything else the same way again. It hurts at first. Your comfortable reality is shattered like broken glass. But then you realize that Wonderland is all around you. And it's beautiful and scary and *breathtaking*. You're in on this amazing secret and you don't see how everyone else can be so *blind*. But you're just as blind, because there is always so much more to learn. The world is always bigger, stranger, scarier, and more amazing than you think."

Everyone stared at Todd, who was looking very embarrassed at his impromptu speech. Even Kira was astounded. She had no idea Todd felt that way. Did he even realize that his continued insistence on being involved could easily get him killed someday?

Jamal, after he had finished gaping at Todd, said, "Well, then I guess I'm in too."

"Right. Like I said, I can't tell you everything. Todd certainly doesn't know everything, and it's taken him months to get this far. But I can tell you some."

Kira gave a cliff notes version of the whole Days (Humans), Twilights (non-humans who can pass as human, or humans with non-human abilities), and Nights (non-humans that are clearly non-human). Then she gave them a slightly more in-depth summary of Weres in general and Werefoxes in particular. She even did a partial shift for them, to erase any lingering doubts that she was some lunatic that managed to pass for lucid. Then, she mentioned the Purifiers.

"They're the ones running the LARP you warned me off of?" Jamal asked.

"That's right. Fairly clever on their part. To be honest, I'm not sure if you would have trouble with them or not. But at the center, a group like the Purifiers is based on fear of those who are different."

Jamal nodded slowly. "I understand. I don't think I'd want to associate with a group like that anyway."

Todd snorted. "You're lucky." That got him stares.

Kira sighed. "We *are* looking for Sakaki. Just because we haven't found her yet, doesn't mean we aren't looking. And even if they don't know anything about that, before she disappeared, she was investigating a Purifier raid on a local Blood. That's a group of vampires. We need info, and I can't join. They'd know I was a Twilight. So I asked Todd to join."

"Wait, wait one second." Shahara raised a hand. "This is a 'game' sponsored by a hate group, may or may not be responsible for An... Saki?"

"Sakaki."

"Right, thanks. Sakaki's disappearance, and is responsible for a 'raid', whatever that entailed, on a group of vampires. And you sent Todd in, alone, to pretend to be interested?"

"Trust me, I'm not happy about it either. Sakaki has always done her best to minimize Todd's exposure to danger. I wouldn't do this if I could help it. But one, we don't have other options. Two, he joined the game. Like I said before, repeatedly, most people never go beyond the game. They certainly aren't going to draw him into the inner circle right away. Third, he isn't alone. I may not be able to walk in and join, but I am watching, ready to cause a distraction."

"What happened to the vampires?" Jamal asked.

Kira sighed. "We aren't sure how the Purifiers found them. They've never been the most informed group. But they attacked the place. It's a burnt-out hulk now. I don't know about Purifier casualties, but last I heard, the vampires had fifteen unaccounted for. Five known dead."

Shahara shivered and Jamal closed his eyes. "Do you think they kidnapped Sakaki?" Shahara asked.

"I don't know. I truly don't. I do know that sitting here wringing our hands does nothing. Besides, Sakaki was 'hired' to find out how the Purifiers found the vampires. It could go very badly for her if the one who hired her finds out she's missing."

Todd's eyebrows went up at that. Perhaps she hadn't told him that part. Whoops.

"Okay, but without backup? What if I went with you?" Jamal asked.

Todd frowned. "I'm not sure if you would have trouble or not. Kira and her great-uncle gave me a fake ID and fake information to join. My cover story includes that I think this is an allegory for immigration. Something I supposedly think should be more stringently regulated. Harder to claim if I bring you in as my friend."

"What if we supposedly didn't know each other?" Jamal asked.

"Not tonight. It would take more time than we have to set you up with an identity. Especially since I would have to explain everything to my great-uncle first. But we can keep the option open for a later time." It wasn't going to happen if she had anything to say about it. One civilian involved was bad enough. At least Todd was semi-knowledgeable and had self-defense training. Getting Jamal to that point would take too long.

Sakaki would probably not thank her for telling Jamal and Shahara as much as she had. *Sensei* would definitely have some things to say about it. But Kira couldn't think of other options. At least they were taking things pretty well. Perhaps even exceptionally well. Then again, they had started with the assumption that something was wrong, and someone was impersonating a friend of theirs. Maybe going in with the expectation of bad news helped. Or maybe their religious background left them more receptive to the idea that reality included more than the known visible part.

No matter how much information you had, no matter how skilled you were at guessing, there was always an element of unpredictability involved when informing someone about the secret. People who should have been fine with it, panicked; and those who should reject it, took it easily. It was one of the many reasons why the secret was so carefully guarded.

Of course, taking it well didn't mean they didn't have a thousand questions. Kira let them ask, answering the ones she deemed harmless enough, letting Todd answer some, and not rescuing him when Shahara scolded him for leaving them in the dark so long. After an hour she put an end to it. "Todd, we've got to go. You have to be ready in an hour."

Todd stood up with a grim nod. Jamal stood up too. "If I can't help Todd infiltrate, can I at least help you with providing backup?"

This was going to go so poorly. "Fine. Shahara, might as well come too. I'll introduce you to my Great-uncle."

***

Kira knew she was going to get a few earfuls from *Sensei* when there was time. But right now, time was a commodity they simply didn't have. She brought them to *Sensei*'s house and started talking immediately. "This is Jamal and Shahara. They're Todd's and Anna's friends, and they figured out I wasn't Anna. I had to explain." She flashed two fingers at him. A level two explanation. They knew most of the basics, but not much more. "Jamal wants to help me back Todd up. So he'll be keeping watch with me? Where's the equipment? Ah, there it is. Okay, we've got to go. I'll contact you by ten. Bye, *Sensei*."

It might not be fair to Shahara, who *Sensei* would politely interrogate. Or perhaps not fair to *Sensei*, who Shahara was bound to enthusiastically ask many, many questions. Either way, she'd be hearing about it later. But later was later and now was now.

Todd let them out the same place he had dropped Kira off last time. Jamal didn't say anything about being led to a slightly run-down hotel, though he did raise his eyebrows when Kira warned him that the owner called her Mary. Fortunately, he knew better than to ask as they walked into the lobby.

"Mary! So good to see you!" The large man swept her into an enthusiastic hug that Kira forced herself not to fight her way free from. She might not have been able to keep so calm if she hadn't prepared for it ahead of time. How did Sakaki manage? She was much more touch-shy unless she was very comfortable with the other person.

"Good to see you too, Leo. How's your granddaughter doing?"

"Carrie is wonderful. I have new pictures to show you." Leo looked at Jamal. "You brought a friend?"

"I needed help with a project." Kira lightly tapped her backpack straps and nodded towards the briefcase Jamal was holding. "He wasn't here. Neither was I."

"No, of course not. Silly me. Talking to no one. But if someone was here, I might tell them that room 275 is free." Leo put the key on the counter. "These keys. Always so disorganized." He bustled around the keys, ostentatiously not looking in their direction.

"If someone was here, they would probably say thank you." Kira took the key and nodded at Jamal to follow her.

He kept his mouth shut until they were in the room with the door shut. "Does he think you're your cousin?"

"Yes. Don't know why 'Mary' though."

"Because she wouldn't tell him her name." Kira looked at Jamal in curiosity. "One of the housekeepers goes to my church. The whole thing got brought up in prayer group a couple times. Leo's daughter and her husband died in a car accident about a year ago, and Carrie was badly injured. Medical bill after medical bill, culminating in needing spinal surgery in order to walk, possibly to avoid breathing problems. Insurance didn't cover nearly enough. Business isn't great, as you can probably see. We did a collection at church, but it only went so far."

Kira nodded but didn't interrupt.

"Well, according to Leo, this woman rented a room for a night. Seemed a little shifty, but hey, she was paying. She was in the lounge, apparently trying to get an internet connection, when Leo heard from the hospital saying that the surgery had to be done within a month for the best effect. He pleaded with them to take her, saying he'd get the money somehow, but he didn't have it then." Jamal smiled. Kira suspected she knew where this was going.

"So apparently, he was on the verge of cursing out the receptionist when this red-haired angel took the phone from him and asked a few questions. Then she pulled out a credit card and paid the whole amount on the spot, only after insisting that their best pediatric surgeon, who she identified by name, perform the operation. When she handed the phone back, the hospital said the whole thing had been paid for. Leo was so shocked and grateful that he immediately ran to tell his wife. When he came back, she was gone. Didn't even see her checkout. He called her 'Mary', and until she came back, he wasn't convinced she wasn't an angel in disguise."

Kira wanted to laugh at that. Sakaki, an angel in disguise. She would have to tell her that when they found her. Sakaki would laugh herself silly. "I'm not surprised. She's done some work that paid very well and believes money exists to be used. And she has a soft spot for kids." Sounded like she hadn't even done it for a favor in return. "But let's get this set up before the meeting starts.

Logic would seem to dictate that two people could set up equipment faster than one. However, that is only true when both people know what they are doing and preferably have helped each other before. When one person does not know what they are doing, and the two have not worked together before, it can be slower than one experienced person working by themselves. Still, they managed. Kira took the parabolic mic herself and gave Jamal the binoculars and camera. "Make sure you get a picture of everyone wearing a black wristband."

***

Todd got a couple smiles and waves he joined the group, but most people paid little attention to him. Fine with him. It was a narrow tightrope. He had to seem capable of being a good inclusion for the inner circle, which meant he had to stand out in a good way. But he also wanted to be invisible enough that no one would seek him out outside the game. He felt like he had to think twice about every word he spoke and every move he made. One more proof that he wasn't suited to undercover work.

Ironically, it was much easier once the game actually started. Everyone knew it was a role, so it didn't matter if he messed up, or if character didn't quite mesh right. It wasn't like he was the only one having that problem. A lot of people liked to put on roles that seemed very different from their normal personalities. It was one of the draws of roleplaying games.

About half-way through the allotted time, Todd noticed a man. Probably in his fifties, but still in good shape, he was talking to a couple of the volunteers. Todd was certain he hadn't been here last week, but he still seemed familiar somehow. From the college? No, Todd didn't think so. The police station? Probably not. Was this someone Todd had actually met? Someone who might know him? He just couldn't remember.

Todd racked his brain trying to place the familiarity while still trying to play the rest of the game. Jackson Brand was trying to get support for his idea of kidnapping someone he suspected might be a Beastial so they could be questioned. It was chilling how easy it was to rally people around this idea. Sure, he knew about mob psychology, but watching it in practice was sickening. Of course, he was pretty sure everyone else would justify it as being part of the game. Their 'characters' were supposed to act this way. No wonder the Purifiers used this to find recruits.

Brand's committee was still deadlocked on how exactly to capture the alleged Beastial when time was called. Two different players congratulated him on taking charge in such a realistic way. Todd accepted their congratulations with a smile, trying to swallow the bile that threatened to rise up his throat.

The man Todd was still attempting to identify came to the front. "Wonderful job, everyone. For those who don't know, I'm Sidney Whitters, leader of this chapter of EFH. This game was a brainchild of mine three years ago; but it has taken you to make it what it is today. I'm so glad you all came today. We couldn't do this without you. I'm sorry for ending the game early tonight, but there are rumors of inclement weather to hit soon and hard. I'm afraid we may have to cancel next week's session too. An email will be sent Sunday, so look out for that. Safe trip home, and I hope to see you all here next time, be it next week or the week after." Sidney gave a beaming smile. "Earth for Humans."

Most answered in kind. Todd didn't. He was looking at the sky. Inclement weather? There was barely a cloud in the sky. In fact, it was prime stargazing weather, if one wasn't in the middle of a major city, of course. True, in South Florida, weather could change in a blink. He distinctly remembered the time he was walking home from the library and got caught in a downpour half-way home. He got home, changed clothes, checked his email, and went back out to blue skies. The whole process had taken about ten minutes.

More interestingly, most of the volunteers and a couple of the players looked particularly alert and edgy. Inclement weather was probably a code. But they wouldn't talk while he was around. Hopefully Kira was listening.

Todd was almost to his car when it hit him. He knew where he had seen Sidney Whitters before. It was a drawing. Kira's drawing. Sidney Whitters was the man Liska identified as being in charge of the raid on the Blood.

Chapter Eighteen

Use your emotions, do not let them use you. –The Kikitsutai
Book of Wisdom

"Um, Todd's leaving."

"He'll wait. Shush." Kira pressed the headphones to the parabolic mic closer to her ear. She wanted to hear this, and it was difficult enough with their electronic sounds to disorient higher hearing ranges. "Make sure to get pictures of everyone who stays."

Vaguely she was aware of Jamal taking the pictures she asked for, but her concentration was on the voices. They were murmuring, which made it even harder to hear. Inclement weather, indeed. Could they use a more obvious code? Not only was the weather perfect, and likely to hold for a couple days, but she couldn't remember the last time she had heard someone who wasn't a meteorologist refer to 'inclement' weather.

She couldn't hear everything, no matter how hard she listened, but she did hear some. A tantalizing puzzle without enough pieces. *Break-in.*

Missing files. Two dead, one hospitalized. Critical condition.

Interesting, but not enough. Yet. Someone was bound to know something. A break-in on Purifiers property? Rumors would be flying already.

"Okay, let's go." There was nothing more to learn here. Packing up the equipment went a little faster than setting it up, but not by much. Todd would definitely beat them to the rendezvous point. It couldn't be helped, and Kira couldn't bring herself to care.

Leo took one look at them leaving and quickly busied himself on the computer, muttering loudly about his budget. Kira left the key on the desk with a folded up twenty underneath.

Todd was drumming his fingers on the steering wheel when they met up with him and immediately went to say something when he spotted them. Kira cut him off before he could say anything. "*Sensei*'s house."

He nodded and drove them without a word. It was a tense silence that wasn't broken until they got inside the house.

Shahara ran up to greet them with an enthusiastic cry. "There really are unicorns! They're real. Mr. Ryoko says he's seen one!"

Kira blinked at that but got past it quickly. Honestly, she had never been quite sure whether or not is was a joke of *Sensei*'s. She had certainly never seen a unicorn herself, nor had she heard any other reliable accounts of a unicorn sighting. Still, she wasn't going to naysay. Maybe *Sensei* was telling the truth. Either way, it really didn't matter right now. "That's great. But business first."

Shahara was serious in a heartbeat. "Did you find anything?"

"Maybe," Todd and Kira said together.

Kira spoke first. "They canceled early. The leader and the true believers stayed. I couldn't hear everything they said, but there was something about a break-in and files were missing. I don't know what was broken into, but if it belonged to the Purifiers, I should be able to pick up some rumors. Or even if it was someplace the Purifiers broke into." Later she'd tell *Sensei*, and maybe Todd, or maybe not, about the fact that the break-in apparently involved fatalities. Probably of guards, which implied a major target. Though it could be a home invasion, which would mean civilian deaths. Perhaps she wouldn't mention the fatalities until she had more details. Jamal and Shahara weren't in deep enough to be told.

"Good. Good. This could be very important." The older Werefox nodded, fingers twitching like he had to hold back from leaping into action. *Sensei* hadn't been on the active list for twelve years, but sometimes it was easy to forget that.

Todd, practically vibrating with impatience, cut in. "Can I see your sketch of the leader from the Purifier's raid?" Slightly curious, Kira pulled the picture from the drawer where it was stored. Todd looked at it briefly and nodded. "I was right. That's him. The leader."

Kira snapped to stare at him, noticing *Sensei* do the same. She had missed that. Then again, it would have been from a distance, and she had given Jamal the binoculars. "Are you certain?"

Jamal looked at the sketch and fiddled with the camera to pull up one of the pictures he had taken. "Yeah, that looks like him." He showed the photo. Everyone agreed.

"We have a name." It was all Kira could do not to gasp. Sydney Whitters. They could look him up, find him and interrogate him in person. This was perfect!

"What did he do?" Shahara asked. "I mean, you said he led a raid..."

"You don't want to know the details. You really don't. I can tell you that he was coolly dispassionate while leading a mob and had no qualms about killing people in very violent ways." Sakaki hadn't even told her all the details.

Jamal put an arm around his sister's shoulders as she leaned into him. "How do you know this?"

Sensei explained. "Sakaki has a mild form of retro cognizance. Sometimes touching an item allows her to briefly end up in the head of someone else who had touched the item while they were in a state of extreme emotion. She touched what was left of a phone, allowing her to see through the eyes of a wraith. That would be like a child vampire. According to Sakaki, her name was Isabelle. Isabelle used the phone to warn the blood that invaders were coming. She was holding the phone when she saw her partner gunned down and was shot herself. It was Isabelle who saw the mob come in, and the leader, the man in that picture, dispassionately tried to set her on fire. Sakaki believes Isabelle bled out first."

Shahara ran off in tears. Jamal swallowed hard a few times and sat down hard on the couch. He almost missed it. Todd, who had heard the story, if perhaps not in so much detail, was pale, but looking back and for the between Jamal and where Shahara had run to, as if trying to decide who he could try to help.

Kira took the decision out of his hands by nodding to Jamal before following Shahara to the bathroom. Shahara had left the door open, but Kira waited outside until the gagging stopped before going in. "Are you okay?"

Shahara shook her head. Kira walked past her and half-filled the bathroom cup. "Here, rinse out your mouth." Shahara did so and rose from the floor, but only as far as sitting on the side of the tub. Kira flushed the toilet, put the lid down, and sat herself. "Deep breaths. You'll be okay."

"Should I be? If you're right..." Shahara shook her head, unable to go.

"Will you're being upset over it change anything?" Kira handed her some tissues.

"What?"

"You can't help Isabelle. She's dead. You can't help Sakaki right now. One, we don't know where she is. Two, even if she was here, I don't think she'd accept your help over this. She wouldn't accept *Sensei*'s help and barely took mine. It isn't your place to do anything about Whitters. That's my job."

A whiff of anger warned her she had said the wrong thing. "So I should just forget about it? Pretend it never happened?"

Yes, actually that would be very helpful. "No. Not at all. Pretending hatred doesn't exist won't make it go away. But wallowing in despair doesn't help either. Right now, you *want* to feel horrible, because you heard something horrible that you can't change. But your feelings don't change anything either. What happened, happened." This wasn't helping. "Look, you want to help? To do something useful?"

"Yes." Shahara dried up her tears, a resolute look on her face.

Good. Great. Now she had to find something Shahara *could* do. Ah-ha! "Come on, I've got a task for you." She took her to *Sensei*'s study. "We're borrowing your computer." Kira didn't bother raising her voice. *Sensei* would hear her anyway. The computer was on, so Kira clicked on the fox icon to pull up the web browser. "I need everything you can find on Sydney Whitters. He seems to be mid-fifties, and we know he lives in or near West Palm. It isn't a common name, so you shouldn't have too much to root through. I particularly want his address, but I'll take absolutely anything you can find."

Shahara nodded and set to work with vim. Kira observed for a moment, but seeing the other girl had things under control, she left to join the others. Stopping in the hallway, she sent a quick text to Tora, asking him to ask his brother to look up Sydney Whitters.

Tora. She hadn't seen him in two months. He had been away when she left for the talks that seemed a lifetime away now. Despite being her betrothed, the decision had been made that he wasn't to know the real reason Kira was still here. It didn't seem fair. While Tora and Ryo were closest to each other, about as close as Sakaki and Kira were, the four of them had all been close. Part of it was because Kira and Tora were expected to marry, but part of it was just that the four got along so well. The quartet had explored all nooks and crannies of their island, and a few nearby, made up their own ridiculous codes and language, played various games to practice tactics and pretend to be heroes, and made general nuisances of themselves.

Even going into different specialties didn't change things. Sakaki had become the most active, specializing in infiltration. Ryo was semi-active, specializing in negotiating and cons, with some hacking. Tora was more support oriented, being a pilot and a better coder and linguist than his twin, though like Kira and Sakaki, the boys could sometimes pass as each other to outsiders. Kira was almost always support, specializing in diplomacy, and occasionally imitating Sakaki.

This might well be the longest she had been apart from Tora. It was certainly the longest she had been away from the island, and Tora seldom was away for long. They emailed at least twice a week, but it sounded like he really missed her. And she was sure that both Tora and Ryo knew something was wrong here.

But mooning over her almost fiancé didn't solve anything. She could see him again when she fixed things here. A small chirp from her phone alerted her to Tora's text. **Got it. U ok?**

Will be.

L ok?

Kira sighed. What did she say to that? She didn't even know where Liska was, let alone her condition. **Working on it.**

Anything I can do?

Not yet. Let you know.

Info w/i 2 days. R busy. NIC. Not in contact. Well, it happened. Life didn't pause just because it felt like it was ending for her.

Kira walked into the living room, noticing that Jamal seemed more together now. "Shahara is looking up everything she can get her hands on about Sydney Whitters. What she can't find out, Ryo can, but he's out of contact for a couple days." If the Purifiers hadn't changed their policy so that new members had a six-week probationary period instead of a month, she'd be able to check herself. Well, some of it. Home addresses weren't kept online. Stupid smart Purifiers.

Kira froze. Home addresses were kept on paper files. There was a break-in, someplace that had to do with Purifiers and files were missing. "I've got to go!" Kira called as she started to run out of the room.

Todd intercepted her, and she forced herself not to hurt him to get him out of her way. "Where are you going?"

"Devil's Fang. I need to know more about that break-in."

"I'll go with you." Todd grabbed his jacket.

It was on the tip of her tongue to refuse, but Todd had been there before, as Liska's 'backup'. Having him there was one more proof of authenticity. "Fine. You drive."

She could hear Jamal asking *Sensei* what the Devil's Fang was.

"Vampire bar," *Sensei* said, calm as if remarking on the weather.

"WHAT?" Jamal and Shahara yelled in unison, loud enough that Kira could hear them through the door she had already shut. Yes, she'd let *Sensei* deal with that.

They drove to Clematis, with Todd parking at the library. It was four blocks from where they needed to be, but it was also the place with the most parking spaces.

She had planned to go after midnight, not barely after ten, but she wasn't sure there was time. If those missing files included addresses, she needed to know, and now.

"Are we making a scene again?" Todd asked, the apprehension and slight excitement in his scent not entering his voice.

"No. No need. I will be talking to Liska's contact. You just stand there and look tough."

"Riiiiigggggght. At some point, they'll figure out that's a bluff."

"You have a UV flashlight?"

"Yes." He tapped a pocket.

"Then we'll be fine. I don't expect trouble. But if he does try to attack, step back and shine the flashlight in his face. I can take it from there."

They didn't go in the main entrance, but to a side door that the owner, Andre, had told Liska to use earlier. That way she didn't have to go causing scenes in the bar, making people suspicious, and undermining Andre's authority repeatedly. The side door led them to a small room; soundproofed, dimly lit, and sparsely decorated, especially for a vampire. Kira spared a small thought for hoping that Todd would be able to see clearly. The light was fine for her and would be for Andre when he got there.

Andre delayed a few minutes. Long enough to make it clear that he didn't answer to her, but short enough that she didn't have a legitimate reason to complain. It helped to know the playbook. "Liska," He greeted her coldly, ignoring Todd completely. "Rex Magnus ordered no further co-operation with you until you show some progress in your... task."

Kira's face didn't change, but mentally she snarled. How was she supposed to figure things out if Rex Magnus closed her avenues of investigation? She didn't want to give out what she knew until she had a chance to investigate Whitters. "I *am* making progress. I've found the leader of the raid. I know his name and face. I'm tracking him down now."

Andre didn't change facial expression either, but she could smell his anticipation and anger. "Who? Give me his name."

"I need to question him first. Then I'll deliver him, gift wrapped, if necessary, to Rex Magnus." Todd didn't like that, but he kept quiet. Good, Kira wasn't taking it back. Couldn't if she wanted to.

"We have prior claim."

"I'm not objecting to that. I simply need something from him first. Now, I want everything you know about the Purifier's break-in."

Surprise turned to satisfaction. "So I know something you don't? Interesting. The name first."

Blasted Bandersnatch! She needed that info. "Swear to me that you will do nothing before I question him."

"I will give your information to my chief, as I must. He is a reasonable man. I am certain he will let you go first, provided you turn him over to us."

Best she was going to get. "Deal." She could smell Todd's fear and disapproval, but she couldn't afford to deal with that now. At least he was keeping his mouth shut. "The name is Sydney Whitters. I simply need his address, should be done by the end of the week. Now, the break-in?"

Andre smirked. "It's intriguing news. Someone, or multiple someones, broke into a Purifier's auxiliary building last night. Two guards are dead. Their throats were slashed, almost to the point of decapitation. One guard was hospitalized with multiple broken bones, and massive internal bleeding. Injuries are consistent with interrogation. Head injury severe enough that even if he lives, which is still in doubt, he'll probably have brain damage. Chances he'll be able to say what happened are in the single digits, if that."

Kira nodded. While it was more details, it was pretty similar to what she heard. "What was taken?"

"Files. Lots of files. Every file the Purifiers had on local groups or suspected local groups, information about non-humans, etc. is gone. Some of it was destroyed there, but some was taken. No one knows what was taken versus destroyed."

Interesting. Very interesting. Not personnel files then. Why take *that* information? Was it so the Purifiers didn't have it? So they could have it? A combination of the two? "Any rumors on responsibility?"

Andre smiled, but Kira smelled his excitement and fear anyway. "The guard who didn't die was found clutching a black origami horse."

Kira hoped her horror didn't show on her face. "A black horse?"

"That's right. Nightmare is back."

Chapter Nineteen

Rumors can make an army of a single horse. – The Kikitsutai
Book of Wisdom

Somehow, Todd had expected that involving Jamal
and Shahara would involve less secrets, not more.
Silly, naïve him. He had enough sense not to ask
Kira about Nightmare while in front of Vampire
Mountain, whose name he still didn't know. But
even waiting until they were in the car, his question
received a terse answer. "Later. Do *not* mention
Nightmare in front of Jamal and Shahara."

Whoever this Nightmare guy was, he
certainly had Kira in a tizzy. Would they even tell
him? He'd just have to see. "What's this about giving
Whitters to the vampires? I didn't know that was
part of the plan."

Kira shrugged. "I don't know what Liska's
plan was, but I don't see a way around it."

"They'll kill him."

"Yes, they will."

Todd swallowed hard. He had seemed nice
this evening, but Sakaki swore that he had tried to

set a wraith on fire while alive. But even if he was a monster, to be calmly discussing his death...

"I'm not exactly thrilled with the idea either. But the truth is, he was dead the moment that he decided to lead that raid. It was only ever a matter of how and who got to him first." Kira wouldn't look at him. "I know for a fact that *Sensei* told Liska to kill him if possible. The only difference is that this way is more acceptable to Rex Magnus."

"That's the *only* difference?" Todd doubted that.

"Fine, maybe not the only one. But Rex Magnus was a hair's breadth from declaring Liska guilty. We gave him someone else to focus on. Don't go mentioning that either."

Todd sighed and pulled into the driveway. Jamal and Shahara were still there, with Shahara showing off the printouts she had found. Todd stayed quiet and listened. Maybe he'd actually learn a few things *that* way.

***

"He's got an unlisted number, and I haven't found his address yet. But I found a few other things. Facebook, LinkedIn, and mentions of him in articles and websites. He's a major donor to the community center, and he writes letters to the editor a lot. I've assembled all the ones he wrote in the past year. Well, the ones they published. Five of them. He works at Tebrow Insurance. I think he's an actuator." Shahara waved the paper in her hand. Kira could smell the excitement rolling off her.

"Excellent. That will be helpful." If nothing else, they could find the address from his job. "How well paid are actuators? If he's a major donor to the community center..."

"His wife had money. She died five years ago. He never remarried. No children. Um, he's fifty-four. Real pillar of the community stuff. Are you sure he's a sociopath?" Shahara asked, confusion and concern cutting through the excitement.

"I'm certain he was the leader of the raid. I'm certain of what Sakaki told me. Maybe he considers himself a decent person, trying to make the world safe from the likes of us." Kira rolled her eyes. "Or maybe this is just the mask he shows the world. We'll find out."

"What are you going to do exactly?" Jamal asked. "You clearly aren't going to the police about this."

"*I* am just going to find out what he knows. How he found out about the vampires, and if he knows anything about Sakaki's disappearance." Kira was mildly glad that wasn't a lie. Not completely the truth, but close enough.

"But, if he... I mean, yeah, you shouldn't take justice into your own hands, and you can't call the police, but he's going to get away with it?" Shahara worried her bottom lip.

Jamal rubbed at her shoulder. "No one truly gets away with anything. You know that."

"Yeah, but it doesn't sit right." Shahara eyed her papers, before looking at Kira. "Do you have a jail for, um...?"

"Non-human matters? No. But that doesn't mean we don't have ways to deal with things. After I find out what he knows, I'll," *hand him over to the Magnus blood*, "report him to the vampire council. They will deal with him according to their laws."

Proving that she knew absolutely nothing about the vampire council, Shahara accepted that answer easily. Jamal was clearly a little more suspicious but evidently decided he didn't want to know or at very least, didn't want to ask in front of his sister.

To put off more questions, Kira started reading the letters to the editor that he had written. Each one confirmed her suspicions a little more. He wrote calmly and rationally, seeming to have well-thought out points. It was only knowing his stance or rereading the letter that one was able to pick out the subtle nuances. The quiet but ever-present call for the 'us' to be ready to stand up and preserve themselves against the 'them', whoever 'they' might be. The 'them' was different in each letter, but clearly Sydney Whitters was not a fan of the different. Be that a physical, national, geographical, or ideological difference, it didn't matter. Then again, she really wasn't expecting him to be open-minded, she simply wished he was less skilled at seeming the calm reasonable voice and was more evident as a raving bigot.

"Did you learn anything?" Jamal asked when Kira put down the last of the letters.

"A little. All their files on various groups and races were taken or destroyed. No way to know which was which." Kira rubbed at an eye. She was going to need reading glasses before long. Or at least magnifiers. "I'm not sure quite the implications on that. Yes, it's good that the Purifiers no longer have it. However, without knowing exactly what the Purifiers knew, who took it, and what they took, I really can't speculate on motives or results. Maybe someone was just trying to prevent another raid or trying to protect themselves. Or maybe this is vengeance for the raid that happened. In either case, this is probably the end of it. Unless the Purifiers figure out who it was and retaliate. Or maybe they want the information for themselves. That could be very bad. Unfortunately, we'll probably have to wait and see." She hadn't even thought to get the address so she could investigate herself. Which might be just as well. The police would be watching now. Liska could manage, but Kira wasn't trained the same way.

"Then why such a hurry?" Shahara asked, putting the papers in stacks according to kind.

"Purifiers keep paper files on their members. Files that include addresses, names, and other identifying information." She didn't have to elaborate, as Jamal winced and Shahara swallowed back nausea. "But it would appear that they weren't interested in that." Which didn't mean they *hadn't* looked at the personnel files, but the likelihood was less.

Finally, she got them out of there and heading home. Todd gave them a ride, but Kira said she'd stay and help *Sensei* sort through things. Todd said he'd be back to give her a ride home. Kira was pretty sure no one was fooled, but no one called him on it, either.

Which mean that she had ten, fifteen minutes at most to fill in *Sensei* and decide what to tell Todd.

***

Todd dropped Shahara off first, then Jamal. "You're not coming up." Jamal didn't even bother making it a question.

"I said I'd give her a ride back."

"Yeah, but that's not why." Jamal sounded calm, but he wasn't completely able to hide the hurt.

"They won't tell me everything either, if that helps."

Jamal shrugged. "A little. But you won't tell us what they told you, will you?"

"Don't know. It depends on what I'm told. They're pretty secretive. It took months for me to learn as much as I have."

"You have to keep their trust. I understand that." Jamal sighed. "Just promise me that if you're in trouble, or they are, you'll remember you can always call on us for help."

"I will."

"Good. Now, go help them find Anna." Jamal stopped. "Sakaki. How different is she from Anna anyway?"

"In all the little things, she's completely different. In the important ways, she's exactly the same."

"And it was Sakaki you were dating? Knowing who she was?"

"Yeah. That was one of the reasons we were having problems. Sakaki has responsibilities and a past that Anna doesn't. But she's amazing. She really is. I hope that someday you'll get to truly meet her." It sounded dumb to say that, but Jamal seemed to understand.

"I look forward to it. So, go find her." Neither of them mentioned that even when, *when, not if,* please *not if,* they found her, she would be different.

Todd drove back and was entirely unsurprised to see that Ryoko-*Sensei* now seemed as wound up as Kira. "So, is anyone going to tell me who or what Nightmare is, or should I try to actually sleep tonight?" He was more likely to drive around at random looking for some clue than sleep, but that sounded pathetic, even knowing they had both done the same thing.

"Sit," *Sensei* said, indicating the sofa. Todd did so, and tried to look quiet and attentive. The older Werefox took a deep breath and began. "Nightmare is... an enigma. About three, three and a half years ago, there was a reporter. He was, I believe your term is, a 'muckraker'. Less concerned with truth than scandal. A poison pen. Unfortunately, while in search of a story, he become perilously close to uncovering our secret. He started looking for more proof. A small team was put on him to lead him astray. As much as possible. We have firm rules in how much we are permitted to interfere with the free press of a sovereign nation."

Todd hadn't known that, but he did appreciate hearing it. Made sense that the Kikitsutai had rules on how much interference they were permitted. He wondered if the rules were self-imposed, part of an agreement with one or more other groups, or imposed by outsiders.

"The team quickly found themselves at a loss. The reporter was much deeper in than we had been informed, had no concern for the consequences of his stories, and was actively enjoying spiting us.

Liska was one of the team, but she wasn't calling herself that yet. She wasn't in charge either. But that's neither here nor there." He shook his head and gathered his thoughts. "The leader of the team, no one you've met, I believe, was asking permission to use more serious measures than they had been authorized for. Sejou was reluctant to agree, as this reporter was too much in the public eye for most of our measures to work well. Too many people knew of him and his personality to hypnotize him, and should he disappear, or even die... well, it would have been a terrible scandal. Possibly validating anything he might have said."

"What happened? What did your team do?"

Sensei folded his hands. "Nothing. While this was being debated, one of his stories sparked a riot. Four people died. Two were children. Trampled. According to the team, the reporter was completely unrepentant that his actions led to that. In fact, Liska claimed he was gleeful to be that influential. She was incensed about it."

She would be. "Then what? Is that when Nightmare showed up?" After all, presumably they would be leading to Nightmare eventually.

"Yes. Though no one knew that at first. As far as we can tell, it started with a black origami horse. One that had 'Nightmare' written on it if unfolded. One showed up in his home mailbox, his work mailbox, and his car glove compartment the same morning. No fingerprints, no clues. Then he started receiving phone calls. The kind with no one on the other line. Our team tried tracing them, but they seemed to be coming from multiple sources. Things started being moved, both in his house and office.

Whoever it was managed to evade both his security systems and our team's surveillance. More and more black origami horses showed up, in places where they shouldn't be. Possibly one or more was doctored with something because he started acting more unstable. His entire bank account was wiped out, donated to children's hospitals and other charities. One day his car was thoroughly and systematically destroyed while inside his building's parking garage. The security cameras had gone on the fritz the day before."

"What about the police? He had to have called them by now." Todd thought he would have called them when the horses first showed up.

"He did. But his proof was missing. The horses he had gathered were gone, the phone records didn't show the phantom calls, even his bank account seemed to be intact. The car was the only thing he could prove. That, I admit, we did have something to do with. The team decided that it would be beneficial to make him seem unstable. That was within their purview. The horses were put in a cupboard in his home. I've seen the video of him opening the door, and them falling on his head." He gave a dark chuckle. "Anyway, the police did take his statement, but with him claiming proof he didn't have, no fingerprints or camera evidence of who damaged his car, and his reputation for trashing the police in his articles, I believe the police decided it was vandalized by someone unhappy with his articles. Person or persons unknown. They didn't put too much effort into it." His smile was small and grim.

Okay, he still didn't get why everyone was bent out of shape yet. "Then what?"

Sensei sobered. "Nightmare either became bored with such childish tactics, or decided they weren't effective enough. The reporter was poisoned, twice, non-fatally. From what we can tell, it was meant to *be* non-fatal. Vandalism continued. He came home from the hospital to find his computer smashed, his plants were exposed to bleach, his fish and cat were gone entirely, we never did find out what happened to them. And there was blood on his bed. A lot of it. The blood turned out to be from one of his editors. Another man we were watching, who belonged to a group much like the Purifiers. Being in the hospital, the reporter was cleared of the murder, but he committed suicide soon after."

"Wow." Todd shook his head. "Was that the end of Nightmare?"

"Not even close," Kira said, speaking for the first time since Todd got back. "He might be the first known causality, but there were others for almost a year. All started with a black origami horse. All had some involvements with Twilights and Nights, many were Twilights or Nights. Not all died, and those that did seem to be mostly accidents or their own hand. We can only find a few instances where Nightmare actually killed someone, and even some of those are disputed. No, Nightmare ruins people. Mind games, exposes their every dirty secret, destroys property, etc. Rarely is there actual physical violence, but when there is, it's often brutal."

Todd frowned. "But you don't know who or even what Nightmare is?"

"Not even if Nightmare is male or female." Kira scowled. "I've heard rumors of both. We're pretty sure Nightmare isn't human, possibly not even a single person. But we don't know why they started or why they stopped. Believe me, we've looked."

"A black origami horse." Todd tilted his head. "That's a pretty easily imitated calling card. Could this be a copycat?"

"Here's hoping." Kira leaned back hard, cushions letting out a puff of air. "Someone did try that once. About three months into Nightmare's run. The real Nightmare took offense. He didn't die, but I'm not sure if that makes him one of the lucky ones or not. Leaning towards not."

Right. Not asking questions about that. "Does this seem like Nightmare's work?"

Kira gave a one-armed shrug. "Without actually seeing the crime scene, or at least the reports, it's hard to tell. More violence than usual, especially for an opening. But it's possible that there was no way to get to the files without killing the guards. I can tell you this much, if this is Nightmare? Things are going to get an awful lot worse. For whoever the target is."

This was certainly cheerful. "Okay, for timeline purposes, Liska was Tisiphone back then?"

"Most of it. I believe she took on the mantle of Tisiphone about three months before Nightmare's first appearance. Nightmare's last known victim was about four months after Sakaki... recovered," *Sensei* said. "We have twenty known, confirmed victims. Rumors of many, many more."

"How did you investigate Nightmare?" Todd asked.

"We started with the team investigating the reporter. Each of them was questioned carefully and repeatedly. After they were cleared, they were assigned to investigate. Then we followed the rumors. But Nightmare was a creature almost completely composed of rumors. Anyone who pales at the thought of an origami horse, and there are many, is afraid because of those rumors." *Sensei* rubbed at his eyes, looking even older than his years.

After a moment, he continued. "Nightmare has become a strange figure to the Twilight and Night communities. He is a protector and destroyer. She is a bogeyman and an avenging angel. We took advantage of it, spreading our own stories. But we *know* almost nothing. Nightmare preyed almost exclusively on those who were a threat to the Twilight and Night communities, even if they were a Twilight or Night themselves. But as far as we can tell, Nightmare was never aligned to any group, following no rules or agenda other than their own."

Which made anyone who wanted or believed they should have control or jurisdiction nervous. No wonder the Kikitsutai were upset. Of course, lone vigilantes were dangerous. "Do you think Nightmare is actually back?" Todd asked.

Sensei kept quiet. Kira took a moment before answering. "Heavens help us if he is."

***

"I'll go through Liska's case files. She was one of the investigators, she's bound to have some information." Kira ran a hand through her hair. "She told me everything at the time, but I don't have her memory."

"She told you everything?" *Sensei* raised an eyebrow. Kira understood his questioning. As close as they were, they still maintained confidentiality on cases. Usually.

"She said she did." Sakaki had been frustrated and needed someone to talk to. She didn't like being unable to figure out puzzles. Not that Kira would have blamed her for keeping information back, but if Sakaki said that she told her everything, that meant she told her everything. It was hard to lie to a Werefox, and it was impossible for either of them to lie to each other, in person, without the other knowing.

Sensei knew that and dropped the subject.

"Anything I can do?" Todd asked.

"Don't mention Nightmare. At all. To anyone. Not unless you're here, and even then, only to the two of us," *Sensei* said.

He smelled of impatience and frustration. "I might, just *might* be able to get the police reports for the break-in."

Kira exchanged glances with her mentor. Those reports would make things much easier, but she wasn't sure Todd could really get them. He might have connections with the police, but that didn't mean that they would actually give him that kind of access. If he tried to get it himself, he'd probably be caught. "How?"

"Ask my uncle."

"What would you tell him when he asked you why you wanted it?" *Sensei* asked. "It wasn't even in newspapers, I checked. He would want to know how you even knew about it."

"That's assuming your uncle is even involved in that case. Does he work homicide?" Kira asked.

"No. Robbery."

"Then he may or may not be involved," Kira said. "It would be helpful if you could do it, but not if you got caught."

"Well, I can keep an eye and ear out anyway. Maybe offer to help my Uncle tomorrow. I do that sometimes."

"After class. You don't want to seem suspicious," *Sensei* said.

Todd nodded, conceding the point.

"Okay, it's a plan. Tomorrow. Tonight, let's get some sleep." Kira stood. Maybe tonight would be better than the last week, or month.

***

Todd awoke to the sound of the phone ringing. Jamal's phone, so he ignored it. Until Jamal answered it and started talking about him. "Yeah, he's here. No. No idea. Yeah, sure."

He rolled over and tried to fall back to sleep. Jamal snatched away his pillow. "That was Shahara. She said that something is really wrong. Get Kira and meet her at the prayer chapel."

"What time is it?" Todd groaned.

"Before seven. But she says it's important."

"Right. Okay." It *better* be important. Waking Werefoxes was risky. Good thing he had *finally* gotten the phone number to Anna's room, and Kira couldn't strangle him through the phone lines. Though it sounded like she wanted to try when he called. Still, hearing it was important, Kira reluctantly agreed to meet them on the second floor of the central building. Todd might have showed Sakaki the prayer chapel, but he hadn't showed it to Kira.

Todd and Jamal got to the central building first, but Kira was coming up the stairs less than a minute later. Shahara was waiting for them in the prayer chapel.

She stopped pacing mid-step and promptly glared at Todd, and then Kira. Mostly Kira. "You *swore* you were just going to talk to him!"

Kira blinked at her. "Who? Whitters? I haven't found him yet."

"Oh yeah? Explain this." Shahara thrust a computer print-out in Kira's face. Kira caught it and forced the paper back so she could actually read it. It didn't take five seconds for her to start growling.

Todd didn't dare take the paper from her, but he did move so he could read over her shoulder.

The print out was from the website of the local paper. Headline read **Man Found Dead in Blaze**.

Chapter Twenty

No information is ever useless. – The Kikitsutai Book of Wisdom

Kira didn't even have to read the article to know what it said, but she did anyway. Sydney Whitters, 54, pillar of the community, was found dead in a house fire. Police would not yet comment on the cause of death or the nature of the fire. It happened about one o'clock last night. The paper must have called in people early to have the story ready by now.

The address made her scowl. The man lived less than two miles from the school. Heck, she had been through his neighborhood at least twice, searching for clues. And someone else had gotten to him first. "Of all the shortsighted..." Anything else she was going to say came out in a growl.

She moved to the side, closed her eyes and concentrated on her breathing. She could not afford to change now. The quarters were too small and none of the others knew how to deal with a transformed Were.

Once Kira was certain she was in control, she turned her attention back to the others. Shahara clearly believed she had killed Whitters, and it would appear Jamal had reached the same conclusion. Todd was upset, but Kira didn't think he believed she had done this.

"I was forced to give one of the vampires Whitters name in exchange for information about the break-in. I attempted to make them swear non-interference until I was finished, but no promise was given." Kira grimaced. They had moved fast, she'd grant them that.

Anger warred with doubt in Shahara's scent. "I'm supposed to believe that?"

"She did. I was there," Todd spoke up. "And unless she continued investigating while on campus, we still didn't know his address last night."

Kira nodded. But it wasn't quite enough for the Jamaican girl. "Do you know what the most binding vow we use in my clan is?" Shahara shook her head. "We swear upon our honor. I swear, upon my honor, that I did not kill that man. This is the first I knew of it."

Shahara deflated like a balloon. "An– Sakaki swore something on her honor once."

That wasn't as surprising as Kira thought it should be. "Sakaki likes you. She trusts you. Maybe she had to lie to you, but I have absolutely no doubt she considered you a friend. Whatever she swore, and I won't ask, she meant it."

"Um, not to break up the sentimental party here, but are we saying that vampires murdered Whitters?" Jamal asked.

"Looks like. I'll have to talk to Rex Magnus tonight." Had he thought to question Whitters first? If he had, what had he found out?

"Won't that be a problem with the police?" Jamal asked. "I mean, forensics are getting better every day, and I thought the whole problem was keeping people from finding out about you."

"That's why the fire. Destroy or damage as much evidence as possible. Besides, I doubt a vampire actually set the fire. They have an instinctive fear of fire and are a little more flammable than humans. Getting a shade to cause the fire, on the other hand... Shades work for vampires as servants, can be invisible and do not leave fingerprints or DNA. There are few ways to detect where a shade has been, and none of them are in common use by police departments."

"Besides, forensics *are* getting better, but it still isn't like in movies or TV shows. And according to my uncle, there are still more cold cases than anyone wants to admit to," Todd added.

"That's one of the reasons why the Vampire Council prevents the rogue killing of humans. Both because humans currently can't detect most vampire methods, and because, eventually, they probably will be able to." Kira massaged her forehead.

Of course, that didn't mean the Vampire Council didn't occasionally sanction the killing of certain humans, like they certainly would have in this case. But they were usually more discreet, and it took much longer to get approval. No, this had skated the rules. Which was difficult, bordering on impossible for vampires, as every vampire had a deep instinctual loyalty to the one who turned them, and each one of them had sworn loyalty to the council and their rules. Moon's light, this was a tangled mess!

Kira took a deep breath and let it out. "Did anyone tell anyone else anything that we learned last night?" She got headshakes and quiet 'no's. None were lying. Not that she really suspected them, but she needed to be able to honestly say that they weren't involved. "And you know I didn't do this?" That wasn't as important, but it would make interaction easier and less strained. Luckily, they all agreed to that quickly. It helped that they wanted to believe. But in this case, it was true.

"I'll talk to Rex Magnus tonight. Todd, be sure to check your email box we set up for the game. There may be an announcement or something about his death. Shahara, Jamal, you do not know this man. You have never heard of him. You have no more than standard concern or curiosity over his death. I'll look up everything I can find and let you know what I can." Kira sighed. "Todd, your suggestion about offering to help your uncle seems even better than it did yesterday. Don't be too curious, but if you happen to overhear something, or the conversation goes in that direction..." Todd nodded.

It would be a long time until dark.

***

Kira had been a bit worried about finding Rex Magnus. Liska hadn't tried to locate where the blood had moved to, lest Rex use that to claim she was up to something. Kira wasn't even sure where to start. As it was, she didn't have to worry. About that.

As soon as she left campus, a dark car stopped in front of her. A large vampire climbed out and held the door open for her to enter. Goody. What would Liska do? Probably something dumb like climb in the car.

Kira eyed the vampire, tempted to ask if her safety was guaranteed. But that would be stupid. Of course it wasn't. Well, it wasn't like she had a better idea. *Remember, be Liska.* She climbed in the car.

She had never actually met Rex Magnus, but she had drawn him once, based on Sakaki's description. So she knew the vampire in front of her wasn't Rex Magnus. Oh, there were some similarities, but it wasn't him. Yet he wore the rings Liska described. Costume jewelry that smelled of brass and steel. Probably supposed to be silver and gold. What was going on?

The car started moving. Kira stayed silent, reinforcing her mask. She was Liska. Which, in a way, was true. 'Liska' was a working name, and she was currently doing Sakaki's job. That made her Liska. Wouldn't be the first or last time a working name was shared.

"No greetings, Liska?" The vampire asked. "Quite rude."

"So is imitating the chief."

He sneered, but his scent was somewhere between annoyed and pleased. A test. So far, she was passing. "I am the chief."

"No, you are a pup, pretending to be a wolf. Where is Rex Magnus?"

"I am Rex Magnus." A lie. Well, at least there wasn't a shake-up in leadership that she hadn't known about. But she had made him angry. She had to be careful.

Kira scoffed. "I will not deal with underlings and jumping through hoops. You can take me to your chief, or we can take a scenic drive through Palm Beach in silence. Your choice." They had crossed the bridge, taking them from West Palm Beach into Palm Beach. But apparently, she wasn't supposed to have figured that out.

The car came to the stop not far from the waterfront. When the door was opened, Kira saw a massive boathouse. Interesting. Most vampires didn't like water. There were exceptions to the rule, but they were almost exclusively vampires who had been humans once. Natural vampires, ones who had been wraiths, all seemed to avoid large bodies of water.

She could ponder later, now she had to follow the large armed guards into the boathouse. When did vampire guards start carrying guns anyway? There was silver somewhere. She could smell it, even if she couldn't see it. Hopefully they didn't have silver bullets. Kira had been grazed by one of those once. It had been agony. She still had a scar on her right forearm from it.

The ground wasn't stable enough to build a basement, but the building had been set up so there were windowless interior rooms. The guards passed her off to another pair, and they led her through a series of rooms. Kira scanned the face of every vampire they passed, subtly trying to maintain a count. There were definitely more than she could see, but she ignored that. A few seemed vaguely familiar, probably from Clematis. The guards handed her off to a third pair, but one of them was Rex Magnus.

Kira gave him a half bow. "Good hunting to you, Great Chief." Postures changed. Apparently seeing if she could recognize him was part of that test. But why test her? Unless... Rex was talking, she had to pay attention.

"So, you have the gall. The gall and nerve to pretend nothing is wrong?"

What was he talking about? What did he know? "And what do you say is wrong?"

Rex moved towards the side, picked up a newspaper and flung it at her face. Kira caught it one-handed and spared it the quickest glance to confirm her suspicions. It was the delayed edition of the paper that had managed to include an article about the fire. "Yes, I wanted to ask you about that. I said I needed to question him first."

"And your questioning required killing him? You promised him to us!" Rex was furious. He hadn't killed Whitters.

"I had every intention of following through. But I hadn't found him yet. So, if I didn't kill him, and you didn't kill him... Who did?"

Rex glowered at her, the confusion in his scent not touching his face or tones. "You cannot lie to me. You killed him to protect your own secrets."

"I swear upon my honor that I did not kill that man. I further swear that I questioned mine, and they did not kill him. Did you question yours?"

"Do you think me born yesterday? Of course I did."

Kira snarled. "The break-in. It was a feint. They destroyed the being files so no one knew they went through personnel files."

"I don't believe you." Despite his words, Rex was at least half-way convinced.

"It's the only explanation. I only found out about Whitters last night, and I didn't know his address until I read the article this morning. I told you about Whitters last night, had you found his address?"

"No." Rex cursed creatively. "Are you saying Nightmare killed Whitters?"

"We don't have any proof that Nightmare is really back yet. But if so, Nightmare always targeted threats to the Twilight and Night community. Whitters was a clear and present threat." She waited a few minutes to let Rex digest that. "Now, why the test?"

Rex eyed her speculatively. "You're slipping, Liska. Some think that you aren't capable of handling this. Some think that maybe you aren't Liska at all."

"Who?" How was she failing now? Or did someone know something?

"You want to know? Find out who killed Whitters." Rex nodded to the guards, who took that as their hint to hustle her from the room. Fighting would only give them an excuse to kill her, so she went quietly.

***

"I'm beginning to think most problems in life are caused, or at least exacerbated by people refusing to communicate." Todd sighed after Kira filled him and *Sensei* in on her meeting with the vampires. "If you and this Rex guy told each other everything you both knew, we might be much closer to solving things. But neither of you are willing to give up your puzzle pieces, so you can't get the full picture."

Kira tried to glare at him, but was too tired to do it right. "While you undoubtedly have a point, there are *reasons* why we don't share our 'puzzle pieces'."

"He knew you weren't Sakaki. Or at least, believed someone who suspect you weren't. Why? I don't think it's because you made a mistake," Todd said.

"Jamal and Shahara saw through me."

"They interacted with you on a daily basis for a month. Even still, Shahara confessed that she wasn't sure until she saw your wrists."

Kira closed her eyes. She did not want to remember that day. The scariest moment of her life was chasing the smell of blood only to find her cousin half-unconscious in a pool of blood, silver knife next to her. Sakaki, barely lucid, had smiled at her and said, "Tisiphone is dead. I killed her." Kira still had occasional nightmares about it.

"Well, thanks for the reassurance, but vampires have ways to observe that your friends don't."

"Or, someone knows something," Todd said.

"Both are possible," *Sensei* cut in. "But right now, we have other concerns. Do you believe you satisfied the vampires that you are Liska, at least for the moment?"

"I think so."

"Good. Todd, what did you learn at the police station?"

"Not a whole lot. My uncle wasn't on either of the cases that we're interested in. Apparently Whitters name isn't anywhere on the lease of the building, because they don't know the two are connected. I did hear a little about Whitters. It's definitely murder. He was dead before the fire killed him, but not before it started. There was smoke in the lungs, but not enough to have killed him. But the body was burned badly enough that it's going to take time to gather the evidence. Right now, they're only eighty percent sure the body *is* Whitters. Not that they suspect anything else, but it will take time to run the DNA test. A lot of the evidence was damaged or destroyed." Todd paused. "We *do* think it was Whitters, right?"

"Honestly, it probably was. But that is an interesting theory. If there is any reason to doubt, we'll look into it." Kira twisted her head in a loose circle to get the kinks out of her neck. "Any word about a black origami horse?"

"I didn't hear anything. But one, they didn't tell me much directly, it was mostly what I overheard. Two, paper would have burnt up quickly in a fire that big. It's a good thing Whitters had a detached house or the fire might have burned two or three others before it went out."

"Or, it might not have been as big." *Sensei* stroked his beard. "If whoever killed Whitters was concerned about collateral damage, they might have been a little more restrained in their actions."

"People after revenge generally don't care much about collateral damage," Todd said. "At least, not according to movies and my psychology books."

"It's true. Revenge tends to be all-consuming. I've seen it before," Kira said. "Of course, that assumes that the motive was revenge. Probably was, but we don't know for sure. You have a profile?"

Todd leaned back on the couch. "Arson, in and of itself, is almost exclusively carried out by men, generally men in their late teens to early thirties. But this was in conjunction with murder, to destroy evidence, which opens up the field. I need to know the details of the murder before I can come up with a true profile. He's daring. Whitters was killed by something other than fire, but the fire started before he died. Meaning the killer either risked Whitters surviving or stayed in a burning building to make sure Whitters died. If this was because of all-consuming revenge, probably the second. Considering the size and nature of the blaze, he could have ended up trapped. Making sure Whitters died would have been more important than being sure to get out safely."

"Sounds like a shade," Kira said. "They have no sense of self-preservation if it conflicts with following an order. And little sense of it at other times. I'm not sure if fire can kill a shade or not. If it is a shade, then the vampires are almost certainly behind it."

"Or, as has been pointed out, it could be someone so focused on revenge that they don't care about their own life," *Sensei* said.

"Or someone careful enough to make sure they had a way out," Todd sighed. Then he sat up. "Oh, there was one thing. It may be nothing, or maybe not. There was sand in the carpet."

"Sand. In Florida. About ten minutes from the beach." Kira felt a little bad for her tone when Todd wilted. "You're right. It could be a clue. Or it could mean he went to the beach in the last week. Was it beach sand?"

"Don't know. It's low priority evidence. I only know because I saw a picture of the scene. They didn't think it was important either."

"If it turns out not to be beach sand, or sand from a beach that isn't local; then it's probably important. If it's ordinary sand from the ocean, then we've got nothing. *I* tracked in sand tonight just from visiting the vampire's boat house." Kira blinked. "That's two possible strikes. Sand and shades."

"But you said Rex claimed to have questioned his blood. They can't go against orders," *Sensei* said.

"No, they can't. I don't think they can lie to him either. He wasn't lying to me. And a wanderer wouldn't have access to that information." Privately, Kira was praying she didn't have to try to convince Rex he had been betrayed by one of his blood. That would get ugly fast.

If only she could actually see the crime scene for herself. There was no point, of course. Between the smell of smoke and fire, and the multitude of people who had already tromped through the ruins, any scent of use would be covered up. Besides, she had never gotten Whitters's scent for herself, so she couldn't even try to use that to double check the identity of the body. Besides, the place was probably still being watched. Maybe Liska could have pulled it off, but Kira would rather not try. Not even in fox form.

Kira's phone gave a robin's chirp. Ryo's text alert. Tora's was a cardinal, and Sakaki's was a crow. Kira unlocked her phone. **Got your info. Better check it. Looks important.**

Checking now. Thanks. "Ryo sent some info. Probably too late now, but he said it looks important. May I borrow your computer?" She was standing even before *Sensei* was nodding.

Ryo had sent her an encrypted email that took two passwords to open. Maybe there was something there after all. After reading, Kira had to swallow twice. "Someone declared war on the Purifiers"

It was a list. A list of events that affected Purifiers, starting with Calloway's death. Their site had been hacked twice in the past month. Three different prominent members started receiving death threats and were flagged as potential domestic terrorists in federal watch lists. The New York group, the literature dispersing arm, was being threatened with auditing from the IRS. The Washington group, which specialized in their technology, had been flooded. Their servers and databases were destroyed beyond repair.

Most interesting was the Florida branch. The local headquarters in Daytona was being foreclosed due to some problem with taxes. They claimed they paid, the government claimed they hadn't. Their website was spoofed, stealing credit card information and member's identities. Considering what it took to even get to the website, it had to be a member.

Five of their members were arrested for unrelated reasons. The Miami headquarters ended up being raided after there were reports of drug manufacturing. Apparently, they had wriggled out of any charges relating to that, but they had to abandon the building, and were again considered potential domestic terrorists. The break-in she had heard about was either the third or fourth break-in of properties connected to Purifiers within the past couple weeks. Different cities, but all in Florida. It was the first where someone died.

Whitters, whose address Ryo did give her, with some apologies about the delay, was not just the founder of their LARP; he was the financial officer of the entire Purifiers organization, and second to the head of the state branch. He was also the only one authorized to keep money files for all Purifiers branches country wide. Which effectively made him even more important than the Florida head, a woman in Tallahassee.

"So the fire wasn't just to cover up the evidence of his murder, it was to hide what files were taken!" Kira cursed herself at being beaten to the punch again.

"But why?" Todd asked. Oh, yeah, he wasn't trained in this.

"Because an organization, any organization, lives and dies by information." Which was why the Kikitsutai made it a point to collect all information they could. "Financial information is especially important, because so much can be found by tracing money trails. Which groups have more money than others tells you who has more members and how generous those members are. He might even have had access to the list of members, since he had to keep track of who was up on their dues."

"You mean, whoever killed him may have a list of every Purifier in the country?" Todd paled.

"Potentially. I must argue your statement, Kira. This is not war. This will be a slaughter." *Sensei* looked like he was carved from stone.

Chapter Twenty-One

Never let your enemy set the terms of engagement. – The Kikitsutai Book of Wisdom

"Um, okay. I know they're like the bad guys and all, but we can't just let that happen? Can we?" Todd asked. Inwardly though, he was a little afraid of the answer.

"No, we can't." *Sensei* nodded approvingly at him. "We hold life sacred. Even the life of our enemies. We do not kill without reason, nor do we allow others to do so."

Todd let out a breath he didn't realize he was holding. "Good. That's... good."

"Besides, a group killing off Purifiers isn't good for us, either. It gets noticed, and not in good ways." Kira didn't look away from the screen.

"Now you sound like Sakaki." *Sensei* smiled sadly. "But first, we must find who is behind this."

"Too big to be one person," Todd said immediately. "There's too much happening too far apart. Also, it seems to be different M.O.'s. You've got hackers, you've got thieves, and you've got thugs. In rough terms."

"True, but at least for the moment, Florida seems to be the epicenter. There's more." Kira pointed to a note at the bottom of the list. **There were other incidents going back at least six months, but nothing as big as this. Working on compiling a list. R.**

"Think that's a clue?" Todd pointed to a line near the beginning of the email. The first hack of the website had been a Trojan Horse that dragged the visitor through a series of websites. Ryo had considerately listed a description of the sites. At first glance, the websites appeared to be relatively random. There was an article on cake decorating, a video file on a surgery done on an eye, two hardcore pornography sites, one on urban legends, one on ghost stories, one screamer video, and a tutorial on how to make origami animals. Knowing what he knew now of Nightmare, the last several sites seemed to be significant. Could be a coincidence, but he wasn't betting on it.

"It's possible. Definitely possible. This is very bad." Kira rubbed a hand across her face. "How did we miss this?"

"Probably it wasn't missed, but none of us were on list of people who needed to know," *Sensei* said. "Or the information was gathered by different people, and it wasn't until one concentrated on looking at Purifiers that all the information was in one place."

"Communication." Todd groaned.

"Indeed." *Sensei* moved away from the computer. "I will make some tea. We will need it."

***

"Hey, everything alright?" Jamal asked when Todd finally got back to his dorm room.

"Not really." Todd sighed and tried to figure out what he could actually say to Jamal. For one, campus dorm rooms weren't the most secure. Two, he wasn't sure how much he was allowed to say.

"Anything you can tell me?"

"You knew that Kira was going to talk to someone about..." Todd just looked to where the day's newspaper was. Jamal nodded, looking grim. "He thought it was her, said it wasn't him, or anyone under him. Kira knows he wasn't lying and says that the people under him can't lie to him."

"Then who did?"

Todd shrugged. "They're making her find out. She's... frustrated about it."

"Is that going to make it harder to find Sakaki?"

"No idea. But apparently this guy was a lot more important than we anticipated. And he had access to information that was even more important."

"Any suspects?"

"Sort of, but I can't say anything about it."

Jamal raised an eyebrow. "Oh?"

"Really. I can't. You know how sometimes when I hang out at the police station, I end up hearing something that I'm not allowed to talk about to anyone outside? Think of it like that. They definitely wouldn't have told me if I hadn't been around when they found out."

A piece of paper couldn't have slipped between Jamal's lips as he slowly nodded. "Alright, I understand. And I certainly don't want to put you in danger. But please, be careful about how deep you go down that road."

"I will."

They stood awkwardly for a moment before Jamal changed the subject. "So, Werefoxes. Can they go to regular hospitals?"

Figures a pre-med student would think of that. "Not really. But apparently, they set up clinics for those who can't go to normal hospitals. I haven't been there, of course, but the girls tell me there is one in the city."

"What kinds of differences are there? Physically, I mean."

Todd smiled. It was nice being the informed one for a change. "Well, I don't know everything. But I do know…"

***

The break-in happened Sunday into Monday. Whitters was killed Monday into Tuesday. Nothing happened Wednesday. Thursday, Kira woke up to find a note had been slipped under her door overnight. The vixen glared at the innocuous looking piece of paper. Sakaki had dealt with notes last semester, but there hadn't been any this semester. Since Atolatar had been behind the notes in the first place, and he was dead, Kira wasn't sure where this one was coming from.

Of course, they knew that Atolatar had a follower in Florida, who was probably the one manipulating him. It was possible that he was sending this one. But he had been keeping a low profile. Why start taunting her now?

Most annoyingly, it had come while she was asleep in the same room. Somehow, she had slept through the note being snuck under her door. All of Sakaki's notes had arrived while she was out of the room, but there was no way she would have slept through a delivery like that. If only Kira had been awake, or had woken up, then she might have seen who delivered it.

Kira tested the paper for traces of chemicals. Nothing unusual other than the fact that the paper had been dabbed with cheap cologne. No powder, no fingerprints. The ink tested normal. The paper smelled like ink, and cologne. Probably a cheap way to cover any scents. That hadn't happened before. Perhaps a different delivery method? Or different messenger?

Most important was the message. There was an address, and below that: **Ten o'clock, Friday night. Nightmare will be there.**

***

"It's a trap," *Sensei* said, squinting at the paper. He had taken the news that Kira was skipping classes pretty well when she started waving around the slip.

"Yes, I know that. But that means that *someone* will be there. Someone who knows something," Kira argued, leaning back in the dining room chair.

"Or they're trying to keep you busy while they do something elsewhere." The older Werefox went back to examining the map. "Or worse."

"Are you saying I shouldn't go?" Kira planned to be there no matter what, so she really hoped he wouldn't order her not to go. She wasn't sure she could obey in this instance.

"You will go no matter what I say. But promise me you will be careful."

"Of course I will, *Sensei*. You know that."

"And that you'll have backup."

Kira winced. "That... would be more difficult." Her great-uncle was in his seventies and twelve years retired. Todd wasn't even half-trained, and she was trying to keep him out of danger. Jamal and Shahara weren't even in the running. She couldn't think of another member of the skulk with the right skills nearby, and getting someone to come in, on this short notice, without questions being asked, was near impossible.

"Is there another active member of the family within fifty miles? Or even a hundred?" Kira asked.

Ryoko-*Sensei* took a few minutes to think. "Not that I have been informed."

"Will you be coming?"

Another pause. "I will come, but I will only be auxiliary help. I am well aware that I am not young enough or fast enough for the type of fight this may come to. But I may still be able to help."

It was something.

"I also believe that Todd can be a useful help."

Another wince. "Respectfully, *Sensei*, I'm not sure that's a good idea."

"Why's that?" Todd asked, coming in from the kitchen. Kira blinked at him twice. He was here? "I showed up twenty minutes before you did. I knew something was up and felt I had to be here."

Kira turned to look at her great-uncle. "You didn't give me a chance to talk. Just came in waving this paper. I figured you needed the lesson in situational awareness. At least this time, it was an unexpected ally. You should have smelled or heard him from the beginning or at least checked the house."

She should have. True, both of them had been around so much that the house had a faint air of each of their scents all the time, but that wasn't an excuse. She definitely should have heard his breathing. "Yes, *Sensei*. I shall strive to do better."

"So, why are we walking into a trap, and why can't I come?" Todd asked, coming over to look at the note.

"Um, how about, because it's a *trap*! That's why you can't come." Kira was not bending on this.

"Maybe. Probably even. But it is vaguely possible that someone learned something and this was the only way it could be passed on." Todd frowned at the map. "I think I know this area."

Kira ignored the last line. "I'm going with the assumption that it's a trap until proven otherwise. And you still aren't coming."

"Yeah, that works really well." Todd didn't back down from her glare. "Look, one way or another, I'm going to be there. I can go with you, I can go on my own, or something may drag me into it. But I'm going. I can feel it."

"*Pre-cogs*," Kira muttered venomously. "Fine. But you do what I say, when I say it. Or what *Sensei* says."

"Fair enough. So, are we going to check out this place? Do a little recon?" Todd asked.

"You're driving." Kira pushed off the table to stand. "Are you coming, *Sensei*?"

"Wouldn't dream of missing it."

Todd drove them to the industrial center of town. "Okay, looks like it's this." He pointed to a small, squat building. The kind that rented out rooms as offices. Four were in use, and there was a 'For Lease' sign.

This could complicate things a little. "Write down the names and what they are for. Stay in the car." Kira climbed out. *Sensei* followed her. "In or out?"

"Out." He moved to a blind corner. A moment later, a fox carefully explored the surrounding area.

Kira tried the door, taking a look at what the businesses were. A lawyer, a real estate agent, a massage therapist, and a nutritionist. Odd combination. It made it very hard to come up with a story about what she wanted.

The door was unlocked, so she went in. The front hall was too bright, and there was a postage stamp of a waiting room. Two chairs and a bathroom. Once again, there was a list of who was renting office space, with a number for what office they had. No receptionist or even a desk for one, and no one was waiting. Kira passed it by, and the door to the lawyer. The hallway split there, left or right. She turned the corner to the left. This led to two other rooms. One had no markings, the other was owned by the massage therapist. Her door was open a crack, and Kira caught a glimpse of a woman reading a magazine.

Silently backtracking, Kira took the other corner to the right. The real estate agent and the nutritionist. The nutritionist, a solid looking woman in her mid-fifties, had her door wide open and gave Kira a big smile. Kira gave her a small smile in return and kept walking. One more corner led to another office. Again unmarked. The door was locked. She hadn't brought her tools, but she could probably pick the lock anyway. But that would take too long, making the nutritionist suspicious.

Kira listened at the door, but there were no sounds. A sniff at the door didn't suggest anyone had been here in weeks. In fact, all she smelled was mold, mildew, and dirt. Someone was coming.

She was absolutely unsurprised to see the nutritionist coming her way. "Are you lost, Dearie?"

British, Northern British from the sounds of it. Sakaki was good enough to pull off being British even to another Brit, but Kira didn't think she was as good. But she couldn't pull off an American accent for long.

"No, I just wanted to see the office space for lease. Do you know anything about that?" Kira asked with her best French accent.

"Oh, yes. You would think Mr. Jackson would be involved in that; he's the real estate agent, you know. But no, he just does houses. Though, between you, me, and the wall, I don't know how he stays in business. I don't think he's sold a house in months. But that's neither here nor there. I'm sure he does his best, bless his heart. But you don't care about that. You want to contact Ace Realty, if you want to lease here. It's not such a bad place, really. The offices are a little small, and that one is a little dank. I think there was some flooding a while back. And you have to be out of here by eight o'clock at night. They are very strict about that. Doesn't seem right to me, but what's it my business?"

Kira put the flood of words aside to decipher later. "How long have you been here? Have you been here the longest?"

"Me? Bless me, no. I've only been here four months or so. Or was it five? No, it was four, because that's when my sister needed knee surgery. She never did listen to me about her diet. I'll bet she wishes she did now. No, longest would probably be Mr. Jackson, I think. Maybe that's why he's still here. Signed a good contract or something. Anyway, he could probably tell you more, if you wanted to rent out the space. What would you need it for? You seem so young to own a business."

"Oh, I'm in web design." It was the first thing she could think of, and it seemed to be a mostly youth oriented business. As long as no one questioned her on it, because Kira's skill with websites was limited to browsing and web searches.

"Are you really? How clever. I've been meaning to redesign my website for ages. I really don't know much about it. RAM and ROM and Search Analytics, it might as well be a different language for me. Never did have much skill in languages. Do you have any business cards on you?"

"No." Kira gave her a sheepish smile. "I keep meaning to get them made, but I haven't gotten around to it. Besides, if I make them before I have an address to put on them..."

The nutritionist gave her a sympathetic look. "Then you'd just have to make more. I understand, ducks. Well thought out of you. Well, if you do move in here, then I'll see you then."

"I don't know, you said it flooded. That's bad for computers, and if it happens again, I could lose a lot. What about the other office, did that one flood too?"

The older woman stopped to think about it. "The other office? Oh, that one. You know, I think that one's owned. Something about storage. I don't know much about it myself. I don't see the need to poke my nose into other people's business."

Potential. Definite potential. "Well, thank you for your help. Ace Realty?"

"Yes, I worked with a woman named Vivian. Lovely woman. So helpful. You'll like her."

Sensei was going to think she got herself kidnapped or something. "I will definitely keep that in mind. Oh, you don't have blue prints for the building, do you?"

"Me? No. But I think they might on the Ace Realty site. Websites are wonderful that way, aren't they? All you have to do is put in the address and the code on the lease sign."

"Excellent. Thank you. I've got to go."

It still took three tries, but she managed to leave without seeming rude. There wasn't enough time to check out the storage office though. She had been inside for almost twenty minutes.

Kira was unsurprised to spot a familiar fox loitering about the door. She didn't make eye contact but walked to the car. She was inside about the same time that *Sensei*, back in human form, came around the corner.

Todd started the car as soon as they were both in. "Anything useful? Should I drive around the block?"

"Sure, can't hurt." Kira waited until they started moving before giving her report. "I didn't detect any traps yet. Six offices. Four in use. One's a 'storage' spot. One's up for lease. The nutritionist's a gossip, may or not be a sentry. The real estate agent seems to have been here the longest and apparently hasn't sold a house in months. This is according to the nutritionist, at least. Everyone has to clear out by eight every night. Should be able to find blueprints online. *Sensei*?"

"Not much outside. Someone who works there smokes. A lot. They have moles; there are small tunnels in various places. There are a few regular scents, but without smelling the renters, I can't tell who belongs there, and who has simply been there a lot."

The drive around the block didn't reveal anything interesting. A few other buildings; three were also buildings to rent offices, and a convenience store on the far corner. All the buildings looked weathered and worn. Like no one cared about their maintenance. It was early afternoon, so there was no way of knowing how effective or bright the streetlamps were. Maybe a night trip.

On the plus side, there were few reasons for people to be around here at night. "How did you know this place? It's not very... traveled."

"Volunteer clean-up day. We picked up trash, painted over graffiti, and repaired windows." Todd made a left turn and headed back to *Sensei*'s. "You can't even tell we were here. It was only a few months ago."

"Happens. But that means it should be easier to break-in."

***

Things would have gone smoother if Jamal and Shahara hadn't decided that afternoon was a good time to come by and ask more questions about Weres, and Twilights and Nights in general. Even then, it might not have been a big problem if they hadn't come while the dining room had been converted into a center of operations. There was a large-scale printout of the blueprints on the table, with a large map of the area, complete with notations, pinned to the wall. A picture and bio of every person who rented an office were spread on a side table, and there was a flurry of papers containing notes and plans and snippets of plans.

Even with all that, things might have been alright if the Werefoxes hadn't sent Todd out to stall them. His paltry attempts to waylay them lasted about two point three seconds before Shahara was moving him out of the way to see what they were trying to hide.

Jamal and Shahara stared slack-jawed at their center of operations. "It looks like we walked into a heist film," Shahara said, picking up a satellite picture of the building.

"That's... not entirely inaccurate. Except I don't think we're stealing anything." Todd turned to Kira. "Are we stealing anything?"

Kira shrugged. "Not currently in the plans, but right now, we should keep our options open."

"Okay, what are we doing?" Jamal asked, reading the bios.

"*We* are doing nothing. *You* are going to go home." Kira nudged Shahara towards the door. Considering Shahara was six inches taller than her and at least twenty pounds heavier, and Kira was trying not to hurt her, she was doing a pretty good job.

"Yeah, I don't think so." Jamal took a seat. "Is this about Sakaki?"

Shahara grabbed the corner of Jamal's seat, giving her enough leverage to push back against Kira's 'gentle' nudging. "Come on, we want to help."

"I don't think you can." Todd was well aware this made him a hypocrite, but he was finally understanding why the Werefoxes kept trying to push him to the side. He certainly didn't want Jamal and Shahara anywhere near this Nightmare person, or whatever trap they were investigating. "It's... complicated."

Shahara picked up a piece of paper. Too late, Todd recognized it as the one that started this whole mess. "Who's Nightmare?"

"No one. Do not ever mention that name again. You never heard it." Kira snatched the paper away. "Do not test me on this. It's for your own safety."

Jamal looked around the room at their plans, then looked at Todd. "Let me get this straight. You are going to some place in what appears to be the bad part of West Palm, because you've been told someone will be there? Someone, who is apparently so dangerous, we can't even mention their name?"

"Well, I'm not sure they're going to let me out of the car. But yeah, essentially," Todd admitted. "Probably best you leave now, actually."

"Is this about Sakaki?" Shahara asked. "You didn't answer."

"Only indirectly. If that much." Kira moved to the door and was rather pointedly holding it open. She was equally pointedly ignored.

"Then how?" Jamal asked.

For a moment, no one answered him. Todd finally spoke up. "This may be the person who murdered Whitters."

The siblings exchanged a glance. "We're not leaving until you tell us how we can help." Shahara's fists were at her hips as she set herself up as an immovable object.

This time it was the Werefoxes who exchanged a look. "Fine. Come back tomorrow at seven o'clock. Bring a first aid kit," Kira said. "But for now, you have to go."

"Seven o'clock. You swear you'll be here?" Shahara asked.

"I swear, on my honor, that I will be here if it is in my power to be," Kira said solemnly.

Sensei gave her an odd look, but Kira said nothing until the siblings actually left. "I know those aren't vows to throw around lightly, but she would not have been satisfied without it."

"I didn't ruin things, did I? Telling them about Whitters?" Todd asked.

"I would have preferred not to have them know, but it's no use worrying now. Perhaps it was even for the best. But give them nothing further," *Sensei* said. "Why did you have them come back tomorrow?"

"Yes. Stupid question, maybe; but they aren't coming, are they?"

"No. But I think we can have them act as home support. Someone has to." Kira picked up a marker. *Sensei* nodded, apparently knowing what she meant. Todd decided not to ask. He's find out. "I'll cross-reference former Ace Realty customers with lists of known Purifiers. Todd, you finish the searches on current office holders. *Sensei*, if you would please continue marking the blueprints..."

***

Jamal and Shahara arrived about twenty minutes early. Todd was glad to see them. He had been there since five and was going quietly stir-crazy. Well, he thought it was quiet. Kira kept shooting him annoyed looks. And occasionally throwing things at him.

Ryoko-*Sensei* was already in place by then, but neither sibling seemed to notice his absence. They did notice that the dining room was clean enough to serve company in. "What happened to all your papers and pictures and stuff?" Shahara asked.

"They got put away. We don't need them out, and you don't need to go through them." Kira led them into the living room. "You can read any book you find in this room, watch TV, we don't care. But stay here. You're manning the base tonight. If something happens and we get separated, we can't risk calling each other, that could put whoever we are calling in danger. Instead, we'll call you. I can call you and tell you where I am and my situation, and you can pass it on to the next person who calls. Jamal, you're our first responder if someone gets hurt. Yes, I know. You don't know how to help an injured Werefox," She spoke over his objections. "Don't worry. We do."

Jamal, a little ashy, nodded. "Hope we don't need it."

"Same here. But better be prepared. Shahara, take this." Kira handed her a sealed envelope. "*Do not open it*! Only, and I do mean, **only** if we are not back and haven't contacted you by one in the morning, are you to open that envelope. There is a phone number and a code phrase. If you haven't heard anything from us by one, call that number, give that phrase, then hang up. After that, pack up what's yours, lock the door, and walk away. You never heard of Werefoxes. Vampires are fictional. You don't know where Todd is or Anna. If we can get in touch with you later, we will. But if not, you know *nothing*. And you will never come back here. Promise me you'll go along with this."

They both promised gravely. Kira nodded, and a small amount of tension went out of her shoulders. "Good. Thank you." She turned to Todd. "Let's go."

"Wait!" Shahara swallowed hard as everyone turned to look at her. "Can we pray for you before you go?"

Kira looked mildly gob-smacked for a moment "Um, okay?"

Todd came over, and put his arm around Kira's shoulders, making sure not to touch her neck. "I think that's a good idea."

Shahara grabbed Jamal's and Todd's hands, leading everyone to take hands. "Lord, I don't know what they're doing tonight, and I don't need to know. You do know, however. They believe it is necessary, and You know if that's true. Please keep them safe and keep their ways right. Please give them wisdom to know the right thing to do and help them not to fear. And once again, I ask that they find Sakaki soon, and that she is safe. Nevertheless, Your will, not ours be done. I pray these things in Jesus' name. Amen."

Jamal and Todd joined her in the "Amen" with Kira a step behind. "Thank you, Shahara," Kira said. "Now, we need to go. Lock the door. We'll call you on the way in."

Todd waited until they were driving to ask, "What's with the envelope?"

"Basically, it's to let the skulk know that a mission failed. Mission failed, and the participants didn't check in. They'll send someone to come over and investigate. Clean-up crew, you could say. The clean-up crew will check the safe, investigate what happened, and figure out the best way to go from there."

Todd didn't ask any more questions. He'd rather not think about how this could go wrong. At seven-fifteen, he parked the car behind the convenience store. Kira was the one who went in with the story about the car breaking down, could they leave the car until their friend came to help? The cashier had sympathy on the teary-eyed woman, giving them permission to leave the car overnight. Since the store closed at ten, there shouldn't be a problem.

By seven-twenty-five, Todd had his sketchbook out, and was sitting on a rusty bench, trying to draw the brick bank in the dying light. It was quickly getting too dark for such an endeavor, but it was the best story they could come up with. More importantly, it gave him a clear view of the door of the office building they were watching. Occasionally, he would catch a quick glance of a cross fox exploring the outside grounds. Kira. He had only gotten a glimpse of Ryoko-*Sensei* as a fox, but his fur was more tan than either of the girls, who were both more orange. Besides, he was stationed across the street with binoculars.

At seven-thirty-three, the first person left the offices. The lawyer, Maria Juarez. According to their research, she was in her mid-forties, and specialized in family law. Clean record, respected by her co-workers, and no known connections to Twilights, Nights, Purifiers, etc.

About five minutes later, the nutritionist left. Beth Walters. Kira had spent a long time investigating her, convinced that she was just too perfectly situated as a sentry to be a coincidence. When they didn't find any known troubling connections, she decided that Walters was probably still being used as a sentry but might not know it.

It was too dark to sketch, so Todd moved to standing by the bus stop. Since the next bus wasn't due until eight-forty, that excuse would work for a while.

Seven-fifty, the massage therapist left. Nora Smith was a black woman in her late twenties and had been certified for three years. She had a comfortable practice but not a thriving one. A few of her clients were known Purifiers, but they couldn't find any proof that she herself was connected.

Which was much the same state for the last of the quartet. Leroy Jackson, the real estate agent. Early thirties, he had several Purifiers as clients, and he played the LARP, but might or might not be a true believer. He was, however, the one who had arranged to rent the extra storage space, and Kira said his financials looked to be tampered with.

Kira had been very interested in that office. According to her, if by some miracle this wasn't a trap, and Nightmare really was coming, it was probably for the contents of that office.

Eight o'clock came and went. Jackson hadn't come out. Had he left before they got there? It was possible. Unlikely, but possible. Eight-oh-five. Eight-ten. Still no sign of him.

Then, at eight-twelve, he left, locking the door behind him. Todd stayed in place. Eight-twenty came and went. Eight-twenty-five.

Kira came to the front door, now in human form. Todd crossed the street to join her. She had the door open before he even caught up to her. Trying not to look like he was breaking in, he followed her inside.

They didn't turn on the lights. Kira didn't need it, and Todd just tried not to walk into walls. It wasn't until they were out of sight of the front door that Kira even pulled out a flashlight.

Todd held the light while Kira picked the lock of the storage office. When she got it, he instinctively held his breath as she inched open the door. When nothing exploded and no traps went off, he looked inside.

Boxes. About twenty or thirty of them. The size used for transporting books or papers. Okay, that was a little anti-climactic, but maybe there would be something interesting inside.

Kira rubbed glove-clad fingers together and moved towards the first box. Todd tiptoed behind her with the flashlight. Her knife made short work of the tape, and she opened the box. As expected, there were papers in it. Papers that didn't make a whole lot of sense to him. Judging by the frown on Kira's face, they didn't make much sense to her either.

She rooted through the box some more, than two others. Similar papers. "What are they?" Todd dared to whisper.

"Deeds, real estate papers."

"It's just stuff for his job?" Well, that was a disappointment.

"No, I don't think so. Walters said he only dealt in houses. More than half of these are for commercial or industrial buildings."

"Purifier buildings?"

"Possible. Very possible." She checked her watch. "Help me get them out of here."

"What? Do we have time?"

"A little over an hour. We'll have to work fast. We definitely don't have time to copy them all."

Fast it was. They ended up opening a window on the far side of the building and tossing them outside. There wasn't enough time to take them to the car, but Kira could fit through the window. Todd stayed inside, tossing the boxes, which she took and hid under a wide-spreading bush. It wouldn't pass inspection in the daylight, but at night, it wouldn't be easily spotted. After hiding the last box, she took a running leap towards the building. Todd caught her arms and helped her inside.

It was five minutes until ten. They got into their places and waited. And waited. Was it a trap? Was it a hoax? Ten o'clock came and went. Todd could feel the minutes dragging on. Little sounds, real and imagined, magnified and rang in his ears. He was almost convinced the sound of his heart would give away his position if anyone came in.

He imagined he heard footsteps so many times that when he did hear them, he thought it was his imagination again. But no, it was real. Breathing slow and quiet through his mouth, Todd waited, even as the footsteps passed his hiding spot. Did they slow? Or was he imagining it? They moved on. Almost. Almost.

A sharp whistle pierced the air. The signal! Todd burst out of the bathroom where he had been hiding, so he would be behind the intruder. Kira was waiting in front, so they would have the intruder trapped between them.

As he came out, Todd hit the lights, as Kira had said. It ruined their night vision, but they were expecting it, so it should wear off faster than it would for Nightmare.

What they hadn't expected was for there to be three people there. But all Todd's attention was on the middle figure.

Kira's too, as she cried out, "It can't be!"

Chapter Twenty-Two

The weakest advantage is still an advantage. – The Kikitsutai
Book of Wisdom

There was fog in her head and buzzing in her ears.
Trying to get past the fog led to pain. For a timeless
moment, she contemplated staying put, waiting for
the fog and pain to dissipate on their own. But she
didn't. Something was wrong. Only if she pushed
past the fog and the pain would she be able to figure
out what.

Gradually, she awoke. Her eyes remained
closed, her body stayed still, and her breathing
maintained sleeping levels. Even her heart rate was
kept steady, through force of will. It was necessary,
because things were really wrong.

Eyes closed, she tried to figure out where she
was, what her position was. The ground was rocking
softly, and the air smelled of salt. She was on a boat.
She had absolutely no memory of embarking on a
boat. At this precise moment, she was lying on a
straw mattress that was covered with a dirty, smelly
sheet. There were bugs in the straw. She could hear
them moving. Hopefully nothing worse than fleas.
The room was bright, very bright. While she would

have to open her eyes to confirm, it felt small and was slightly cold. No sounds or smells of anyone else currently in the room. A low buzzing, just within the edges of her hearing range, changed pitch just enough that she couldn't tune it out.

Her clothes were gone. All of them. Instead, she seemed to be clad in an oversized shirt. She ignored her fury, refusing to react. When she found out who had done it, and why, then she could figure out the appropriate response. Until then, it would have to wait. There were sensors. Just a couple, probably measuring heart rate, maybe breathing.

Her smell had changed. She smelled... pregnant? No. She smelled of Solium, one of the two chemicals that were only naturally occurring in Weres. Solium stabilized them so they weren't constantly changing. She had been dosed high enough that she couldn't transform. Normally only heavily pregnant Weres would smell so strongly of Solium. That's why she had initially thought of pregnancy.

Last, there were bands of metal at her wrists and ankles. A slight shift confirmed her suspicions. Chains. Heavy, strong chains. *Well, I'm in trouble.*

Liska cracked an eye open. It shut immediately as the room was just as bright as she had suspected with her eyes closed. On her third attempt, she was actually able to see a little.

The room was small, probably less than ten foot square. There was a toilet in one corner, and a tray strapped to the ground in front of her. Bolted onto the tray was a dog dish labeled 'Precious', containing chicken and rice. To the side was a metal pitcher of water laced with Solium. Clever. It would take a good week and a half, maybe two or three, for her current dose to wear off. If she had to keep re-dosing herself, it would take a lot longer.

A camera was watching her, and there were some controls over by the door. Probably connected to the chains; to give her slack or tighten them so she couldn't move. Very clever.

Someone had put a lot of time and effort into catching her. Whatever their goals were, they planned to keep her alive for a while. But what where their goals? She couldn't know the proper response until she knew what they wanted.

There were two ways to handle being captured. One was to put all your efforts into surviving long enough to either escape or be rescued. It meant going along with any torture and mind games the captor might play, whatever it took. Just survive. The other way was to try to get killed before being able to reveal any information. But whichever option was chosen, it was important to make up one's mind in the beginning.

So, what should she do? There were certainly plenty of things she knew that she would die rather than tell. But that may or may not be what her captor wanted. Fine, until she had reason to believe it was a bad idea, Liska would hang onto survival, and to making whoever did this pay.

Liska closed her eyes again and thought of all the tortures, all the mind games, all the horrible fates that could possibly be done to her. Any time her mind shied away from a thought, she forced it back, imagining it as vividly as she could. She thought of them, imagined them happening, and took a moment to actually feel the pain and fear. It probably made the heart monitor go crazy, but it couldn't be helped. Then she put them aside, one by one. *If this happens, I can handle it.* Maiming, blinding, burning, rape, silver, any one of a thousand horrible deaths, etc. Then she calmed. Anything she could make herself handle in her mind would be easier to handle if they tried it physically.

The exercise was necessary, but if they truly had a heart sensor on her, there was no way to convince anyone she was still unconscious. So Liska slowly sat up, looking around the room. The chains did retract and extend, and if she was interpreting the complicated series of gears and pulleys correctly, they were currently at or near their full length. Standing was difficult. She was still fighting off whatever drugs had been used to knock her out, and wasn't used to standing on a boat.

With the chains extended as they were, she could walk as far as the toilet, or the wall on the other side, but only halfway to the door. She walked the perimeter of her area twice. The locks on the chains could be picked if she had her tools, but she didn't. Her clothes were nowhere in sight and even her hair had been hacked short, almost to her ears. Someone was going to be paying dearly for that.

As angry as she was about being stripped and put into an oversized tee shirt, she could understand the purpose. They had to make sure to get all her tools and weapons away from her. At least with the tee shirt, she wasn't completely naked. The tee shirt was practically a dress on her. But there was absolutely no reason to cut her hair. It had taken two years to grow it that long.

Liska returned to the straw mattress, only to discover there wasn't a comfortable way to sit down. No matter what, there was straw poking her uncomfortably. It had been while she was lying down too, but she had been concentrating on other things.

Nothing else was in the room. Nothing to reveal who had taken her or why. So what did she remember? She remembered T– Kira. She remembered calling Kira. Kira had come, surprisingly fast. They were both exhausted, and Kira suggested they sleep. Then what? She couldn't have been taken from her dorm room, could she? No, she was missing some things. Driving. There was something about driving. She was driving. Why? She didn't like driving.

It was no good. She couldn't remember. Probably it was a side effect of the drugs. Like the chemical headache. Well, it would clear up and she'd remember more in time.

The room had no windows, but according to her internal clock, it was probably about three or four in the afternoon, of the same day. While she didn't know how close or how far they were from land, she was relatively certain that they were still within fifty miles of West Palm Beach, heading south, slowly.

In the meantime, there was nothing to do but wait to find out who captured her and what they wanted. Maybe then, she'd be able to figure out how to escape. It was someone who knew about Werefoxes. Knew a lot. And had access to Solium, which was hard even for Weres to get a hold of.

It was extremely unlikely that she had been captured by a human. Solium was both difficult and expensive to synthesize, and to the best of her knowledge, less than a hundred humans in the entire planet knew enough about Solium to even attempt to synthesize it. The fact that she was on a boat made it less likely that she had been captured by a vampire or a Were. In most cases, neither liked being on the water long term. Some claimed that both had a connection to earth that made them more vulnerable on water or air, which was why they didn't like boats or planes. Liska didn't think it went that far, but it was true that most vampires avoided water and planes, and Weres were seldom sailors and almost never pilots. Tora was one of five pilots in the entire skulk. Five fully trained, at least. About half had enough training to handle a plane in an emergency. On the other hand, vampires who had been human, especially a human who had traveled frequently by boat or air, had fewer problems.

Dragons, ghouls, and fae were totally out of the question for various reasons. Dragons were too big to fit in a room like this, and weren't prone to mind games. If a dragon attempted to kidnap her, she would have woken up in a dragon cave with the dragon present or not woken up at all. Ghouls rarely left their haunts and usually weren't smart enough for something like this. Fae were smart enough, but they didn't like boats, especially ones made of iron or steel. Also, they wouldn't need to drug her so she couldn't transform. They would use magical bindings to prevent it, or that would stay even if she changed.

The various water-based creatures hated boats with a passion and would probably have accidentally drowned her trying to get her to wherever they wanted her. Intelligent or not, most of them never quite got how dependent air breathers were on air. Flying creatures would be more likely to take her somewhere high, not a boat.

So, who would use a boat? It was a clever move. Not only did it put her at a disadvantage, but she would be much harder to find. Even if she did manage to escape this room, getting back to land safely would be a challenge. Probably that was why they were on a boat, even if it wasn't the preferred method of travel for whoever took her. It was unlikely to be a coincidence. Clearly her captor knew enough about Werefoxes to know about Solium, to know the right frequency of noise that would drive her crazy, to know that she would be more sensitive to bright lights than she would be bothered by dark.

The cold wasn't a problem, at least not at the moment. Maybe they didn't know that her cold resistance was much better than her heat tolerance. Or maybe the room was naturally cold. Or maybe it would get hot later. She would have to wait and see.

There was a lot she would have to wait and see.

***

By her reckoning, she had been waiting for about two hours when the door opened. In that time, she had thoroughly mapped out her space three times, eaten a little of the chicken, and moved everything that could be moved, even if it was just a fraction of an inch. That made it *her* territory. Maintaining some form of control was important, even if it was mostly illusion.

When the door opened, no one was visible, no one came in. Liska went with it anyway. "About time. I would like to make a complaint about my accommodations. No one brought clean towels, and someone forgot to leave a mint. I expect better service than this, or I shall take my business elsewhere."

There was a deep chuckle in an unfamiliar male voice. Slowly, a figure entered. Male, looked about fifty-ish, with the crooked look that happened sometimes to formerly human vampires when they reached beyond the fifth century mark. He was short, not more than a couple inches on her, if she were standing. Probably Eastern European descent.

Being a human turned vampire explained a few things. He was one of the few who didn't mind water. Perhaps a former sailor. Happened a lot back a few hundred years ago. The newly turned sailors were better adapted to a sailing life, and for the first decade or so, often had a little better sun tolerance. Of course, sailors also tended to be superstitious, and would notice things like a sudden difficulty with sun, and change in dietary habits, so many of those vampire sailors didn't last more than a couple years.

Whatever he was once, he was certainly someone to be reckoned with now. Not tall, not handsome, probably no one of status when he was human; he had an aura of power and control now. She could do that same thing, but where she used cheap tricks and bits of psychology knowledge, for him it was either natural, or so long practiced it was ingrained.

Possibly he had been an Esper before he was turned. It happened occasionally, especially when the gift was one in high demand or considered useful. An Esper turned vamp had a fifty-fifty chance of losing his gift or it becoming stronger. No one knew why.

"You must pardon the staff. They get a little over-excited." The vampire came closer but stopped about two feet shy of the limits of her chain. She could reach him if she stood there, but he'd be gone before she got there.

Liska didn't move. "I can tell. Don't think much of your beautification staff, either." She ran her fingers through the remnants of her hair.

"You will likely find short hair practical. With the fleas and all."

"Of course. I can see you went out of your way to provide me with an authentic sea voyage. So, where are we going?"

He smiled at her. She did not like that smile. At all. In fact, she really wanted to throw that stupid dog dish at him and try to knock out some of those teeth. Probably just as well the dish was bolted to the tray. "Nowhere in particular. I want to stay in this area. Maybe a supply run or two."

So far, so good. She had learned a few things, without giving anything away or incurring any new pain. Time to push it a little. "Do you have a name, or should I just call you 'Porter'?"

Even from a few feet away, she could hear his teeth grind. There were a few whiffs of irritation, but his face didn't change. That was a definite nerve.

Important to know. Even more important, he was able to restrain himself from reacting to what he considered a serious insult.

"In time, you will be calling me Master." Liska didn't bother to scoff. "Until then, I am Cazimir."

It only took a second of riffling through her mental database to make the connection. "Ryasmus's second in command?"

There was a pained grimace. Ryasmus must have turned him, but it still galled him to admit subservience. "I was part of his blood, yes."

"Then you became Atolatar's flunky." She wasn't surprised by the slap, but the speed and strength were a little more than she expected. There was blood in her mouth and her vision swam briefly. Worse, she hadn't seen him move. Not someone to underestimate.

"Are you so easily led then? He was. To believe that an infant like him could possibly take control of even a fraction of the blood like that. Oh, he would have had potential. Eventually. But I knew he would never come to much. No vision." Cazimir strode from one side of the small room to the other, just out of her reach.

Liska didn't move and refused to let herself smile. Cazimir might be a formidable adversary, but he was a terrible interrogator. "So, the whole blowing up a peace conference was your idea?"

He gave her a haughty glance. "I was led to believe you were smarter than this. No, it was his idea. I knew it was unlikely to work. But it accomplished what I wanted."

Atolatar gone, and he could either lead openly, or manipulate his newest cat's-paw. "What was that?"

The ancient vampire shook his head. "You may not be suitable for my plans after all."

Fine with her. Chances were good that even death was preferable to whatever plans he had for her. "What do you want, anyway?"

He gave her a malicious smile. "If I told you, you wouldn't be able to give it to me. Eat your meal. You'll need your strength." He swept out, the door slamming with a dull thud.

Chapter Twenty-Three

A cage can imprison the body. Only a person can imprison a mind. – The Kikitsutai Book of Wisdom

After Cazimir left, Liska sat motionless with her eyes closed for a long time. Every single detail about her current circumstances and the recent encounter were analyzed and re-analyzed.

Cazimir was in charge, or at least, believed he was in charge, of this plan to kidnap her. Someone else could have used that streak of entitled arrogance to manipulate him. Like Cazimir had manipulated Atolatar and possibly even Ryasmus before him.

To a limited extent, she could use that streak. It was precarious though. He'd see through it if she were clumsy, and it would then be harder to manipulate him in the future. Plus, if she miscalculated, she'd risk injury by provoking his temper. Still, she would have to take the risk.

He believed her young, wild, reckless, and stupid. Good, let him. Let him believe she had succeeded by luck and the training of others. Let him underestimate her. She'd already laid the grounds, now she just had to keep him believing it.

Cazimir said that if she knew what he wanted, she wouldn't be able to give it to him. Not that she would refuse, but that she'd be unable. What could he possibly be referring to? Well, he was a lousy interrogator. She'd figure it out.

He had said she'd call him 'Master'. The fox in her growled at that. He was not her alpha and never would be. But perhaps she could fool him, make him think he'd brought her to heel. In would be difficult, both because it went against everything in her, and because he wouldn't believe it if she capitulated too fast.

He would have to believe he had broken her. It wouldn't be a quick or painless process. Her training had included resisting torture and brainwashing. She'd needed it before, and it looked like she'd need it again.

Slowly, silently, she refined her plan. If she performed a series of minor rebellions, probably being 'punished' for each; then managed a major rebellion, there would be a major punishment. Probably major enough that she could fake being cowed, especially if she 'weakened' in the face of the smaller punishments. But she had to convince Cazimir he had broken her, without actually breaking.

This was going to really hurt. But it was her best option. Kira and *Sensei* would know she was missing, if not yet, then soon; but Liska couldn't count on a rescue. They probably didn't know who had taken her, and almost certainly didn't know she was on a boat. Any rescue would be slow in coming, if it came at all. Now would be a wonderful time to be on good terms with a nearby telepath. Unfortunately, telepaths were extremely rare, and tended to be arrogant, difficult to work with people. In fact, the last telepath she met had gotten himself killed as a direct result of being arrogant and difficult to work with. No, she didn't know any telepaths within a hundred miles, let alone one she could count on for help. She was on her own.

***

Hours came and passed. Liska didn't move, didn't eat. No one came. Her first mini-rebellion. Either Cazimir or some underling would come in and punish her for not obeying orders, probably by taking away and withholding food; or they were waiting until she ate so they could 'praise' her for 'obeying'.

Liska weighed both sides of the equation. On one hand, she couldn't be too quick to give in. On the other, *not* eating didn't gain her anything. If they *did* withhold food, she could have some problems. She might make a point of carrying around a protein bar or two, but her clothes were gone. Perhaps she could eat the fleas. Wouldn't her captors love that? Besides, that was a good way to get parasites.

The dog bowl was a bit of an irritant, but since it was so obvious that they had gone out of their way to try to humiliate her, she could almost laugh at it. Cutlery would have been nice though.

After about four hours, Liska decided it was probably in her best interest to eat, even if she had been 'ordered' too. The delay was enough to show that she wasn't going to acquiesce quickly, and the food hadn't been tampered with. It was possible the next batch would be. All the more reason to eat this time.

The chicken was easy. Cut up pieces with no bones that she could easily eat with her fingers. Bland, but most foods were to her. Besides, she would have been more surprised if they had tried to make it appetizing. The rice was a little more difficult. With no fork or spoon, she only had two options. Scooping it up with her hands, or actually putting her face in the dish like a dog. Much as the latter might amuse her captors, Liska preferred to use her hands.

Her hands were a mess by the time she finished, but she still had the pitcher of water. She poured water first on one hand, than the other, and rubbed them together. Then, reluctantly, she drank some of the water. She would have to at some point anyway, why make things worse by getting dehydrated?

She'd barely put the pitcher down when the door opened. So they had been watching. As she thought. "Come in," Liska called. They were going to come in anyway, might as well pretend she had some say in it. Control, even the remnants of it, was important.

Cazimir strode in and pretended astonishment at the empty dish. "Oh, you did eat? Good girl."

Liska snarled with a little more irritation than she actually felt. Cazimir reeked of smug satisfaction. Good.

"Was your meal satisfactory?"

"Not particularly. Bland. The rice was undercooked, the chicken overcooked. Cutlery would be nice. Unless we are going for Ethiopian cuisine. Anyway, maybe some steak next time?"

Fortunately, Cazimir seemed amused by her continued acting like she was at a resort that simply wasn't up to snuff. "I'll have a word with the cook."

Liska nodded as if satisfied. "You can also have a word with someone about this mattress. Or at least a few blankets." She poked a piece of straw back through the sheet and pretended she didn't hear insects scurrying away. Blankets weren't necessary for heat, but they might provide a little more protection from bugs. Liska had already acquired at least half a dozen bites. This was going to be fun. So very much fun.

Really, why straw anyway? They probably had to go out of their way to get it, and it would rot eventually. Cazimir could have given her nothing, leaving her with the cold floor, or just a couple blankets, but they had gotten straw. Probably collected the bugs too.

"Your accommodations will improve as you earn them." Cazimir smirked.

Yes, she had expected this. It was definitely one way to know how well he thought she was 'breaking'. "Am I supposed to swab the deck? Or maybe batten the hatches? Because I have to admit, I never did figure out what that meant. Also, I seem to be," she rubbed at a wrist cuff, "indisposed."

Cazimir seemed slightly amused by her 'ignorance'. "We'll start with something easy. Remember this: I am your master. You obey me. You have been here forever."

Liska arched an eyebrow. "I see."

"How long have you been here?"

"I'd say about half a day." She braced for the slap and wasn't disappointed.

"You have been here forever. How long have you been here?"

He couldn't possibly expect her to capitulate that easily. "Half a day."

Oh goody, her lip was bleeding. She licked at it, even as she saw him stare at the drop of blood. He recovered quickly. "You have been here forever. How long have you been here?"

This continued until her vision was swimming, even after she blinked to clear it. "How long have you been here?"

Head bowed, she didn't answer. Cazimir shook her, sending shards of pain piercing through her brain. "How long have you been here?"

"Ooh, pretty lights..." Liska drawled, unfocused eyes staring loosely over his shoulder. Disgust filled her nose as he dropped her back onto the infested straw mattress. But he left, even if he took the tray and water with him. She hadn't given in yet. One point for her. Now if only she could clear out the pain in her head.

***

For the next three or four days, Liska was pretty sure it was four, things followed that pattern. Cazimir would come in, try to get her to say part of his mantra, and leave when any more punishment risked serious damage. She still hadn't decided whether or not it was a good thing that he seemed to want her in one piece. Probably not.

For her part, Liska had stopped pretending that she was complaining about an unsuitable hotel after the second day, and let herself seem a little more afraid every time he came in. He wouldn't believe her sudden 'compliance' unless she built the proper foundation first. Besides, it wasn't like she wasn't scared. She was being held by a crazy vampire who had no qualms about torture. Of course she was scared.

Cazimir might be crazy, but he wasn't stupid. Since beating her to the brink of unconsciousness, or past it, wasn't working; he clearly decided it was time to try something else. So, day five, he put down the tray, complete with drugged water and semi-cooked ground beef in that stupid dog dish. Liska's lips twitched at the scent. The food was drugged too. Nothing lethal, she'd bet, but she'd probably be awfully sick.

"Eat."

Yeah, no thanks. "Not hungry," she lied. He had waited longer than usual before bringing the food. It was bad enough that he only brought food once a day when she *needed* to eat at least twice a day. Stupid small stomach.

He clapped her ear, causing her to rear away, hand protectively over it. Was her ear bleeding? No. But, *ouch*, that hurt. Shouldn't have caused permanent damage. Not with just one incident. Hopefully that wouldn't be his new favorite tactic. "Eat."

"You first."

Cazimir grabbed her hair, short as it was, and yanked her head back, painfully exposing her neck. "I am your master. You obey me. You have been here forever. Now, as your master, I command you to eat."

Liska swallowed painfully but managed to blow a raspberry at him. The next second, a strong hand grabbed her neck and slammed her into the wall. Reflexes kicked in, causing her to scratch and pull at the hand. It wasn't working. He was too strong and she didn't have the leverage. In less than a minute, she didn't have the air.

As black encroached on her vision, he dropped her. She hit the mattress with a dull thud. "One last time. Eat."

Liska didn't move, didn't speak. She was too busy gasping in air to find a decent response.

"Fine. We'll try this later then." Cazimir left, taking the tray with him. No food. No water.

***

He didn't come back until the next day. Liska spent the interval as she had spent most of her time here. She walked the limits of her circuit whenever she got restless, or just to make sure she stayed in good enough shape to take advantage of whatever chance came. Eventually one would. The rest of the time she spent mostly inside her own head. Reliving favorite memories, trying to remember her favorite stories or movies, or imagining new adventures with Kira, with Tora and Ryo, with her parents, with *Sensei*, even with Todd or Jamal and Shahara. Even all of them at once, no matter how nonsensical it might seem.

In her head, she showed Todd, Jamal, and Shahara around Kikitsutai Island; a more in-depth tour than Todd had seen before. She showed them her favorite spots while Tora and Ryo made up the most outrageous lies about what had happened there, and Kira alternated between scolding them and egging them on. That grew into all of them playing tourist in Japan. Father would show them Tokyo, Osaka, and Okinawa; showing them the historic buildings, the gardens, and some of the technological advances. Mother would suggest some of the natural reserves. Fox Island was a must, of course. So many wild foxes, a few Werefoxes would fit right in. For the humans, they would probably enjoy Naru Park. Tourists could feed the small deer, who knew it and got very pushy about their food. They definitely had to go to Rabbit Island, where one could literally be mobbed by over a hundred rabbits.

She could picture it so clearly. *Sensei* would sit on a bench, pretending to be above such foolishness, but his smile would be evident as some of the bolder rabbits sniffed around his shoes for food. Father would pretend to be grumpy, but never once say anything about leaving. Mother would have a video camera. Tora and Ryo would pretend to try to catch the rabbits, joking about a rabbit dinner, while Kira sat on a rock trying to lure some bunnies to her. Todd and Jamal would be surrounded by a sea of bunnies, looking a little bewildered, while Shahara would actually be sitting on the ground, practically covered in the furry lagomorphs. And she... well, maybe some of the bunnies would ignore the scent of fox and let her pet them.

The picture made her laugh out loud. Her captors were probably wondering if she was going crazy. Good.

In other visions, Liska was showing her parents her dorm room at the college, and giving them a tour of the school. They followed her to classes, and afterwards, praised her for how well she was doing. Somehow, that felt even less likely than a group trip to Rabbit Island.

Not all her imagining was of fuzzy feel-good thoughts. Cazimir figured prominently in some too. Of course, in her imagination, *he* was powerless, or at very least, less powerful than her.

However, Liska was a little surprised at how few of her fantasies were revenge-oriented. She spent much more time imagining her family, her friends. Even remembering the exact wording of textbooks took up more time than thinking up exactly what she would do to Cazimir when she got free.

Part of her worried about that. Having a concrete plan for 'after' was important for survival. On the other hand, Cazimir wanted power. Hating him gave him that power. Maybe ignoring him was for the best

The vampire in question interrupted a pleasant fantasy of a camping trip in the Blue Ridge Mountains. She had been there once and enjoyed it immensely. On this imaginary trip with her were Kira, Tora, Ryo, Todd, Jamal, and Shahara (who kept complaining about the ugly hiking boots). They were roasting marshmallows, which the non-Weres planned to turn into s'mores. Liska didn't open her eyes. Maybe she could stay in the fantasy. Hm, Tora or Ryo should offer one of the humans caramel-covered crickets.

The smell of water intruded on her fantasy. No, it was a stream. They were near a stream. Always have a campground near water if possible. She was thirsty. Her mouth wasn't quite completely dry yet, but it would happen soon. Even her perpetual headache was worse from dehydration.

The water wasn't drugged. That had her opening her eyes. On the tray in front of her was that dumb dog dish with the same meat from yesterday. It had been refrigerated at least. Still tampered with. The pitcher wasn't there.

Liska looked up at Cazimir. The pitcher was in his hand. She didn't get water until she ate. Of course.

The food would make her throw up. Probably a lot. That would dehydrate her too. She ran her tongue around her mouth, swallowing a little saliva. Cazimir didn't bother to say anything, just smirked at her.

Slowly, Liska leaned back and closed her eyes. So, after Ryo, it would probably be him, tricked someone into eating caramel-covered crickets, what would happen next? Shahara would throw a fit. Todd and Jamal, one of them would have been the one to eat it, and the other would laugh hysterically. The other Weres would voluntarily take a few crickets, it being a favorite treat of all of them. Then they would tell ghost stories. That was what one did in the summer, especially around a campfire.

Small smile on her face, Liska almost didn't hear Cazimir leave, taking the tray and water with him.

***

Lack of water was becoming an increasingly severe problem. Her tongue felt like sandpaper, and her mouth hurt from being so dry. Dull, throbbing pain echoed ceaselessly through her head. Her urine had been dark and smelled strongly of chemicals the last time she had been able to urinate. Liska was pretty sure she couldn't now. Pity the toilet used chemicals instead of water. Plus, there was no reservoir of water she could access.

Hours passed. They had gone through so much effort to keep her alive, surely they wouldn't just let her die of dehydration this quickly. Would they? It had been at least forty-five hours since Cazimir had taken the water away. Maybe they underestimated how long she could go without water.

If they had, then they were probably getting a clue. She hadn't even bothered to get off the mattress today, choosing to doze. That sounded much better than slipping in and out of consciousness, which might be more accurate.

A loud sound brought her closer to awareness, but despite the feeling that she should know what it meant, she didn't. Then there was another sound. Not as loud, but longer. And she was moving.

Looking around dazedly, Liska realized her chains were being shortened just before she slammed into the wall, spread-eagled. Someone was in front of her. She tried to dredge some answers from her remaining brain cells, but before she could try to think, someone grabbed her face roughly. Cazimir. That's right. He forced her mouth open and poured a small amount of water into it.

Liska spluttered but managed to swallow the majority of the water. Like turning on the power of her brain, she found she was able to think. Cazimir was here with water and a sports drink. Clearly he knew that she was too dehydrated for just water to be sufficient.

After a minute, when she didn't throw up the water she had been given, he gave her some more. Too much at one time. She choked, and some of her precious water slipped from her mouth. Once she had swallowed what she had, Liska tried to lick at what fell.

Cazimir sneered at her. But he gave her some of the sports drink. Didn't taste as good as the water, but she didn't complain. He alternated between the two until they were both gone.

Now Liska was thoroughly aware, but she was still weak. Why had he even bothered to restrain her? She couldn't have fought him right now.

"You disobeyed my order and insulted my hospitality," Cazimir almost purred, still holding her face hard enough to bruise. Liska declined to point out that the rules of being a good guest don't apply to hostages and remained silent. "I try to teach you, and you reject it. I am merciful, but you must learn. Be thankful I gave you water before your punishment."

Oh dear. Cazimir let go, causing her to hit the wall. She was going to have a permanent headache for the rest of her life at this rate. Of course, at this rate, her life was only going to be another week or two. Still, she remained silent and expressionless, other than a slight wince. Cazimir went to the door and tossed both bottles outside only to come back with something small. Her vision hadn't completely come back yet so it wasn't until he was halfway to her that she was able to make out the hypodermic needle in his hand. Oh, grand. She *hated* needles.

She could try to fight it, but right now, if she wasn't chained to the wall, she wouldn't be able to stand. Her limbs were shaky enough that one of those rabbits from Rabbit Island could take her on. Whatever was in that syringe, Cazimir was going to succeed in injecting her with it. The only thing her 'struggles' could do would be to risk the needle breaking off in her skin.

Cazimir, being a vampire, had no problems finding a good vein in her arm. Vampire doctors were particularly good at finding veins and identifying circulatory issues and blood-borne diseases. Of course, Cazimir wasn't a doctor, to the best of her knowledge. But she had lost some weight, which she really couldn't afford.

"I don't even need a tourniquet," Cazimir remarked as he plunged the needle in. Liska let her head hang. Not looking, not reacting. It was better than outright defiance sometimes, because he couldn't be sure if she *was* defying him, or not really aware of what was going on.

No showing pain. It was probably only her imagination that her arm was burning. It took time for most serums to take effect. The fact that she didn't know what she had been injected with worried her, but there was nothing she could do about it. She'd find out.

***

The serum gave her extremely nasty flu-like symptoms for the next six hours. Cazimir left her chained to the wall as she shivered so hard it felt like her bones would snap. Fire and ice alternated in racing through her veins, and anything that was in her bowels liquefied and came out, explosively. Liska managed not to vomit, as much through force of will as anything else. She'd probably choke to death if she did. Not having anything resembling food in her stomach probably helped a little.

Her brain was being squeezed in a vice, she could feel it. Her ears were ringing painfully. But it wasn't until blood started dripping from her nose that she wondered if she was going to die here. Die chained to a wall by a psychotic vampire who *still* wouldn't tell her why he had kidnapped her.

Just as she was beginning to wonder if death might be the better option, the symptoms began to abate. She was still in pain, and was thoroughly dehydrated again, weaker than a newborn fox kit, but the flu symptoms were gone. No more fire or ice, no more nose bleeds. Nothing was left in her system to evacuate one way or the other, but the bile stopped creeping up her throat.

About an hour later, Cazimir came back. With a hose. First, he washed away the floor, clearing away her mess, ruining the straw. Maybe she'd get lucky and it would kill all the bugs.

Then he turned the hose on her. She closed her eyes and turned her head away from the stinging spray. He would use salt water, wouldn't he? And she had so many small and large injuries that there probably wasn't a square inch of her that didn't sting under the salt. Then there was the pressure. Getting sprayed by a hose on full blast at close range really hurt. She couldn't even drink the water left on her face because it was salt water.

Couldn't open her eyes right away either. First there was the force of the water, then there was the salt making her eyes sting. Finally, she had her eyes back under control.

Cazimir was standing there, waiting. He smirked as she saw the water bottle in his hand. Liska swallowed involuntarily. Oh, she needed water.

"How long have you been here?"

The fox in her bristled and growled. How dare he? Liska breathed through chapped, bleeding lips. She licked them once, even though it hurt. Then she swallowed again. Her eyes slipped shut. "Forever."

Chapter Twenty-Four

Even lies have truths inside. – The Kikitsutai Book of Wisdom

After her 'capitulation' things got a little better. Sure, she had been left chained to the wall, dripping wet in a cold room; but once the floor dried, Cazimir moved out the now ruined straw and brought in an old, beat-up, smelly mattress. At least it didn't have bugs in it. While far from comfortable, the springs didn't come out and poke her like the straw did. Reeked to high heaven, but oh well. She'd get used to it.

Cazimir started alternating whether or not the water was drugged. Unsurprising. It wasn't like she could wait long enough for the Solium to wear off, so why spend so much on expensive chemicals when he didn't need to? Besides, eventually, it would be very toxic. She was still being fed from a dog dish, and while the food was far from appetizing, it hadn't been drugged to make her sick. Cazimir hinted that it would get better when she 'learned her place'.

It irked her, a lot, to even consider playing along, but Cazimir's patience was running out. Soon he would figure out she wasn't as broken as she let on. If at all possible, she would really like to avoid another 'flu' session.

Liska tried to tell herself it was just words. Lying was very familiar to her, to enemy, to friends, even to family. She was lying to him now. For example, ever since acquiescing to his claim that she had been here 'forever', she had been particularly careful to keep track of how long she had been there. Ten and a half days by her count.

But it wasn't just words. Even a liar like her knew that. Words have power. Ask any Fae. Every lie held a kernel of truth. If she called him 'Master' enough times, even she would start to believe it. Besides, she wasn't sure she could say it without gritting her teeth or sarcasm. On the other hand, maybe that would work. If she steadily showed fewer and fewer signs of revulsion from the words, he'd believe it was succeeding. Maybe.

A storm was coming. Even in a windowless room she could tell that. It wasn't enough to make the waves choppier yet, but she knew. The atmospheric pressure had increased. She could feel the electricity in the air.

Liska wrapped up in her sheet. She knew the cameras watched her, but she wasn't sure if there was audio or not. Probably. "Hey! There's a storm coming. Is this boat moored?"

She never got an answer. Within ten minutes, the surf got rougher. Soon she could hear the wind. This was going to be a bad one. Hopefully it would be short. It was right on top of them. A couple times

Liska thought she actually heard lightning. There was no mistaking the thunder. Even covering her ears, each roar reverberated through her bones.

That was distracting enough that it took her almost twenty minutes to realize she was getting very seasick. Grand. Todd had mentioned once that he enjoyed watching storms. He probably wouldn't enjoy it so much if he was experiencing one while in a boat. A metal boat. Hopefully her mattress would be a poor electrical conductor.

She was pretty sure that she was actually at low risk for electrocution, there had to be a way boats dealt with that. After all, cars were safer to be in than out in the open. But she didn't know the physics behind it, or even really care. It wasn't going to solve her misery.

The storm finally blew itself out, but it took a lot longer for her stomach to settle. While she was waiting for that, the door opened briefly, and someone she couldn't see tossed a blanket in the room. It landed a good two feet from her, but she had just enough range on the chains to grab the edge. The blanket was wool and smelled strongly enough of ship oil that she couldn't pick up the scent of whoever gave it to her. But it was warm. When she wasn't wet, the room was bearable, but it always had a mild chill to it. Liska cocooned herself in the blanket and sheet and waited.

Cazimir didn't come for hours. Between two and a half and three hours, if her internal clock was right. Liska prayed it was still accurate. If she lost that, then she'd be on the way to losing herself.

When the elderly vampire opened the door, Liska invited him in, as she often did. He took two steps in and eyed the blanket. She couldn't read his expression, but she could hear the sniff of disgust, and hear the mutter of, "Soft."

As the blanket was actually pretty coarse and scratchy, he probably wasn't referring to the blanket as soft. So, not only had Cazimir not been the one to give her the blanket, but he hadn't ordered anyone else to give it to her either. One of his underlings, or possibly (unlikely), his superiors, had gone behind his back to give her something that wasn't necessary to her survival. Interesting. She had gained someone's sympathy. While she couldn't count on her 'benefactor' going against Cazimir directly, or disobeying an order, it was nice to have even a partial and reluctant ally. If she knew who it was, or how to contact them, it would be even better.

Cazimir, despite his disapproval, made no attempt to take the blanket away. He tried another tack. "As you can see, I am merciful. The gracious master who takes care of those who are his. If you weren't so rebellious, I wouldn't need to treat you like this."

Liska didn't call him on it. "Thank you for the blanket," She said, more to the camera than to him.

"Well, you can have manners when you choose. How long have you been here?"

Ten and three-quarter days. "Forever."

"Who do you obey?"

She hadn't answered that one to his satisfaction yet. Cazimir was smart. He had focused first on getting her to claim she had been there forever. Something he knew she would object to less than saying she obeyed him, which in turn was easier than calling him master. He was worming his way in.

What should she answer this time? She had to give him the answer he wanted sooner or later. Should this be that time? No. Not yet. "The one I choose to obey."

Cazimir sneered, but didn't hit her, to her surprise. "You aren't half broken enough. Not yet." He swept away. Liska tried to ignore that pit in her stomach that told her something very, very bad was coming.

***

Cazimir stormed through the ship, ignoring the wraiths and shades that threw themselves out of his way. Sometimes literally. He knew exactly who was to blame for this rebellion. He found the guilty party playing solitaire in his quarters. The younger vampire looked up, flushed guiltily, and tried to pretend he hadn't.

"You, Pup, gave the fox a blanket." Cazimir didn't make it a question and made sure to use the younger vampire's hated nickname.

Eric tried to stammer out denials. Cazimir backhanded the stripling. "So you ordered another to give it to her. I care not. It was still you."

"Well, you don't want her to get sick, right?" Eric tried to justify. "You never said not to."

Cazimir hit him again. "I turned you. You do not go against me. Understand? And I'm telling you right now, you do nothing to or for that *vixen* without my say-so."

He nodded quickly. Cazimir wasn't an empath, but he could tell that Eric wanted him to leave, preferably now.

"Is she breaking or is she faking it?"

"Well, it's a lot more complicated than–"

Cazimir silenced him by pushing him into the wall. "Is she breaking, or is it an act?"

Eric was too soft, but he was useful. Since Cazimir had turned him, he was loyal first and foremost to him. So, eyes on the floor, Eric swallowed and admitted, "Mostly fake."

"How *much* is she faking it?"

He flinched. "Almost completely."

Cazimir snarled. He had been certain he had been making progress with her. She was good. And when he was done, she'd be magnificent. "This calls for something... *special*."

***

When Cazimir came in again, about an hour after he had left; Liska did not invite him in. He came in anyway, the scent of silver with him. Oh, this was bad.

Once again, her chains were retracted so she couldn't move. Only after that did Cazimir come close. While his face was sorrowful, his scent was gloating. "You force me into such stringent measures. Why do you make me do this?"

She could argue that she wasn't 'making' him do anything, but hey, power was power. "I guess I'm just stubborn." Liska was pleased to note that her voice was steady. Silver may scare her more than almost anything in the world, but she wasn't going to give him the satisfaction of knowing that. Not if she could help it.

"You are. I'm sorry to do this." *Lie*. "But you leave me no choice."

Cazimir pulled out a silver necklace. It was big, quarter of an inch wide at the smallest, to a couple wide long in the front, meant to be worn like a collar or choker.

This time she fought. Not that it did her any good. The vampire held her fast, and wrapped it around her neck, even if he had to fasten the clasp at the side of her neck.

Don't scream. Don't give him that satisfaction. Do not scream. Burning agony around her neck. She couldn't breathe. The collar was choking her. *Don't scream. Don't give him that satisfaction. Do not scream.* It was acid on her throat. It was fire inside. Her vision was gone through a fog of pain and tears. She could smell blood, but wasn't sure where it was coming from. *Don't scream. Don't give him that satisfaction. Do not scream!* It was only then she realized she was already screaming.

***

Liska didn't know how long she screamed. Everything was wrapped up in pain. She was on fire, and there was blood in her throat. Then it stopped. The necklace, collar, *shackle*, was removed. She could breathe again. Barely. Apparently, she had screamed enough to cause her throat to bleed and pop a blood vessel in her nose. That wasn't the only blood. Liska had banged her head against the wall long enough and hard enough that there might be minor brain damage, and there were definitely bruises. She had writhed and pulled against all the chains enough to scratch her limbs up.

It took her a few moments to even see Cazimir in front of her, and there appeared to be two of them. Proof of her clear concussion, for a moment, she was actually concerned that there *were* two Cazimirs. Her thoughts focused, even if her eyes didn't.

"How long have you been here?"

Liska tried to gasp out 'forever'. She truly did. But all that came out of her abused throat was a groan that would not have been out of place in a Frankenstein movie, coming from the monster.

She tried again. No better. Cazimir scowled at her in disgust. Liska tried whispering, but that hurt even more. She was not wearing that thing again. She mouthed it.

"I suppose that will have to do. For now. Now, who do you obey?"

Having learned her lesson, Liska mouthed it again. *You.*

"What was that?" She tried again. Cazimir smirked. "I'm not sure I understand. Do you want this again?"

Liska shook her head frantically. For about two seconds before the pain exploded again.

"Who do you obey?"

She knocked her right hand against the wall. When Cazimir instinctively looked towards it, she pointed at him.

He smiled wider. "Me?"

She nodded, much more carefully. The pain increased, but not as badly.

"You will say so tomorrow." Cazimir left, extending her chains to let her drop as he left.

Chapter Twenty-Five

To see the future, look at the past. – The Kikitsutai Book of Wisdom

It took a long time for Liska to move. To gather her shaky limbs to herself, and burrow under the blanket so completely that she had to re-adjust it to let in air. Tears continued to seep from her eyes, but she didn't sob, so it didn't count as crying. It was simply a natural response to pain. That's all. And, oh, she was in *pain*! If only that buzzing wasn't around, she would withdraw into her own mind where she couldn't feel it. If she did that now, she might never come out. Right now, she had trouble thinking that was a bad thing.

That buzzing made sleeping difficult until exhaustion kicked in. She simply couldn't tune it out because there was just enough variety to keep her on edge. Cazimir clearly meant to have her sleep deprived, which she was, but did he know or suspect that it prevented her from mentally retreating too?

She would have to 'break' and soon. Probably very soon. If she held out much longer, it might not be pretend. Would he believe that today was enough? Especially after everything she had been through so far? Possibly. She would find out tomorrow. Liska wasn't sure if she would even be able to speak tomorrow. Another thing she would find out tomorrow.

Exhaustion overwhelmed her, and a shallow sleep moved in. She dreamed. Kira was there. She said they were both tired and should sleep. They turned into foxes and curled up for a nap on Sakaki's bed. Kira slept, but she had trouble. Liska kept thinking. Trying to avoid certain thoughts, she ran through her mental notes on the vampire case. Something clicked. What was it?

By now, Liska realized she was dreaming, but tried to stay in the dream. She wasn't very skilled at lucid dreaming, but she had done it before. As long as she could keep from waking up when she realized she was dreaming. What had she been thinking? Lists. She had been going through lists. What had she found?

On the lists, she had been looking at who helped the Magnus Blood after the attack. The first one to step in who wasn't a known Wanderer from the area, was a vampire who called himself Rimat. She had heard that name before, associated with the Lyonoko Blood. Ryasmus's Blood. Apparently he was near the sea.

A sense of urgency filled her. Rimat might be Atolatar's follower. If not, he would probably had some information about who was. She needed to talk to him. Liska sprang to her feet and transformed. Kira didn't stir. She must be exhausted.

When Van delivered the lists, Liska had given her a burner phone. A way they could contact each other that wouldn't be obvious. Liska paid the bills, and promised she would ever only text Van, instead of calling which could get her in trouble. They had never used it but now was as good a time as any.

Liska went into the kitchen so she didn't wake Kira with her texting. *What do you know about Rimat?* Honestly, Liska didn't expect an answer for hours. Van was probably asleep right now and would be until nightfall. But to her surprise, she got a reply back inside of five minutes.

Not over the phone. There was an address a few miles away. Liska sent back a confirmation code before looking at Kira. She trusted Van, but it was a bad idea to go without backup. But compromised backup could be worse than none. Well, she would have to borrow *Sensei*'s car anyway. She'd ask his help.

Only, he wasn't home either. Liska tried waiting for him, but her impatience got the better of her. If she was careful and subtle, it should be fine. Maybe just a little recon. She borrowed the car and left alone. Once she knew more about Rizmat, she could send them information. No point in spooking Van anyway.

Liska was awake by now, but at least she remembered how she had gotten into this mess. She didn't remember anything more than that, but it looked like she had found Rimat. Or he found her. Rimat was probably a *nom de guerre* of Cazimir. Grand. Why hadn't she left enough in her notes for someone else to follow her tracks? Idiot!

Though it might not have helped much if she had. Even she hadn't known he had a boat, or even that he had been human and might be willing to sail. Who knew what name the boat was registered under? Heck, she didn't even know if she was on a boat or a ship.

But it did ease most of her lingering worry that someone else had been grabbed when she had. No, she was pretty certain she had been alone. But how had she been captured anyway? Had Van betrayed her? Somehow, she didn't think that was the case. Was Van in danger? Had that been Van on the other line?

The memory tickled but didn't become clearer. It would come. In time.

***

Liska woke with a throbbing ear. She had clearly been laying on it. Most of her muscles were sore too. The fetal position was not comfortable to hold for long periods of time. Her wrists and ankles were itchy and grimy. Actually, most of her was grimy. She had tried to clean herself a couple times. But there was no cloth other that the shirt she wore, her sheet, and her new blanket. The sheet took a surprisingly long time to dry in this room, and the blanket was certain to be worse. Besides, being wet made the cool room uncomfortably cold.

The healing bug bites were itchy too, along with a myriad of other small scratches and scrapes, and in a few places, cracked skin. Her head was a dull pain instead of a sharp one, so she supposed she should be grateful for small favors.

She turned her head slightly to ease pressure off her ear. Then promptly remembered exactly how very *much* her neck hurt. So much so that she had tried to drown it out with a million minor aches and pains. It didn't work for long.

After the pain eased about as much as it seemed like it was going to, Liska slowly sat up. She swallowed some water, which hurt; and ate a little bread, which hurt even more. Finally, she carefully tried speaking. The first attempt was not only painful, it was also incomprehensible. The second was equally painful, but less incomprehensible. By her fifth try, she graveled out a perfectly understandable, "The fox that runs under the moonlight shall be ever free." In Fox, of course. She wasn't going to risk any other language while being recorded. Besides, Fox involved a larger vocal range than any human language. If she could manage that, she should be fine.

So, she could still talk, albeit with pain. It was possible she would never be able to talk without pain again. Perhaps her voice would return to normal eventually. Maybe with surgery. Or maybe it wouldn't. The scar certainly wouldn't go away. Not on its own. Liska didn't dare touch it.

One, it would hurt a lot. Two, she was afraid to know how deep it went and how big. Maybe it was only on the surface, or maybe her neck was a blackened mass. She would find out in time. Surely Cazimir would show her a mirror eventually. He would want her to see his handiwork.

Scars were problematic in her line of work, particularly big, memorable ones. Big, memorable ones that would be impossible to hide unless she became in the habit of wearing scarves or high collars, both of which she avoided. Even when she was the one putting it there, she disliked pressure on her neck. Still, no one was going to forget seeing a scar like this, so she would have to do something. Maybe a skin graft would help. Something to worry about later.

This was another clue. Cazimir didn't care if she was in pain or if she was permanently marked but still wanted her in decent physical condition. So, what did he want? Atolatar had claimed to have Tisiphone under his thumb, a lie that was probably to draw her out. Though she did wonder how he knew she had been Tisiphone when she didn't know herself. Perhaps Yoshiro had told him.

She had guessed that Cazimir might plan to make it look like she worked for him. It would explain a few things. Why he didn't want her completely incapacitated but didn't care about scars or anything she'd quickly heal, not to mention the whole calling him 'Master' bit. But it didn't explain why he said if she knew what he wanted, she wouldn't be able to give it to him. Liska still hadn't figured out what that was supposed to mean.

Perhaps he wanted to show off to others that he had managed to break her. In which case, the collar scar would only increase his apparent power. Liska had made a fair name for herself in her time working. Not that she had actually done everything attributed to her, but her name was known in certain circles of the Twilight and Night community. Ironically enough, probably her biggest credit was 'killing' Tisiphone. Still, while she was considered a rising star of the Kikitsutai, she wasn't top tier yet.

If Cazimir wanted the infamy of breaking one of the Kikitsutai Ninja, then she would be a poor choice. Detractors would claim that she had broken so easily because she was a half-breed, or female, or still so young that she wasn't fully trained. Not to mention, he would earn the undying enmity of the Kikitsutai. Of course, that was a given.

So, why target *her*? If it was just a Werefox he wanted, *Sensei* might have been a better choice. Not because he wasn't capable of defending himself, but because he spent so much time alone, it would take longer to notice he was missing. And if Liska was starting to earn fame, well, *Sensei*'s preferred name, The Ghost, was still whispered about with respect and fear over a decade after his retirement. Not that Liska wanted anything to happen to *Sensei*, she was quite glad he was safe. But why? Maybe Cazimir thought she'd be an easier target.

Maybe she was easier. For all she knew, she had knocked on his door and started asking questions. But he had been prepared. Sooner or later, he was going to grab a Werefox. Or at least, some kind of Were. Solium was neither easy nor cheap to synthesize, and chains were not typically built like this. Not to mention the hay and the bugs. If Cazimir had to move his schedule up, it wasn't by more than a day or two.

Cazimir had implied knowing at least a little bit about her on first meeting. He said that he had been led to believe she was smarter than she was acting. He also acted like it was their first time meeting. Of course, she did first, but he didn't seem confused or surprised. So perhaps she didn't just get taken while questioning him.

It looked like she had been targeted specifically. Interestingly enough, she didn't recall a single instance of him mentioning her name. Any of them. He might well know she was Sakaki, being the one to have sent the shade to deliver notes. Or this could actually be a case of mistaken identity. Liska doubted that one though.

But there was more to this. She was sure of it, if not what it was. Surely Cazimir didn't just wake up one day and decide, 'I want a pet Werefox.' Or if he did, then the vampire was clearly insane. He wanted her in good enough shape to do something. Or perhaps, good enough shape to have done something. Now, that was an interesting train of thought.

What if she was being held here, not so she would do something for him in time, but so she wouldn't have an alibi when he framed her for something? Rex Magnus would certainly be impatient if no progress was made on who betrayed his blood. Progress she couldn't make while here. He had wanted to blame her already. What if Cazimir framed her for something else? Possibly even presenting her body as proof? Certainly, there would be inconsistencies if one cared to look. But he could probably come up with a story about her hair, or her injuries, even the silver burn. As for the deeper things, the evidence of Solium, possibly remnants of whatever drug he had used on her if any remained in her system, well, Rex wouldn't dig. Her family could argue, but that would lead to a diplomatic nightmare with the vampires. They might decide it better to let everything lie. Nor could she even blame them for it.

Still, if that was what Cazimir intended, he was being very sloppy. Rex might not argue, might not dig, but he would know there was more than he was being told. So would anyone else. Chances were, sooner or later, everyone would know she was just a scapegoat. Vindicated by history wouldn't be her preferred fate, but she'd take it over going down in history as a traitor.

But she didn't think that was the plan. Maybe she was wrong, but odds were that if Cazimir wanted that, he would be more careful about obvious marks. Especially the silver. It would be extremely difficult to convince anyone that any Were would willingly maim themselves with silver or injure their neck. Of course, Liska was a semi-exception. She had slit her wrists with a silver knife three, going on four years ago. Even now, she couldn't remember exactly why she had thought that a good idea. The silver knife part. She knew exactly why she had tried to kill herself. But for some reason, in her frenzy, there was an insistence that she use a silver knife. There were only three on the whole island. Two now.

Never mind that. Focusing on the past didn't help her out in the present. Or did it? She had been Tisiphone, the one who killed Ryasmus. Ryasmus was the one who turned Cazimir. Cazimir would therefore have been undyingly loyal to Ryasmus in return. It was nigh on impossible for a vampire to disobey even an implied order from the vampire who turned him. There were even claims that if a vampire, particularly a young one, tried to turn on his 'parent', then he would weaken and eventually cease to be a vampire, probably dying in the process.

Not that Liska could think of a single proven instance where that happened.

Assuming Cazimir knew she had been Tisiphone, which was very likely, then this was probably at least part revenge for killing Ryasmus. Honestly, for a pacifist, Ryasmus sure had a lot of people willing to kill her to avenge him.

But there had to be more. She had mentioned Ryasmus to him before, and Cazimir barely reacted. Even that reaction seemed to be more annoyance at having to admit subservience to the other vampire. *Seemed to be.* Maybe she had misinterpreted. Not every emotion had an easily identifiable scent. Sometimes she had to go by context. He had been irritated. She had heard him grind his teeth. Heart rate sped up. But there was no sorrow, no fury. No sign that he was willing to risk war with the Kikitsutai to avenge his mentor.

Atolatar had known she was Tisiphone and sent notes taunting her about it. There was no way Cazimir *didn't* know. Unless by some ridiculous twist of fate he thought she was someone else. Statistically improbable. Not impossible, but not much better than the odds of Cazimir coming down right now to unchain her, offer her a cup of hot tea, and say he had changed his mind and she could go as soon as they made landfall, oh, by the way, here are your clothes.

Okay, laughing hurt. Lots and lots. *Let's not do that again anytime soon.* Footsteps intruded as Liska tried unsuccessfully to soothe her throat with cold water. Cazimir was coming. She would bet her best katana that he wasn't here to offer her hot tea.

Judging from the small smirk at the flash of fear she allowed to show, the way his smirk widened when he saw her neck, and the complete absence of either a key or a mug in his hands, it looked like her best katana was safe. "How long have you been here?"

"Forever."

He seemed pleased by her croak. "Who do you obey?"

"You."

"Say it."

She just did. "I obey you." Her voice broke twice trying to say it. Had she permanently damaged her vocal cords? Only time would tell. Weres were good at healing, but they had limits.

Now would come the hard part. "Who am I?"

Did she give in now? Was this the right time? Forget the right time, could she even do it? Could she call him 'Master', even to fool him? Her lips moved. No sound came out.

Cazimir scowled. "Who. Am. I?"

Liska took a breath and tried again. Air came out, but no sound.

He grabbed her, right on top of the burn. She couldn't scream, she couldn't even think. Distantly she was aware of words, but she couldn't tell what they were.

Cazimir moved his hand, evidently realizing she couldn't answer. "Last chance. I grow weary of this. Who am I?"

He meant it. She had exhausted his patience. This might well be life or death. "Mas..." The word dissolved into a wheeze. Coughing hurt too. Good to know. Liska licked her bleeding lips. "Master."

She closed his eyes so as not to see his smile. It did nothing to shut out the smell of his satisfaction. She had him convinced he had broken her. But she wasn't convinced he hadn't.

"Good. Good." He pet her hair, and Liska forced herself not to move away. "Kitten. That will be what I call you. You will answer to it."

A humiliating nickname. One that made her sound weak and dependent on him. She knew this step. "Yes, Master."

More satisfaction. He really liked being called 'Master'. Odd that he chose to call her 'kitten'. Foxes were canines, even if they were the most feline of canines. Of course, young foxes were called kits. And cubs, and pups.

"Good. Now, good kittens get treats."

"Thank you, Master." It stuck in her craw to call him that, but it had him convinced she was broken. Which meant that eventually he'd let his guard down. Then she would strike. Kitten, was she? Well then, he should remember just how vicious a cat could get. No one truly tamed a cat.

Cazimir left, takin the food tray with him. When he returned, there was food, decent food, on a plate, with cutlery. And the water was untainted. No clothes though. On the other hand, she couldn't put clothes on while chained up anyway.

He stood there, watching her eat, for reasons Liska knew better than to question. Every once in a while, he would call out, "Kitten?" Liska made sure to at least look at him each time.

She knew what this was. He wanted her responding instinctively to his name for her. It was a way of trying to shape her identity. Unfortunately for him, Liska frequently had trained herself to respond instinctively to different names at certain times, but not at others. Kitten was just one more. Once Cazimir left, she would spend some time forming an identity for Kitten. Kitten could be the broken, frightened girl who wouldn't dream of doing anything that might make Master mad, all while Liska waited and planned.

"Kitten?"

Kitten looked up, pausing from her food. "Master?"

"Do you like your food?"

"Yes, Master." She could add a 'thank you', but surely Cazimir didn't think she had succumbed to Stockholm Syndrome so quickly. No, she could add it in time. For now, this would be sufficient. If he considered it important, he would prompt her.

Cazimir nodded. "Isn't this so much better than when you were disobedient?"

"Yes." He glowered at her. "Yes, Master."

"Who am I?"

"Master."

"Who do you obey?"

"I obey you."

"How long have you been here?"

"Forever."

Cazimir was clearly pleased. "Good. Good, Kitten." He started to leave.

"Master?"

"Yes?"

"Why did you betray the Rex Magnus Blood?"

Chapter Twenty-Six

Even the strongest steel can break. – The Kikitsutai Book of Wisdom

Cazimir spun to stare down the impudent Werefox. He had been surprised she had called after him at all, but this was the last thing he had expected from her. But when he looked at the newly dubbed Kitten, he saw no condemnation, no sign she was digging, simply curiosity. By the power of the Blood, how had she figured that one out?

"What?"

"Why did you betray the Rex Magnus Blood?" The tone and inflection were exactly the same as when she asked the question the first time.

If she wasn't certain he had done it before, she was now. It was a good thing she would never have the chance to tell Rex Magnus. Rex wasn't as old or as powerful a vampire as Cazimir himself, but he was clever and vindictive. He would have no choice but to speed up his plans to kill Rex and incorporate what was left of the Magnus Blood into 'his' own.

Not that it would be difficult, but he didn't want to move too fast. Not yet. None of Cazimir's own followers knew he was responsible for giving Calloway directions and a layout of the building; not after he ordered the shade he used to destroy itself. Nor would they appreciate finding out. Not that he couldn't keep them under control, but it would add complications he didn't need right now. Not when he almost had the Were where he wanted her. She wasn't yet as broken as she wanted him to believe, but was closer than she realized. And he knew exactly how to throw her over that edge.

"I did not betray the Rex Magnus Blood." After all, what loyalty did he owe them other than the loyalty to vampire kind? If the Blood could be found and decimated so easily, then clearly they had poor leadership. They needed a strong leader.

For too long vampires had followed the council. A group of vampires that hated each other, and spent more time trying to shore up their own position than protecting and strengthening vampirekind. Perhaps it had worked well enough in the past, but it wouldn't for much longer. There were simply too many humans, too many ways that vampires could be exposed to the world, and more reaction like the Purifiers would come. Yet the 'council of the wise' couldn't stop their bickering!

The solution was obvious to him. Rule by a group was unwieldy and slow. History had proven again and again, that in the most difficult times, extraordinary changes were almost always caused, or at least spearheaded, by a single exceptional person. Often a strong leader who wasn't afraid to rule with an iron fist. Vlad Dracul was never a vampire, but he gave a peace to his land, internal and external, that was practically unprecedented. Even now, he was a respected figure in his native lands, no matter how reviled he might be in the world at large. Or Ivan the Dread. Called 'Terrible' over most of the world, the Russians still believed him to be what a leader should be.

If he could unite the vampires under him, a united force against threats from the humans, the Weres, the Fae, or any other who would try to control them, it could only be for the better. For the vampires, and possibly the world at large. Ryasmus had dreamed of peace but never realized that the only way it could be accomplished was if everyone was afraid to challenge you. Even from the beginning, Cazimir had understood that. Which was why whenever Ryasmus gave him orders, Cazimir was able to keep the end goal, peace, in mind, and work towards that goal, even if it meant going against orders. It had taken him the better part of two centuries to realize that other vampires couldn't do that. He was extraordinary. All the better. He would be the extraordinary one to unite the vampires.

Of course, that meant that eventually Ryasmus had to die. It was unfortunate. Cazimir even liked the strange vampire in his own way. But he was simply too weak to be the glue that held the vampires together or even appear to be that power. It had provided a problem for Cazimir. No matter how much he knew that Ryasmus would have to die for the betterment of vampires as a whole, for that peace that Ryasmus loved so dearly, he couldn't actually kill him. Perhaps it was the loyalty of a vampire for his parent, maybe it was his own fondness for his mentor, but every time he even thought about killing Ryasmus, Cazimir found himself paralyzed with nausea.

He tried to think of other methods. Ryasmus had actually let him turn some of the vampires, only proving how weak he was. When Cazimir was in charge, he would insist on personally turning all new recruits. But he couldn't order or even suggest that one of his 'children' kill Ryasmus. None of them were strong enough to be successful. Or even be able to see the necessity of killing a Master Vampire.

Ironically enough, the method that eventually worked wasn't even one he had done deliberately. Ryasmus had chastened Cazimir for his ruthless streak, but never to the point that Cazimir had held himself back from loosing it when he wished. Oh, he had gone by a different name sometimes, but Rimat was barely different enough to be considered a pseudonym. So his own violent actions were assumed to be sanctioned by Ryasmus. Which led to the Kikitsutai sending the girl in front of him to eliminate Ryasmus. It had fallen into his plans so nicely that Cazimir almost regretted the necessity of breaking her. But it was only broken that she could serve him, for the good of all.

"Then why tell the Purifiers where the Blood was?" The girl asked. Only calm curiosity in her voice, but there was a spark in her eye. She knew.

He backhanded her. The girl didn't even blink. "You do not question me. Do you understand?"

"Yes, Master."

Cazimir swept from the room, straight to the camera room. No one was there. No one had seen. Good. None of his current crew would understand the necessity. Not yet. They wouldn't tell even if they knew. He had ordered all of them not to say anything to anyone about their 'guest', or anything that happened or that she said while she was here.

He erased the footage reluctantly. He had wanted to keep today's video. Proof of when he finally broke the fox's spirit. Of course, it wasn't broken yet. He'd be able to keep the footage of *that*. When would he do it? Not yet. Give her a couple days to recover, to be lulled into complacency. He wanted her broken, not shattered.

***

One vampire hid in the shadows as Cazimir strode past. In his hand, he clutched tightly at the thumb drive in his hand. The thumb drive that held a copy of the footage that Cazimir was currently deleting.

This was a dangerous game he was playing, having made that copy. Even doubting his parent was painful. But how could betraying other vampires be a good thing? Cazimir had denied it, but the fox was certain. It was her ability to detect lies versus Cazimir's trustworthiness. *Listen to the Father. Trust him. He knows best.* But did he? It was borderline blasphemous to even think it. He certainly didn't say it.

But Cazimir was destroying the footage. Did that prove anything? Or was he simply hoping to avoid something like this? A young easily-led vampire questioning him. He was only alive thanks to Cazimir! He owed him everything!

The footage didn't *prove* anything. He should just dispose of it right now. Or give it to Cazimir, confessing everything. That was exactly what he *should* do. And he stood there, thumb drive imprinting lines in his hand, wondering what he *would* do.

***

Cazimir was clearly more dangerous than she had anticipated. Far, far more dangerous. Kitten bent over her food, eating slowly, never looking up. Liska used the time to think.

She still wasn't sure why she had asked him about betraying the Magnus Blood. While the thought had occurred to her how convenient it was for Calloway to have been used both to attack her and the Magnus Blood, or that Rimat was there to help the survivors so quickly, it wasn't until she actually saw his reaction that she *knew* he was responsible.

For a vampire to turn on another blood was unprecedented. Almost unthinkable. But somehow Cazimir had twisted it in his mind as acceptable, probably necessary, maybe even a good thing. Liska knew her mind had twisted paths, but she wasn't sure she *wanted* to understand his logic. This was the right-hand man of the world's most famous pacifist vampire? How had he managed to twist things with Ryasmus?

Vampires were funny. They were as intelligent as humans; as capable of thinking, reasoning, and problem solving. Except when dealing with the one who turned them. Once, as a practice exercise in how to work around issues, Father had set a table with six cups on it, telling her not to touch the cups until he explicitly said she could. He then told her to move the cups to the other side of the room. First, she moved the table. After Father forbade that, she picked up the tablecloth. When he ruled that out, she puzzled for a while before finding a small balloon. She inflated it while in the cup, transported the cup, and let the air out when it was there. Father had actually laughed and congratulated her on using a solution he hadn't seen before.

The average vampire following the same test could easily figure out her solutions or others. Unless the test was given by the one who turned them. Then they would be paralyzed by confusion and indecision. Following two contradictory orders? It simply couldn't be done. If Cazimir was able to disobey his parent, or even twist things to disobey the spirit of the law while obeying the letter, than he was rare, and all the more dangerous for it.

Well, she had figured out who betrayed Rex Magnus, even if she didn't know why. Maybe she'd actually live long enough to tell him.

***

Her sense of time was fading. No clock, no window, even Cazimir's visits were at random times, so she had nothing to keep it in balance. Heartbeats and breaths were too small and variable to measure more than a couple minutes. Her hair grew too slowly to use for anything shorter than months. She had expected to lose her internal clock eventually, but she still dreaded it. Was this day fifteen or sixteen? Or was it day twenty? No, not that long. She thought. But she couldn't be sure.

Fine. It was day fifteen. Didn't matter if that was right, this was day fifteen. Maybe it would be easier to keep track of the days if she didn't spend so much of her time half-asleep, but there was nothing else to do, she didn't have the energy to do it if there was, and lack of true sleep kept her exhausted.

Since becoming Kitten, she had gotten better food, but not more of it. Quite frankly, lack of food was definitely taking its toll. Her arms and legs looked more like sticks than anything else. Part of her was half convinced that her elbows were sharp enough to just pop through the papery skin on top if she bent her arms carelessly. With the camera on her, she didn't examine the rest of herself, but she knew her bones were jutting out more than usual.

If Cazimir wanted her to do something, he was either going to have to get her to do it soon or start feeding her more. Liska was voting for the 'more food' route. Mother frequently said she looked like a strong wind would blow her away. Now it would probably only take a sneeze.

Cazimir came in. No tray. He was smirking and staying by the door. Something had changed. That was never good for her.

Faintly, a smell reached her. A familiar smell. What was it? Cazimir was speaking. It sounded like it was through water. "I've brought you a surprise."

Kitten responded, but Liska didn't bother to pay attention. A memory was nagging at her.

Cazimir moved to the side and shortened her chains. Enough that she was against the wall but not suspended off the ground. "Come in, Pup."

Slowly, hesitantly, another figure came in. Liska pulled in a breath.

She had pulled into the address Van had sent her. It had once been a bait shop but looked like it had been closed for years. A vampire was huddled in the shadows. Four o'clock was still early for them to be out. What was Van doing up and about this hour?

Liska was halfway to the store when she realized that the vampire hiding in the shadows wasn't Van at all. "Eric? What are you doing here? And what made you think I'd be willing to talk to you right now?" Where was Van? Was she late, or hiding because Eric was already here? Or had she sent Eric on ahead because she couldn't make it.

As Liska approached, her warning senses prickled. Something was very wrong. Eric knew too. He was really scared. He fidgeted, eyes darting everywhere, hands checking his hood and sunglasses. "I'm glad to see you. Thanks for coming."

Despite herself, some of her irritation faded. Not that she let it out of her voice. "What are you doing here?"

He held up a familiar phone. "You texted me."

She knew she should be furious, but she wasn't. "That's not your phone."

"I know. Whose is it? I want to get it back to the owner, but I'm not sure who owns it. Or if they're supposed to have it." He gave the phone a

light toss and caught it. Trying to play casual. Even if she couldn't smell his terror, she wouldn't have bought it.

"I'll return it. I know the owner." Liska extended an arm, not getting closer than she had to.

"I thought you wanted information?"

"Do you have it?" Eric couldn't have been a vampire more than ten, fifteen years. Twenty at most. It was very unlikely that he knew anything about Rimat.

"No, but I need you to meet someone who does."

Yeah, the alarm bells were ringing long and hard. "I'm busy. Give me a number and I'll make an appointment."

"No, you need to talk to him. It's important."

"You aren't in the position to demand things. Twenty seconds or less, why do I need to talk to this guy?"

Eric sputtered for a second, as Liska just stared him down. Something was wrong. She didn't want to be here. She took two steps back before realizing she had moved. "Fine, text me a name and number. I'm gone."

There was movement to her side, by the door of the shop. Liska turned to it, hand reaching for a dagger, even as chloroform tickled her nose. One hand grabbed her hair, twisting her head painfully, while the other came with a rag, blanketing her mouth and nose.

Holding her breath, Liska brought up the dagger, only for another hand to grab her wrist. Eric. The betrayal caused her to inhale sharply.

That was a mistake. Faced with her betrayed glance he only mouthed, "I'm sorry." Then there was black.

Eric glanced at her before staring at the floor, reeking of misery. "I... I was ordered."

Cazimir laughed. "Yes, you were. But so what? It wasn't like you actually cared for the vixen. Just her bed. Did you succeed at that?"

Blood drained from her face, even as Eric winced and slowly shook his head.

"No? Do you want her now? The chains mean she won't be able to fight."

Her breath was fast. Too fast. Blood was rushing in her ears.

"No. The challenge is gone." Eric finally looked up, though he wasn't looking at her.

"Challenge? What challenge? You're an empath who used your gifts on girls to get into their beds. Don't think that makes you any less of a rapist than the one who chains the girl down to sleep with her." Cazimir waved a hand dismissively.

"I'm not–"

"I don't care. I don't care how many girls you use. Whether you call it seduction or rape. It doesn't matter." Cazimir turned his attention to Liska, who was trying not to hyperventilate. "He was useful, Eric was. Without him, you wouldn't be here. I wouldn't care about you. You wouldn't be what I need."

The words meant nothing to her, pebbles against her skin. The room was spinning. Eric had betrayed her. Probably been planning to betray her the whole time he was in West Palm Beach. And she had sensed nothing. *I can't deal with this!*

Instantly, she heard a voice in her head, *Then let me.*

Liska closed her eyes.

Nightmare opened them.

***

"It worked," Eric said quietly, feeling the shift in personality. The swirling morass of fury and vengeance that Sakaki kept on the back burner had come to the fore. Even her stance was different. Not the bent, cowed stance of Kitten, or the confused, shocked, barely standing Sakaki. This woman stood rigid, murder in her eyes.

Cazimir smiled, not realizing how he radiated satisfaction. "Perfect. Hello, Nightmare."

Nightmare gave Eric the briefest glance, then turned from him with a dismissive sniff, to glare at Cazimir. "I hope you know that you will die for this."

The old vampire's smile widened. "Perhaps. But until then, you will work for me."

"Why?"

"Because you hope that in time I will let down my guard enough for you to kill me. And because until that time, you will be taking down the Purifiers."

Eric felt her considering it. "Agreed." When Cazimir looked his way, he nodded. She was telling the truth this time.

Cazimir actually laughed. "Excellent." Then he turned to Eric. "Are you planning to rape the girl or not?" Eric hurriedly shook his head. "Then I don't need you here. Go."

Eric left, hoping he got as far as his quarters before he was sick. He didn't.

Chapter Twenty-Seven

Some goals make even enemies, allies. For a time. – The Kikitsutai Book of Wisdom

Nightmare was a very different captive than Liska had been. Liska had been working on fooling Cazimir into believing he was succeeding in breaking her. Nightmare knew she was broken and didn't care. Liska worked on figuring out what Cazimir wanted and how to get away. Nightmare had been told what Cazimir wanted and was simply waiting for her chance at revenge. Getting away afterwards was secondary. If it happened, great. If not, that was fine too.

Nightmare was also treated better. She was given more food and occasionally let off the chains to exercise. The annoying noise that made it so difficult to sleep was turned off. She celebrated by sleeping for most of a day, and they left her alone to do so. After all, there was a job to do, and she needed to be in good enough shape to do it.

Cazimir, for reasons known only to him, decided that Eric would be the one in charge of monitoring her exercises. Maybe he thought she wouldn't kill him. Maybe he hoped she would.

Whatever he wanted, Nightmare mostly ignored Eric. When she did look at him, it was with the same look someone would give a half-squished slug. It was days before she even spoke to him.

Eric came in with her tray. The water had Solium this time. The food was actually herbed mussels with angel hair. Nightmare didn't bother to scoff at that, even while she wondered what he was playing at. Was he trying to irritate her by reminding her of the date he had sabotaged? Was he trying to win her over with a fonder memory? Was this Cazimir's orders? Probably. It didn't matter.

He didn't look her in the eye, hadn't been able to since Cazimir brought him in to rub her nose in her stupidity. So, he felt guilt. So what? What good did that do her?"

Eric put the tray down and paused as if unsure if he should stay or leave. Nightmare ignored him, taking a small bite of pasta. No wine in the sauce this time. Idly she wondered if he had gotten it from the same restaurant. They had pulled into land for a few hours today.

"Do you hate me?" The question was quiet, and judging from the surprise in his scent, Eric hadn't meant to ask it.

Nightmare chewed the pasta in her mouth and swallowed, spearing a mussel with her fork. "You're the empath. You tell me."

"I... I can't tell. You feel a lot of anger and hatred right now."

And he wanted to know how much, if any, was directed at him. "You aren't worth the energy to hate."

"I had my orders. I couldn't..."

Nightmare could understand orders, even bad ones. Even without the vampire loyalty to their turner, Sakaki wouldn't disobey direct orders from her father. She could almost forgive the kidnapping. Well, understand it at least. "Were you ordered to seduce me?"

From the corner of her eye, she saw Eric flinch. "I wasn't..."

"Were you ordered to manipulate my emotions?"

"If necessary."

"To do what? Get me to Cazimir?"

"Yes."

"*Did* you manipulate my emotions?" Because looking back, it seemed very suspicious that Sakaki's emotions for Eric were so much stronger than he was around, and much more manageable when thinking about it later. Some of that was typical, but this was a suspicious amount, now that she knew.

Eric didn't answer. He didn't have to. The answer was obvious.

"You weren't manipulating me to meet Cazimir; you were manipulating me to fall in love with you." Only falling in love with Todd first had saved her. But even Todd had changed his mind.

"I..."

Nightmare plucked another mussel from its shell. "He was right. You are a rapist."

Eric made some peculiar choking sounds, but Nightmare didn't look up. "I am not!"

"You tried to push lust on me, didn't you?"

"That doesn't make me a rapist!"

"If I had tried to sleep with you, would you have accepted?"

"Well, yeah." He didn't say 'of course', but she heard it anyway.

"Despite knowing that I wouldn't want to if you hadn't manipulated me?"

"But..." Nightmare stayed quiet, staring at him. Not letting him off the hook. "It's different. You would have wanted it then."

"Only because of your manipulations. Tell me, how many other girls have there been? Girls who only slept with you because you imprinted emotions on them." Eric was silent. "How many of them would have slept with you if you hadn't done that?"

"I don't know."

Nightmare nodded. "Rape."

Eric sputtered, but Nightmare ignored him. The food was good at least. She reached for the pitcher to drink some water. Eric snatched it away from her. Now she looked at him.

"I'm not a bad person."

A bitter laugh escaped her before she thought about it. "Clearly. We're only arguing over whether your manipulations make you a rapist, while I'm a prisoner of a vampire you helped to capture me. You've done so much to help me in the meantime."

"I got you that blanket."

She had wondered about that. "A blanket? Oh, you must be in the running to be nominated for sainthood!"

"I had no choice in taking you. Cazimir ordered me to."

"How did he even know about me?"

To her surprise, Eric flinched hard enough to drop the pitcher. Maybe there was more of a story than she thought. The pitcher didn't break, but all the water spilled out. Eric muttered something that might have been an apology and scurried off with the pitcher. He returned a moment later, put the pitcher on the tray and left. Nightmare took a small sniff. The water didn't have Solium in it.

***

"I have a mission for you." Cazimir swept in, looking like he needed a cape to swish behind him.

"What kind of mission?" Nightmare remained stoic, even as her mind raced. A mission. She was a mildly skilled hacker at best, though she had been better a few years ago. Most of her missions, for any of her working names, involved actually physically going somewhere and doing something. Which would get her off this lousy boat. Sure, Cazimir would have plans to keep her from escaping, but maybe she'd be able to slip past his net anyway. Or at least leave some kind of message.

"Physical infiltration. That is a specialty of yours, is it not? I need you to get into the Purifier's headquarters in Miami. You will be gathering information and planting evidence."

"Purifier's buildings aren't easy." She could do it, at least when she was in top condition, but even then, she considered them a challenge.

"You will have assistance, of course."

Ah, not sending her in alone. Of course.

"You have blueprints?"

Cazimir did. And he had plans on exactly what he wanted. After reviewing the plans, Nightmare thought she could do it. "I'll need clothes. And some of my tools."

"Of course. Get some rest. I want this done tonight."

***

When Cazimir came back, he had clothes, tools, and weapons. He also had what appeared to be an explosive collar, but she could smell the silver. "There is silver dust in this." He waved the collar. "One of your assistants will have the remote. You will not know which one. If you do not follow orders precisely... Well, I understand that silver poisoning is a terrible death for Weres."

She snarled as he drew nearer. Cazimir scowled. "You aren't going anywhere without this."

"But you can't put it on me." There was no way she would be able to let him. Growling, she swallowed as much distaste as she could, which wasn't much. "Give it to me."

Cautiously, he handed her the collar. The collar itself was steel, so at least that wasn't a problem. It was difficult to put it on, both mentally and physically. Pressure still hurt on the slowly healing silver burn. At least she could talk without pain now. Actually, the wound was healing better than she had feared. Discoloration and blistering but not blackened.

Latching the collar shut was one of the hardest things she had ever done. Obviously it wasn't meant to come off without some specialized tool or key. One she didn't have, and she'd bet her right hand it was meant to go off if tampered with. "Satisfied?"

"Very." The chains were removed. "Get dressed."

He actually gave her back her own clothes, the ones she had been wearing at the time of her capture. From the feel of it, they still had her toys in them too. Good. She was more comfortable with her own weapons and tools. For a few seconds, she considered killing Cazimir right here and now. Sure, she'd be dead a few minutes later, but she'd take him down with her.

No, not yet. If this opportunity arose, there would be others. Maybe one where she wouldn't have to die such a horrible death to kill him.

Cazimir didn't leave and was unlikely to turn around just because she asked. Better not to let on she was bothered by his scrutiny. Instead, she took a couple steps to the side so she wasn't in view of the camera and dressed as quickly as she could. "I'm ready."

Two shades glided in a moment later. They were visible, for a change, but that was probably for her sake.

"These will be your assistants. They have been ordered to obey your directions on this mission so long as they do not contradict my own. When your mission is finished, you are to return. They *will* kill you if you do not do as ordered."

Nightmare nodded. Shades, huh? She couldn't kill shades. Not really. She didn't know where these had come from or why, so there was no solving that to dissipate them. They avoided or withdrew when confronted with blessed salt, but she wasn't sure that actually hurt them. Certainly wouldn't kill them. She also didn't have any. On the other hand, shades weren't very intelligent. They would follow orders, generally to the letter, but that was because they couldn't think around things.

Nightmare could work around the shades in ways she couldn't work around a vampire or wraith, and they might not even notice. But she wouldn't be able to escape them. It didn't take brain power to push a button, and she couldn't stop them, kill them, or even knock them out.

It might be easier if she was working with wraiths or vampires, but Cazimir knew that too. On the other hand, more complicated missions would probably need more intelligent backup. Nightmare said nothing for now.

"What is your mission?" Cazimir asked.

"Find out where the Purifiers keep their paper files, particularly data files and personnel files. Photograph as much as possible, taking none. Leave the drugs you give me behind." She wasn't sure where Cazimir had gotten ahold of three kilos of cocaine, but that was easier to get than Solium, so she didn't ask.

Cazimir nodded. "You may also want this." He pulled out a very dark, probably black, square of paper. "I trust you know what to do with this."

Nightmare accepted the paper without comment. Interesting, he actually wanted her to leave a calling card behind. That meant the Kikitsutai would be getting involved, sooner or later. Of course, that would cause trouble for Sakaki. Even if they believed she didn't know what she was doing, she would not take well to discovering that she had another personality that she never suspected. But that would be dealt with later.

"We make landfall in twenty minutes. It will be almost midnight. Eric will drive you and your assistants to the target location. Once there, you will have two hours to complete your mission before you are deemed in rebellion and terminated. Do you understand?"

Two hours should be plenty. The building wasn't that big. Most of that time would be spent memorizing as many details as she could find. "I understand."

"Excellent. Follow me."

It was her first time leaving the room since her capture, so Nightmare intended to learn as much of the layout of the boat as possible. Sooner or later, she intended to be free of Cazimir and his crew. The more options she had, the better.

There wasn't much to see. They passed three other doors before climbing a spindly metal stair to what was clearly the top deck. Nightmare thought she saw a stair that went down too, but she didn't get close enough to confirm.

Above board, it was clear the boat was about forty or fifty yards long. She noted the location of the life rafts. Always a good thing to know.

Nightmare closed her eyes and breathed in the night air. Salt water, metal, ship oil, the soft smell of blood that vampires always exuded, and a hint of rain in the offing. It was such a relief to be out of that room. She had been cooped up for far too long.

Miami. Miami should have a strong Coast Guard presence, on the lookout for illegal immigration, smuggling, etc. Had Cazimir taken that into consideration? The shades could go invisible, but anyone taking one look at her would know something was wrong; even assuming she didn't do anything to tell them or get their attention. So she better not get spotted. Cazimir probably wouldn't care about killing any witnesses, and she would prefer not to be the cause of death for some innocent security official just doing his job.

"How are we avoiding the Coast Guard?" Nightmare asked.

Cazimir smirked. "Easily, actually. We are pulling into a small dock, one we've been seen at a few times in the past. You and Eric will disembark, the shades following invisibly. Officially, you are doing an emergency supply run." He frowned at her, before taking a lump of cloth from a wraith standing nearby and tossing it at here. "Put that on."

'That' turned out to be on overlarge hooded sweatshirt. When she had the hood up, the collar was barely noticeable. Anyone catching a glimpse of metal would probably assume it was just a necklace.

"Say nothing to anyone. Eric does any necessary talking."

A bit of a mistake there. Nightmare was certain she could spin a convincing tale better than Eric, but Cazimir couldn't afford to take any challenges. "Understood."

Fifteen minutes later, they were at the dock. "Showtime," said Cazimir.

Chapter Twenty-Eight

Good intentions do not always lead to good results. – The
Kikitsutai Book of Wisdom

Eric led the way down to the dock.
Sakaki/Nightmare glided silently behind him,
almost as if she were a shade herself. The dock
minder was one he had run into before. Only time
would tell if that was good or bad.

"Hey, Jack. Late tonight, aren't you?" The
minder greeted him. Eric thought his name was
Tom, but he wasn't sure.

Nightmare didn't even blink at him being
called a different name, or to Tom staring curiously
at her, trying to figure out what was up with her.
Then again, she was staring at the dock itself,
perhaps she hadn't noticed. Or maybe she was
trying to get her land legs back. She had been on
board that ship for weeks.

Eric carefully sent feelings of indifference to
Tom. Slowly he felt the curiosity recede. "Yeah, a
little. We won't be long. Just getting supplies."

"At this time of night?" Todd looked at his watch.

"Yeah, well, someone had the bright idea of going to the Keys." Eric shrugged. It didn't answer the question, not really, but Tom didn't ask anymore.

"Well, you know the drill."

Eric nodded, showing his ID and signing the fake information they had given for the boat.

"Her too."

"Huh?" Eric asked.

"If she's coming ashore, I need her ID too."

"Oh, right. Um..."

Out of the corner of his eye, he spotted Nightmare move. A jolt of fear ran through him. What was she doing? As he spun around to stop her, he noticed that she pulled a small plastic ID from her pocket. Oh. That was what she was going to do.

Feeling a little silly, Eric relaxed as Tom leaned forward to read it. "School ID, huh? Don't have a government issued ID?" She shook her head. "I guess I can take this. But better bring something official next time. Anna Andrews? Okay, that's good." He wrote it down. "Right, I'll need to see them again when you leave. Good luck with supplies."

The two nodded, and Eric led the way to the car Cazimir had arranged to keep stored at the dock. No one was around, so Eric didn't have to come up with some ridiculous excuse for opening the rear doors for the shades. They could open doors themselves, but Cazimir had ordered them not to do things like that when they were invisible and could attract attention.

Nightmare opened her own door, and buckled up before staring out the windshield, clearly ignoring her surroundings.

"It's not far," Eric said, as much to break the silence as any other reason. Unfortunately, that only seemed to accentuate how awkward the silence was. There was a slight rustle of cloth that might or might not be from Nightmare nodding. The shades were ordered not to talk unless specifically questioned or ordered. But that was more of a relief than anything else. Shades were not good conversationalists. Like water wasn't very flammable.

He tried again. "Are you nervous?" A very minute shake of the head. "Um, good."

Eric started driving. The silence got louder and more oppressive with each passing minute. "What's your plan?"

They were stopped at a red light, so he was able to see the annoyed look that she turned and leveled at him. "What?"

Nightmare pursed her lips together but said nothing.

"I don't understand."

She jerked her head to the back, indicating the shades. What was she trying to say? "Something about shades. Orders?" She nodded. "Oh! You were told not to talk. But that was just to outsiders."

Nightmare raised an eyebrow and cocked her head back again. A clear 'Do they know that?' Considering the intelligence level of shades, that was a good question. He couldn't blame her for not wanting to risk her life on a possible misunderstanding. Before he could say anything of the sort, she turned forward and pointed. The light had turned green.

It took approximately twenty minutes to reach the former men's club that the Purifiers were supposedly running a dog kennel out of. The dog part wasn't a complete lie. Problematic, but Cazimir insisted on her infiltrating this place first. He knew that Weres and dogs didn't get along. Well, there was nothing Eric could do about it. It was totally out of his hands.

Almost totally. He turned to the backseat and spoke in the clear command voice that worked best when dealing with shades. "She will need to speak to give you orders. You will listen and obey those orders so long as they fulfill the mission. Do you understand?"

There was a moment of silence, like unspoken conferring. Finally, a whispery voice answered, "We obey the master's orders."

Eric frowned. That didn't answer the question. "The master's orders were to assist her. To follow her orders. She will have to speak to give those orders. Do you understand?"

A longer pause. "We will listen to the fox. We will obey the master's orders."

Eric let out a breath. "Best I can do," He said to the silent Werefox. She didn't respond, nor did he expect her to. "Twelve-thirty. Meet back here at two-thirty or before. I will be getting supplies, but I should be back within the hour."

She climbed out of the car, stopping long enough to open the back door.

"Right. Good luck."

Nightmare gave him a look of studied disdain before melting into the shadows.

***

For a supposed dog kennel, there was a *lot* of security. Two security cameras on each wall, and according to the blueprints, there were even more inside. Because it had been a 'gentlemen's club' there were no windows, probably why they picked this location. If Cazimir's report was correct, there should be two guards and at least ten to fifteen dogs inside. Grand. She hated having to make do with someone else's information. She hated dogs. And she really hated having to work for Cazimir.

Nightmare closed her eyes, bringing up a mental picture of the blueprints. Rectangular building, with the door in the right corner, leading to a small lobby. From the lobby, taking up the majority of the space, were the kennels. The left section of the building was walled up, hiding everything the Purifiers didn't want found. That's where the security office was, and files she needed. No way to get there without going through the dogs. Nightmare stifled a shiver. She did *not* like dogs

On the far side of the building was a fenced in yard for the dogs. Supposedly, one guard would be back there, while the other stayed in the room watching the cameras. First things first. She wasn't going to manage anything staring at the building.

Two cameras on each wall made it so they could see anyone walking up to the building no matter which side they came from. With a little time, effort, and probably hacking, she could figure out where the blind spots were. But there wasn't time for that.

The Purifiers had never hired someone like her to test their security. If they had, they would have done something about the large oak tree that spread branches over the building.

"Follow me," she breathed on the wind, before appraising the tree. This wouldn't be an easy climb. No low-hanging branches, no good foot rests, and the trunk was too thick to get her arms around. Still, Nightmare was part of Sakaki, and Sakaki had been climbing trees since she was big enough to hold onto the branches without falling off.

Who says foxes can't climb trees? First, she stabbed the tree with her dagger, whispering a quiet, "Sorry, tree." Then she pulled out a ten-foot length of paracord and a small bottle of hand sanitizer. Tying the sanitizer on one end to weight it, she boosted herself up, standing on the handle of the dagger and threw the weighted end of the cord. It took two tries, but she got it to wrap around a sturdy looking branch.

With the cord to help pull herself up, she only needed the occasional foot hold, before climbing onto the branch. She let down the cord. "Can you climb up?"

There wasn't a verbal answer, but the cord jerked, and after a minute or two, she felt a sense of presence, and the smell of decay grew. "Wait here a moment." Nightmare unwound the cord from the branch and aimed for a higher branch. This was an easier climb because she could use other branches for leverage. "Now climb up." She tossed the free end of the cord, making sure it was near the original branch. Nightmare would be the first to admit that she wasn't an expert on shades, and that included how well they could climb. The answer appeared to be 'reasonably well' as the shades joined her a minute later.

Nightmare eased further out on the branch so she was over the building. "One of you wait here, one come with me. The one who waits, when we come back, you lower the cord for us. Understood?"

There was a long wait, while Nightmare tried to figure out if that was too complicated for a shade to understand. Before she could figure out another way to word her orders, she got a reply. "Go with fox."

A slightly different voice whispered, "Stay. Lower cord."

"Good. Now." She jumped onto the roof, landing slightly rough on her ankles, before practically flattening herself against the roof, trying to avoid being seen by anyone. She felt more than heard the shade join her. "Check the yard. Is anyone there?" Nightmare pointed to the far end of the building.

She had almost made it to the skylight when the presence returned. "Guard. Kill?"

"No. No deaths."

The shade didn't like it. "Blood. Kill."

"Cazimir didn't say to kill. No evidence but the horse."

There was a hiss from the shade at her side, but Nightmare ignored it. She had reached the skylight. It was alarmed, of course, but it was a surprisingly outdated alarm. Perhaps they had forgotten about it. The silver rim of the skylight would be a little more difficult, but she had gloves.

The alarm took forty-two seconds to disarm. She could have simply cut the wire, but that might have alerted somebody. Nightmare put an ear down next to the glass, but there was no sign that she had alarmed anyone. Looking through the glass, she saw cages and cages of dogs. At least they were all in cages. There was a door in the wall where she needed to go. It was only a few feet from the door to the outside. On a table in between, there was a half-full coffee pot. This might work after all.

"Move this. Carefully." Nightmare ordered the shade. She could move the hatch herself but wanted to make sure the shade could.

There was another hiss. "Salt."

Of course there was. With careful sniffing and a very thin knife, she was able to remove enough of the salt to let the shade through. The hatch was moved. It was dark inside, but that wouldn't bother either of them.

The dogs were starting to shift nervously. "Go down there, put this in the coffee pot. Do not be seen." Nightmare handed the shade the second powder that Cazimir had given her, waited until she couldn't feel the shade, and replaced the cover.

Moving to the side, Nightmare lay on the roof, listening. As she suspected, the presence of a shade stirred up the dogs, to the point that someone came to check it out. It was an internal door, so not the guard outside. A man yelled at the dogs to be quiet. It worked. Enough that she could hear the faint sounds of liquid. Someone was drinking, walking back the way he came. Nightmare waited an additional five minutes for the sedative to take effect. If that shade had completed his part. But there was no way to check. She would have to risk it.

Once more, she opened the hatch. The dogs were barking up a storm now. She waited a minute, but no one came in to check it out. She ought to be clear. With a grim smile, Nightmare jumped in, landing on a cage that held an extremely aggressive looking Doberman. Goody goody gumdrops.

They can't hurt you. They can't get out of their cages, and you aren't going to be sticking things in there. The dog tried to snap at her feet but couldn't get them through the bars. She quickly hopped off anyway. Too many dogs. There were far too many dogs. No time to panic. Get the job done and get out.

There were loads of video cameras here, and she had to be visible on some of them. It was inevitable. But no one was reacting. Which meant that either the guard hadn't noticed, was in no condition to do anything about it, or was waiting for her. The dogs were making too much noise for her to trust her ears, and she wasn't close enough to pick up subtle smells. She was going in blind.

Nightmare forced herself not to flinch from various dogs. Partially because pulling away from one made her closer to another. Partially because she wasn't stupid enough to think that Cazimir wouldn't be interrogating the shades about everything. He didn't need to know she was afraid of dogs. She definitely didn't need him to know that.

A sound that wasn't barking penetrated. It was the scraping sound of metal on stone. By the time she figured out what it was, it was almost too late. The outside guard was coming in.

"What has gotten into you?" A woman asked. Unsurprisingly, none of the dogs told her. "Quiet!" The dogs quieted but still paced nervously. With a click, there was a flashlight on, scanning the room. Nightmare flattened herself on the floor, letting the beams go over her head.

There were at least two rows of cages between her and the guard. Some of the cages were occupied, some weren't. *Nothing to see here. Go back outside.* Judging by the sounds of footsteps, it wasn't going to be that easy. Stationary targets are harder to spot, but she was in the middle of the floor. On the other hand, if she moved, she might be overheard or spotted. Besides, there weren't any good places to hide in a hurry. At least the guard wasn't turning on the overhead lights. Or looking up to see the open skylight.

The footsteps went to the door where the Purifiers hid everything they didn't want seen. "Carl? Everything alright?"

No answer. She knocked again. Finally, the guard moved away with a quiet mutter, "Old fool's probably drunk again."

Nightmare heard liquid being poured, and the scent of coffee intensified. Listening carefully, she could hear something being drunk, then the close of a heavy metal door. She didn't move for a hundred heartbeats, but as far as she could tell, the guard was gone.

The dogs started barking again as soon as she moved, but Nightmare ignored them. She wasn't frightened of them. Sure, her vitals were a little fast, but that was adrenaline, Okay, maybe she was sweating a little, but so what? She was in Miami wearing an oversized hooded sweatshirt, of course she was hot. The chills? Well, they did have the air on.

Both guards *should* be neutralized. *If* Cazimir was right and there were only two guards. At least twenty minutes had passed since she started the mission. There wasn't time to waste.

Nightmare passed by the closest door to the hidden room for the one closer to the guard room. If the first guard was still in any shape to fight back, she didn't want to be so far away that he could shoot her before she got close. The doorknobs were silver. Good thing she was still wearing gloves. Standing to the side, she opened the door quickly, pulling her arm back immediately. Nothing.

Nightmare stood quietly for a moment, before she could sense the presence of a shade. "Scout inside. Can you see the guard?" She whispered.

"Salt."

Of course. "Look inside. Do you see anyone?"

"See no one."

Ducking down, she wiped at the threshold, dislodging the line of salt. "Now?"

"Scout."

Nightmare waited. A minute passed. Another. A third. "No guard. Room."

Right, the guard was in the camera room. Made sense. "Follow me." She walked briskly towards the camera room. No point in stealth. It was either useless or unnecessary. "Open the door." Shades wouldn't die if shot. She was pretty sure, anyway. If they did, well, then she was down one problem.

The door opened. Nothing happened. "Guard asleep. Kill?"

"No kill. Leave him." Nightmare looked herself. Sure enough, the drugs had been effective. Good. According to the cameras, the outdoor guard was out too. Excellent. She would cover up the footage when they were ready to leave.

Once more, she broke the threshold of salt, this time she reached in and turned off the UV lights too. "Watch him, tell me if he starts to wake." She had information to gather.

***

Eric tapped his fingers over the steering wheel. Twenty minutes to go. He hated waiting. Really hated waiting. But it wasn't like he had the training for this. Or would even be able to get in. Why did Cazimir want him involved in this anyway?

According to him, it was because Eric knew Nightmare best. Eric pretended not to see the dig in that. It was certainly true. He hadn't been a vampire for five years when he met Sakaki. He had only met a couple Weres before, and never one his age. Well, maybe younger. He still wasn't sure how old Sakaki was. His first guess when meeting her was that she was about nineteen, but between her panicking when he tried to kiss her, and that she was still posing as a college student three years later, she might have been a little younger.

She was pretty, but the quiet pretty, the kind that acts like she doesn't know she's pretty. Fine with him. The girls who knew they were beautiful were generally a little more demanding. Young enough that she probably didn't have much experience with love, especially as a Were. He didn't buy the whole 'only fall in love once' story that Weres claimed, but if she believed it, then she was probably a virgin. Eric did like a moderate challenge.

The first day was groundwork. He had realized quickly that he wasn't going to get far that night. But he could build a foundation. Find a baseline for her emotions, and start reinforcing the idea that being around him made her feel good. He had done it dozens of times. But it didn't work quite as well as normal, and he couldn't figure out why.

First, he couldn't get a definitive promise to meet again. Usually that was easy. He would get either a promise, or a coy 'maybe' that meant yes. But her maybe meant maybe. Since he couldn't get a promise, he'd have to look for her to see her again. She might come back to him but might not.

Secondly, even knowing her emotions, he couldn't predict her actions. She was young, she should be ruled by her emotions. But apparently, she wasn't. Of course, the fact that he wasn't sure of his success only made him more determined to succeed.

But there was something that made him hesitate. Eric hadn't sensed it at first, only catching the edges occasionally, but there was something else there. Something dark. When he actually looked, making sure she was too distracted to notice, Eric found himself actually frightened. There was anger there. Fury, vengeance and hatred. Sakaki kept it away from her, possibly didn't even realize she was feeling it. But it was there, her emotions, not ones forced on her. Who was this girl?

That was actually how he found her the next day. Something had stirred up that swirling mess, and Sakaki was barely keeping the reigns back. With an easy smile, pretending he couldn't feel the fiery whirlwind, he approached her, only slightly surprised that whatever was wrong was strong enough to affect her physically. It took most of his strength to get her to a bench without looking like he was dragging her.

The problem was these emotions. They were caused by something deeply rooted, and she couldn't remove them. But what if he could help her contain them? Eric touched her forehead, centering himself in her emotional tempest. The emotions he was looking for were as painful as hot knives. He separated them from her other emotions, then pushed them back, further and further into her psyche, finally forcing them into the equivalent of a cage.

It was a difficult process, but not a long one. Less than five minutes passed between start and finish. That's when he noticed that Sakaki had passed out. Not surprising, and perhaps for the best. He certainly didn't want to admit to manipulating her emotions.

Eric took her back to his place, telling anyone who saw them that she had had a little too much to drink. Every time he wondered if it would have been better to have stayed on the bench. But an unconscious woman was going to attract *attention wherever she was. If they had stayed on the bench, someone would have insisted she go to the hospital. Even taking her to the local Twilight/Night clinic would have caused more complications than Eric wanted to deal with. He didn't think anyone would be able to tell what he had done, but better not to take the chance.*

Once they reached his apartment, he placed her on the bed, dropping her bag by the door. There was a passing curiosity about what she had in her bag but he knew he'd better leave it alone. Weres had a much better sense of smell than vampires did, and he had long learned that some girls were very possessive about their things. Then he settled down to wait for her to wake up.

She took the whole 'moved to a strange apartment while unconscious' better than he had feared, though he noticed the way she sniffed about to check his explanation. Then she was determined to leave. Not that he was surprised about that, but he didn't want her to leave yet. Eric wasn't so low as to sleep with an unconscious woman, but she wasn't unconscious anymore. Maybe they wouldn't get as far as sex tonight, but he should be able to at least get her topless. Hadn't he done her a favor?

Saying it was stress that caused her to pass out, even if he knew that wasn't true, gave him his opening. Eric forced himself to go slow. She was more confused than aroused, but her fear was a surprise. He certainly didn't expect her to lash out at him. Or to run.

Good thing she stopped. He could easily have followed her, but not so easily explained how. But he was worried. Luxemburg was a pretty safe

418

place, but she was not at full strength. Plus, he needed to at least try to recover some ground. She let him walk her home, but Eric knew he had lost some progress.

It wasn't until the next day he realized what else he had done. Still reeling at the news of the assassination the night before, Eric left a vampire club, only to stop dead as he felt that mass of emotions again. "It can't be," he whispered. He had locked them up. They couldn't... then he spotted her.

She was across the street and hadn't noticed him. There was a harshness in her face and a danger in her walk that he hadn't seen before. When she passed a window, he caught a glimpse of her face. The murder in her eyes.

Closing his own eyes, Eric tried to sense her emotions. How had they gotten out? Why were they stronger? The answer hit him like a sledgehammer to the gut. Before, those emotions were mixed in with all her other feelings. By separating them and isolating them from the rest, he had strengthened them, allowing them to cohere, and form something else. Whoever this person was, she wasn't Sakaki. Not right now.

What could he do? How could he fix this mistake? Eric walked away. He wasn't going to try to talk to her tonight. She probably wouldn't even recognize him. Cazimir. Cazimir would know what to do.

It was agonizing. Trying to explain everything, trying to put a good spin on how he had deeply manipulated her emotions without her knowledge or permission, how he had accidentally broken her mind. Cazimir listened patiently. Then *tossed the drowning vampire a life raft. "All will be well, Eric. I can take care of this. But you need to bring her to me."*

"I don't think I can get her to Switzerland."

"I can't leave here right now, and it is important to deal with this as quickly as possible. Find a way."

She hadn't gone, of course. Then she disappeared and he heard nothing. Eric hadn't known enough to connect her to the Kiktsutai and he had never connected her to Nightmare. Cazimir did though. Eric had barely thought about Sakaki for a year before he got to West Palm Beach. Cazimir hadn't warned him until he got there. It took him two days to figure out a way to approach her.

Nightmare wouldn't exist without him. Eric had tried to deny that, but it was true. Yes, Sakaki's emotions were a mess, but she was dealing. She wouldn't have split off a sliver of her psyche if he hadn't done it to her first. Even then, Nightmare had been inactive for years. But Cazimir woke her up again.

Eric had trusted him. He trusted Cazimir would help when Eric explained what went wrong. He believed Cazimir would help when Eric confirmed that yes, this red-headed Werefox was the same one he had met in Luxemburg. He had thought Cazimir's almost obsession with finding her through the past couple years was so they could fix his mistake. It wasn't until Cazimir commanded Eric to kidnap her that he really began to doubt his mentor. And now it was too late.

The car door opened, tearing him from his thoughts. They were back. "You got it?"

Nightmare nodded.
"Okay. Let's go."

Chapter Twenty-Nine

Who is worse; the murderer or the one who commissions the murder? – The Kikitsutai Book of Wisdom

Nightmare looked up as Cazimir sauntered into her cell, but remained sitting on the mattress. Things had improved since her mission in Miami. She got to keep her clothes and was often only chained by one ankle now. There had been two other missions on Purifiers buildings, but not headquarters. They were a little easier, and more importantly, got her off this stupid boat. However, she was now wearing the collar full time.

Eric was a bit of an enigma. While he still caved at the first frown from Cazimir, there were hints that he might be a little more than a spineless slug. Twice more he had brought her water laced with Solium, only for something to happen and he replaced it with ordinary water. Another week or so, and it might be out of her system enough for her to change. To the best of her knowledge, Cazimir had no idea. Which meant that Eric was somehow figuring out how to countermand orders from his 'parent'. Interesting and troubling. Maybe they didn't know as much about vampires as they thought. Perhaps it had something to do with them having been humans first. Cazimir had clearly been human once, and she strongly suspected Eric had been as well.

Cazimir stopped halfway across the room. "I have another mission for you." Judging by his anticipation, there was something unusual about this. Something she probably wouldn't like. "It's in West Palm Beach."

Nightmare didn't even blink. "Target?"

"It's a Purifiers auxiliary building. Plans are a little different. We're making a statement."

Goody goody gumdrops. "How so?"

"I want all the vampire files they have. Destroy any files they have on any of the other races. I also want pictures of all the personnel files of the officers. Don't leave any evidence that you were in those." Cazimir eyed her another moment. "Get the names of everyone involved in the raid on the Magnus Blood. And kill the guards after you get the information you need from them."

Sakaki would probably care. Dangerous bigots or not, she never did take well to killing someone who wasn't actively trying to kill her or someone else. Nightmare had fewer qualms. These people were a threat to her and hers. But it was the first time Cazimir had told her to kill. He had always specified no deaths before. He was getting bolder. Was that significant? "Understood."

Cazimir smiled.

***

The auxiliary building had three guards. Either they had increased security after the rash of break-ins, or this was a more important building than the others. Once more, Nightmare had two shades to work with, possibly the same two shades. They were more restless tonight. Probably because Cazimir promised they could kill today.

This building didn't have a skylight, so they were spying from a window. The auxiliary building was one big, open room. While there were cameras, someone, and Nightmare hadn't bothered to ask Cazimir who, had hacked the security feed to put them on a loop. They were to take the footage when they left, but this way the Purifiers didn't know they were here.

The window frame was silver, which she could only touch with gloves, and under the frame was salt, so the shades couldn't pass. Worse, the window couldn't be opened from the outside.

Nightmare watched for several minutes while trying to keep the shades under control. It didn't take long to establish the patterns. More importantly, she recognized one of them. The tallest guard had participated in the mob attack on the Magnus Blood. She pointed him out to the shades. "I will question him. Do *not* attack him.

There was a muttered hiss. "Master says kill."

"I'll take care of him."

"We kill others."

It wasn't a question. Refusing would probably be considered going against Cazimir's orders. Which would lead to *her* death. "You can take the others, but not until I say. Just leave him. Follow my plan. Wait for my signal. Remember, I'm allowed to talk."

Nightmare backed away from the building, looking for a large rock. Instead, she found a baseball. Even better. With a solid throw, she pitched it through the window.

Less than thirty seconds later, two of the guards ran up. The ones that she told the shades they could kill. Hopefully they wouldn't move too soon.

Both guards were armed, and had withdrawn their guns, but nether were quite willing to wave a gun at her just yet. Nightmare gave them a sheepish, slightly scared smile, hands out placatingly. "I'm so sorry! My ball just got away from me! I can pay for the window; just, please don't call my parents."

The guards, a woman in her mid-thirties, and a man in his upper-twenties, exchanged a look and slowly holstered their guns. "I think you'd better come inside," The man said.

Nightmare shot a nervous look at the guns. "Um, why? Do I have to? I mean, I can give you the money for the window... Maybe not all right away, but–"

The woman cut in. "We just need to straighten a few things out, come up with a payment schedule, etc. Maybe we won't have to call your parents after all."

Biting her lip, she walked ahead of them, as indicated. When they got to the door, she tripped on a shoelace and kissed the ground. "Ooft! Dumb, homicidal shoes!" Neither guard helped her up. Neither noticed that she wiped the salt from the threshold either.

The room was filled with filing cabinets. Lots and lots of filing cabinets. It would take a very long time to go through all of these. Much longer than she had.

"What color are her eyes?" The guard who hadn't come out, the one she had ordered the shades not to touch, asked.

"What? My eyes? Brown." Nightmare looked around as if confused. "What does that have to do with anything?"

The man who had come out grabbed her face roughly, turning to peer into her eyes, while his female partner trained a gun at her head. "Amber. They're amber."

Mob guard pulled out his gun, now also trained on her. "Silver."

"What? What are you doing?" Nightmare shrieked, as the man let go of her face, only to pull out a silver bracelet. No prizes for guessing what he meant to do with that. If the shades weren't in position, she was dead. "Now!"

She grabbed the man's arm and tossed him into his partner before launching herself up and over the closest row of filing cabinets.

Blood was heavy in the air. The shades had done their work well, too well. She had to get to the one guard before they killed him too. "Louis! Jessica!" The voice was taut as piano wire. Not surprising, considering he had seen two co-workers, if not friends, cut down by something he couldn't see.

Thunder split the air. Multiple times. Smart plan. Fire a spray, hoping to bring down the invisible assassins. Too bad it wouldn't work. She had asked. Shades were either impervious, or the next best thing, to bullets.

It would take a couple minutes to get her full hearing back. Good thing they were small caliber bullets, or it would take even longer. But the guard was so afraid that the scent of his fear was almost as strong as the scent of blood. There was a soft thump as he backed into a filing cabinet

"Who are you? Where are you?" Surely, he didn't actually expect her to answer that, did he?

Footsteps. He was running in her direction. Perhaps he was just trying to get away from the shades, or maybe he had guessed, correctly, that she would be more vulnerable to bullets.

As he turned the corner to her, Nightmare brought up her collapsible baton, smacking him straight in the nose. Even through the baton, she felt the cartilage crumple under the force.

Dazed and in pain, he dropped the gun on automatic, backing away, hands coming up to his nose. Nightmare didn't give him a chance to recover. A solid kick shattered his kneecap.

Screaming, the man collapsed to the ground. Nightmare kicked the gun away then stood with one leg on his chest, waiting for him to recover enough to realize she was there. It took a few minutes for the haze of agony to change to hatred. There was fear there, and lots of it, but if she couldn't smell it, couldn't hear his heart racing, she might not have known. "Kill me and be done with it."

She gave him a chilly smile. "Not until I get the information I came for."

"I won't tell you anything."

"Oh, yes, you will. Sooner or later, everyone does."

***

Eric hadn't had chauffer duty, so he didn't see Nightmare and the shades until they returned to the ship. Even before he saw them, he could smell the blood that surrounded them like an invisible cloud. Nightmare had blood on her gloves and a bit on the leg of her pants. Eric thought it was probably a good thing he couldn't see the shades.

Cazimir approached them, and Eric listened in shamelessly. "All dead?"

"Two dead. The third, I questioned. He was alive when I left, but he might not be now. I doubt he'll ever wake up. Definitely won't be able to talk."

Cazimir frowned. "I ordered them all dead."

"The heart might be beating, but his mind is gone. You want to send a message? Trust me, that's scarier than killing out right."

The older vampire was quiet for a moment. "And the other two are dead? You are certain?"

"The shades practically decapitated them."

Cazimir smiled at that. "You got the names."

"Twelve names, and the address of the leader. This guard was number thirteen."

"Good. The files?"

Nightmare rolled her eyes at that. First expression she showed since returning. "The ones you want are in the trunk of the car. Mostly. Backseat, too. It took a lot of trips. Shades aren't good at carrying things."

No, they really weren't. Eric didn't know if anyone had actually tried to measure it, but he couldn't remember shades lifting more than fifteen, twenty pounds at one time before.

Cazimir's brow furrowed. "How many files were there?"

"Three filing cabinets. I grabbed anything that even seemed to mention vampires. Probably you don't need it all, but..."

"No, you were right. I'd rather you bring me papers I don't need than leave anything I might need."

Nightmare gave a sharp nod.

"Any complications?"

"No."

"How long did it take to get the guard to talk?"

"I didn't time it."

"A guess, then."

She shrugged. "Eight minutes? Ten?"

"You left the horse?"

"Clutched in the guard's hand."

Cazimir turned to the shades. "Is she telling the truth?"

"Fox says truth. No lie."

Eric swallowed hard. Cazimir was in one of *those* moods again. Not good. But there was nothing he could do.

"Excellent. It sounds like the mission went well." All expression fled from Nightmare's face. Apparently, she could sense the coming storm too. "*However*, I cannot have you getting creative with your orders." Cazimir backhanded the Were, who didn't even flinch. "You do as I say. Do you understand?"

"Yes."

He smiled a soft smile. The kind that always made Eric want to hide. "I don't think you do. But you will." Cazimir turned to Eric. "Chain her back up. Then give her a shot of Punishment."

Eric winced. He didn't know what was actually in the serum, but the name was enough of an indication. It gave both vampires and Weres intense flu symptoms for several hours. Sakaki had been given it once before, just before she started agreeing she had been here forever.

Orders were orders. He couldn't disobey. Nightmare looked at him, disdain dripping from her gaze. But she followed him without a word, without hesitation. He didn't say anything to her until they were back in her cell. "I don't have a choice."

She didn't say anything. Eric snapped a shackle around her ankle. After a moment's thought, he left the other limbs free. Cazimir said to chain her back up. She only had the ankle chain before.

When he came back with the syringe, her eyes widened briefly, before shuttering, looking dead. She recognized it. But Nightmare didn't move.

"Orders. I have to obey."

"Do you?" Nightmare asked, not looking at the arm where Eric was finding a vein. At least she wasn't fighting him.

"I don't have a choice."

"There's always a choice. Not always a good choice, but always a choice."

Eric bit his lip, inserted the needle and stabbed the plunger in with more force than he anticipated. Once empty, he withdrew the syringe and backed away quickly. She had closed her eyes. "Sakaki?"

She glared at him, hate and fury in her eyes. "Leave. Now."

It was the only thing he could do.

***

"Pup!"

Eric froze. "Yes, Cazimir?" A shallow emotion scan revealed that his 'parent' was a short ways outside his quarters and in a good mood. One of those good moods that meant trouble.

"Got a job for you."

Eric put down the flash drive he had been fiddling with, and turned, hand over the drive. Cazimir wasn't looking at him. He nudged the drive under his pillow. "What kind of job?"

"Talk to Derrain. Tell him there was a break-in at a Purifiers building tonight. Give him the agreed upon details, but don't tell him we had anything to do with it. While you are ashore, talk to Rex Magnus. After all, 'Liska' isn't being very successful at tracking down this lead."

It was probably best not to point out that she was failing because Cazimir had kidnapped her. It was more than his life was worth to point out that apparently she had still figured it out. Eric no longer had any illusions that Cazimir would hesitate to end him if he found out that Eric had overheard that conversation, let alone had a copy of it.

"While talking to him, point out that many of the Kikitsutai are rumored to be able to pass for each other. How does he even know that the current 'Liska' is the same one as before?" Cazimir smirked.

Eric nodded silently. He had seen the Werefox who had taken Sakaki's place but never gotten close. From a distance, the appearance was uncanny. But he didn't know if she could pass if put to the test. He didn't actually know anything about her, except that she was clearly pretending to be whatever role Sakaki had taken on at the school. The human was helping her. Honestly, he tried not to think about the fake Sakaki.

"Good. I want you back by dawn."

Cazimir left. Eric delayed only long enough to securely hide the flash drive before leaving as well.

Chapter Thirty

The offspring of Fear and Hatred is Death. – The Kikitsutai
Book of Wisdom

Nightmare didn't even look up when the door opened. Seven hours of vicious flu symptoms had left her shattered and exhausted. As soon as the symptoms abated enough, she slept the sleep of the drained. Nightmare thought she had gotten about four hours of sleep and an hour or two of semi-sleep, but it wasn't enough and she was trying for more.

Judging by the smell, it was Cazimir. Grand. Nightmare didn't bother opening her eyes.

"Get up."

Now she opened her eyes, just long enough to glare at him. He was serious. Enough so that refusal would get her hurt. Probably more seriously than the rebellion was worth. With a groan, she shifted to a sitting position. It was the best he was going to get right now. Honestly, she wasn't completely sure she could stand steady right now.

Cazimir scowled but didn't bother chastising her. "I have another job for you. Tonight."

"Should have thought of that before you rendered me inoperable." It was a quiet mutter, but the vampire heard anyway, backhanding her hard enough to make her see stars. "Hitting me won't make me better able to work."

"You *will* do this, and tonight." Was he scared? Anxious, at least. Why?

Nightmare tried to assess her status. Breaking into another Purifier building was just plain out. But if he had something simpler, maybe requiring less physical intensity, perhaps she could pull it off. "What am I supposed to be doing anyway?"

Cazimir smirked. "Oh, you'll like this one. You are going after Sydney Whitters."

She could practically feel her ears trying to perk up. "The leader of the raid?"

"The same. He is the financial officer for all Purifiers. I want all his records. Burn the house down when you're finished. Oh, and Nightmare? Make him suffer."

"I'll need help."

"You will have your usual assistance."

Nightmare shook her head. "Shades won't do it. I'm weak right now. I'll be a little stronger in a few hours, especially if I eat. But not enough to move boxes of files. Purifiers are paranoid enough to not have that kind of information on a server that could be hacked. It will all be paper. A lot of paper. Shades aren't strong enough. I need at least one wraith or vampire."

Cazimir eyed the ceiling, probably considering what she said. "Very well. I will arrange something. Food will be brought soon. Regain your strength. No horse this time."

Odd, but not worth questioning him over. Besides, he was already gone.

***

Nightmare did feel a little better after a couple hours, but she would definitely be pulling this job handicapped. Cazimir came in to her cell with a vampire and a shade trailing him. "Jared will assist you tonight. It is your responsibility to ensure nothing... *untoward* happens to him. Same rules as before. Your orders go unless they contradict mine. Remember, you can be killed in a heartbeat." Cazimir looked back and forth between her and the vampire. "You will ask no questions about the assignment, and listen to nothing she might say about it, except to follow her orders," He told the vampire, before glaring at her.

The message was clear. No mentioning that Cazimir had arranged the raid on the Magnus Blood. Just as well, Jared would probably refuse to believe her anyway. She could try to plant a seed or two, but it probably wasn't worth it.

Cazimir was talking to her. She tuned back to listen. "Do you understand?"

"Yes. Get his files, kill Whitters, burn the house."

"Whitters should suffer. I expect you to get... *creative.*"

Nightmare nodded. *Sensei* had told her to get rid of him if she got the chance. Well, told Liska. Close enough. At least she could obey his orders.

It didn't take long to reach their destination. Whitters turned out to live in a freestanding house in an affluent neighborhood not far from the school. Risky, there was a chance of someone recognizing Anna. She would have to be alert to act if that happened. On the other hand, she probably didn't look much like Anna anymore.

Her hair had grown about an inch since it had been hacked off, so it was almost chin-length instead of around her ears. She had lost probably about fifteen pounds, leaving her looking skeletal. There was the wide, dark burn scar around her neck, though it might not be visible around the control collar. To be honest, she probably looked like a homeless drug addict.

Would the vampire or the shade hold the controls to her collar? A vampire would be able to reason out a situation, make judgement calls, and were very loyal. Shades were even more loyal and couldn't be killed. There were positives and negatives to both. She could worry about it later. Right now, she had a job to do.

It was nearly midnight, but Whitters was still awake. She could see him in his living room, reading. A quick circuit around the building didn't suggest any evidence anyone else was there. Even his home proclaimed him a Purifier. The door handles and window frames on the first floor were silver. Probably salt there as well. The outside light was a UV light. A clove of garlic and a string of peppers hung in a dimly lit alcove by the door. Peppers? Really? Did he expect to be attacked by djinns? Only the ones from Eastern Europe reacted to peppers at all, and they were less aggressive than the average goose.

The second circuit around, she found the security alarm. An expensive one with a good reputation. She could crack it, but it took time. Or at least, it would if he had actually turned it on.

"Stay out of sight," she whispered to her companions before she walked up to the door and rang the doorbell. Through the sheer curtain, she could see him jolt up and look uncomfortably at the door.

He hesitated, and she rang the bell again. After a moment, he came to the door but didn't open it. "Who's there?"

Nightmare spoke. Nonsense words at just the right volume that he could hear she spoke but not what she said.

There was the sound of metal hitting metal. The door opened a crack, chain in place. "Who is it? What do you want? Do you know what time it is?"

"I know it's late, but I need to talk to you. You're Sydney Whitters, head of Earth for Humans, right? Please! You've got to help me!"

He tried to object, but she talked over him. "I know who robbed your building!"

The door yanked open as far as the chain would allow as the porch light came on. "Who are you? What do you know about that?"

Nightmare flinched away from the lights, putting a hand up to shade her eyes. "I'll tell you everything, but you have to let me in! They'll kill me if they see me!" She put her hand down and looked around wildly, as if searching for assassins. At same time, she signaled the shade and vampire to wait in place.

Scowling, Whitters closed the door enough to remove the chain, opened the door and stepped back. Not verbally letting her in, just in case. Nightmare walked in and kicked the door shut.

"Now, start explaining. Who are you? How do you know about the building? Who robbed it?"

Nightmare smiled. "Why, I did, of course."

Before he could respond, she drove her knee into his groin. Whitters doubled over moaning. She kicked his ankles out under him, then used a power cord to tie him up while he was distracted. It wouldn't hold long term, but it didn't need to either.

Nightmare put on her gloves and opened the door, swishing her foot around to disrupt any lines of salt. "Come in." She wasn't the owner, but Jared had been ordered to go in by Cazimir, who might well have turned him. Together, it should be stronger than any threshold protection.

Jared and the shade came in a moment later. To the shade, she said, "Scout around. Make sure no one else is here." To Jared, "I need all the accelerants you can find. We need a big fire."

"The notes first."

"Of course. After I persuade Whitters to tell me where they are."

The shade returned, confirming that no, no one else was there. Jared was still gathering whatever flammable things he could find. Nightmare sniffed once. Paint. "He painted recently. See if you can find the leftovers. That's probably flammable."

Whitters was finally coming back to his senses, so she knelt next to him. He squinted at her until his eyes focused. "Who are you?"

"Me? I'm just a Nightmare."

The name meant nothing to him. Didn't matter. "You're a freak. A violent, vicious freak," He spat.

She raised an eyebrow. "*I* am? I'm not the one who calmly led a mob to destroy a bunch of people who only wanted to be left alone." Whitters gulped. "Did you think no one would find out about that? Do you ever think about the woman you set on fire? More of a girl, really. Her name was Isabelle. Did you know that? I'm betting you didn't."

Whitters was pale, sweaty, and shaking. "No, they were monsters."

"Monsters? They weren't hurting anyone. They left you alone. No, the monster was you. You and your crew." Jared came back with a couple partially used gallons of paint. Nightmare pointed up at him. "He's a vampire, just so you know. We've been ordered to burn your house down. Tell me what I need to know and we won't leave you to burn to death. Where are the Purifier financial files?"

"I don't kno— AAARRRGGGHH!" Whiters tried to pull his newly broken ankle away from her grasp. All that accomplished was more pain as she shifted it a bit more.

"Care to try that again?"

"What fin—" He didn't scream, but he did hiss as she took a knife and almost lazily scored it down the side of his face, starting at the corner of his right eye.

"Ever hear of the death of a thousand cuts? I've never actually done that before, but I've been told how it's done. There are variations, of course. The way I was taught goes something like this. You start by removing the eyes." She pressed the knife just hard enough to break skin as she traced from the tear duct of one eye, down under the eye, over the nose, to the other eye. "Then you go after the fingers." She pulled backwards at the little finger of his right hand until it broke. "And toes." Since he was wearing shoes, she didn't try to get at his feet but pushed hard on his broken ankle. "I think you cut off the nose and ears too, but I can't remember." Nightmare grabbed his left ear and scrunched it in her fist. "Then you start carving up the victim." She cut off a small bit of flesh from the top of his hand.

Whitters was hyperventilating and kept looking to Jared like he wanted to beg for help. Help that wasn't going to come. She almost had him.

"Done right, it usually takes three or four days for the victim to die. Like I said, I've never tried it. Are you volunteering to be my first practice?" She twirled the knife with a flourish.

"No, please! I'll do anything. Don't hurt me!"

"Where are the files?"

"Upstairs! My office. In the brown filing cabinet. Everything's paper. It's all there, I promise. Don't kill me. Please, don't kill me."

Nightmare turned to Jared. "He seems to be telling the truth but check to make sure."

Jared nodded and left. A minute or two later, she heard the obvious sounds of a filing cabinet being opened. Listening carefully, she could even hear the papers being rifled through. "It's here."

"Good. Start moving it. And tell the shade to spread around the kerosene upstairs." Then she turned to Whitters. "I want to check some information with my new friend here."

"Please–"

"I want the names of everyone who participated in that raid. Names and addresses. And before you get some noble idea of trying to spare them? I *will* know if you lie. Besides, you're not my only source."

Whitters hesitated for about ten seconds, nine seconds longer than she expected, before rattling off a list. It was identical to what the guard told her less than twenty-four hours ago.

"Calloway gave you this information?"

"Yes. Couldn't believe the drunk idiot stumbled upon a nest like that, but we took advantage of it."

"Did you kill Calloway?"

Whitters stared at her in surprise. "Calloway died in a DUI. I didn't have anything to do with that."

Probably Cazimir then. Or maybe it was a genuine coincidence.

"Papers are moved." Jared stayed in the hallway. "If we're starting a fire, I want to be outside.

Nightmare nodded and started to stand. A wave of dizziness came over her, likely an after-effect of the drug she had been given earlier. Whitters, probably sensing his death approaching, rolled into her while she was off balance. "You can't leave me here!"

Suddenly knocked off her feet, she put her hands out to catch herself, only to realize too late that she was going to put too much force on her right wrist. Sure enough, it jammed hard enough that she was literally seeing stars for a moment. Biting her lip, Nightmare stood, massaging her wrist. She didn't think it was broken, but it would definitely swell and bruise.

"Can you walk?" Jared asked, no concern in his voice or scent.

"Walk, yes. Drive, no."

He nodded. "Need anything?"

"Slop the paint around. The propane tank is fine. Then leave. I can light a match."

Whitters was screaming mix of curses, denials, and begging for mercy. He was ignored. Once Jared and the shade had left, Nightmare smiled at Whitters, which made him burst out in tears.

A few minutes later, she was going through the house, making sure the accelerants were set up in such a way that the whole house would burn down. Starting upstairs, she nodded approvingly at the kerosene doused bed before carefully lighting a clean corner of the sheet. Just to be sure, she pulled down one of the curtains, setting it so one end was on the bed with the other on the dresser. Which held cologne. That should be flammable. She splashed some over the curtain. It hadn't caught fire yet but should soon.

In the bathroom, she mixed ammonia and bleach, and simply left it at that. In his office, she took some papers from his desk and stuffed them inside the computer tower before turning it on.

When it didn't seem to be lighting a minute later, she pushed in a lit match, then took another to the cord. Fire traveled quickly over wires.

By the time she went back downstairs, she could smell and hear at least two different fires roaring away. The stairs had kerosene and paint slopped on them, and she lit the third step after she reached the bottom.

Whitters was still screaming, but she ignored him to go to the kitchen. Taking a small metal mixing bowl, she put it in the microwave and set it for five minutes. Then she turned the stove to clean, draping a kitchen towel half inside, with the door open a crack. This room probably wouldn't burn very well. That was alright, the garage should more than make up for it. Especially when she set his camp stove under the gas tank of his car.

Going room by room, she continued to start small fires or set things in motion to start a fire or simply burn. By the time she returned to the living room, smoke was heavy in the air. She had pulled up a handkerchief and safety goggles a few minutes earlier.

Whitters was sputtering but still begging weakly; when he saw her, he redoubled his efforts. "Please. You promised. If I told you, you wouldn't kill me."

Nightmare stared down at him. "I never said that. I promised if you told me, I wouldn't leave you to burn alive. So I won't." She ripped the leg off a side table. "I'll show you the same mercy you showed Isabelle." Nightmare stabbed the leg through his heart, then pulled it out.

Whitters jerked in shock and surprise, confused eyes on her. The life was fading.

Nightmare couldn't bring herself to care. "You should be dead by the time the fire hits you. Probably." She lit the table leg and placed it on the paint splashed table next to the mostly full propane tank. Then she walked away without a backwards glance.

Chapter Thirty-One

One enemy on the inside is more dangerous than a hundred on the outside. – The Kikitsutai Book of Wisdom

Cazimir took almost two days to isolate himself to study the stolen files. Eric expected it to take longer, so he was a little surprised that Cazimir sent him back to Rex Magnus on Wednesday to find out his reaction to Whitters's death.

"Right, shall I visit Derrian too?" Eric asked. He tried not to show any signs of nervousness. When he visited on Monday, Rex had told him that Whitters was the leader of the raid and was making plans for his revenge. 'Liska' had told him. While Eric knew better than to ask, he was certain that was why Whitters was now dead.

Cazimir waved a negligent hand. "I don't care what you do. Simply remember what I said about what to tell him."

Eric nodded. He was learning, slowly, how to get around Cazimir's orders, but it was so hard. Every time he tried to stretch them, he felt horrible, emotionally and physically. Even worse, he could feel the bond start to fray. There were rumors, more of horror stories, of young vampires who strained the bond by trying to disobey their parents. Pulling too far, they painfully reverted back to what they were before. If they were lucky. Other times, they died or became some horribly mutilated monster. But even if he was lucky, even if he reverted back to a human; he would be a human with an inoperable brain tumor and about three months to live. No, he wouldn't even think about it. He would obey Cazimir. He would obey his parent. So, it was a good thing Cazimir gave his permission.

Derrian perked up when Eric came in. "You're here! I'm glad. I've been lonely."

Eric gave him a small smile. "Sorry about that. Cazimir keeps me pretty busy."

Derrian frowned at that. "I know it's taking a lot of work to fix things after Atolatar..." He swallowed hard. "But you'd think he'd keep me informed. I have a right to know what's going on."

Eric ruffled Derrian's hair. "I know. He said... he said things were falling into place." That was pretty accurate.

"Tell me what he's doing?"

"I can't."

Derrian scowled. "For all that I'm supposed to be in charge of the Blood, no one tells me anything."

Eric tried not to wince. Derrian was nominally the head of the blood, but everyone knew it was Cazimir. Sometimes even Derrian knew that.

"Tell me what's going on." Derrian tried again.

"I can't. Cazimir ordered me not to."

"But I'm in charge of the Blood."

Eric didn't say anything. Derrian was smart. He'd pick it up.

"The only loyalty stronger than the one to the leader of the Blood is the loyalty to the turner," Derrian continued.

"True."

"That loyalty fades when the turner dies. Ryasmus is dead. So, I should be your highest loyalty." Derrian nodded as if stating that affirmed something deeply important.

"If Ryasmus turned me, then you would be right," Eric said.

Frustration turned to confusion. "Huh? Of course Ryasmus turned you. He turned all the vampires for the Blood." There was a very long pause. "Didn't he?"

Eric shrugged. "Cazimir said not to talk. I've got to go."

There, that was the best warning he could give. Derrian would read the writing on the wall, or he wouldn't and Cazimir would depose him and put a new cat's-paw in his place. Eric just hoped that if Derrian *was* stupid enough to confront Cazimir, he wouldn't mention Eric's part in enlightening him.

***

As ordered, Eric called the boat to report rather than going in person. That left him available to run any errands needed while still on mainland. Because Cazimir had a twisted sense of humor, and because it was secure, Eric was still using the phone that he had used to lure Sakaki into a trap. Had Van ever realized he had pickpocketed her? He didn't know, he hadn't seen her since.

"What did Rex say?"

"That Liska passed all the tests and swore on her honor that neither she nor hers killed Whitters. Rex Magnus is livid." Eric hadn't even talked to the vampire leader. He had stayed well back and listened to him rave for almost an hour.

"So, the imposter knows how to pass. Ah well, it matters little. They'll be at each other's throats sooner or later."

Eric said nothing.

Cazimir noticed. "No questions why I would want them fighting?"

"No. I trust you have your reasons." Eric *knew* he had reasons. They just weren't the same reasons he wanted to believe a month ago. "Do you have any orders for me?"

"I do, actually. According to the files I've been looking through, one of the things the Purifiers are paying for is a monthly rental for an office in a small building on Flagler." Eric wrote down the address he was given. "It's being rented through one of their members to store files of Purifiers buildings all over the state. I'm sending Nightmare to get them in an hour or two. Check out the security she'll have to get through."

"Doesn't she have a sprained wrist? She can't go out tonight or tomorrow."

There was a heavy silence as Eric feared he had over stepped. "Very well, Friday will do. But no later."

"What time will she be going? Midnight again?"

Cazimir was quiet for a moment. "We've developed a pattern, haven't we? Everything between midnight and three. No, earlier this time. Ten, I think. Make arrangements."

"I will." Eric hesitated but spoke. "The Kikitsutai are going to investigate this, you know. The other 'Liska' knew Nightmare was active again."

There was a rumbling on the line, like static. Cazimir was chuckling. "Let them come. I'll be ready."

Eric was left with a dial tone. *Let them come.* Well, if that was what Cazimir wanted...

***

"Move boxes of files?" Nightmare stared incredulously as she rubbed at her wrist. It was not only swollen to almost twice its' normal size, but it was also visibly discolored. That said, it was better than it had been yesterday. She had wrapped it in the bandages provided and was trying not to move her wrist or use her hand unless she absolutely had to. Moving her fingers caused random shooting pain up and down her arm, providing further incentive.

Cazimir glowered. "*You* were the one careless enough to get injured."

"Which probably wouldn't have happened if you hadn't made me go out just after being sick like that." Before Cazimir could argue, she continued, "Not that it matters how or why I'm injured. The fact is, I am. If you want boxes moved, you need someone else to move them."

"Fine. A vampire will be sent along with you."

"How many boxes do you want moved?"

Cazimir considered it. "Two vampires then. But don't think for one second you will be permitted not to pull your weight. Jared said he moved all the papers himself."

She raised an eyebrow. "I was busy."

"You had already gotten your information."

"Confirmation. Whitters led the raid. If someone was involved that the guard didn't know about, then Whitters would."

"Was anyone?"

Nightmare shrugged. "Apparently not. He didn't tell me anything I didn't already know." About that.

"Then it was pointless. Be ready in an hour." Cazimir swept from the room.

Nightmare, very maturely, stuck her tongue out at him. Then she went back to glaring at her wrist. The same stupid wrist that she had broken months ago. She hadn't caused permanent damage, had she? Probably not. Not yet. It wasn't broken, but it was a very bad sprain. She'd have to be careful with it. Ice would be useful, but they hadn't given her any, even when she asked.

She took a drink. Nightmare didn't even how Eric managed it, but she hadn't been given Solium since the first time he switched out her water. Did Cazimir know? It was almost out of her system. Of course, the last few days would be nasty. If he hadn't caught on yet, he probably would then. But if she somehow managed to keep it from him, then she would be able to transform. Changing into a fox would be near impossible if she was chained on every limb like she had been in the beginning, but there was only ever the ankle chain now. She could probably slip out of that, and the control collar. It would be a challenge; she was on constant video. But perhaps on a mission...

The door opened, and Nightmare snapped her thoughts back to the deep reaches of her brain. Eric walked in. She hadn't seen him since he injected her with that serum. He was... twitchy. Something had him jumpy. Perhaps he was afraid of her reaction after last time.

Nightmare leveled a poisonous glare at him. But nothing changed. He was no more or less nervous than before. Okay, whatever had him upset, it wasn't her.

"I brought a brace. Figured you could use it." Eric held up an elastic wrist support wrap. Probably for the best. The less flexible kind either wouldn't fit or would be too painful to wear.

He helped her put it on. She held still, moving only when necessary, trying not to show any reaction. Once, pain caused her to close her eyes and keep them closed, but she didn't make a sound or bite her lip.

"It's time to go. Are you ready?" Eric unchained her ankle.

Nightmare stood, ignoring the proffered hand, and walked away without looking at the vampire.

Until he called after her. "Hey, good luck. Just... stay alert. And good luck." Then she looked at him. Very twitchy. Nightmare was beginning to have a bad feeling about tonight. Before she could decide if it was even worth trying to question him, he was gone, practically fleeing from her.

Cazimir was on deck already, with two vampires she didn't know. Both were tall, muscular, and near identical in appearance, though the taller one was fair haired, and about three inches taller than his dark-haired companion.

"I want all the boxes from that office. Bring them here, leave a horse, and get out. No creatively interpreting orders. Neither of your 'associates' will hesitate to break you in half if you do."

No introductions this time? Not that she cared. Nightmare simply nodded. "Who's driving?"

The shorter one drove. Neither of her associates were talkers, and not a single word was exchanged throughout the trip. Fine with her, she didn't feel a need to make friends, especially not with people she might have to kill later. After all, even if she managed to escape from Cazimir without killing anyone, it wasn't like he would give up. He would send his people after her.

Which meant she might end up killing Eric. Cazimir would almost certainly send him after her, perhaps believing she would be reluctant to kill him. Was she? Nightmare didn't have any fond feelings for the manipulating empath. Sakaki might care, but Nightmare currently didn't. On the other hand, he was the only one who actually treated her like a person. He hadn't once hurt her, except when he had been explicitly ordered to. He gave her a blanket and substituted clean water for tainted. He didn't hate her, even if he didn't care about her the way Sakaki had thought he did.

But Nightmare was still very angry with him. He had used her and betrayed her. All in all, Nightmare was pretty sure that if Cazimir ordered

Eric after her; to kill or even just kidnap her again, she would kill him without hesitation, but probably not without regret.

The car came to a stop. Nightmare looked around but didn't see anything that fit the description of the building they had come to rob. The silent twins exited the car, Nightmare following them, making sure her hood was up. Sakaki had been warned repeatedly that her red hair stood out.

No one bothered to tell her where the building was, so she simply followed the silent vampires across three blocks. That was a bad idea. How could they make multiple trips carrying boxes across three blocks without being obvious? There wasn't a lot of traffic, but there was some. She'd mention it after she cleared the building.

The vampires led the way to the porch of a small building that advertised various offices. This must be it. Once they got to the door, the vampires stood to the side and stared at her. Clearly, this was her job. Nightmare bent to examine the lock.

And instantly caught a familiar whiff of fox. She wasn't the only Werefox to pick this lock tonight. Kira!

How? Was she still inside? Had she somehow found out or guessed that Sakaki would be here tonight? How could that be possible? Had she gone after the files herself?

Then she recognized the other scent. Todd. He was here too. Both had gone in about two hours ago, and neither of them had left through this door. There wasn't a back door on the blueprints. So, either they had gone out a window, teleported, or they were still here. Neither of them knew about

Nightmare. This was going to get tricky. Very, very tricky.

None of this showed on her face as Nightmare straightened up and pulled out her tools. Because the lock had already picked once tonight, she had to be especially careful. It may or may not be locked right now. If it wasn't, then that would make her vampire 'friends' suspicious.

Suddenly very grateful she hadn't bothered to learn their names, Nightmare fiddled with the lock some, not enough to either lock or unlock it, before trying the door. It didn't open. They must have locked it. Sensible.

A little more effort and she had it unlocked. Nightmare opened the door and waved for the vampires to precede her. Neither moved. Well, alright then.

She walked in first, not surprised in the slightest when they fell in slightly behind her, one to each side. Which one had the controller? She needed to know, and her odds were only fifty-fifty.

She walked heavy, making sure her footsteps were audible, instead of the near-silent footsteps of her relaxed walk, or the silence she was capable of. It was a little bit of a challenge, because the floor was carpeted. Both Kira's scent and Todd's became clearer. Particularly Todd's. Had he doubled back? She walked another few steps.

Breathing. She could hear breathing that wasn't hers. Vampires don't breathe. Her steps slowed a bit almost involuntarily as she eyed the place. There was a door to one side. He must be in there.

Nightmare kept walking, ignoring the door. Neither vampire looked in its direction, probably because she was ignoring it.

There was only going to be one chance at this. Whatever Kira had planned, and it had to be Kira's plan, she would be startled and taken off guard at Sakaki's appearance. Nightmare pulled down her hood, so that Kira would be *able* to recognize her right away. Hopefully the vampires would be equally startled at whatever Kira did.

Nightmare palmed a dagger in her left hand and wished she had something to cover her nose and mouth with. Any second now. Any second.

Movement. Movement that wasn't their party. Nightmare forced her injured hand to cover her nose and mouth.

The next few seconds were both a flurry of activity that was almost impossible to interpret, and a long drawn-out series of events that seemed to take forever to end.

Kira's whistle pierced the air, with the banging of a door behind them and the lights coming on less than a second later. Nightmare hadn't expected the lights and was semi-blinded, but she didn't need to see.

As Kira exclaimed in disbelief, Nightmare plunged her dagger into the heart of the vampire on her left side, the shorter one, she thought. As he dissolved to ash, she turned to get his companion.

The one with the remote in his hand. He pressed the button just as she stabbed him. The ash and silver dust fell at the same time.

Chapter Thirty-Two

Worry has never solved a problem. – The Kikitsutai Book of Wisdom

Shahara gave up the book she had been trying to read when she realized she had been staring at the same two pages for at least thirty minutes and *still* had no idea what it was saying. Discarding the book, she stood up and started pacing. Again.

Jamal had tried to get her to stop pacing and sit down the previous three times. This time he said nothing until Shahara shrieked at him with frustration, "How can you be so calm?"

Her brother sighed and looked up from his medical textbook. "Will going nuts help anything?"

"Well, no."

"Then we just have to wait." He went back to the textbook. Shahara was about to snap at him until she recognized the diagram as being the same one she had seen the last time she had been pacing. Jamal was just as worried as she was.

She slumped down on the couch next to him. "We should have done something."

"Done what? We don't even know where they went, let alone what they were doing."

"Yeah, I know."

Jamal put an arm around her shoulders. "You prayed. It's in God's hands now. Try to leave it there."

Shahara sighed. She didn't like it, but Jamal was right. "It's hard. I hope they're okay."

"Me too." His voice was normal, but the arm on her shoulders seemed to tremble some. "I still can't believe Todd got involved."

Shahara closed her eyes and wished she had kept her big mouth shut. Todd was her friend, yes, but he was Jamal's best friend. Had been for years. He had to be feeling it more than she was. She looked at her watch. Ten-thirty. Wasn't everything supposed to begin at ten? What was going on?

The phone rang, causing both siblings to jump. Shahara got to the phone first by virtue of leaping over the coffee table instead of going around it. "Hello?" She forcibly bit her lip to keep from asking questions. If it wasn't Todd or Kira, then she shouldn't be letting whoever was on the line know anything was up and she didn't belong there. If it was Todd or Kira, then asking questions would take up valuable time that could be better used hearing the answers to those questions.

"It's Kira. We're heading back. Todd and I are fine. Tell Jamal to standby. We're about ten minutes out." There was a click of the phone being hung up before Shahara could ask anything.

Jamal was behind her, shaking out his foot. Vaguely Shahara remembered him barking his shin on the coffee table. "Well?"

"I'm not sure. She said that she and Todd were fine, but that you should standby."

Jamal let out a quiet breath, but she could see the panic in his eyes. Pre-med or not, he had never been solely responsible for an emergency before. "Okay, maybe that means there are only minor injuries, like bruises and stuff. Or maybe the older guy, what's his name? Maybe he got hurt."

"Oh, yeah, she didn't mention him." Shahara bit her lip. "Mr. Ryoko. I hope he's okay. I think he's like in his sixties."

"Anyway, we'll find out soon enough." Jamal opened his first aid kit, separating out the bandages, hydrogen peroxide, and hot/cold packs.

Shahara went to the window and took door duty. How could ten minutes drag on for hours? Surely it had been longer, even if her watch was lying to her. Then a car drove up and parked in the driveway. Her first instinct was to turn on the outside light. But if someone was hurt, that would just attract attention. Besides, according to Todd, Werefoxes had great night vision.

Dimly she saw people get out of the car. The tallest, who had to be Todd, went around and started to pull something out of the backseat. To her horror, it looked like a person. Wait. Three people got out of the car, so how could Todd be carrying someone?

She opened the door as they got close. It *was* a person. Todd set her down on the couch. It couldn't be. There had to be some mistake. Shahara looked closer.

It was Anna, but it wasn't. The girl unconscious, *please be unconscious, she can't be dead, she can't be,* on the couch looked awful. She was skeletal with all her bones jutting out. There was blood on the lower part of her face, especially the nose and mouth. Her right hand was spotted with red, like she had been splashed with droplets of acid, and the wrist was swollen and red, wearing a brace. Shahara was sure she didn't want to know what caused the wide, vivid red scar across her throat. It was partially hidden by some weird necklace. Her face was bruised and her eyes were sunken in. Her hair looked like it had been brutally hacked off and was just starting to regrow.

Jamal gaped for a moment. "Anna? Sorry, Sakaki?" He looked to Kira and Todd. "What happened?"

Kira sighed, looking like she had aged ten years. "We found her. Apparently, she had been tortured and forced to work for someone, we don't know who yet. We really haven't had a chance to talk to her. She's been exposed to silver dust, and I'm not sure why she's unconscious. How badly is she hurt?"

After slight hesitation, Jamal picked up a stethoscope and started to listen to her heart. "Heart rate is about forty-five beats a minute. Is that normal for an unconscious Were?" Kira gave a so-so gesture with her hand. Jamal took off the stethoscope and hovered his hand over her mouth and nose. "Breathing is slow but steady. Any sign of broken bones, other than her wrist? Back? Neck?"

"No. I checked back at... where we were," Todd spoke up for the first time, eyes fixed on the unconscious girl's face.

Jamal peeled open the eyes carefully. "Pupils are equally dilated, that's good. She probably doesn't have a concussion. I hope." He examined the swollen wrist gingerly. "I don't *think* this is broken, but I recommend x-rays to be sure. Um, I'm going to have to get at least this sweatshirt off to examine her. And frankly, these clothes are probably beyond saving."

Kira nodded and handed over a pair of scissors. "What do you need?"

"Hold her head steady. Shahara, keep her right arm still, I don't want to jar it more than we have to." The sweatshirt was hard and awkward to cut through, but they got it off. Sakaki didn't react at all. Not a move, not a moan, not even an eyelid flicker. Underneath, she was wearing an extremely grimy white tee-shirt. No blood. Since she seemed have been wearing the shirt for days, if not weeks, hopefully that meant that she wasn't bleeding underneath.

"I have no idea what caused this," Jamal said, carefully not touching the scar on her neck.

"Silver. Someone put silver on her for at least an hour to cause that." Ryoko looked like he very much wanted to find whoever did that and expose him to something equally painful for at least an hour.

"Um, little scared to ask, but I think I have to." Jamal ran a hand over his right eye into his hair. "You said she had been exposed to silver dust. What is that going to do? Can that be fatal?"

"Yes, but if she was exposed to enough to kill her, she'd be dead by now. The silver dust is why there is blood on her face. Might be some in her lungs, but it wasn't enough to choke her." Kira's words would sound harsh if it wasn't for the utter relief that saturated them.

Jamal nodded. "Any way to counteract the silver?"

"No. We can treat the irritations, but that's all we can do," Ryoko said.

"Okay. I can't check for more injuries while she's clothed. But I don't want to move her any more than we have to." He eyed the scissors again.

"There's no infection. I'd have smelled that in a heartbeat. The smell of blood isn't strong enough to be much more than we've already seen, and we already checked for broken bones or warm patches. I think the rest can wait for her to wake up," Kira said.

Jamal let out a breath. "Okay. I'll get some ice." He was back in a minute and started wrapping it. "She's dirty, malnourished, I suspect dehydrated and sleep deprived as well. Bruised, scraped, and her wrists are chapped."

Kira removed Sakaki's shoes and socks. "Ankles too, this one's almost raw. Probably chained, and they rubbed a lot. Also, she was given a chemical to prevent her from changing into a fox. I can smell it on her. Not a high dose. They probably couldn't afford much of it. Should wear off in a week or so."

So why was she unconscious and what happened to her?

***

Kira checked Sakaki's pulse again. It was the same as the last two times she tried. Slowly, she was beginning to accept that yes, this was real. They really had found Sakaki. And somehow or other, Sakaki had truly been Nightmare, without ever realizing it.

Kira stared in horror. Coming to a building where she expected a trap at worst, to confront a mysterious and skilled enemy at best; only to run into her kidnapped cousin, who might well be dying right now.

Slowly, the familiar/unfamiliar girl dropped a swollen hand, now dotted with tiny silver burns. There was blood by her nose, and as she coughed, blood flecked on her lips. "I don't, don't think it was enough," *coughing,* "to kill. I made sure to exhale."

"What if you're wrong?" Todd asked, quietly enough that he might not have been aware he spoke.

She didn't turn around to look at him. "Then I'm already dead."

Kira inched closer, afraid. What if this was a dream? What if she walked forward to touch her cousin, and she faded away like mist? Or worse, what if this wasn't a dream, and Sakaki died in front of her? "Sakaki?"

There was a smile on her face that she had never seen on Sakaki before. Wry and tired malice. "Nightmare. Always have been. Sak—" *She coughed until she had to gasp for breath.* "Sakaki never knew. She can't know. You can't tell her."

"Um, I can't–" Todd cut off as Nightmare raised a shaking hand.

"She swore. No more hidden bits. No more dangerous secrets. One way or another." She held up her left wrist, silver scar forward. "She can't know."

"What does she know?" Kira asked, trying to find a way to refute that Sakaki was Nightmare, had always been Nightmare.

"She remembers being captured, and about half the captivity. On a boat. Tell her... Tell her she tricked him, managed to escape." Nightmare coughed some more. "She'll wake up next."

With that, she slumped to the floor. Kira and Todd were kneeling at her side instantly. The door opened. Kira snapped to attention, only to relax at the sight of Ryoko-Sensei. He stared at them in shock. "What? How?"

"She tricked her captors. She's hurt. We have to take her back to your house." Kira did a quick hands on examination. Nothing stood out as urgent. She had to figure out something that Sakaki would believe, swear Todd to secrecy, and find out who kidnapped her in the first place. No one else was going to find out about Nightmare. Not if she had anything to say about it

"Okay, perhaps an explanation now?" Jamal asked. They had made Sakaki as comfortable as they could and had food and water for her when she woke up.

"I don't know what I can tell you. She was obviously tortured." Kira took a deep breath. "She didn't get a chance to explain what was going on. There was someone there with her. When we appeared, she took him down, but he triggered the ugly collar on her to release silver dust."

"So, it was cooperate or die?" Jamal asked. "And do I want to know what 'took down' means?"

"Exactly. And no. She didn't say what they wanted her to do or if she had done this before. I'll talk to her, and I'm going to ask that you *not* ask her about it. At all."

"Did she really kill–" Shahara started to ask.

"Whatever she may or may not have done, it was out of necessity. Don't ask her."

"What about the note that said–"

Kira cut Shahara off a second time. "Copycat. Don't mention that to her or anyone else either."

"Right. Well, can we stay until she wakes up?" Shahara asked.

Kira turned to *Sensei*. It was his house, after all. "I do not know when she will wake, but I see no reason you cannot spend the night if need be." Then he turned to Kira. "Why don't you help me make some tea?"

She followed, knowing that he wanted to talk to her privately. Once in the kitchen, she started the water boiling, before turning back to him.

"Weren't there two guards?" Kira nodded. "Do we need to clean the scene?"

"They were after files. We tossed them out the window and hid them under a bush, but it will be obvious as soon as morning hits."

"How many files?"

She shrugged. "We took them all. There were at least thirty, forty boxes."

"Anything else?"

"I relocked the doors and scattered the ashes with my feet. With a little luck, they'll vacuum before they notice anything. Even if they don't..." Most humans wouldn't figure on vampires, and even if they did, it wouldn't link back to them.

"Vampires?" Kira nodded again. "Did you recognize them?"

"Barely saw them. All my focus was on Sakaki." She shook her head. It was still unbelievable to her.

"Any chance they were anything other than minions?"

"None in my mind."

"She didn't say who?"

"No." Which meant they had to stay on high alert.

"My car is still near there. I will ask Todd to drive me there and retrieve my car and make sure we didn't leave anything there. You stay here with her."

"Yes, *Sensei.*" Kira took the kettle off the burner just before it started to shriek.

Neither Jamal nor Shahara seemed to think anything of their excuse. Todd agreed immediately, seeming to realize both parts of the plan.

"If she does wake up now," Todd shook his head wryly, "She might be slightly less than happy to see me at the moment."

Oh, yeah. She had almost forgotten the whole reason Sakaki had called her down in the first place. "I think she's had other things to think about. But you might be right." Then, trying not to wince, she turned to Shahara and Jamal. "She might also be slightly less than pleased that you know who she is. Or at very least, she'll be confused."

"Understood. If she seems agitated, we'll leave. We just want to know she's alright." Jamal let out a breath. "I wish you'd take her to see a real doctor, a real hospital. I don't know near enough."

Kira hummed, more in acknowledgment than agreement. Yes, they would take Sakaki to the clinic, but probably not tonight. She needed to make sure *Sakaki* woke up first. But the clinic would help. If nothing else, there would probably be someone who could remove the ugly collar.

It was something she would never be able to explain to a non-Were, the deep visceral reaction she had to seeing that collar around Sakaki's neck. It made her so angry to see it, almost worse than everything else combined. There were signs that she had been wearing the collar for days, and Kira was betting that Sakaki had not once been able to forget or ignore it. Even with a little room, it would feel suffocating, constricting with every swallow, every breath. It was more than a way to control, it was an insult, a way to humiliate, a denigration that could drive one mad. How had Sakaki coped?

Maybe they didn't have to wait as long as the clinic to take it off. As gently as she could, Kira rotated the collar so the latch was in the front. A specialty key and probably made to go off if tampered with. But it had already gone off. Tampering with it more couldn't hurt, right? "Before you go, *Sensei*, do you think you could pick this?"

He knelt down to squint at it. "Possible. It will take time though. I need my tools." Kira fetched his picks and a large magnifying glass, while Todd strewed cushions and pillows on the floor. Shahara held the magnifying glass steady while everyone else reluctantly kept back, to stay out of the light.

Kira went back to pondering. They needed to know who had kidnapped Sakaki before they took her to a clinic. Yes, the clinics were neutral ground, and a sanctuary for all. But that was more tradition and common sense than any binding rule. Well, that depended on race. Supposedly the vampires were bound, since the Vampire High Council had sworn to protect the neutrality of the clinics.

But there were too many irregularities going on for Kira to be comfortable with 'tradition' as protection. Who were the vampires with Sakaki? Were they part of the Rex Magnus Blood? If so, did Rex know about them? Had he ordered this? How much of 'Nightmare's' latest spree of terror had actually been Sakaki, and what happened to make her resurface? Could she do it again?

But those were questions that she wasn't going to have answered right away. Some might not be answered ever. And if she got Sakaki back, Kira could live with not getting those answers.

Except for who did this. That they needed to know. If Rex Magnus had anything to do with this, Kira was going to destroy him. Actually, whoever was responsible for this was dead. Kira didn't care if it *did* risk war between the vampires and the Weres. No one got away with hurting her cousin. Even if it meant setting the world on fire and watching it burn.

Chapter Thirty-Three

Escaping the enemy does not always mean escaping the enemy. – The Kikitsutai Book of Wisdom

It took almost twenty minutes for Ryoko-*Sensei* to remove the collar. Todd was relieved to see it gone, and he was pretty sure that his reaction was mild compared to the Werefoxes'. After that, they went to fetch the boxes. With two cars, they managed to fit all the boxes in their respective trunks, but it took almost an hour. Still, no one questioned them when they returned. Todd found himself holding his breath as he walked into the living room. But she was still out cold. The ice had been replaced with fresh ice, and someone had put lotion on her hand and face, with some kind of waxy substance on her lips. Probably for the silver irritations.

"Any change?" Todd asked, as he gingerly took a seat on the coffee table. When the wood didn't react to his weight, he relaxed a little and went back to studying her face.

"Nothing. I wish I knew why she was unconscious," Kira said.

"Well, she's clearly been through a lot of stress. Maybe her brain just needs a vacation. Besides, I'm sure she's dehydrated." Jamal swished his lower jaw back and forth, thinking. "Do you have any sterile sponges I can take apart? We might be able to at least hydrate her a little."

Ryoko-*Sensei* rummaged around until he found a clean natural sponge. Jamal pronounced it okay and cut it into smaller wedges, calling for a cup of water. Shahara came back with one just as Jamal stuck one of the wedges on a tongue depressor. Getting the sponge wet, he held it to Sakaki's lips. Her mouth opened. When he stuck the sponge in, she sucked on it.

"Is she waking up?" Shahara asked.

"Not necessarily. It's a reflex reaction. Even people in a coma can respond to this." Jamal dipped the sponge back in the water. "It won't be enough to properly rehydrate her, but it should help. If need be, we can give her honey through a different sponge. A little nutrients. But, once again, I *strongly* recommend taking her to a hospital. I can't do an IV for starters." He gave her a little more water.

"I can, if we have supplies. Which I'm sure we do," Kira said, still kneeling on the floor next to her cousin. Jamal and Shahara stared at her. Todd didn't bother. It didn't surprise him at all. "It's not like it's that hard. We all have emergency medical training. Sakaki actually did a tracheotomy once."

"I've had to do amputations on two separate occasions." The older Werefox placed another cup of water next to Jamal.

"Right. Well, I don't think either of those will be necessary at this time, but we'll keep the IV idea in mind." Jamal gave Sakaki some more water. "I just wish she would wake up."

It was a sentiment they all echoed.

***

Unconsciousness was fading, but she grasped at it with all her might. She didn't *want* to wake up! No more cold, bright room with chains and sadistic vampires. No more drugged water, too dangerous to drink but even more dangerous to refuse. No more torture.

A few days ago, Liska had had a nightmare. A bad one. Blood was everywhere. She was drowning in it. Everywhere it touched her, she started to bleed and burn. Her fault, all her fault.

She had woken up gasping for air, gradually realizing that she was breathing. It was just a nightmare. And her actual situation was even worse than her dream.

Not this time. She was staying in this fog of unconsciousness. It was warm, she was semi-comfortable, and she could imagine hearing voices around her. Voices of friends, who were concerned about her. As long as she could stay unconscious, she could imagine that if she woke up, it would be to friends.

Liska had dreamed scenarios like that before, until it just hurt too much. Every time she dreamed of a rescue, or even just being somewhere else, safe and with family or friends, it was more painful to wake up a captive, mistreated and alone. So, she had stopped. But apparently, she hadn't stopped. Because she was dreaming now.

It was a bad idea on her part. She honestly wasn't sure that she could handle that disappointment again. Even when she had deliberately imagined it, there had been a sense of disappointment when she stopped pretending. Waking up, opening her eyes, being back in that room, she wasn't sure she could take it this time. It might snap whatever remnants were left of her sanity. Or maybe it would depress her enough to try suicide through whatever methods were available to her. She had figured out three possibilities, using only the resources available on her first day of captivity, just in case.

No, she would stay asleep. Maybe forever. Which probably counted as a fourth way.

"I just wish she would wake up." Jamal? It sounded like him.

"Me too." Kira. Well, if Kira and Jamal were in the same room, then she was definitely dreaming. Well, if she was dreaming, she was going to enjoy it. Shahara would be there, Todd too.

"She'll wake up. I'm sure she will. I've been praying." Ah, there was Shahara.

Liska felt something. Her hair was moving. Someone was moving it. Part of the dream. It was part of her dream! "Good. We need it." Todd's voice. It was close. Pretend it was him smoothing her hair. Yes, she could handle that. A Todd who hadn't decided that he couldn't accept her life. Accept her. Yes, this was a nice dream. Except everyone was sad.

"Is there any change?" Ryoko-*Sensei*. As if she needed more proof this was a dream. Only in her dreams would they all be here together.

Briefly, she wondered if she was deeply enough into the dream that she would see them if she opened her eyes. But she didn't dare. No, that would wake her up and put her back in the nightmare world, where nothing made sense and pain was as constant as breathing.

There was a splash on her forehead. Water and salt. A tear? Who was crying? Probably her, if she woke up.

"No change." Todd. His voice was thick. Another splash. Her cheek this time. "Is there anything we can do?"

There was movement by her leg. Sudden enough that she almost reacted "Maybe. Just maybe." Kira. More movement. Liska had a distinct feeling of someone leaning over her. "Clover," Kira's voice whispered in her ear.

It was their word. The code to pull each other from a trance. Everything was safe now. But was it? If it was a figment Kira telling her, and she woke up to a nightmare again... But if it wasn't a figment, then she couldn't *not* respond. Liska was terrified, but she couldn't be a coward.

Liska opened her eyes.

***

Todd almost fell backwards when Sakaki's eyes fluttered open. "Sakaki?" It seemed too good to be true.

Those eyes met his before looking around the room. "Still dreaming. Thought I stopped."

Kira ignored her confusion and picked up the cup from the table. "Here, can you sit up a little? I have some water. Left hand."

"Is it drugged again?" Sakaki asked, even as she accepted Todd's help to sit up. "Oh, right. Dream. In reality, the water is drugged." Her left hand was shaky as it took the cup. Sakaki sniffed the water, before sipping slowly.

"Better? We've got food too." Kira turned to Shahara. "Get some crackers. Cabinet over the stove." Shahara ran off without a word.

"I like this dream. But I have to stop dreaming this."

Kira silenced the room with a look before turning back to Sakaki. "Why do you have to stop dreaming this?"

"Because each time, it's harder to wake up and face reality. More painful."

Kira nodded, taking the crackers from Shahara and starting to open the box. "What if this wasn't a dream.

Sakaki looked around the room again, paying particular attention to the humans, before looking back to Kira. "I've dreamed this so many times. It could only be a dream."

"Maybe. Or maybe, while we were looking for you, I had to take your place. Maybe Jamal and Shahara were observant enough to figure out I wasn't you, and dumb enough to confront me about it." Jamal squawked an objection and was completely ignored. "Maybe I had to explain things to them."

Sakaki tilted her head like she was considering that. "Can I have some crackers?"

"Sure. Start slow, okay?" Kira passed over three crackers. "Do you want more water?"

Sakaki nodded. No one said anything while Sakaki slowly ate half a box of crackers and drank two cups of water. Then she looked at them again. "I'm tired."

"Sleep. We'll all be here when you wake up. Then you'll know it wasn't a dream," Ryoko-*Sensei* said, pulling a blanket over her.

She was asleep almost before she finished agreeing. No one spoke for a few minutes, until Shahara broke the silence. "Um, well, that... I have no idea. Is this a good thing or not?"

"From a health standpoint, I'd say mostly good. She woke up, was lucid and at least semi-rational. There were no signs of serious injury that we missed, and pain seems manageable. From the mental standpoint?" Jamal shrugged and started to clean up the trash. "Mister psych major?"

Todd shook his head. "Beyond my level, but I think we're mostly okay there too. She's been through a traumatic situation, and it may take time for her to fully come to grips with the fact that she's out of it. Besides, she wasn't expecting you two at all and might not have been expecting me. We'll see how she's doing tomorrow. See if she still thinks it's a dream. She'll need therapy, no matter what. But hopefully not over that." He sighed. "In the meantime, do you mind if we camp out in your living room tonight?"

"As I promised that you would all be here tomorrow, I do not see how I can say no. I do have a couple guest rooms if anyone would rather not sleep on the floor."

Despite Ryoko-*Sensei*'s offer, everyone seemed to prefer proximity to comfort. The coffee table and chairs were moved to the edges of the room or out entirely, and the linen closet was thoroughly raided. With several layers of blankets and pillows on the floor, it actually wasn't that uncomfortable. Both of the uninjured Werefoxes transformed into foxes, making it an easier fit than it might have been. Kira fox curled up on the end of the couch by Sakaki's feet, while Ryoko-*Sensei* claimed the recliner.

Shahara took the end near the wall, while Jamal settled in near the middle. Todd was closest to the door, making sure there was still a path if anyone needed to get up in the middle of the night. The last thing he saw before falling asleep was the peaceful face of Sakaki. They had found her. Now came the hard part.

***

As far as he could tell, Todd was the first to wake up in the morning. Nature was calling too loudly for him to bother to do more than a cursory check. Once that need was soothed, he came back to the living room.

Jamal and Shahara still hadn't moved, and Jamal was lightly snoring. The foxes seemed to be asleep, but he wasn't sure about them. On the other hand, Sakaki was looking at him, no expression on her face.

He tried to be careful not to wake the others, but speed was more of a priority as he hurried to her side. "Hey. You scared us."

"Is this a dream?"

Well, that was better than yesterday. "No. No, it isn't. You're really here."

She looked at the sleepers on the floor. "They know?"

"Some. We had to tell them. They're pretty worried about you."

"I... I don't remember. How did I get here?"

Todd winced. He had no idea what to tell her. He couldn't lie, but how could he tell her the truth? "Do you trust me?" The moment it was out of his mouth, Todd felt like kicking himself for asking such a dumb question. After what happened just before she disappeared, why would she trust him?

"Yes."

Okay, he hadn't expected that. "Good. Thank you. I can't tell you everything. I don't know much myself. I do know you managed to trick someone and escape, though you got hurt in the process. Try not to move your right hand more than you have to. But I don't know where you were or who took you."

After a moment, she nodded. "I remember who."

The fox at the edge of the sofa had opened her eyes but wasn't moving. Probably Ryoko-*Sensei* was awake too. But for some reason, they were leaving this to him. For now. "Do you want to talk about it?"

"No. Not yet. Later."

"That's fine. Whenever you're ready." Todd racked his brain for something else to say but she beat him to it.

"What's the date?"

"The date? March twentieth. You've been missing for over a month and a half."

"Oh, I lost track." She was so quiet. So subdued. Like someone had drained all the energy and spirit out of her. Quite frankly, it was scaring him.

But she had been through a traumatic experience. That changes people. He would have to be patient and adapt. For now, they had her convinced that she wasn't dreaming. It was a start.

"Can you help me up?"

Todd blinked. "Up?"

"My legs are fine, aren't they? They seem fine. Ish."

"As far as I know, they're fine. But are you sure you should be moving?"

"I need the facilities. And a shower."

Fox Kira suddenly stood up, stretched, leapt to the floor and dashed out the room. Sakaki followed with her eyes. "And Kira will make sure I don't overdo it."

"Okay, here. You support yourself with your left hand and I'll..." He cupped a hand around her right elbow and gave a little lift when she was ready.

She nodded in thanks and walked out of the room on semi-wobbly legs. Kira, now in human form and wearing a robe, met her at the door.

Water running woke Jamal and Shahara. Ryoko-*Sensei* left to transform, and judging by the smells, make breakfast.

"She's awake?" Shahara asked, spotting the empty couch.

"Awake, convinced she's awake, and taking a shower."

"Good. Excellent." Jamal leaned his head back in relief. Then brought it back to face Todd. "Is there another bathroom?"

There was, and everyone had put themselves at least semi to rights by the time Sakaki came back down, wearing clean clothes.

"I'm so glad to see you!" Shahara squealed, rushing forward to give the Werefox a hug. But she stopped several feet short when Sakaki reeled back, staring with wide eyes, hands coming up defensively. Kira immediately got between them.

Shahara took a couple steps back. "I'm sorry. I should have realized. We're all glad to see you. We've missed you and been really worried." She took another few steps back. "Your uncle is making breakfast. Do you think you're up to it?"

Sakaki paused for a moment before answering. "Breakfast? Yes. I can eat something."

Jamal didn't try to approach her, but he did give her a broad smile. "Your cousin explained, well, not everything, but enough. We know your name is really Sakaki, that you aren't human, etc. We are still your friends. We understand why you lied and won't tell anyone. Promise."

"Thank you. I appreciate it." Another pause. "I'm supposed to apologize for lying now, aren't I?"

Shahara laughed. "Ideally, yes. But I'd rather you not apologize than give an apology you don't mean. And I don't think you're sorry for lying."

"Comes with the lifestyle." Sakaki slumped into a chair at the kitchen table.

Breakfast was quiet as it became increasingly obvious that Sakaki simply wasn't up to dealing with so many people at one time. Or much of anything else at the moment. Ryoko-*Sensei* was the one to say that after breakfast, the humans would go home, and Sakaki was going to the clinic. She didn't argue or complain.

That surprised Todd a little. He wouldn't have imagined that Sakaki would be an easy patient. Not the way she went out of her way to hide or deny weakness. Judging from the troubled look that Kira and Ryoko shared, this compliance wasn't her norm.

If Sakaki noticed, she didn't say anything. She barely looked up from her toast and thinned oatmeal. She didn't even argue over being given that while everyone else had eggs and bacon.

After breakfast, Ryoko put the food away, Kira did the dishes and Sakaki seemed to have fallen asleep in her seat. The humans put away the blankets and pillows and put the living room back to rights. Sakaki was still asleep, so they quietly passed on their well wishes to Kira and left, promising to stop by later.

***

Liska sat quietly in the car, eyes closed behind sunglasses to block out the light. She hadn't fallen asleep while at the clinic, but neither had she felt particularly alert either. Why was she so exhausted? It was weird. Everything felt either one step removed, like it wasn't happening to her, or like it was happening to her, and she was extra sensitive.

Todd being there didn't feel real. She knew she should feel something about that, but she didn't. Couldn't even figure out what she was supposed to be feeling. But when Shahara tried to hug her, she panicked, like the other girl would attack her. Even knowing that Shahara was as likely to attack her as a giant sinkhole was to swallow the house at that very moment, even knowing that she could have stopped Shahara in her tracks if she *did* try; Liska had been afraid. Good thing Kira stepped in, for both their sakes.

It was like she couldn't figure out what she should be feeling or what should be important. Like the clinic. As much as she respected their purpose, as grateful as she was for their existence, Liska hated going to the Twilight/Night clinics. They were a massive sensory overload. Too many smells, too many sounds, and way too many upset people.

But today, she hadn't cared. Hadn't responded to anything but the most direct stimulus. Liska was aware that her behavior was worrying Kira and Ryoko-*Sensei* but couldn't work up the energy to do anything about it.

"We're here." Kira was at her side. "Do you need a nap?"

"Yeah. I think so. Then I need to tell you what happened."

"Okay. But you can sleep first. Todd and the others will probably come by later. Do you think you'll be up for a visit?"

Liska shook her head. "No. No visitors. Not until I manage to get a handle on things."

Chapter Thirty-Four

Those who love you will stand by you in your weakness. –
The Kikitsutai Book of Wisdom

"It's been three days. I understand that recovery is a long, slow process. I understand that she may not want... witnesses to her 'weakness', especially people who don't know what she's been through. But we just want to see her, let her know we're thinking about her. Maybe just a quick stop?" Todd tried not to pace his dorm room. There really wasn't space, and his cell sometimes dropped calls if he went too close to the window.

Kira's voice came through slightly distant, like there was interference on the line. "I don't think so. I've asked her. She says she's not ready. And the solium is still flushing out of her system. Believe me, that's not a pretty process. It's better not to agitate her right now. I'll tell her you called though. Hey, I have to go to class today. If you wanted to send a card or something, I'll make sure she gets it. Best I can do."

"Right. Thanks, Kira." He hung up.

"Still no go?" Jamal asked from his side of the room.

"You got it. Kira said she'd deliver a card, but best not to see her in person yet."

"Shahara should have a bunch of cards. I'll ask her." Jamal sent a quick text, which was answered even quicker. "Yup, says we can each send one if we want."

Todd nodded but didn't say anything. He hadn't had a chance to really talk to Sakaki and had no idea where they stood now. Not that he planned on asking her right now. That would be selfish. No, she needed some recovery time first.

But he wasn't sure if Liska didn't want to see them because she wasn't feeling up to it, or because she really didn't want to see *him*. Sending a card, while it may be the only form of contact she would currently accept, seemed hollow.

"Card not good enough?" Jamal asked while not asking.

"Not really."

"You could write her a letter."

Todd reluctantly shook his head. "I'd say the wrong thing or word it wrong or something. At least if I talk to her in person, she can usually get some idea of what I mean even when my words are wrong."

"Okay, so maybe a care package."

A smile slowly grew on his face. "Now that has potential."

***

Ryoko-*Sensei* looked up as Kira came in carrying two shoe boxes and a large teddy bear. "School seems to have changed somewhat since my days."

Kira gave him a small smile, more in acknowledgement that he had made a joke than because she found it funny. "Care packages. Todd, Jamal, and Shahara seem to have decided that since they can't visit in person, they would make their presence felt this way." She set the bear on the chair and put the shoe boxes in front of it like the bear was holding the boxes. "We're lucky. Shahara couldn't get the balloons she wanted." Then she got serious. "How is she?"

Sensei sighed. "Her fever's up. I think some of her injuries are infected and the antibiotics the clinic gave her simply aren't helping. She was lucid, last I checked, but... If she's not showing improvement by tomorrow, then I think we should take her back."

"Where is she now?"

"Asleep in your closet."

Kira nodded. Werefoxes were still animal enough to want to isolate themselves when badly injured or sick, and the burrowing instinct could get strong. Rather than dirt, most burrowed under blankets or clothes, often in a closet or under a bed. "I'm going to go check on her."

Even without directions, Kira could have found her easily. Sakaki's breathing was labored, even though there was no evidence of anything wrong with her lungs. The door to the closet was open a crack. Kira pushed it open a few more inches.

On the floor, Sakaki turned glassy eyes to her. "It's just me," Kira said, before sitting cross-legged on the floor. "How are you feeling?"

"Kira?"

"Yeah. It's me."

"Did he capture you too?"

"No. We got you out. You're safe." It was at least the fifth time that Kira had to tell her that. *Sensei* had told her a few times as well.

"Is he dead?"

Now Kira had to restrain her emotions. Sakaki had managed to debrief on her captivity before falling victim to, well, everything. Cazimir was going to receive a very painful lesson on the loyalty of Werefoxes. No one hurt her cousin and got away with it. *No one.* "Not yet. But he will die. I swear." Sakaki looked at her. "If you recover soon enough, you can have first shot at him."

"Dunno. Maybe Rex wants it."

Kira shrugged. "You two can come to some sort of arrangement."

"Need proof."

"We'll figure something out."

"I'm tired."

"Okay, you rest. I'll get you some more water." Kira picked up the mostly empty water bottle by Sakaki's side.

Sakaki nodded. Her eyes drooped, but she was not relaxed or asleep. She smelled of sweat, heat, and pain. It didn't escape Kira's notice the way Sakaki's eyes opened a crack, as if to make sure she really was there. Or that she really did bring back her water. Kira wasn't sure which.

It would be faster to get water from the bathroom tap. If Sakaki was fine, that was exactly what Kira would do. But in this state, she was sensitive to the chemicals in the tap water. Which was why they had bought a few gallons of distilled water, keeping one in the refrigerator. It took about two minutes longer. Which was at least one minute too long.

As Kira was coming back up the stairs, a howling sound erupted from her room. The water bottle fell from her hands, and she vaguely heard it hit a couple stairs and roll, but she was busy running. She almost ripped the closet door of its' hinges forcing it open as far as it would go.

Sakaki was curled up in a fetal position, tears streaming from her eyes, and grabbing her legs hard enough that Kira was briefly amazed she wasn't breaking at least one limb. The pain Kira had smelled earlier had intensified by a power of ten. Worst of all, Sakaki seemed to be transforming back and forth involuntarily. She never got all the way to fox form, but she wasn't changing back to human form either. As Kira watched, the tail appeared, and fur started to appear on her arms. Sakaki whimpered.

Sensei darted into the room. "I have painkillers for her." He held up a bottle. Kira recognized it as the painkiller given to a child for their first few changes. Commonly considered by Weres to be the most painful thing anyone ever went through.

"Is it strong enough for an adult?"

"The clinic said to give her a double dose. But I'll need you to hold her."

Kira didn't bother to respond. She snagged the comforter from the bed and wrapped it around her cousin before sitting down next to her. Then she dragged Sakaki to a semi-sitting position, trapping her against the wall. Unsurprisingly, Sakaki tried to bite her. One of the trials of dealing with a sick Were.

Even though Sakaki didn't know she was there, Kira tried talking to her. Nonsense words, more to let her know that someone was there than to tell her anything. "It's going to be okay. *Sensei* has medicine for you." She arranged Sakaki in a more sitting position, pulling her hand back when Sakaki snarled at her. "None of that now. You don't need that. Just take this medicine. You'll feel better." *Sensei* had the dose in a cup. "Open your mouth." Sakaki, currently getting furry in the face, just growled at her, no recognition in her eyes. "Well, if you're going to be like that..." Kira forced her mouth open, and *Sensei* quickly poured in the liquid. As soon as it was in, Kira shut her mouth and held it shut until Sakaki swallowed the medicine.

Kira didn't move yet. "Please tell me that *was* a double dose."

"It was."

"Good." Sakaki was still fighting her. Kira carefully got up, keeping an eye on Sakaki's arms and teeth. But once she started to move away, Sakaki didn't seem to consider her a worthwhile threat. Or at least, it would be more trouble or painful than it was worth to attack her.

Kira turned to *Sensei*. "How much longer is this supposed to last?"

He closed his eyes and shook his head. "Between two and five days, depending."

"I'm not sure we're going to make it."

"Neither am I."

***

Kira woke suddenly, not sure what had woken her. After a moment of listening, she heard a moan. In her rush to get up, she didn't move the sheet back enough and fell to the ground. With a grunt, she pulled herself free from the blankets and crawled to the closet. "Sakaki?"

Sakaki gave a pained whimper.

"Can you hear me? It's Kira."

Slowly Sakaki's eyes rose to half-mast. Kira wasn't sure if Sakaki was seeing her or not. "Do you need something for the pain?" No answer. "Water? Food?"

"K...Kira?" She sounded like a little fox kit.

"Yeah, it's me." Kira started rubbing her back gently. Sakaki was radiating heat. How high was her fever anyway? "What do you need?"

"Hot. Everything hurts."

"Let's give you a cool bath. That will help you feel better."

About halfway through being helped up, Sakaki seemed to forget who was there and what was going on, pulling away with a growl. Kira readjusted her grip so that Sakaki didn't fall and she was less likely to get bitten. "It's me. Kira. I'm trying to help you. Let's cool you down."

That seemed to stump Sakaki enough for Kira to escort her to the bathroom. "Sit here." Kira sat

Sakaki on the closed toilet and started the water. She needed cool but not cold. Once she had what felt like a good temperature, she put in the drain and turned back to Sakaki.

Sakaki, meanwhile, had picked up *Sensei*'s hand soap dispenser, and was examining it like she had never seen anything like it before. There were several gobs of foam on the sink and two on her hands, as Sakaki experimented with it.

"Right, how about we leave that alone for now." Kira pried the dispenser away. "Come on. You can't take a bath in your clothes. Can you get undressed?"

Apparently not. Kira helped her cousin stand, strip, and climb into the tub. Or tried to. As soon as Sakaki put one foot in the tub, she stopped and refused to move. "Come on, in the tub. You'll feel better."

Sakaki didn't move but seemed to be getting more agitated. What was going on? Kira tried to remember everything that Sakaki told her about her captivity. Nothing stood out as an answer, so she went further back. But nothing that she could remember would explain her freaking out about a bath.

Kira was about to give up when Sakaki went completely limp. It took all her effort to keep Sakaki from hitting her head and getting her semi-gently on the floor. "Sakaki?" Sakaki started to spasm. "*Sensei*, call the clinic! Emergency!"

The spasms were over by the time *Sensei* had come in the room, and Sakaki was conscious. Unable to get off the floor, and not lucid, but conscious. "What happened?" *Sensei* asked, phone in hand.

"She had a seizure. I know she didn't hit her head, but she's..."

"Am I on the floor?" Sakaki asked, in French.

"Out of it." Kira sighed. "Yes, you are on the floor," she replied back in the same language. Behind her, she could hear *Sensei* hurriedly filling in the dispatcher on the other line of the phone.

Sakaki blinked as if surprised to see her there. "Did you get your duck yet?"

"Yes. Don't worry about it." She turned back to *Sensei*. "Please tell me they're sending an ambulance."

"Already en route."

"Good. No, don't try to stand up yet. Just lie down."

"Why am I on the floor?"

"You fell." Kira picked up a large towel and draped it over Sakaki.

Sakaki fingered a corner of the towel. "I have clothes. Usually. Don't I?" She was speaking Arabic now. Not one of Kira's better languages.

"Yes. You do. But not right now."

"Oh. Am I on the floor?"

Kira and *Sensei* exchanged a look. "I'll go let the ambulance in," *Sensei* said, leaving Kira to continue with Sakaki.

"Yes. You are on the floor."

There were four more repetitions of 'Yes, you're on the floor', three explanations of why she was on the floor, three reassurances that yes, Sakaki did have clothes, she simply wasn't wearing them right now, and a few more comments about some duck Kira was supposed to have, all in about five different languages, before the ambulance arrived.

"I'm riding with her," Kira said, allowing no argument.

The Fae EMT gave her a quick look. "You aren't even dressed."

"I have a bag. I can change at the hospital. I'll have my shoes on before you can have her downstairs."

The vampire EMT didn't look away from checking Sakaki's vitals. "If you can be ready, then you can ride with us."

Like Kira really cared about going to the hospital in her nightgown. Still, she took a moment to pull on a pair of pants and her shoes. She was still downstairs waiting by the door when the EMTs were bringing Sakaki down on a brace board.

"I will meet you at the hospital," *Sensei* said.

Kira stayed out of the way while the paramedics did their work, but she watched everything. Every technique, every tool, every procedure. Even memorizing all the medical jargon that went over her head.

Sakaki's fever had escalated too far, which was what caused the seizure. But solium leaving her system wasn't helping. Because she kept changing, it was hard on her body and keeping her overheated.

When they got to the clinic, Kira refused to leave Sakaki's side, until the nurse, also a Were, agreed to let her fill out the paperwork while sitting in Sakaki's room. Though that might have had something to do with the fact that the one time they did make Kira leave, Sakaki had gotten so upset that they almost had to sedate her before Kira forced her way back in.

Sensei arrived about twenty minutes later. "How is she?"

"They've got her on medication to bring down the fever. They wanted to strap her down so she didn't hurt herself because of the solium, but I convinced them that would be a bad idea." Not only was being restrained the last thing Sakaki needed, Kira wasn't sure that she would be able to stop herself from maiming the moron who tried it. And if she didn't hurt him, *Sensei* would. Fortunately, it hadn't taken much to talk them out of it. Though the doctor did make sure to remove the scalpel and ordered security to keep an eye on her. Seriously, she hadn't even touched him.

"Anyway, they're definitely keeping her overnight, and probably all of tomorrow as well. Possibly until the solium stabilizes."

Sensei nodded slowly. "It may be for the best. You should sleep while you can. You have class tomorrow."

Kira let out a humorless laugh. "I'm not going anywhere, and you know it."

"You should still rest. Is she likely to wake?"

"Probably not. They said the painkiller had sedative properties." Kira tried unsuccessfully to swallow a yawn. "You may have a point." There was an unoccupied cot in the room. "You take the cot. I can sleep in the chair."

"There is a room where families of patients can get some rest."

"I'm not leaving her. If you want to sleep there, be my guest. But I'm staying here."

It took another few minutes, but Kira got *Sensei* to agree to her plan. As she tried to find a comfortable position in the hospital chair, she happened to glance at her watch. Two-fifty. It was going to be long night.

Chapter Thirty-Five

There are no shortcuts to recovery. – The Kikitsutai Book of Wisdom

Todd didn't think too much of it when he didn't see Kira for one day. Their schedules only overlapped because they made a point of seeing each other. Kira was undoubtedly spending as much time as she could with Sakaki, so she probably wasn't at school much beyond classes. When he didn't see her a second day, he grew more concerned. Especially when Shahara said she skipped English.

"I'll call her. See if there's anything..." They already knew Sakaki was in bad shape. Asking if something was wrong would be stupid. "Anything we can do."

"I want to be there when you call her. Maybe we can talk to," Shahara looked around the cafeteria, "her cousin."

"Worth a shot," Jamal said.

"Fine. Upstairs? It's quieter." Todd finished the last of his dinner.

Everyone followed his lead, and a few minutes later, they were upstairs. Todd dialed Kira's number. The phone rang three times before she answered it. "Todd, is that you? Seriously, she's not up for visitors yet."

"Actually, we're all here. You're on speakerphone."

"Thanks for the warning." Kira sounded tired. "Sorry, but she can't talk right now. I really can't either."

"You haven't been here for two days," Shahara said. "Did she get worse?"

"Kind of. Her fever went up, and the chemical is making it worse. We had to hospitalize her. They say she might be able to go home tomorrow, but that depends."

"Can she have visitors?" Jamal asked.

"No. One, the clinic is particular about their privacy. Two, it's family only. Three, she doesn't recognize *me* half the time. Trust me, we're dangerous when sick. You don't know the signs to watch for." Todd wondered a little about how vague Kira was being until he realized that she was trying to be careful in case anyone overheard. Something he should have thought of in the first place.

"But she's getting better?" Shahara asked.

"Yes, she's getting better. Slowly. Give her a little more time. I'm sorry, but I haven't given her your care packages yet. I will when she can appreciate them. Nothing time sensitive, right?"

"No. There's some candy, but that won't go bad too fast. As long as you don't have as big an ant problem as the campus does. Everything else is non-perishable." Todd took a deep breath. "When she's up to it, tell her that we wish her better and look forward to seeing her, please."

"I will. I have to get back to her now." Kira hung up.

***

"Okay, we're home." Kira looked back at Sakaki, who nodded but didn't open her eyes. While she hadn't been delirious for over a day, she had been extremely quiet. The doctor warned them that she would probably be easily fatigued, prone to mood swings, and oversensitive to stimuli for a while. Part of it was withdrawal from the solium, part of it was normal reactions to recovering from trauma. Nutritional deficiencies weren't helping either.

Kira unbuckled her seatbelt, let herself out, and walked around the car, opening Sakaki's door. That, at least, got Sakaki moving enough to unbuckle her own seatbelt. Then she looked at the car. "This isn't *Sensei*'s car."

"Oh. Cazimir faked your death. *Sensei*'s car crashed with a body in it. The body was identified as you. We knew it wasn't but haven't figured out who it was. Anyway, *Sensei* got a new car."

"He killed someone else? Because of me?" To Kira's horror, Sakaki was starting to tear up at the thought.

"That is *not* your fault. Cazimir is just a sadistic nutcase. Besides, we don't know for sure he killed someone. He may have somehow stolen a body." Sakaki just looked at her. "Come inside. Please."

She did. "How come I didn't notice it was a new car before?"

Kira shrugged. "I don't know. I guess you were distracted. It is the same kind."

Sakaki sank into the sofa, eyes closed. "I hate being sick and weak."

"You'll be better soon. Hey, if you're up to it, your friends from college made up some care packages for you." Sakaki didn't say anything, but she opened her eyes and looked interested. Kira even caught a whiff of curiosity. Better than she had gotten for a while. "Stay there. I'll get them."

They were right where she had left them. "Here." Kira handed her the bear first.

Sakaki took it with a smile. "A teddy bear?"

Kira shrugged, not admitting that she knew Sakaki secretly loved stuffed animals. "I think it's a normal get well gift in this culture."

Sakaki tucked the bear next to her and took the first box. It had been taped shut, so she turned her fingernails to claws to slice the tape. It was good to see her have the control back. Of course, the clinic had insisted that she demonstrate the ability to change into a fox and back again voluntarily before they discharged her. Much to Sakaki's dismay, neither Kira nor *Sensei* agreed to let her sign out Against Medical Advice.

When she opened the box, the first thing visible were cards. Two purchased cards, and one hand designed, probably from Todd. Kira had almost forgotten Todd was an artist. Sakaki read the cards before putting them on the coffee table and moving on to the rest of the box. If she wanted Kira to read them, she would have handed them to her. If she didn't want Kira to read them, she would have put them next to her. By putting them on the coffee table, it was Kira's decision. Perhaps later.

Also in the box was a paperback novel, historical fiction from the looks of it, some puzzle books, and a gift certificate for downloadable songs. In the other box there was some candy, a notebook and pen, a certificate for downloadable apps, some Silly Putty, and a stress ball. Sakaki immediately picked up the stress ball and started to fiddle with it. "So, they really did find out."

"I couldn't pass as you long enough. Came close, but they confronted me almost a week before we found you. Something about my not having your scars."

"Shahara saw my wrist." Sakaki stared absently towards the window, not seeing Kira's shudder. Which didn't mean she didn't know it happened. "Sorry."

"Not now. Just... not now." Not when she was trying to figure out a way to avoid the same outcome. It was hard to figure out a solution when she didn't dare think about the problem when she was around Sakaki.

"This was really nice of them. I should thank them."

"Probably. They would like to see you. When you're ready."

Sakaki closed her eyes and shook her head. "Not yet. Maybe soon. I'm tired."

"Okay. You rest."

She was already half-asleep. "Then we plan. Rex Magnus."

"When you're awake." Kira draped the blanket over her cousin, smiling as she noticed Sakaki was instinctively cuddling the teddy bear.

***

"Rex Magnus is going to be a problem," Kira said. Liska forced down her irritation at the obvious statement. "Any ideas how we can prove that Cazimir betrayed him?"

Sensei pressed his fingertips together. "Are we admitting what happened to you?" He asked Liska.

She shrugged. "Only does any good if he believes me about Cazimir. Otherwise, we just tricked him."

"He suspected something. He put me through a test to see if I was actually you. Probably wouldn't have passed it if I hadn't drawn him based on your description. Maybe... If that was suggested by someone he knew was associated with Cazimir or Rimat, or whatever he was calling himself that day, then that might help."

Both *Sensei* and Liska disagreed. "You're underestimating vampire loyalty. We'll need a *lot* of proof." Liska leaned back and thought. "There was a camera. They were filming my captivity. I asked him outright why he betrayed the Magnus Blood. He denied that, but not that he told Calloway how to find them. Even that wouldn't be *enough*, if we had that, it might be a start. But I don't even know if it still exists."

"Do you know the name of his ship?" *Sensei* asked.

"No, I never saw the outside. Or if I did, I don't remember it."

"Look, we'll figure this out. We know who it was, we just need to get proof." Kira gave her a small, unconvincing smile. "We will figure this out."

Liska smiled back, trying to help Kira believe it. She was exhausted again. "Until then, you're me." And probably for some time afterwards. Right now, Kira looked more like her than she did. She could wear a wig to hide the way her hair had been butchered, but people would notice that she was suddenly about fifteen pounds lighter and had a giant scar across her neck. *Sensei* was working to get her scheduled for cosmetic surgery to minimize it or cover it up, but she had be better and stronger first. "What did we tell the skulk?"

"Officially, you never went missing and Kira just stayed to assist you in avenging the Magnus Blood. Now... Your parents know the truth. No one else yet."

"Right. What happened to my phone?"

"It was found in the car accident. Destroyed. I've ordered you a new one, and Kira has most of your same information, doesn't she?"

"Most." And what Kira didn't have, her notes should. Liska forced her neck straight when it started to fall forward. "I think I'm going to crash again."

Someone said something, but Liska didn't hear it. She didn't wake up until she heard Kira answer the door. Voices. Todd and Shahara. Meaning Jamal was probably here too.

"She's asleep." Kira.

"No, I'm not." Liska forced herself to sit up and rubbed at her eyes. "I can take a short visit." She had been out of the hospital for two days and couldn't completely isolate herself. Even if part of her wanted to.

Kira leaned into the room. "Are you sure?"

"Quick visit." She stifled a yawn. "Really quick."

Soon Todd, Shahara, and Jamal were sitting across from her in the living room. Kira sat on the couch next to her, probably to offer a little protection and kick them out if she got too tired.

There was an awkward silence as everyone tried and failed to come up with something to say. The silence was almost tangible when Liska broke it. "Thank you for the care packages. That was very kind of you."

Shahara gave her a huge smile. "You're welcome. You enjoyed them?"

"Yes, I did. Or do." Which was grammatically correct in this language? "I'm not awake yet."

"It's fine. We understand. But we wanted you to know that we were thinking about you. Do you need anything?" Todd asked.

"I can't think of anything."

"Are you coming back to school?" Shahara asked.

"Not this semester. I can't pass for Anna yet. After... I haven't really thought about it." Which was a complete lie. She had thought for hours about whether to go back to school or just give up on it, but she hadn't come to any conclusions yet. So far, for her freshman year, Kira had taken almost as many of her classes as she had. School was looking more and more like a failed experiment. And if she kept thinking of that, she was going to get very depressed. Not here. Not in front of them. Later.

"Right. Um, this is probably insensitive, but I'm not sure how to avoid it." Jamal took a deep breath. "We aren't going to ask you about... what happened, but if you want talk about it, we'll listen. Or if we're reminding you of something and you want us to stop, just say something and we will. No questions asked."

Liska nodded solemnly. "I'll keep that in mind. But I'm not really talking about it now." She never did subscribe to the theory that talking about things a lot made them better. Sure, maybe talking to one or two people helped, but after that, it was more like obsessing. Sometimes talking to more people just meant more time thinking about the problem. Besides, they didn't have enough frame of reference to understand. "Anything interesting happening at school?"

She listened with half an ear as they told her little things about school. How one dorm managed to steal another dorm's mascot and displayed it on the Green, wearing the dorm colors of the dorm that stole it. How one professor, for reasons rumors disagreed upon, had taught classes for a day while wearing a sparkling pink ball gown. According to Shahara, he looked rather fetching in it. The squirt gun battle one guy's dorm was doing, pitting the floors against each other. Two teachers in the Humanities department were getting married near the end of the year. The ceremony would be in the chapel and students were permitted to attend. The school play almost didn't open on opening night because something happened to all the costumes. What happened wasn't clear. Either some prankster had hidden them all and only been persuaded to confess at the last minute, or they were misplaced and only found at the last minute, or they were given to a laundromat and there was some delay or miscommunication there.

Shahara mentioned how her roommate woke up a few days ago with a lizard on her face. Jamal told her about seeing an egret crossing the street in the pedestrian crosswalk. Todd briefly described a class where his professor brought in his pet ball python. Liska gave him a sympathetic grimace for that, remembering that Todd didn't like snakes.

Everything was fine until Shahara started telling her about one of the prominent trees on campus which had been struck by lightning and was now dead. Liska found herself starting to tear up.

"They're looking into tree removal specialists. Probably going to do that when the semester ends, since that's a little under a month away. But for safety's sake, they're telling everyone not to go near it. And... are you crying?"

Liska shook her head, even as the tears started to run down her face. "I'm sorry. I don't know what's wrong. I..."

Kira immediately stood up. "Okay, she's tired. We need to let her rest some more. Thank you for coming, we both appreciate it."

No one objected to being hustled out. There were a few well wishes and goodbyes that Liska barely responded to. As they got to the door, she heard Shahara ask in whisper, "Is it my fault, for talking about the tree?"

"No. She's just... stressed. And tired. Don't worry about it."

Good. Shahara shouldn't blame herself. Liska didn't honestly know why she was crying. She didn't even know which tree Shahara was talking about. And it was possible she would never find out. Probable, actually. Now she was really crying. Oh, she hated being this moody.

Kira was back, trying to comfort her. Right now, she didn't *want* comfort. She wanted to be left alone. But it would be rude to tell Kira that. It seemed to take an age before she had the tears under control. "I have no idea why I did that."

"Do you feel better?"

No, she felt like she had been crying. Her head throbbed, her throat ached, and her eyes burned. "Maybe a little. I really am tired. I think I'll go upstairs this time."

Kira frowned but agreed. "Call if you need anything."

Liska walked upstairs, aware Kira was watching her for any sign that she might fall or need help. At least she didn't say anything about Liska trying to get some space.

It was the first time since coming back from the hospital that she had gone upstairs. Last night she had crashed on the couch. To her annoyance, that flight of stairs was enough to leave her slightly dizzy. She would have to work on building her stamina back up.

Sleeping in fox form was tempting, both because she hadn't been able to for a long time, and because emotions were much simpler in that form. Foxes didn't feel multiple emotions at the same time. But while the solium was almost back to its normal levels, and she *could* change, it was still high enough that full changing was awkward and uncomfortable. Besides, her wrist was still acting up and changing with an injury was a bad idea.

It was too warm for blankets, but three or four sheets gave her the feeling of burrowing without overheating her. She pulled them over her head, leaving only a small opening for air. There was no reason to be depressed. She had friends who cared enough to stick around even after finding out she had lied to them, that she wasn't human. They cared enough to send gifts and to visit.

Todd hadn't spoken much. Hardly anything. Friends, they had said. But he was awkward with her, not knowing what to say. She was going to lose him. Completely. At least this time she knew why she was crying.

Chapter Thirty-Six

Anger adds strength to the muscles and subtracts wit from the brain. – The Kikitsutai Book of Wisdom

"I think I'm going to tell your friends that they shouldn't visit again. Not for a while, anyway," Kira said, as Sakaki reached the end of the staircase, turned around and went back the other way. For the third time.

"Why?" She didn't sound upset. Or relieved. Or anything, really.

"If they're upsetting you like this..."

"Like what?" Sakaki took a seat in the middle of the stairs. Like a puppet with its' strings cut. "I have to build my stamina back. You know that. I can't just be like... *this* forever."

"No. I understand that. But I think you're pushing it."

"The faster I recover, the faster I can stop Cazimir. Right now, even if we found him, I'd be a liability. I will *not* be a liability or left on the sidelines." There was a light in her eyes that Kira had prayed she would never see again. Then it faded, and her cousin was back. "I just... At very least, I don't want to give him the satisfaction of breaking me."

"Alright. I can understand that." Kira sighed. "Just, please be careful. None of these exercises while someone isn't here, just in case?"

"Fine."

It was only later that Kira realized that Sakaki never objected to no more visits.

***

"Look, I'm glad you're trying to get stronger, but I don't think you're up to running around the block yet." Kira handed a panting Sakaki a water bottle.

Sakaki took it, rubbing sweat from her forehead. After a few minutes, she had drunk enough water and gotten back enough breath to answer. "Four."

"Four what? Four *blocks*? You ran around four blocks? In the afternoon? Are you crazy?"

She shrugged, still winded. "Probably. But I've got to do this."

"You haven't even been out of the hospital a week! Would you please cut yourself some slack?"

"I can't! Don't you understand? I *can't* be weak like this. And I will be unless I push."

But do you have to push this hard? Kira didn't bother to say anything. She recognized a losing argument when she saw one. "Just don't push yourself into a relapse. And if you must go running, don't do it in the heat of the day. That's not good for you at any strength."

Sakaki might have been about to say something, but she was interrupted by the phone ringing. The vixens exchanged a look. *Sensei* had been called out of town for a weekend. Kira answered the phone. "Hello?"

"Liska. Have you made any progress in figuring out who betrayed my Blood?"

"Rex Magnus? How did you get this number?" *Sensei* hadn't had any contact with the Blood, though they surely knew he was in the area. Sakaki wouldn't have given it to him. She stood nearby, listening alert and attentive. Focused. It was almost good to see.

"Don't underestimate my sources. Or try to evade my question. Have you made any progress?"

'Tell him?' She mouthed to Sakaki with a shrug. Sakaki held her hand level and shook it back and forth, in a 'sort of' gesture. "Yes. I have."

"How much progress?"

"I have a name. But I can't give it to you yet. Accusing without overwhelming proof would get... messy."

"Then hurry up and get proof! I need answers." The connection closed with a click.

"Well, that was pleasant." Kira put the phone back.

"Something's up. I'm not sure what, but something is definitely up." Sakaki swallowed the last of her water. "I don't like this. At all."

"Yeah, me neither. Stay close to home, okay? Until we know where to find Cazimir. Rex Magnus might be watching this place."

Sakaki frowned but agreed.

"You keep telling me you have things well in hand, but you won't tell me what things you're doing. I don't like it. If I'm supposed to be running the Blood, I need to know what is going on with the Blood."

Cazimir forced himself not to react to the insolent whelp's demands. Perhaps putting Derrian nominally in charge of the Blood wasn't such a good idea. "Of course. But unfortunately, there are so many things going on that to stop and explain would take a very long time and possibly interfere with the projects themselves. Perhaps I can delegate a few people to summarize the various projects and plans and explain them?"

Derrian thought about it for a moment. "Acceptable. But I want it by the end of the week. Particularly your plan about stopping the Werefox. You are certain she's the one who killed Atolatar?"

"Absolutely certain. Don't worry. I have a plan in mind for her. You will have your revenge." Derrian had no notion of what he had already done to the fox, but he would probably approve. Or perhaps not. Derrian was young. Young and soft.

"Right. One week. You are dismissed."

Cazimir bowed and swept from the room. Derrian was going to be trouble. He either had to put him in his place or remove him entirely. Either way, it would have to be soon. Before or after he had incorporated the remnants of the Magnus Blood?

Eric saw him and stopped still. He had been apprehensive since Cazimir had captured the

Werefox, but since she escaped, the boy had been downright jumpy.

"Well? How did it go?" Cazimir demanded.

"You were right. Rex Magnus does know the number to her uncle's house."

"Which you now know, correct?" The Pup had better have gotten that number.

Eric nodded quickly. "Yes. I memorized it."

"Good. What did she say?"

"That she had a name but wouldn't give it without proof. Rex Magnus ordered her to get that proof."

So, she had made it to reinforcements. He suspected as much when her body didn't turn up. He hadn't been able to check the clinic records, they were too protected for that. But that put him in a bit of a situation. Having her under his thumb was better than having her dead, but having her dead was better than having her free and able to wreak havoc.

An idea came to him. An idea that had a high chance of eliminating or leaving both Rex Magnus and Derrian in his debt. If he was careful and/or lucky, he could probably either eliminate or recapture the Werefox as well. "Tell Rex Magnus that Derrian would like to meet with him. A leader's convene."

Eric frowned. "I thought you were avoiding things like that, because Derrian doesn't know how to hold his own in one of those."

"And he won't learn without practice. Rex Magnus owes us and he knows it. You can't get a more sympathetic audience than that. You *do* want him to become a good leader, don't you?"

"Of course, but—"

"Do it! Get him to agree and I'll tell you when and where. I have things to prepare." Pup might be getting a little too independent too. Well, if he survived the purge, he'd work on him.

***

"Have you seen Sakaki recently?"

Todd looked up from his textbook. He hadn't even heard Jamal come in. "No, Kira keeps saying she isn't ready yet. Why?"

Jamal shrugged. "Just wondering. I mean, you are dating her. Aren't you? The break-up was a ploy because she went missing, I thought."

"Actually, it's a little more complicated than that. I need to talk to her about it, but I don't think now is a good time. Really don't think now is a good time."

"Well, I can't blame you for that. Don't want to overwhelm her."

Todd nodded and turned back to his book. He really did want to talk to her, even as he was afraid of messing everything up for good. But it would be selfish to put his wants before her recovery.

If you don't talk to her now, you will never get the chance. The thought came out of nowhere, smacking him in the case like a snowball. He took a moment to try to decipher if it was a random fear or his precognition talking. After a moment, he still wasn't sure, but he decided he'd rather do something rash from fear than ignore a possible precognizant warning. "You know, I think I'm going to go visit her. At least briefly." Even if they didn't discuss *that*, it would be good to see her.

He was out the door before Jamal finished asking him if everything was okay.

***

"If you get Silly Putty all over my keys, I'm going to be upset."

Liska ignored the brush of anger and depression she felt at Kira calling the keys to Anna's dorm room hers. It wasn't like she would ever see the room again. "Technically, they're my keys. Besides, it comes off." She continued making key imprints in the putty.

"Are you bored? Because seriously, we can put on the TV or music. Or I can find you a book."

"I'm fine." She wasn't fine. She was frustrated, snappish, and chomping at the bit to *do* something, anything. But there wasn't much she could do as a semi-invalid who had to stay in the house. So, she was annoying her cousin by playing with her keys.

There was a knock on the door. Both Werefoxes snapped alert. Kira palmed a throwing knife as she went to open it. Liska stayed out of sight, fingering the handle of her dagger until she recognized Todd's voice.

Her first reaction was a leap of hope and warmth. That quickly gave way to trepidation and even anger. Perhaps this wasn't a good time to see Todd. Not while her emotions changed at the drop of a pin.

But Kira let him in, so she would do her best not to be rude. "Hello, Todd." She gave him a neutral smile. The same one she gave half the skulk, the ones who were neither friends nor enemies. Kira frowned, obviously recognizing the smile.

"Hey. Um, how are you feeling?" Todd seemed to be asking his shoes.

"I'm getting better. Slowly. Too slowly." She slashed the key across the putty with a little more force than was necessary.

"Good. I mean, that you're getting better. Not that... Oh, blast it!" The vixens stared at him. He turned to Kira. "Would it be possible, I don't want to be rude–"

"I have some things to do on campus. You two play nice. And Todd, even with a sprained wrist, she can still kill you at least six different ways, so if she tells you to leave, do so." Kira smiled a chipper smile. "I may like you, but I like her more. I *would* help her hide your body so no one ever found it."

"Deal."

Before Liska could object, Kira was gone. Oh well, she'd be back soon for her keys. Of course, for now, she was stuck with Todd. "Kira likes you?"

Todd shrugged. "We worked together a lot while you were gone. With your uncle too." He took a deep breath and sat down opposite her. "How are you feeling, really?"

"Not up to deep emotional discussions." She wasn't. At all. She would cry or scream or throw things at him; and she'd rather not do any of those, or get the police called to *Sensei's* house.

"Ah, right. Okay. Will you tell me when you are?" She glared at him. "I don't mean tonight. I mean, whenever. Three in the morning if you want. Though preferably not the night before an exam."

Before she could come up with some kind of polite non-committal response, or even a reasonable brush off, the phone rang. *Sensei* was still away, so Liska answered it. "Hello?"

"Hello, Sakaki."

Liska growled. "Cazimir. You... *fangless leach.* What do you want?"

Todd looked alarmed. Had he been told about Cazimir? It didn't matter.

"I challenge you. Vampire to Were. A fight to the death. Bring any weapons you like. Bring all of them, if you want."

Trap. Definite trap. And right now, she was mad enough not to care. "When and where?"

He named an address. "I'm already there. It should take you about twenty minutes, if you don't get lost."

Never let your opponent set the terms of your conflict. "I'm on my way." She slammed down the phone.

"Please tell me you aren't doing what I think you're doing?" Todd asked, horrified.

"I'm taking my kidnapper up on a challenge."

"Look, even *I* know it's a trap. Please don't do this."

"He knows who I am, he knows where I am. If I don't go to him, he will come here."

"Home field advantage."

"Less useful when your opponent blows up your house or sets it on fire." Liska wrapped a brace around her wrist while slipping on her shoes. "I think I can pull a few surprises out of my sleeve."

"Call Kira. Ask her to back you up."

"No. This is *my* fight. So, stay out of it." She started arming herself.

Todd groaned in frustration. "At least let me drive. You'll hurt your wrist if you drive."

He had a point, and even through her haze of anger, she could recognize it. "Fine. But only driving. No going inside."

"Great. Let me leave a note."

Liska nodded. If they didn't return by the time Kira came back, then chances were either she would need backup or she would be dead.

***

"Hey, I'm back. I forgot you still had my keys." Kira walked in the house, and promptly noticed it was too quiet. It felt like no one was there. She did a cursory search of the downstairs anyway. Nothing. This was not good.

She came back to the living room. No sign of an unusual mess. Sakaki's shoes and her sometimes brace were gone. And there was a piece of paper from Sakaki's new notepad in the middle of the table with her name in large letters and underlined.

It wasn't Sakaki's handwriting, but it might well be Todd's. Kira snatched it up.

___Kira___,

Sakaki got a call from someone named Cazimir, who challenged her to meet him at the address at the bottom. I couldn't stop her from going, so I drove. We left at 7:17.

Todd

It was seven-thirty. Kira was running before the note hit the table.

Chapter Thirty-Seven

Revenge is a bitter meal. – The Kikitsutai Book of Wisdom

Todd parked the car in the dingy, littered parking lot in a warehouse complex. "Why is it always abandoned warehouses?"

"It isn't. Not by a longshot. But warehouses do have their advantages. Wide open spaces, and secret places to hide. Besides, warehouses are often not near residential areas." Sakaki, Liska now, checked herself over. Probably to make sure she had everything. "At least the bad guys stuck to warm climates this time."

Todd winced. He had forgotten complaining about that.

She climbed out of the car, and Todd exited too. "You should leave," she said.

"Not happening. I'm not leaving you alone." When she started to argue, he continued. "I promised not to go inside. And I won't. But if you aren't out in ten minutes, I'm calling Kira."

"Fifteen."

"Ten. I'm not backing down."

Liska glared at him. "Fine. But you promise me you won't go in, or I swear I will lock you in the trunk."

Todd decided not to mention that Ryoko-*Sensei* had made both him and Kira practice using the internal trunk release to escape the trunk until they could do it blindfolded in under a minute. Then he made them practice with Todd's car. "I promise not to go in." He took a deep breath. "Just... Promise me you'll come *out*."

For a moment, the hard mask of Liska faded. "I'll do my best. Be careful. Maybe stay in the car with the doors locked." She glared at the warehouse. "I have work to do."

Todd watched as she disappeared through the doorway, calling himself every manner of fool. Then he looked at his watch. Seven-thirty-five. She had ten minutes.

***

"Are you sure I can do this, Eric?" Derrian asked. "What if Rex Magnus laughs at me?"

"He won't laugh at you. You'll do fine. Just remember what we told you." Eric looked around the room. Why on earth had Cazimir insisted on the convene being held in a warehouse? "Don't be nervous. Don't be arrogant, but don't be a pushover either."

Derrian nodded. "He really wants to meet me?"

Is that what Cazimir told him? What was he up to? *Trust the Father. He knows best.* That was wearing awfully thin. Eric just gave Derrian an encouraging smile. "I'll go see if he's coming."

He had barely gone ten yards when he heard something. Someone... breathing? Did Rex Magnus bring a wraith guard? Eric went to check it out.

***

The first floor of the warehouse was a huge but empty room. No one was there. Liska walked the perimeter anyway. No people, no obvious traps. The second floor was a maze of smaller rooms. This was going to be a nightmare.

She heard and smelled the vampire at the same time. Not Cazimir, but...

Eric turned the corner...

***

And promptly met Nightmare's fist. Sprawled on the ground, Eric cradled his broken nose and stared up at her in horror. "Give me one good reason why I shouldn't kill you right here, right now."

Eric gaped like a landed fish.

"Nothing?" She pulled a sword.

"I told them where you'd be!" Eric cringed. "I did what I could to help you."

Nightmare glared at him, malice glittering in her eye. "What's Cazimir doing? What's his plan?"

"I don't know, I swear! He just told me to get Rex Magnus and Derrian here for a leaders convene."

"Who's Derrian?"

"The kid he's using to pretend to be head of the Blood."

"A puppet."

"It's not Derrian's fault. He's just a kid."

Nightmare snarled, pieces falling into place. "Is Rex Magnus here yet?"

"I don't think so."

"Stop him from coming in! I don't care how you do it. Cazimir's going to kill us all at once!"

Eric didn't argue. "Derrian! He's–"

"I'll get him. But, Eric? If I see you again after tonight, I will castrate you before breaking every bone in your body. Do you understand?"

Eric nodded quickly.

"Go! Get out of my sight!"

Eric ran the way she had come, and Nightmare followed Eric's former path.

***

Two minutes to go. Todd alternated between glaring at his watch and staring at the door Liska had disappeared through. He had almost convinced himself to call Kira early when a car screeched into the parking lot, stopping a few yards from him. The smell of burnt rubber and hot metal assaulted his nose.

The driver's door was open before the car stopped, and Kira was out so quickly that Todd wasn't sure she even put the car in park. "Is she in there?"

"Yeah, eight minutes ago."

Kira nodded, already sprinting for the warehouse. "Stay here! Do *not* go inside."

Todd didn't bother replying, she wouldn't have heard him anyway. Instead, he sighed, leaned back on the car, and wished he knew what was going on.

***

Following Eric's scent trail, Nightmare grew alarmed when another scent started to overpower it. Semtex. Yup, she was right. And she was an idiot. And she had to get this 'kid' out before the building went up.

The first bomb went off seconds later, knocking her off her feet. She wasn't hurt, but the building was now on fire. And if Cazimir was half as smart as she thought, he probably had more.

Nightmare forced herself to her feet and ran. Eric had come from a room around this corner. Which one, ah-ha!

She yanked the door open, spotted Derrian, and froze.

***

Cazimir frowned at the thermal readings. The Werefox was still moving, he must have set off the wrong bomb. No matter, he would just set off the rest. Pity he hadn't gotten Rex Magnus; but the posturing, arrogant vampire hadn't shown up yet. If he came alone, Cazimir could kill him and claim he had been caught in the explosions. If not, well, Cazimir would use the cover story on him.

The crazy Werefox, determined to wipe out the vampire clans, had somehow found out about the convene and blown up the building. But she had gotten caught in her own blast. If he played his cards right, Cazimir might actually be able to use this to take down the Kikitsutai. While vampires and Weres were close to even matched, Werefoxes were only a small portion of the Weres, and the Kikitsutai were only one clan of Werefoxes. The largest and best organized, but not the whole of them. It would take careful planning, but it might be possible.

He was about to set off the next bomb when the door slammed open, startling him into dropping the detonator. A black-haired twin of the Were he had kidnapped two months ago stood in the doorway.

"No one hurts my cousin and gets away with it. *No one.*"

***

Eric had called Derrian a 'kid'. Knowing that vampires aged slowly, Nightmare had been prepared for the 'kid' to be older than her. She had not been prepared for a wraith who looked about eleven. In a wheelchair. One she had put him in, three years earlier. "You!"

He recognized her too. "You! You're the one who did this to me! You killed my brother! Eric! Help!"

Smoke was filling the air. There wasn't time for this. "Hate me later. The building's about to blow up."

"Why are you trying to kill us?" He grabbed at the wheelchair handles, fighting as she tried to pull him out.

"I'm not. Cazimir is!" She yanked him free, slung him over her shoulder and started running. She would have to trust that Eric stopped Rex from coming in. Cazimir would have to wait.

Derrian kept struggling, hitting her and squirming. He didn't kick, though. Paralysis? Could be. She didn't have time to feel guilty now.

The fire cut her off from the stairs, and there had been only one staircase. She could barely see through the smoke. After another minute or two of trying to find a way out and her passenger fighting and screaming the whole way, she stopped and put him down.

"What? You can't leave me to die!"

Nightmare rolled her eyes but didn't respond as she tied a handkerchief around her nose and mouth. Then she scooped the kid up again. At least he wasn't fighting her anymore.

Finally, she found an outside wall. "Hang on, kid. This is going to get bumpy." She put him down long enough to grab an office chair and throw it through the window. Then she picked him up, grabbed the side of the building with one hand, climbed up to the windowsill, and kicked off the building.

***

Why had he agreed to wait outside? What could have possibly possessed him to promise that he would stay put? What was going on in there?

Todd nearly had a heart attack when he realized that the loud sound he had heard was an explosion of some sort, and the building was now *on fire*! Where was she?

He was about to try to go in, promise or no promise, when he jumped a foot when something came flying out a second floor window. Was that a chair? A moment later, there was a person. He was already running before he realized it was Sakaki.

***

There are several good ways to minimize injury while falling, even from the second floor of a building. There are significantly fewer ways to fall well when carrying someone.

She managed to roll with the fall, taking most of the impact herself, before coming to a dazed stop about three yards from the building. It was a rough landing, and it took her a moment to breathe. Vaguely she was aware of Todd running towards her. Bad idea. The building might explode. Nightmare turned to yell to him to leave, but before the first syllable left her mouth, there was a sharp, stabbing pain, and all the air left her lungs at once.

Looking down, she saw the dagger. It had just barely missed her heart. Still deadly though. Todd pulled Derrian away from her, but he was staring at her in horror. Nightmare smiled at him. The edges of her vision were going dark, but she could still see him. She had to explain, then he would understand.

"Sakaki!" He was pressing around the knife with his jacket. "Hang on!"

"It's okay. Tisiphone's last victim."

She couldn't see him anymore, but she could smell him. She wouldn't die alone.

***

"No, you really don't want to go in there." Eric stood in the doorway, blocking Rex from entering.

"I have been asked to a leader's convene. If you do not let me pass, I will consider it a declaration of war." The building shook. "Never mind. What is going on?"

How could he even explain? "Cazimir–" Eric doubled over suddenly, pain running through him. Was he dying? No. "He's dead. Cazimir's dead," he said in a daze.

Rex inclined his head gravely. "You have my sympathies."

"He's dead. I can tell you."

He scowled. "Tell me what?"

"That it was him! He told the Purifiers about you. He kidnapped Liska and tortured her and was going to brainwash her into working for him, and he's behind these recent 'Nightmare' appearances, and he was going to kill you and Derrian, and Liska tonight." It was dizzying.

Rex stared at him a moment, trying to decipher the words before speaking. "That is a very serious accusation. Do you have any proof?"

"Yes, actually I do." He finally knew what to do with his data stick.

***

Todd was trying to stop the blood flow without actually touching the knife, but Sakaki was fading fast. Kira came running up, took one look at them, and took off. "I'll get help! Keep her alive until I get back!"

Right, like he wasn't trying to do that right now. In the background, he heard the boy he had dragged away crying, but Todd couldn't bring himself to feel sorry for him. He hadn't hurt the kid, though part of him had wanted to. But the kid wasn't even trying to move now.

"It's supposed to be better now. She paralyzed me. She killed my brother. But it isn't better. It's worse."

So that's what she had meant. "Welcome to the wonderful world of revenge, kid. It doesn't fix anything. Ever."

"Derrian!" Eric seemed to appear out of nowhere. "Are you alright? She got you out." Then he spotted Sakaki. "What? What happened to her?"

"Ask your friend." Todd nodded, bitter towards the boy.

Eric closed his eyes and sighed. "Cazimir. This is his fault. And mine. Thank you for not hurting Derrian." He looked at Sakaki. "Is she dead?"

"No." Not yet. Not ever if he could help it.

"I'm not a healer. There are only two things I can do for her." He knelt by Sakaki and put a hand on her forehead. Todd couldn't tell what the vampire was doing, but it seemed to be strenuous. He looked a couple years older when he finished. "Nightmare formed when I isolated parts of her psyche from the rest. I've reintegrated it into the rest of her personality. It won't have the power to take over again, but she will have to deal with the memories. There aren't any other hidden parts. I checked."

Slowly, as if in pain, Eric stood and picked up Derrian. "I'm taking him to the vampire homeland. I doubt either of us will leave in your lifetimes."

"But... shouldn't she have the choice?"

Eric shook her head. "She already chose you."

"I saw her kissing you."

"No, you saw me kissing her, when I knew you were watching. When she pushed me away, it was your name on her lips." Eric met his eyes. "She won't care but tell her I said goodbye. Rex knows the truth now. Most of it. I told him that Cazimir was behind Nightmare." He was gone before Todd could say anything more.

Sakaki was barely breathing and his jacket was soaked with blood. With his free hand, Todd pulled out his cell, and pressed speed dial three.

Jamal answered on the second ring. "Long visit. How's she doing?"

"What do I do about a knife stabbed in the chest? Might be heart."

"What? Please tell me this is hypothetical!"

"I really wish." Todd stuck the phone between his shoulder and ear so he could use both hands. She was still breathing, wasn't she? Yes.

"You call an ambulance!"

"And if I can't?"

Jamal let out a strangled sound of frustrated hysteria. "Is the knife still impaled in the victim?"

"Yeah, I knew better than to pull it out."

"That's something. Lot of blood?"

"My jacket's soaked, but she's still breathing."

"What hap– never mind. Doesn't matter. Look, she needs a hospital! Now!"

"Yeah, well, I don't know–" Sirens. Coming towards them. An ambulance swerved into the parking lot. "Oh, Kira's got an ambulance. I'm putting you on speaker."

Kira drove past them so they were at the back of the ambulance, before stopping and running around.

"How did you get an ambulance?" Todd asked, as Kira opened the back and started to drag down a gurney.

"I asked nicely."

"Asked nicely?" Jamal practically shrieked on the phone.

"Asked nicely. Threatened at sword point. Same difference. I'll hold down the jacket, you get her on the gurney."

They had her moved and even set up a blood transfusion in under two minutes. Apparently Sakaki was AB+ blood type. Universal recipient. That was a stroke of luck. The only one they currently had. Sakaki's breathing was slowing, but there was an oxygen mask inside. "I'll drive. You... do whatever you can," Kira charged him, before slamming the door shut.

Todd exchanged his now ruined jacket for bandages, keeping the knife in place. "Come on, Sakaki. You've got to hang on." He brushed hair from her face. "You can't die. I love you."

Chapter Thirty-Eight

When all crumbles around you, take a breath, and begin again. – The Kikitsutai Book of Wisdom

Sakaki stared at the tiles over her head for a good two minutes before realizing she was awake. Alive too, which was a surprise. In a hospital, which probably accounted for the 'alive' part.

Being a hospital, her nose was mostly numb from all the medicine smells around. It was disorienting, but not an insurmountable obstacle. She just had to use her other senses a little more.

For example, she was in pain but clearly being medicated. Since her last memories included a deadly knife wound, neither fact surprised her. The incision was no longer bandaged and appeared to be about a week or so old, judging by her usual healing speed. If it healed normally, the scar would be near invisible unless one knew to look. There was an IV on her arm, and a healing scab where there had been another. Her wrist seemed to have finally healed and only gave an occasional small twinge when she moved it around.

Nobody was in the room with her, but there was a book on the table by the chair. So she had at least one frequent visitor. Who could read French. Three flower arrangements were on the table, in varying stages of freshness.

Someone was walking in the door. Sakaki looked at the door, amused to see Kira jump when she saw her eyes open. "You're awake? Seriously, in a coma for eight days, unconscious for another two, and you wake up in the five minutes you're left alone?" She hurried over to the bed and poured some ice chips into a cup.

"It's been ten days then?"

Even through her dulled nose, she could smell Kira's relief. "Yes, pretty much. What's the last thing you remember?"

Sakaki sucked on a couple ice chips while considering it. "Letting Cazimir goad me into walking into a trap, telling Eric to stop Rex Magnus from coming in, did that work?"

"Yes. I've talked to Rex since. You finish first."

"Not much more. Rescued the kid and got stabbed. What happened to the kid?"

"Todd said Eric took him. Said they were going to the vampire homeland. Possibly for a century or more."

Sakaki nodded. "Good. Maybe they can heal him there."

"Maybe. Who stabbed you? The kid?"

Todd hadn't told her. "Wasn't his fault. I didn't get Cazimir."

Kira smirked. "I did. Sorry, I know you wanted him, but..."

But she understood. She would have gleefully ripped apart anyone who hurt Kira too.

"So, you remember everything?"

"Oh, yes. Everything. Nightmare, too."

Kira winced. "I didn't want to keep that a secret from you. I just–"

"I know. You didn't lie to me. I never asked enough that you had to." She didn't want to talk about it. Not right now. Maybe not ever. "How much longer is the semester?"

"A little under two weeks. The doctors think you'll probably be up for going back to Japan by then."

"Well, that's good."

"Very good. Apparently, *Sensei* managed to book you an appointment for cosmetic surgery for your scar."

Excellent. She wanted it gone, yesterday. "When?"

"Two days before my semester ends, actually. That's two for two, my taking your exams, you know."

Sakaki gave her a tired smile. "I'm sorry about that. Especially since I don't think I'll need them now."

Kira leaned forward, frowning. "You're giving up school?"

"Look at the facts. In the past school year, I've missed more days than I took; we had to bring three people into the secret; and I've," she waved her hands weakly, "broken. More than once."

"I admit it's been a bad year, but I don't think it had anything to do with the school. How about this? Don't say anything to anyone else yet. I'll finish the semester. If you decide you're done, you'll have plenty of time to drop out during the summer. If you decide after a month or so that you want to continue, you'll have that as an option."

There was sense in Kira's suggestion; even if Sakaki didn't think she'd ever want to go back. "Okay, we'll table it. So, what did I miss?"

Kira offered a few more ice chips, then sat back. "Okay, Rex Magnus knows Cazimir betrayed him, and kidnapped and tortured you. He knows that Cazimir 'faked' the Nightmare appearances, I don't know if he knows you were involved. Eric gave him some of the footage of your kidnapping. Between that, Eric's word, and mine, he's decided to believe it and not dig any deeper. So you both can save face, the official story is that you discovered and eradicated a dark 'cancer' on the vampire race. He won't tell about your kidnapping, we don't tell about him being played."

"Fair enough. The skulk?"

"You got into trouble with an unspecified villain. You were hurt, but have managed to avenge yourself, and somehow help the vampires at the same time. Details are scarce. Your parents, my parents, Tora and Ryo, all know most of the details. *Sensei* knows everything except that you were Nightmare. He's been visiting too. Todd knows, I think, pretty much everything. He visits when he can. Probably be here this afternoon. Jamal and Shahara know that there was some sort of encounter with your kidnapper. He's dead, and you nearly died. Because they're humans, they can't visit so easily." Twilight/Night clinics were reluctant to let Espers in, let alone ordinary Day humans.

"And the most important question..."

"They'll let you leave the hospital when you meet their criteria. Probably three to seven days. The nurse can give you the list. You are very lucky, you know. Your heart kept beating until we reached the hospital and they could safely remove the knife. Then they had to give you two blood transfusions. Almost three." Kira shook her head. "Technically, you died. Twice, I think. And look at you. Not even brain damage. Well, more than you had before, anyway."

Sakaki rolled her eyes. "Yes, I know. I shouldn't have let Cazimir goad me into a challenge. Especially one where he set all the terms."

"True. But if you hadn't, he would have killed Rex Magnus, Eric, and that kid, and gotten away with it. Was Eric working for him?"

She shrugged. "Cazimir turned him. Plus, I don't think Eric knew exactly what he was doing until too late. He said he told you where to find me?"

"So *he* left that note. That explains a few things."

Her eyelids were getting heavier. "I think this drug is wearing me out."

"Get some rest. You need it."

***

Despite the pressure of final projects and exams coming up, Kira and Todd visited daily, and even Shahara and Jamal were able to sneak a quick visit, with Kira and *Sensei* vouching for them. It took four days for her to get out. Kira let her know that she gently squashed plans of a welcome home party when Liska was released. Since Liska fell asleep in the car on the way home and barely woke enough to move to the couch to sleep more, she had to agree Kira was right.

Instead, they had a quiet year's end party before Sakaki had to go to Japan for her surgery. She was able to stay awake for the whole thing which was an improvement.

"You will be coming back next year, right?" Shahara asked. Liska noticed Kira, on the other side of the room talking to Todd, perk up.

Probably not. "I haven't decided. Honestly, I'm trying not to think about it. So far, school has been... unsuccessful."

Shahara frowned. "I hope you do."

"Well, even if I don't come back, we can still stay in touch. I travel a lot, so I may be back in the area even if it's not for school. Just give me your email address."

Shahara quickly wrote both hers and Jamal's. "You have Todd's, right."

"I do."

"So, what happened between you and Todd?"

She didn't want to talk about that. In fact, she had actually faked sleep on at least two occasions to avoid talking to him. "Well..." She trailed off as she heard Todd coming up behind her.

"Hey, can I steal Sakaki away for a moment?"

Shahara flounced away with an air of satisfaction. Liska turned to Todd. Yes, it was going to be *that* conversation. There was absolutely no privacy in the house. "Back yard?"

"Sure, that's fine."

Liska didn't want to talk to him, certainly not about this. But it wasn't fair to Todd to go back to Japan without clearing the air. Not that this was going to be easy. She didn't have the energy for this. She took a seat in one of the deck chairs, while a flustered Todd took the one across from her.

She was not going to be the one to break the silence. Todd opened his mouth and closed it at least three times. "I'm sorry. I've tried a million times to figure out what to say to you. Everything sounds stupid." Liska didn't say anything. "Right. I wanted to apologize."

"For what?"

"Back before you... disappeared. When I told you I thought we were better as friends. I'm sorry. I didn't even mean that. But I saw you and Eric..."

That explained a few things. "He kissed me."

"You didn't stop him. I thought you made your choice and it wasn't me. So I was trying to back out gracefully. But I lied. If I had just told you what I saw and left it to you... I..."

"You were being a gentleman. Maybe things would have been solved faster if we had just shouted at each other, maybe not."

"Right, the point is," he took a deep breath. "I don't want to only be friends. I want more than that. I love you."

Someone less paranoid than Liska probably would have said, "I love you too." The two would have fallen into each other's arms and maybe kissed. Like a movie or something.

Life wasn't a movie. "What did Kira say?"

"What do you mean?"

"You were talking to Kira before. Did she put you up to this?"

"What? No, of course not!"

"You told me before that you couldn't handle my life. Do you really think you can now? That you can accept waiting to find out whether or not I actually got out alive of some situation or other?" His face was neutral, but the smell of horror and guilt gave him away. "Did Kira tell you why I called her down?" More guilt. She saw it now. Kira told him that she loved him. Todd, in his guilt and chivalry, was determined to make good his old promise to be there for her forever, even though he no longer wanted to.

"Sakaki–"

"No. I understand, I don't blame you. But I won't have your pity. We'll keep in touch." Sakaki stood up and slipped inside while Todd tried to come up with words. *Sensei* saw her come in, and she gave him a quick sign that she was tired and going up to rest. He'd keep the rest away.

Upstairs, she pulled out the drawing that she had been working on when no one was watching. She was leaving for Japan tomorrow and wanted it finished first.

***

As soon as Todd finished his last exam, he headed for Ryoko's house. Even with the tension between him and Sakaki, Kira and Ryoko hadn't rejected him. In fact, they seemed to want to help him fix things. Good, he seemed to need all the help he could get.

"Hi, Mr. Ryoko. Oh, hi, Kira. Did you finish your exams?"

Kira stretched like a cat. "All finished, all moved out of the dorm. You?"

"Almost all moved out. Have you heard from Sakaki? How did her surgery go?"

Ryoko smiled. "She's home now. They think that when she's healed, the scar will be near invisible.

"Good. I'm glad. She must be happy about that." He eyed the boxes in the living room. "So, is her stuff going to stay here until next semester?"

Both Kira and Ryoko grew grave. Kira was the one to answer. "Actually, she said to bring it back with us when we go. She doesn't think she'll need it here again."

Todd sank into a chair, bile rising in his throat. "She's not coming back? At all?"

"She asked me to give you this after exams." Kira handed him a manila envelope.

He opened the envelope and pulled out a thick piece of paper. On the paper were detailed charcoal drawings of two flowers. Flowers she had included a sample of in the envelope. Having the flowers to compare to, he could tell she had done a very painstaking job. As Shahara would say, it was a masterpiece. And possibly a message. "I recognize sweet pea, it's my mom's favorite flower. But what's this one?" He held up the cluster of small yellow flowers.

Kira gave a quick sniff, nose wrinkling. "Smells like rue."

"Sakaki knows the language of flowers, right?"

"She does, but I don't."

"Fortunately," Ryoko interjected, "I have the book she learned from."

Sweet pea turned out to mean 'gratitude'. Rue, on the other hand, was 'regret, sorrow, and repentance'.

"I need to talk to her. I tried before she left, but she didn't believe I was sincere. I *need* to talk to her." Todd ran his hand through his hair, trying to think.

"How will you do that?" Kira asked, face blank.

His thoughts raced a few minutes. "Shahara. She has an emergency credit card that she's never used. If I tell her why I need it, promise I'll pay her back every penny, even the interest, she might just let me borrow it."

"How will you explain to your family that you're disappearing into Japan?" Ryoko asked.

"I don't know. Um, another art contest?"

"Are you absolutely *certain* that you're serious about her? Forever?" Kira asked.

"With all my heart." Todd forced himself not to flinch back from their interrogative stances and looks.

Then they relaxed, and Kira smiled. He had passed some kind of test. "Then I think we've got a plan."

Chapter Thirty-Nine

Distance is no obstacle for the determined soul. – The Kikitsutai Book of Wisdom

Sakaki tossed the book away, bored. She was back home. For good. Ish. Luna Liska would continue to travel and take jobs, of course. Hopefully Nightmare would never be needed. But right now, she felt at loose ends. Father had made it quite clear that she wasn't taking any jobs until she was fully and completely healed. Mentally as well as physically. She wasn't planning on going back to school, which she could admit was a bit of a disappointment. So, now what?

Moping in her room solved nothing. Maybe doing something would help. Who was home? Father was in his study. The soundproofed, even against Were hearing, study, with the door closed and locked. Maybe she'd find out what he was doing later. Maybe she wouldn't. Mother had gone out visiting before Liska went upstairs. She sniffed around, but it smelled like she was still out.

Kira would probably come back in a day or two. The semester still had a few days to it, but she thought that exams were done. Or would be done today, or something like that.

Maybe she should do some visiting herself. Tora was flying to the states to bring Kira and *Sensei* back, but Ryo was between jobs, she thought. Maybe he'd be in the mood for a visit. Or she could find someone else. Or maybe just take some time to herself.

Liska heard the lock disengage from the study upstairs. Ah, Father was done with his business. She decided to stick around a little longer, just in case he needed or wanted her for something.

There was a knock at the door. "Sakaki, would you answer that?"

He didn't sound surprised, he must have been expecting a visitor. Sakaki opened the door. And stared in shock.

Todd stood there, wearing the traditional kimono of one who came to beg a favor.

"What are you doing here?"

He ignored her rude, sputtered greeting, and bowed. "I seek an audience with the chief."

Behind her, Sakaki heard and felt her father approach. When she turned, she couldn't even be surprised to see that he was also wearing his most official clothes. "I grant you an audience with Sejou the Dragonclaw." He turned to Sakaki who was still standing there in shock. "Sakaki, some tea for our guest?"

"Yes, of course." Her shaky legs led her into the kitchen, while she shamelessly spied on the men. Father took his seat, while Todd knelt in front of him. She couldn't watch anymore, since she needed to set a tray, but she listened attentively.

"Great Chief, please grant me permission to ask my request."

"You may ask. What is your wish?"

Where had Todd learned this? She had never taught him. She hadn't even seen a ceremony like this since she was a small child.

"I must beg your permission to ask your daughter for her hand in marriage."

CRASH! Neither man even looked in her direction. She called out a distracted, "Sorry!", and swept up the broken cups in a daze.

"Do you know what it is you ask?" Father asked.

"I do." Todd's voice was clear and steady.

"She is a jewel without price. What makes you believe yourself worthy?"

"No worthiness on my part, Great Chief. I can only plead love. I love her." For the first time since he walked in, he looked at her, as she came in carrying the tray of tea and refreshments. "And I believe she may love me."

Sakaki set the tray down between them, and knelt to the side, eyes down. She would think she was dreaming, but not even in her dreams would she think up something like this.

"I see. Sakaki?" She looked up into Father's unreadable gaze. "Do you love this man?"

"I..." She swallowed as her throat closed up. "Father?"

His face was blank, but her nose always told her more than her eyes did. Regret, compassion, hope. "All I ask is that you answer honestly."

"Yes, Father. I love him."

He nodded gravely, then turned to Todd. "You have my permission to ask her. But to win her heart, that you must accomplish."

"Father?" This wasn't possible. How?

He looked at her, with a sad smile on his face. "It is not the path I would have chosen for you, but as has been pointed out to me, repeatedly, only you can choose the path you would take. If this is what you want, then I give you my permission. And my blessing. But be sure this *is* what you want." Then he stood and left the room.

Sakaki didn't bother moving from her kneeling position. "How?"

"Kira and Ryoko. I convinced them, so they let me come on the plane. They grilled me on my intentions and explained the ceremony. Then arranged for me to talk to your father on the phone. For an hour. I'm not sure if he would have given me the time of day if Ryoko hadn't vouched for me. I know he questioned both of them in Japanese." Todd shook his head. "I have something for you." He stood, walked to the front door, and reached outside for something. Sakaki stood while he was coming back. A bouquet of primroses. "I don't have a ring, but Kira told me that Weres don't typically use permanent jewelry. This will have to do. I never got the chance to give you the first bundle, so I was shocked that Kira found it in your room. I know you know the language of flowers. I've been trying to find the right meanings." Eternal love.

"Todd—"

"Let me finish, please? I finally figured out what to say." She nodded and waited. Todd took a deep breath, then placed a hand on hers. "Sakaki, you have changed my life more than anyone else ever has or ever could. You not only opened up a whole new world to me, you took me deeper and deeper into it. So much so that I don't even recognize who I was before. In the past year, my deepest joys have been felt at your side, and my deepest fears were the fears of losing you. I want you part of my life forever. And I want to be part of your life, forever. You can't say I don't know you. Your family filled me in on anything that might drive me away. I can't say you don't know me, because I'm sure you know me as well as my parents do, if not better. I love you. I thought I did in Moscow. I was sure in West Palm. And I would stake my life on it now. *I love you.* Please, Sakaki, marry me."

She had to wipe away the beginnings of tears before she spoke. "I can't change who I am. I am an active ninja. You can't just stand to the side and wait to see if I survive."

Todd nodded. "You're right. I can't. That's why the one thing I ask, is not that you give up being what you are, but that you don't leave me behind again." He held up a hand when she started to object. "I know, I would be a liability at the moment. But teach me. Train me enough that I can help you. If you are going to take risks like that, and I know you have to, then I'll take them too."

Sakaki took a sip of tea to give herself a moment to think. It wouldn't be as simple as that, but Todd was sincere in what he said. "Are you absolutely certain of this?"

"I am. I don't know what I'll tell my family, but I am absolutely positive. I want to spend the rest of my life with you."

He did know her. He knew about Nightmare, he knew about Tisiphone. He still wasn't scared off. Not even by having to keep a secret from almost everyone he knew. Sakaki took a deep breath. "Yes. Yes, I'll marry you." Todd let out an exhilarated, shaky laugh, that she couldn't help but join in. "When?"

He smiled, and took her teacup, putting it to the side. "What, give you a chance to change your mind? Now." Before she could parse his meaning, he opened the front door and shouted, "She said 'yes'!"

There was an answering cheer. A very loud, multi-voiced cheer. "What? Who knew you were going to ask?"

"By now? Probably everyone." He didn't get the chance to say anything else, as they were separated by a large group of people.

Kira and Mother led a small group of women and older girls as Sakaki was swept back upstairs. "Come on, you can't get married in that." Kira pushed her into her bathroom. "Take a shower, a quick one. Then dry your hair as best you can. Don't put anything else in it. Then come out. We'll have your clothes ready."

The door was shut before she got a chance to argue that her hair took forever and a day to dry. Except, it wouldn't because thanks to Cazimir, her hair wasn't yet shoulder-length. Getting close though. At least she had gotten a professional haircut so it looked like it was supposed to be that length, rather than looking like she had gotten into a fight with a rogue barber.

Sakaki took the quickest shower she could, all while trying to convince herself this was really happening. It seemed so much like a dream. But her dreams were never this... happy. Or strange. Even when she thought about the idea of marrying Todd, she was sure it would be against the wishes of the skulk. Who would have guessed they would be so favorable? Who would have guessed that Father would approve?

To her relief, only Mother, Kira, and Kira's mother, Aunt Yukina, were in the room when she walked in. "The others will help you get ready once you're dressed," Mother said. Then she opened the large box on Sakaki's bed. "This was mine, when I married your father before the skulk. I think it only appropriate that you wear it today. If you wish."

Kira gave her a wink behind Mother's back. She knew that Sakaki had mentioned a wish to wear Mother's wedding kimono at her own wedding. But she hadn't actually thought she would. Mother's kimono had cost a small fortune to make, even in a place where a woman's kimono could easily cost more than a new car. Mother's kimono was more expensive than her college tuition for the year.

Completely hand-sewn, a silk, twelve-piece garment. Mother said it was white with white embroidery. The embroidery was of cherry blossoms, with hints of a fox, and even a moon.

"Are you sure?"

"I'm very sure. No one has worn it since my marriage. It should be used again."

She had only worn a formal kimono twice, so Sakaki gratefully accepted the help to put on the elaborate garment. Before they put on the outer layer and the *obi*, Kira let in the other women who were supposed to help her get ready.

Before she knew it, she had Mother putting makeup on her, Aunt Tomo weaving flowers into her hair, Kira massaging a lotion into her feet, and cousin Kaede rubbing the same lotion into her hands. There were at least half a dozen others present, and everyone was offering her all kinds of advice.

"Let him think he wins most of the arguments. Male egos are fragile."

"Never go to bed angry at him or let him go to bed angry at you."

"Be honest with him, but not too honest. Maintain an air of mystery."

"Never stop flirting with him. You have to be his wife, and his lover." Mother blushed slightly at this advice but didn't argue.

"Don't expect everything to be easy now. You'll have to work at it. What it is, is irreversible."

"Make sure you tell him you love him."

"Make sure you tell him you respect him."

"Remember to be friends, always."

Mother stopped the flurry of chatter. "Sakaki, you know most of this already. Yes, you are inexperienced, but you will learn. Don't expect perfection, on either of your parts. Just love him and accept his love in return. Everything else you can work out."

"Yes, Mother."

Mother flushed but swallowed her embarrassment. "You do know how sex works, correct?"

Sakaki was pretty sure she managed not to blush. "I've been instructed." Even if she had never done anything along those lines.

"Good. We'll drop that subject, shall we?"

Kira snickered. "Everything else is being prepared now."

"Prepared how?" She certainly hadn't been making plans.

"C'mon, don't you remember how we used to plan our dream weddings?"

"You remember that?" They hadn't done that in years. Even a dream wedding to Yoshiro had been unappealing enough that she couldn't enjoy making plans.

Kira just smiled enigmatically.

***

Todd very much appreciated the help in changing from one formal kimono to an even more formal kimono. From the English snippets of conversation he heard, weddings in the skulk weren't normally this formal. But Sakaki was the only child of the chief. That probably ramped things up a little. Besides, everyone seemed to be having fun. Todd was given a great deal of advice, some of which he was sure Sakaki would never forgive him if he actually followed.

Kira and Ryoko had explained how the wedding ceremony would work, after making sure he had down the ceremony for requesting a boon.

Judging by the way even Ryoko seemed surprised in a few places, he suspected Kira knew some of Sakaki's wishes on how she wanted her wedding. Good. If they were going to spring a surprise wedding on Sakaki, then it should be one she would cherish. The Werefoxes asked if there was anything he wanted included, but Todd pointed out that they would probably have to have another wedding in the States to make it legal. As legal as it could be when one party was using a fake identity because she didn't legally exist. Anything truly important, he could have included there.

Before he knew it, everything was ready. His kimono was elaborate and had many pieces to it, but it was apparently simpler than a woman's kimono. The guests would also be wearing kimonos, but much simpler versions than either of them would be wearing. According to several people, the first challenge the married couple had to face was getting each other *out* of the kimonos.

His kimono was midnight blue with blossoms of some sort overlooking a mountain. Possibly Mount Fuji. The sash, they called it an *obi*, was brilliant red. Odd compared to the usual suit of a Western wedding, but he didn't care. He was actually getting married, how could he care what he was wearing?

There was a brief sunshower before the wedding. Rain without clouds. Ironically enough, that turned out to be called a kitsune wedding shower in Japan. More than one person called it a good omen. That may be, but Todd was still glad it ended before the ceremony which would be outside.

It was just before sunset when Ryoko led him to a clearing on the island where a large flat stone lay. A small white canopy was over it. The canopy symbolized the shelter the couple was to provide for each other. Red cloth surrounded the rock, which was being used as a table. That cloth symbolized the community that was their foundation.

There was no seating, all the guests stood in a circle around the cloth. Suddenly, following some signal that Todd didn't catch, everyone started to sing. He made a mental note to ask Sakaki what they were singing later. That, and learn Japanese.

When the singing started, Ryoko nudged him forward. Todd walked eyes down then knelt when he reached the rock. On the other side of the crowd, Sakaki did the same, but according to tradition, it was bad luck for them to look at each other until the ceremony was over.

Sejou walked around them three times before coming to a stop between them. He spoke first in Japanese before repeating himself in English. They would be doing that all ceremony, because Todd was informed that a ceremony completely in English 'wouldn't count'.

"Today is a momentous day. For Sakaki and Todd, but also for all of us. Todd and Sakaki have come to join their lives in love and marriage. We have come to witness that. It is love that brings us here today. Love brought a man across the globe to ask for a woman's hand in marriage. Love brought that woman to agree, even though it meant leaving the home of her birth. Love will bring this couple through the rest of their lives, if they let it."

He paused and spoke again. First in Japanese, then in English. "Who bears witness to the love this couple shares?"

A woman's voice spoke up, but it wasn't until she translated to English that Todd recognized it was Kira. "I bear witness to their love. I watched them grow together. I have heard their declarations."

He saw her red kimono slip back into the circle, then someone else spoke up. Ryoko. "I bear witness to their love. I have questioned it and found it true."

Sejou spoke again. "Marriage is a joining of lives and of blood. Do you share your blood willingly today?"

Todd picked up the ceremonial knife on the rock. "I share my blood this day and swear to be loyal and to protect you until my blood is gone." He made a slice in his finger, then passed the knife over to Sakaki, still without looking up.

He saw her hand as she took the knife. She quoted his words, first in English, then in Japanese. When she had made her slice, they pressed their hands together and kept them there.

"They have shared blood. Who will bless this joining of blood?"

Tora had volunteered for this part. "I bless this joining of blood. I offer these daggers. May they always be used to protect each other, never against each other."

The daggers, like all wedding gifts, would actually be given to them later. It was time to separate their hands. Thanks to the pressure, his cut wasn't really bleeding anymore.

"Marriage is a joining of sorrows. Will you share your sorrows with each other, comforting and accepting comfort in turn?"

Todd reached for the goblet in the middle. "I will share my sorrows with you and take up your sorrows in turn." They had warned him the drink was bitter, but it was stronger than he expected. He didn't choke, which was good, because that was considered bad luck. Sakaki took the goblet, said the words, and drank from the same spot he had.

"They have shared their sorrows. Who will bless this joining of sorrows?"

"I bless this joining of sorrows." Sakaki's mother came forward. "I offer this tea set. May they never forget the solace of a listening ear, and shared food and drink." She stepped back into the crowd.

"Marriage is a joining of joys. Do you swear to share your joy and always strive to increase the joy of each other?"

Todd reached for the bowl of sweetened dumplings and picked one up with the provided chopsticks. "I will share my joys and strive to increase your joy." Using only his peripheral vision, he managed to feed Sakaki the dumpling, then hand her the chopsticks. She did the same for him with more grace.

"They have shared joys. I will bless this joining of joys. I swear that a shelter will be given them. A roof over their heads, and a sanctuary for their joys and sorrows. Bless this couple with me." Apparently as chief, it was his prerogative to assign housing for every couple when they married.

Both Todd and Sakaki stayed kneeling at the rock while the crowd circled them singing. It was a different song, but clearly everyone knew it.

When Sejou stopped, he was on the other side of the rock, but still between them. "Marriage is not simply between a couple. It is a matter for the whole community. Share with us your love and passion."

Sakaki waited until after Sejou finished in English, even though she understood him in Japanese; but in unison, they took the unlit candles in front of them and lit them from the lit candle in the middle. Then they stood and started lighting the candles of guests. Those guests started lighting the candles of those around them, and soon they were surrounded by a ring of flames.

Then and only then were the couple free to look at each other, now recognized by the skulk as husband and wife. One look at Sakaki and Todd had a theory on why they weren't supposed to look at each other beforehand. She was so beautiful, he wouldn't have been able to talk. Not for the first time, Todd regretting that kissing the bride was not part of the Kikitsutai ceremony.

She looked like something out of a fairy tale. A white embroidered kimono, a wreath of flowers woven into her hair. He recognized white carnations, peach blossoms and pear blossoms, later he'd ask if there was any significance to them. Best of all, she seemed pleased by him too.

He wanted to tell her how beautiful she looked, but he couldn't talk. Not that it mattered much. The crowd was ushering them on their way. Kikitsutai tradition, as soon as the couple was married, they took off in a boat to a small nearby island, appropriately named 'Honeymoon Island'.

The guests had a reception without them, starting with lighting floating lanterns to see the couple off. While the couple was away, it would be decided where they would live, and any gifts anyone wanted to leave the couple would be deposited there. It had seemed odd to Todd at first, but he thought he understood it now. Right now, he didn't want to be at a party or have to deal with a million details about setting up a new life. He was actually married, amazingly enough, and all he wanted was to be with his wife.

A food hamper, and two bags of supplies were already on the small motorboat waiting for them. Actually, he had been informed that one bag was supplies and the other was 'supplies'.

Suddenly on the boat, alone with Sakaki, Todd found himself inexplicably shy. She smiled at him. "Don't worry, I know the way."

"Good, because I don't."

She pointed at an island he could just barely see in the growing darkness. "That's it. Oh, look!"

The floating lanterns were filling the sky behind them. "It's beautiful. The whole ceremony was beautiful. But not as beautiful as you." He looked at her. "Will we end up in an accident if I kiss you now?"

"We might. But I'm not sure I care." She grabbed the neck of his kimono and pulled him down so she could kiss him. When they both let go, she said, "That's the first time I ever kissed someone."

"But hopefully not the last."

"No." She turned back to steering the boat. "Not the last. We're actually married. I don't believe it yet."

It took about ten minutes to reach the island, and a few minutes after that to tie off the boat and walk to the cabin. Someone had taken the time to stock it for their arrival and turn on a couple lights. Considerate. Sakaki could have found it in the dark, but he couldn't.

"Jamal and Shahara wanted to come, but they couldn't come up with a way to explain disappearing to Japan on such short notice."

"The ceremony tonight was taped and photographed. We can show them that. Besides, we'll have to have some sort of ceremony back in the states for legal purposes." Sakaki started looking through the bags. Whatever was in them was causing her to blush. He wanted to see that a lot more often.

"Shahara told me that I was to tell you that your drawing was a masterpiece. What is that about?"

Sakaki took a moment, before laughing. "I'll explain later. First things first. The first duty we do as a married couple."

"Help each other out of these kimonos?"

"Absolutely."

Also Look For:

Those Who Go Do Not Return

By H. J. Harding

The king summoned four people to his elaborate throne room to assign them a quest. Lakara, a scholar who has spent almost her entire life in the palace. Davorin, the best and youngest known necromancer in the land. Sir Jors, a knight who has served for ten years, but who may have been rendered a liability and is on his last chance. Kita, an outsider and thief who is given the choice of going on the quest or being executed. All four are ordered to find the Jewel of Ishni, a gem with no powers of its own but desired by the gods who fought over it.

With no trust and every one of them concealing secrets that could mean death or failure, they must learn to work together, or Death may claim them all.

Also by the Author

Moonlit Memories Series:

Secrets of the Moon Fox

Nightmare's Revenge

Ring of Blood

Hyde Chronicles:

The Pawn's Play

Knightfall

The Bishop's Decoy

Other books:

Those Who Go Do Not Return

Non-Fiction:

Lavender: An Essential Guide